WORLD ONE

WORLD ONE

VAIL HENRY

MOXIETASTIC
moxietastic.com | Fairfax, Virginia

This is a work of fiction.
Names, characters, organizations, places, events, and incidents are either the products of the author's imagination or used in a fictitious manner. Any resemblance to actual persons, living or dead, actual events, actual places, or actual organizations is purely coincidental.

ISBN 978-1-948279-00-0

Printed in the United States of America

First Printing, November 2017

With gratitude—

A number of people reviewed part or all of the second draft of this book: Shannon Woods, Kirstin Nickerson, Laura Sheldon, Heather Fagan, Sandra Henry-Stocker, Scott Rosenkranz, Alan Centa, J., LaMishia Allen, Jacki Newbery, Kevin Inouye, and Doug Wilson. It took five rewrites to incorporate the practical, detailed feedback of some of these people—and five years to absorb the encouragement of the others. I needed both for this story to emerge.

—Vail, *November 2017*

WORLD ONE

Chapter 1

In TruWrld2, through the fluorescence of his pride, User 1,893,241 received an old-style message—the kind you have to tap to open. He scoffed. There was a lot to snit about in this sim: the shabby-chics who adored themselves but fumbled their slipstream controls; the weepy babies who complained of fairness and how hard it was to make a life; the zongie-eyed zombies plunking away at menial tasks without enough human staffing to notice abuse.

Scratch that, he smirked. He liked the zongie-eyed automatons. With absent owners, they were the best entertainment this side of chickens. That was, in fact, why his avatar stood in front of this particular sim-mine.

Approaching the dark blot of the opening, User 1,893,241 stirred with excitement. With no personalization, no monograms on the wooden support beams, and no name, the mine was a digital hole in the hill and a mere number on the TruWrld2 map. He knew what he'd find inside; he knew the owner wasn't paying attention. What he didn't know is that somebody else was paying attention.

"Welcome, good sir, to our mine," greeted a coal-stained automaton in default auto-dialogue.

"Fraplit soulless peanut," answered User 1,893,241.

"A peanut, sir? There is nothing to eat at this location; however, you are free to tour the premises so long as you do not remove goods."

"Stick yer unction up yer nether."

After performing a swift linguistic assessment of this series of syllables, a regional TruWrld2 server attempted to make the miner answer, "Pardon, I do not understand your meaning." However, the server was not able to make the automaton speak. Instead, it returned an error: The miner in question no longer appeared on the logs of sim-entities capable of communication.

User 1,893,241 ordered his avatar to kick the automaton's severed head away, field-goal style. "Fraplit drone-bones, all of you!" He laughed at the complete lack of response as the head rolled forehead-over-chin and came to rest on one ear. Even the nearest drones kept droning; they had no programmed response for what had happened: User 1,893,241 had used his Heraldic Sword of ZiprothAr—a trophy item, one of only a thousand licensed in TruWrld2—to perform a decapitation of an unmanned character. Satisfied for the morning, he trotted his avatar out of the cave. He looked around at the sunny field, leaning on his sword like a cane, wondering what to do next. A light flickered at one corner of the screen.

"Piss your text, freak," said the user, tapping on the oddball, text-only message. The content was only five words. It took the entire four seconds before the note vanished for User 1,893,241 to comprehend what it said: *This isn't your world anymore.*

Many kilometers away, another man—one who also avoided using his real name in sims—grinned his swarthy face. It wasn't that Sodi had worked hard for today's entertainment: Soon-to-be-ex-user 1,893,241was nobody, just one of a series of people Sodi noticed. Users were no better than what his victim had thought of as *zongie-eyed zombies*: they reacted so predictably that Sodi could write programs to accomplish the perfection of timing and twist that he would now execute by hand. But the squirming of a victim lasted only a few moments, and the squirming delighted him.

"Where'd the text go?" User 1,893,241 asked the nothingness, which answered by accretion. His avatar stumbled to the right, collapsing to his knees before the user realized that the sword, too, had disappeared. "You jellyfish kissers!" he yelled aloud, as though the administrators of TruWrld2, who he blamed, could hear. He retreated from the sim locale and re-entered his admin zone to check what else had evaporated in the assumed technical glitch.

Much has disappeared. His sim account had been emptied of kash. Then the kash account itself disappeared, as though it had never existed.

Spewing the sort of curses that inconveniently triggered verbal blocking in TruWrld2, User 1,893,241 checked the rest of his settings. With relief, he saw that his real estate list remained intact even though his entire weaponry was gone. The screen shifted. One of the sim properties deeded to him vanished from the list. By the time the user blinked past his fury, two more parcels of sim real estate had vacated his list.

"No! What's—this don't happen!" The fourth and last piece of real estate disowned him, leaving the account as barren as a new subscriber. "Administrator! How do I—? My stuff is going! Administrator! I can see my stuff disappearing! Please—" he spoke, but before TruWrld2 could connect an administrator, the screen froze. It darkened. A tiny hourglass flashed momentarily, and delivered him to the welcome screen for TruWrld2. His login did not work.

As a baseline policy, unowned real estate in TruWrld2 had a standardized per-acre price set at thrice the development cost of the region divided by the number of acres in it. By the time a given region in TruWrld2 swelled in popularity, the market value of the virtual property often exceeded this baseline by a large margin. This discrepancy created an opportunity for entrepreneurship. At any given minute of the day, an average of 713 people searched TruWrld2 for unclaimed real estate.

The vacated ownership on each of User 1,893,241's parcels

was discovered and claimed within twelve seconds. The sim world processed on. Data overwrote itself. Change was.

Checking that his own TruWrld2 kash account had grown by a fraction, Sodi switched off his monitor. His toying always ended the same. Users posed no contest: Sodi's tracks were too clean. It did not interest him to watch how the details cleaned themselves up. Standing, he walked past the expensive light generators in his studio to gather up the laundry.

Ex-user 1,893,241 threatened legal action when he was finally able to reach an administrator, but she laughed. "We have no record of you owning sim-estate, sir, and besides: World One laws only apply to World One. We have our own laws here."

"But I paid my subscription with World One money!"

"No, sir. TruWrld2 runs on kash credit, not World One funds. If you bought kash with World One funds, that should have been credited to you. Any legal claim beyond the point of conversion falls within our jurisdiction based on the past thirty years of legal precedent. But you're free to discuss this with an attorney if you wish."

"Yes, I want to."

There was a silence. "Sir, if you want legal service, you need to call an attorney on your own."

"How do I do that? Wait, is that gonna cost me?"

The administrator disconnected.

Chapter 2

In the world where grass died if you didn't water it—and died in the way that made it sharp and crunchy under your own biological feet—Kat avoided her friend's scowl. She defended herself: "Whatever his join date is, he has sixteen Arabian horses, a villa in Shahaim, an apartment in New South Manhattan, and an Italian grape arbor. He's active." *Active in TruWrld2*, Kat added to herself. Mez always seemed more interested in speaking of the digital worlds than the one they now shared.

"How many digits in his core user number?" Mez asked.

Kat tapped her fork against her hundred-gram mini-rack of hot potato wedges. The way they lined up in neat rows looked wrong to her. She knew diners like this had to run on robotics to survive their slow business, but those starchy bits of geometry did not belong in the real world—or at least not in *her* real world, which was World One, where your *join date* was your birthday. Kat prodded a potato out of place. "Only five."

"That's what gets me about this guy. He's almost an original—old blood. That's all he's got?" Mez laid her spoon on the orange tabletop. "Most of the originals are royalty sultans and whatnot. Anybody can get sixteen ponies if they have time. He should have the Taj Mahal. He should have two of them."

"But I like him, Mez. We get along."

"Kat, it's all wrong. Either he's lazy or he's been elsewhere. How can you send him a permanent heart if he can't account for his life? Kat, that's serious. He'd get to use all your resources, and you can't take it back."

He's been elsewhere, Kat let repeat in her mind. This seemed true of almost everyone to her, even here, sitting with her best friend on a beautiful day on earth, but unable to drive conversation away from a sim. "Yes, you can. You just need an administrator."

From a separate booth across the aisle from Kat and Mez, the only other customer at Big Dee's Café glanced up at the two strangers. Her sagging posture slumped over weather-chapped elbows, hiding her brilliant, glittering eyes. Eva's thoughts sprinted: *Not only is she eating lunch outside her home, but she's mentioning an administrator?* She studied the woman who'd been called *Kat* in short glances. Concealing her wrist in her lap, she jotted on her mini-tab: *Kat, 35ish, dark hair, 10-inch braids, offwhite blouse, shin-cutoff jeans, blue rubber-soled moccasins. Big Dee's, Wednesday, 2:17 p.m.* Eva made no notes about the woman addressed as *Mez*.

Not noticing the stranger, Mez continued to speak to Kat, "Call an *administrator*? That could take 24 hours! He could do anything in that time. With access to your resources, he has access to you. Serious, Kat, he could lay you out. He could be a serial account killer. You could be dating a sim-scarrer."

"They take care of those," Kat tried to quiet her friend.

Mez scowled, shoving her plate over the stained polymer of the table's trash-take conveyor. "Well *maybe* he's been around long enough that he knows how to cover his tracks!"

"I can't hear this," Kat said. She slumped forward and swiped her mini-tab for distraction. "Maybe he's just putting more into other sims," *or World One*, she added mentally.

"Exactly! Don't p-heart someone who won't be around."

"Mez, I like him. I *don't* think he's a sim-scarrer. And if I'm wrong? There are other sims."

There are other sims, Eva thought, near fumbling, and chanced a long look at Kat's wrist. The lower right corner of a mini-tab typically held the security app for housing. She strained at the icon and took notes: *Purpl 4 yell strps horz gren at bot rt fern?* The app changed *horz* into *horn* but corrected the rest well and processed her notes into an image of an access app icon and an address of the building that app was developed for. This was a World One building. It was a place people lived in the flesh, and it wasn't that far away.

"There are other sims, but there's only one TruWrld2. You're okay losing everything, just being gone, just dead? I still remember tenth grade, we signed up to the same sim-classes and dressed our avatars in identical skins. Kat, there is nobody else I'd stump out to some retro slopshop for. You don't even care if you let some wack rob and kill you?"

Kat's voice weakened. "I could start over."

"Ridiculous! You'd have to do grunt work for a year nonstop before you'd get any of your life back. Kat! You can't! I don't want to lose you! I have a bad feeling."

I don't want to lose you, either, Kat thought, *but sometimes I'm not even sure I have you at all anymore. We can't seem to talk about anything but TruWrld2.* "Look, we'd still hang out, I'd come by, whatever. *I'm* not going to literally die. I just..." Kat frowned at the stranger stabbing at her mini-tab. "Hey Mez? Let's leave."

—

Eva sent half her avocado sandwich into the trash-take to leave first. It made it less obvious she intended to follow them. Outside the diner, she turned toward the intersection more likely to keep her waiting. In spite of the power in her sinewy legs, she kept her steps slow. By wiggling her ankles in her low-heeled, short boots, Eva feigned being unused to walking in such gear. The practiced act looked real.

She's already like one of us, Eva considered. *Already trying to prove to someone that there is something worthwhile in the real world—*

in World One, she corrected herself to popular language. *And she's doing it alone. And who knows for how long, without support, without affirmation. She needs us. She belongs among us.*

Eva heard a door open and voices emerge. They did not grow fainter: The two ladies from the diner were coming the same way. To stall, Eva scanned the walker button at the intersection as though she were unfamiliar with it, waiting for the signal even though no vehicles were passing over the cracked pavement.

Kat walked half a step ahead of her friend until Mez, needing support, grasped the only live crepe myrtle tree on the street. The disturbed white flowers drifted down on her like giant dandruff. "Why did I let you convince me to walk? Your place is what, hours from here?"

"Only the way you walk, Mez. Seven blocks."

"I just ate, you know!"

Kat sighed. "We can go to your place instead. You're never going to see my apartment, are you?" She held out her hand. Mez grabbed her upper arm instead, breathing, and waggled her other hand in complaint that the next three tree-grates in the sidewalk stood barren—nothing further to lean on.

Eva's walk light changed. Reaching the opposite curb, she dropped a shoe off her heel to stall and risk a glimpse of where the women were going. Mez let Kat into the Kazali Servi-Mod apartment building on the corner.

Satisfied with the information she'd gleaned, Eva fitted her shoe back on and reversed her direction with strong, stable strides.

—

Sodi opened the door to a bright apartment. "Welcome back, sunshine."

"Thanks," said Eva.

"Are you busy now?"

"Not too much," Eva smiled. "What have you got?"

"The leaf!"

"There's only one? Their budget must be tight."

"No," he laughed, rocking back on his heels, which strained white linen across the happy swell below his navel. "It's just the mother leaf, sunshine. Of course the city council will have me design others, but this one is the model for the rest." He stepped closer to trace the lines in Eva's shoulder with the back of his index finger.

She smiled. "What kind did it turn out to be? American chestnut?"

"No, they didn't choose your favorite. But sunshine, this tree was extinct before it ever grew. Don't feel the loss."

"I see." The extinction of the American chestnut, even in a simulated form, weighed on Eva. She slid her bag of equipment under a rotund sidetable with long legs. "Sounds like a downright unhistorical marvel."

"I like it. It's not authentic."

Eva rolled her eyes while Sodi brought the winning leaf up on the living room screen—an outmoded panel that came short of human height. Half of the asymmetrical shape of the leaf looked like maple, but shaved down to concave arcs. The other half curled around in one complete turn of a spiral before ending in a sharp tip that dipped down under gravity. Up the stem, a pair of simple, cotyledon-style leaflets finished the edge.

"That would never survive. It would block its own sun. Are they serious?"

"You have to watch it in motion. And in groups." Sodi then spoke to his workstation in the next room, "Lillian! Forty leaves, animate them." A group of forty leaves appeared on the living room screen and seemed to blow in a gentle breeze. The spiral portion of each leaf fluttered and sparkled with simulated sunlight. He watched Eva's pretty, appraising eyes. She seemed disappointed, which he disregarded. Flipping a thumb toward the room he used as his studio, Sodi invited with a sly grin, "Wanna come see them in three dimensions?"

"This is good enough, thanks," she spoke in a flat voice. Sodi stepped behind her and settled his hands on her waist. She paused, then overlaid her hands on his. "They're pretty. Not authentic, but they dance."

He spoke close to her ear. "That's why it passed. It plays with the low-grade breezes more than any other style I showed them."

"Why was that important? If they want leaves to flutter, why don't they crank up the wind speed?"

Eva could hear him smile as the warm curve of his cheek brushed the top of her ear. "You can't underestimate how sensitive people are to that," Sodi said. "The average person can guess a simulated wind speed to within twelve percent—which is seven percent more accurate than the same study five years ago. And most people still want some things to feel authentic. They don't want a ten-kilometer-per-hour breeze on their face, but a thirty-kilometer-per-hour breeze in the holograms."

"I hadn't thought of that."

"That," Sodi said, twirling Eva around and kissing her between the eyebrows, "is because you definitely don't sim enough."

"Uh huh."

"A below-average gamer. In fact, you are downright deficient," he grinned, warmth in his eyes.

"Oh no, I can't tell a breeze from a gale in a holographic tree. They'll come to document me as a subversive any time now."

Her voice was flat, but she smiled at last and kissed him back.

"My tooth is looser!" Still clad in black pajamas, Sodi's son cropped the corner as he sped into the room, small feet padding over the knots of old, beige carpet. Lifting his face up toward Eva, he opened his mouth and prodded an undersized dentition. It cocked at angles, hinging at only one place on the gum.

"Hey, it's about to come out!" Eva cheered.

"Maybe," the boy responded, withdrawing back into thoughtfulness. His expression skewed as his tongue prodded the strange window of flesh under his tooth. Eva released Sodi, squatted down, and encircled the boy in her arms. He seemed not to notice he was caught until she pressed the bridge of her nose into his cheek, her forehead on his temple.

"Your temperature feels so much better, baby. Did you sweat again?"

"Yes. I got new pajamas. I'm not a baby."

Eva lingered at the child's temple until he leaned away. She asked Sodi, "Did he eat?"

"Some. Enough."

"And kept it down?" she asked. Sodi nodded at her. "What did he eat?"

He smiled a little. It was not that Eva mistrusted him, at least not on this. It's that she was always too vigilant. Sodi enjoyed her predictability, the impatience in her face, her deep brown eyes questing for reassurance while steeling themselves for things to go wrong. "Third of an apple, minus the skin. Small glass of water. Half-slice of dry toast. Hour ago."

He watched her calculating his answer. Her eyes unlocked. "I'm glad."

"It was enough," he repeated. The boy wandered off to a

shelf of paper books. "Your work: good?"

"I met my commitment. Two last hours for this week, plus the fifteen support votes I needed to keep my numbers." Eva watched his son pluck a thin volume off the shelf. She walked across the room and arranged two pillows for him to recline. The child traced an apostrophe on the cover of the book. "And, of course, there were a few countervotes," she continued. "One lady came by with seven—*seven*—dogs."

"Ah. How'd those dogs look?"

"No, Sodi, they were great. If dogs could smile... and she walked all seven of them herself..." Eva touched the mini-tab on her wrist. "I was sad to lose her confidence."

"Found her, sunshine. Didn't lose her; someone else can follow up."

"Of course; I took notes. It's just... she'll never like me. I chose my message. I want to believe it's sound enough not just to keep some income flowing, but to screen through people and find the ones we need. Or that need us."

"You do that," he reassured, "and dozens of times. Starving artists appreciate your income."

"Thanks, but I wish more of the recruits liked me. She definitely won't now that she's heard my service message 'Run It Over.' It sucked."

"Someone else will get to her. Did you eat, sunshine?"

"Yes. No. I went to Big Dee's, but there was another candidate—"

"Two in one day?" Sodi's incredulous voice brought Eva's chin up a bit.

"Yes! Two in one day." She sat down on a red, gadget-free sofa and took off her ankle-boots.

"Did 'Run It Over?' go better with the second?"

"I didn't pitch. I was eating lunch. I overheard her talking to her friend."

"'Her'... they're both women," Sodi mused, eyes twinkling.

"Yeah, good luck with that!" Eva balled up her lacy socklet and chucked it at him. Sodi caught it, shook it out flat, and kept it. "So this *woman* was having lunch with yet another *woman*—the world is full of *women* today—and she... I think she's in love... beyond the sim." Her fingers found the hem of her shirt and outlined its repeating pattern of embroidered triangles. The shirt was old. "But not in love with you," she teased—somewhat.

"I didn't figure. Woman wants to be in love with me, I tell her right away, 'Don't eat lunch where my lady does.'"

"Good strategy."

"Did you get to talk to her?"

"No. They went into a Servi-Mod. But the candidate didn't live there; her access app—" Eva pulled up her notes and the icon of the app the mini-tab had suggested. It displayed on the living room screen. "Here it is. Got an address for the building it goes to. She wasn't the Servi-Mod type. Taking risks, starting over, losing a sim—it didn't matter to her. She was just in love."

"But with a sim," Sodi cautioned.

"*Through* the sim, *through* it. There's an opportunity with her, but it may be short."

Sodi memorized the address. "Is there an opportunity for me to get your other sock? I've got a whole load of whites raring to go."

Eva threw it, face alight.

Chapter 3

The Servi-Mod chain of apartment buildings succeeded where Santa Claus failed.

For almost fifty years, engineers and scientists had fawned over the nascent technology of 3-D printers that could manufacture in any substrate: a Santa Claus machine. Highly niche goods—a plate to match grandmother's heirloom set, a brassiere to match that perfect-but-discontinued style, a child's favorite stuffed animal (pre-worn to exactly the desired condition)—no longer required effort or patience to acquire. They could simply be fabricated.

By employing a fleet of coordinated, localized Santa Claus machines, the company Santa Source provided this unlimited array of made-to-order goods before their eventual collapse. They were heralded as the most significant revolution in economics in a century: the "long tail" of low-demand goods had finally coalesced into a streamlined, high-quantity, prime market. Hundreds of thousands of part-time entrepreneurs were made obsolete, along with their inefficient and complex network of intrusive advertisements, sim storefronts, and global shipments.

But Santa Source wanted more. Pumping cash into its R&D, the mega-corp sought to compete for the market of common, daily-needs goods—and to fabricate them on demand and on site. They envisioned a leased Santa Source machine in every home to provide all the daily food, paper products, linens, and clothing the family required. Unused goods or leftovers could simply be recycled back into the machine for sanitary re-processing.

Environmentalists applauded the efforts: Farms could be released back into wild land. Transportation-related pollution could be reduced to the minimum required to deliver raw materials for the Santa machines.

Over twenty-five years, Santa Source mortgaged itself into a pinnacle of debt as it developed the capacity to Santa-produce foodstuffs, and to do so with minimal wait time. Their machines self-sterilized, delivered hot or cold, and even provided the utensils and dishes required to consume each meal. However, the resulting first-generation machines were so massive that they outsized the average residence.

It became apparent that Santa Source would not bridge the size leap before the hollowed-out company collapsed under its dissipating stock values.

The mega-corp launched one of the most intense marketing campaigns ever seen to push communal use of the household Santa machines. The first wave of installs evidenced that, because of the long regeneration time between uses, each machine could only serve three families—and only if they coordinated their meal times to be offset by a minimum of 70 minutes. Few families were so eager to have on-demand, on-site goods that they were willing to cooperate with others.

A renegade group of anonypreneurs—entrepreneurial black-hat publicists who worked incognito via whisper-root campaigns in the sim worlds—launched a vicious counterstrike. "Bubba's backwash in my brew" was graffitoed into sim farm fields, on sim buildings, into the patterns of movement in the clouds and water rivulets, and (in a few controversial instances) into the play of light in avatars' eyes. Within hours, users across the worlds were seen standing in motionless pairs as players examined each others' eyes for evidence of hacking. Analysts estimated that the widespread pausing cost sim worlds trillions of kash dollars from asynchronous stoppages in sim-global economies. In short: It got everyone's attention.

Out of cynical glee, replica slums of three-family tenements operating on a Santa appeared across the sim-worlds. Avatar drones were sent to live pre-programmed lives consisting mostly of requesting a pint of sim-Santa-fabricated beer, swigging half, and casting the backwash remnants back into the machine for the next drone in line. Many of these parody slum Santas were abused to produce greenish beer tinged with visible microbes, which caused the drones to vomit directly into the machine. The most hideous examples were viewed by 72 percent of all sim users. The "sick Santa" image became a global icon more famous than the true Santa Source logo.

Back in the real world, Santa Source never released a second generation of their breakthrough machines. The global company was parsed by bankruptcy into regional facilities that were run independently without R&D budgets.

Popular belief said that the anonypreneurs were shadowy members of Santa Source's disorganized, real-world competition. This was not true. They were five individuals—all children of poor ex-dealers of antiques and artisan goods—who could still recite the stories of how their families lost everything to Santa Source's short-lived success.

Sodi never knew who the other four anonypreneurs were. Neither did he profit from the Retail-iation Movement that followed:

Retailers discovered that the call for "pure" foodstuffs now coincided with an unparalleled demand for on-site daily goods. People didn't want to leave the sims set up in their homes, but they needed sustenance. A standing inventory of pre-produced goods therefore appeared unavoidable, but business analysts wished to eliminate costly point-of-sale stores and the hassle of ordering. After all, nothing value-added could be spun from the need to bail on your sim and walk a block just to get a bagel. From this realization, another innovation in business was born: the Servi-Mod apartment.

—

The door retracted as Mez approached it. She and Kat stepped off of the movilator and into the main room of Mez's Servi-Mod. At first glance, the walls appeared to be covered in three-dimensional art backlit with a warm, offset glow. Most of the oval room's illumination came from a section on the short left end, where rows of lights picked out a series of grumpy-looking, fresh pears. "I know you've seen these apartments before," Mez limped to a curved sofa in the center cockpit of the room.

"I have," Kat admitted. "I looked at a Servi-Mod a few blocks from here. I couldn't afford the rent, not in comparison." Kat held mute on her other reasons for avoiding the most modern housing option. She hadn't found words for the deep unease the living units gave her. She feared the loss of boundaries. *If a home is a commercial location,* she wondered, *what do the people in it become?*

"I keep telling you that you could afford more if you'd just take the time to develop your sim-come."

"I hate that word. Either it's real income or it isn't. You can't pay for a real home with fake money." She stopped at another section of backlit shelves and examined the wares. "What does pomegranate juice taste like?"

"I don't know. Have one," Mez shrugged. "They're just on my selection plan this month. All this crap is supposed to be healthy. And of course you can pay for a real home with sim-come, Kat. Please! Just because *your* building isn't owned by the biggest sim-to-real currency exchanger in the world doesn't mean you can't cash your kash." A series of display panels ignited around Mez. Each bested seven feet. Semi-translucent when off, they did not quite create a visual barrier in the room. Recessed lights awoke above the cockpit into a rain of white. Kat grunted at the sudden change.

"Do you like the Natur-Lite?"

"What?"

"It's so they don't have to put windows in here. The health thing, depression. It comes on automatically for... however long to replace sunlight. But I've been outside today. Hey Barnabie!" she called at her home robot, "Kill the lights already!"

A series of wall LEDs twinkled in obeisance. The Natur-Lites switched off. Kat uncapped a fat bottle of fruit juice. "Why don't they just put in windows?"

"Hello, maybe *glare*?"

Kat sipped at the nectar. She passed a clutch of canned peaches, single-serving boxes of varied breakfast cereals, and sheathed breads. As she came to the short end of the room opposite the pears, the lighted shelf held toilet paper, two cans of spray disinfectant, bottles of shampoo, four kinds of soap, and folded towels.

"Do you have to buy the towels every time?"

Mez shifted her bulk to mash a pillow behind her lower back. "I don't know. They just put the towels there. It's integrated laundry or it's printed. You pay when it comes off the shelf again. Nothing here is paid for until I use it, until I take it off the shelf."

Kat rounded along another wall. "These drawers?"

"Socks. No, that's shirts." Mez glanced up and laughed at Kat's expression as she held up underwear. "Girl, I don't do a stitch of laundry. Why should I? I have money to make."

"Do you always get the same... socks... back?"

"They're clean. I don't know. I make my selections, and the clothes are always here."

A windchime tinkled. Mez turned her attention back to the display panels. On one, a lithe, purple humanoid with wings danced and waved her hands around a coppery sapling, which bulged with iridescent red fruit. A second panel showed a flannel-clad man closing the hatch on a train car full of watermelons. The third panel, which had chimed, bore the face of an attractive young man dressed as though he were an attendant in a ladies' club. With luscious professionalism, he informed Mez to stand and stretch, pick out a healthy lunch—*the pears are near peak ripeness*, he advised—and take her thyroid medication.

Mez rolled her eyes and waved her hand dismissively at the screen. The Barnabie robot interpreted her natural body language by slipstream control and withdrew the alerts before Mez complained, "Already had lunch, stretched enough for a whole week, Barnabie." She shook the wrist with her mini-tab as though this would fix the failed activity sync, then turned to Kat. "Hey, hand me that bottle. Further up." She watched Kat pass her finger along a high shelf, pointing in succession. "Yeah, that one. Actually, I just need one pill. Thanks. I hate getting up once I'm comfortable, whatever the Reg Man says."

"So what else do you have on Life-Regs?" asked Kat, handing her the medication.

Mez rolled her eyes and popped the tiny disc in her mouth. The Barnabie robot recorded that she took it as the sync caught up. "Well, just anything. I mean, I get wrapped up in stuff. I have a lot going on. Like, yeah this is a pretty modest setup, but when I'm in full swing, I've got two guys on each panel, and some of them are bosses of a bunch of automatons I'm also running, just so they can feed their income to the bosses. Just grunt stuff. But keeping them all busy takes a lot of brain, Kat. I have to be on the ball. And if I'm caught in all those lives, well, it's true: Sometimes you forget to change your socks. Just like they say, nobody's giving you sim-come for changing your socks; why should I remember it?"

"So the Reg Man tells you to change your socks?"

"Yeah," Mez smiled, "and my drawers. They do such a good job; he's always got some amusing way of bringing up the subject. I swear, sometimes I haven't even realized a whole day has gone past."

"Don't you sleep?"

"When I need to."

"Does he tell you when?"

Mez exhaled an exasperated breath. "What else is he for? Tells me everything. Drink eight ounces of water. Get some rest. Look away from the screen for a couple minutes—I'd delete that one if I could, nobody listens to it anyway. Actually I make him say that in Swahili because it sounds pepperminty. Uh, what else? Take a bathroom break. Check yourself for—"

"You have Life Regs tell you when to use the bathroom? Mez, that's low."

"No, it's isn't. Kat, how are you still so backwards? Nobody's got time to think. I've got things to do. I work constantly to run all these lives. World One stuff is ridiculous: It's just bio-maintenance. If it weren't for the Reg Man, I wouldn't even notice until it was critical, and then I might not be able to slip away without stalling things, and definitely losing some of the sim-come. I realize you're ignorant of it, but maximizing sim-come is really delicate. You have to be right on for some of the exchanges. You can't keep dozens of yourself waiting; it'd be a waste."

Mez quieted down and refocused on the panels. On the fifth one, a woman of unlikely proportions approached and began to converse with her avatar on the sale of a filigree diadem.

"I guess you give up a lot of sim-come to spend time with me," murmured Kat. Mez heard but offered only a soft silence as answer. Mez said *64T* and nodded at the fifth panel to slipstream her counteroffer. There, in subtitles and in quiet, sing-song auto-dialogue, the smiling avatar said, "This would look so elegant on you, Madam Keloti. I will part with this for only sixty-four thousand."

But before Madam Keloti had made an equally eloquent auto-spoken counteroffer, Mez's attention had already returned to screen one, where the winged purple avatar had finished her spell, and was now examining the largest of the fruit droplets. Glancing back with a frown, Mez noticed the text *35T* had appeared under Madam Keloti's avatar. She spoke *58T final*, slipstreamed the command, then muttered, "another cheap beggar; why do I bother." At the same time her counteroffer appeared on other user's screen, her avatar voiced, "Fifty-eight thousand is the final price I can offer you. Do we have an accord?" Mez rolled her eyes at the unnecessary speaking; nobody ever listened to it; auto-dialogue was too slow. Before the spoken words finished playing, Mez had already logged the contract on the watermelons and returned the farmer avatar to the field.

Kat blinked off the lull of watching Mez sim. She wondered if she'd been standing there for five minutes or twenty, then realized she didn't even know what day of the week it was. She'd never lost the sense of *today* and *the day after tomorrow*, but years had passed since *Friday* or *weekend* translated into the warm, rushing glee of *I get to play outside all day*. Kat capped the juice, trying to stem her feelings. "Bathroom?" she said, afraid to interrupt Mez.

"There," Mez dismissed, waving a finger to a break in the shelves near the pears. There were four such breaks in the room, and each led to an area with an odd, acute shape that fit into the corners left over by the main room's oval. Sprouting from the center of the bathroom ceiling was an auto-sudsing shower head that would clean both the occupant and the room. This was the sole feature of the apartment that Kat envied.

As Kat came out of the rest room, she noticed Mez had

activated another panel. A pink ogress in a golden tiara and war bikini was announcing the news. In a grunting voice, she reported, "...rise in popularity of user-created 'make something happen' events may change the TruWrld2 economy. Anti-bugs and sim-potions could become scarce. But the bigger question is: Who is making these effects? And who is making their solutions? Experts say n—" Mez skipped to the next news story. "In World One, three more permanent road outages in the region have cut off another two hundred rural residences from the transportation grid. Authorities suspect subversive groups are responsible for the coordinated effort that left rural routes 203, 627, and 62 impassable after explosions destroyed portions of the road bed."

"Those subversives better *never* come to the city. I am *not* leaving my home," said Mez as she moved her purple, winged character to dance over a small patch of glowing lima beans. "Servi-Mod would just have to find a way to get my stuff restocked in here without roads."

The news continued, "Corporate giant Servi-Mod has again stepped in to re-home the victims of attacks that authorities seem unable to stop."

A rectangle opened in the sim, showing a video clip from World One. A clean-shaven man in a yellow tie, identified as the communications executive for Servi-Mod said, "We are pleased to give these individuals and families the solace of comfortable and convenient homes during their time of crisis."

Mez called over to Kat, "You know, those people never leave Servi-Mod once they're in. Those roads never get fixed. There's no budget. The subversives know which roads aren't important enough to fix. That's why they choose those to blow up. I don't understand why we haven't taken out all those unlegitimized creeps yet. And anyway," her farmer avatar reached the field, and she set him to work filling the water troughs for livestock, "Why would those re-homed people leave Servi-Mod? It's a better life."

Kat wanted to leave Servi-Mod. Trying to be polite, she looked at the other three doors. One was the entryway. One, she guessed, would be a closet. Kat peeked into the final door. Beyond it was a bedroom so small that the mattress had been custom-made to fit. Every bit of floorspace was taken up by either this triangular bed or by the area needed to open the door. But this room also had the one feature that Kat longed for: a window.

"Go in if you want," Mez called out, "but close the door. Gives me glare." Kat obeyed, sat on the edge of the bed with her feet in the small well of floor space, and looked out of the window.

She was on the sixteenth floor. The world outside emptied out before her like a broken heart. To the west she saw a segment of road grid designed to usher crowds of sizes she'd only seen in historical photos. Today, as every day, the streets carried sparse traffic. Two Servi-Mod trucks lurched around a corner; one overran the curb. Crews of city workers in orange-and-yellow-striped jumpsuits huddled around empty sidewalk grates where street trees had long ago died.

She turned her gaze to the east and saw nothing but the adjacent wing of the Servi-Mod building. One stripe of windows extended up the wall, and none of those windows contained other faces. She felt lonely. She slept.

Kat woke in dimmer light and stumbled from the bedroom. "I need to go home, Mez; it's near sunset."

"It's what? You didn't have dinner. Kat, just stay. I never sleep in my room anyway. I can spare panels six and seven for you."

"Thanks—but I gotta be home."

"At least take some dinner with you. I hate to think of you

going back to an apartment without any food in it."

Kat overlooked the unintended insult. She picked up a package of fig tarts and turned it over, looking for the embedded transi-tag. "Mez, do people ever just leave the food packages on the shelf? I mean, so they don't have to pay?"

"No, silly." For the first time since Kat re-emerged, Mez took her eyes off her sim panels. "If they did that, they wouldn't get re-stocked, and they'd run out of food. You might as well be in a retro apartment." Mez's brow wrinkled with concern. "You don't look all there, Kat. You sure you won't stay?"

"I have to go. I promised." But her friend was already engrossed in the sims again.

"Goodnight, Mez. Thank you."

"Yup, 'night."

Kat walked through the hallways to the tiny front lobby, hardly bigger than a hallway itself. The exit carousels let her out to the streets. She saw nobody. She turned toward home.

Chapter 4

The child's fever returned that night. "Hold my head down," the boy rasped, a little voice in the darkness. "It is going everywhere." Eva could feel him more than see him. His aura of heat congealed into a five-centimeter-thick cocoon. She pressed a cold cloth to his head, willing it to wash out the heat and the strange ideas she thought of as *daymares*.

"We'll keep your head on, baby. Rest. You're with mama." Turning her head, she saw Sodi standing aloof in the doorway and flinched at being overhead calling herself this child's mother—again.

Sodi noticed her reaction even without physically seeing it. He did not object. He never had. "Lunchtime, I gave him the last dose of antibiotic. Five rounds now. I can't get more. I'll take him to the hospital. Flat-out carry him in." He watched Eva's expression harden. He'd known it would harden just as he knew how this conversation would end.

Sodi used his charisma and intuition to, as he called it, *program people* as liberally in his private life as in his clandestine side-work. He saw no sign of such laughing lawlessness in his son, which posed a problem quite apart from the recurring fevers: His child's organized, logical obedience meant he would need to belong somewhere—not just to the wind and whim in which Sodi placed his own inconstant allegiance. Aside from the child's health, this is why he would press Eva into returning to the Moma.

At that moment, Eva was glancing down at the exposed fraction of her outer right thigh. Sodi recognized that she had guessed at his aims and would need a little time to think old thoughts before he could continue. Embedded in the soft crease of Eva's outer thigh, the tail of her scar curled in one complete turn of a spiral, pointing back at itself. It wasn't an injury. This scar had been made for art and for membership in the Moma, who did not require digital identification credentials. They did not require digital anything.

It was this difference that led to groups like the Moma being feared. They did not participate in sim lifestyles, in digital commerce, in sim-based education programs, or in politics. Aberrant, they became generally mistrusted because mainstream people could not understand how they lived. As World One's society changed too quickly, as tax bases and infrastructure destabilized, there came a need for scapegoats to blame for emerging problems. The wide variety of unrelated aberrant groups were collectively blamed for bridge collapses, for outbreaks of disease, for acts of erosion, for reservoir losses, and even for deaths. Images of people in strange clothes with dirt on their faces became iconic for terror, anarchy, and filth in World One. They became implied criminals.

The media gave aberrant groups no voice, so in time, society gave them no rights. The legitimization laws passed after a strangely coincidental series of horrific acts were blamed on the collective of unrelated groups that lived off-digital. These laws mandated digital identification records and early enrollment in approved sim-education programs—else a forfeiture of citizenship. While excellent at polarizing digital society against non-digital lifestyles, the legitimization laws did nothing to stop the flow of tragedies. Outrage intensified until the political climate reached a break limit. Then the laws leveled up.

Eva could still remember, as a child, watching the newscast when the change happened. Spittle had flown out of the mouth of the bald man in round glasses who had yelled from a podium. "We spend resources and time protecting renegades who attack us," he'd said. "Not one more day will we honor those who destroy us. Not one more day will we preserve rights for those who undermine our rights." Young Eva had watched this, not understanding why the loving hand on her shoulder grabbed so tightly that the nails dug. A cheer sounded from the newscast. Amid that fanfare, basic human rights became contingent on citizenship—and citizenship was only available to legitimized persons.

"What does it mean?" she had asked.

"It means you're starting school tomorrow. In a sim."

"Why?"

"Eva, do you love your dolly?" She had answered only by nodding because the voice trembled, and the trembling had scared her. "You will go to school so anyone else who likes your dolly can't just take it away."

But another voice then spoke, darker: "Eva, do you love your sister?"

Young Eva could not answer. She squeezed her doll against her chest.

"Eva, do you love your sister?"

Eva shook off the memory and raised her eyes to Sodi, who was still watching her patiently, expressionless. She tried to remember the last thing he'd said. It had been about hospitals. "So your plan is to walk in the hospital and say, 'Hi, I had a son seven years ago; please cure his fevers that don't respond to any medicines we've been able to lie for or steal.' And they'll say, 'Why is there no record of this child? Who are you? Who is his mother?'" Eva clamped her eyelids shut as though to push back on another memory.

Sodi's posture and voice stayed relaxed. "I'll say you're his mother. You have every right to get medical care."

Eva shook her head. "He's so old and still not legitimized.

They'd take him from us for neglect. They'd take him and educate him until he forgets everything else." *Until he forgets me,* she thought.

"So we enroll him. He's already getting the best education in the city."

"They'll still be suspicious. God forbid they examine me and get a look at my thigh, or check into your background more closely. We would lose him. I might lose you. A lot of people could lose what they love." Eva covered her eyes with a hand. There was so much she did not want to see again. "You know about risks. You know. There has to be another way."

Sodi did know. "Of course there is."

"I can't go back to them. They're wrong." She sat a long time at the foot of the child's bed. Sodi found no reason to speak or move his tall frame from the doorway, so Eva continued, "I don't know what else to try. I'll take him with me tomorrow. Fresh air may help. It's been worse than this. Maybe he's getting better."

Here at last Sodi's voice calcified. "Better today? Maybe. Better last week? No. How much worse will you let it get? The Moma will help."

"We need to stay here. We're still too few. We have to find more members. I don't want your son to be abandoned."

"Boy can't be abandoned if he has a place with the Moma. He's not going out tomorrow."

"Sodi, I think he's getting better. Besides," she glanced up with a weird expression of plaintive hope, "I need him. The trust thing. Authenticity. That woman Kat has seen me too recently. She will think I'm stalking her."

"You are."

Eva huffed in exasperation. "You understand."

"Quite well." Sodi had not anticipated this part of the conversation. He gauged the scenario, took a long look at the still-sweaty face of his only living child, and came to a conclusion. "Eva, this is a gamble. You want a gamble, I want a bargain: You take him tomorrow. We get help from those that can help if fevers keep on."

"From your people."

"Yes," he said too loudly, "from those who can help." In spite of the talking, the child had fallen asleep. One small hand jerked up and landed, palm-up and defensive, on his own chest. Sodi intuited Eva's mind squirming by the tension in her neck. He dismantled her imminent objection by urging, "You say he's getting better. If so, this bargain is good for you. If not, he goes anyway."

Eva held her breath as long as possible before giving in with a quiet *yes*.

Chapter 5

"I have a headache without pain. It's like my mind is trying to go in three directions at once," Kat said, transmitting her exact words into TruWrld2 in a voice very much like her own.

The other avatar in her simplistic, two-monitor corner console asked, "Is that why you logged in so late? Did you see a doctor?" His voice was set to a slightly thin baritone. He was designed to look mid-forties, dignified grays dusting through his hair. They stood in a TruWrld2 limbo park with a sapphire blue stream punctuated by tufts of grass. This meeting space existed disjointed from the rest of TruWrld2—a locale apart from the normal digital geography—where users could meet regardless of their home location. There was no industry here, no commerce, and no access to personal effects. Few other avatars dawdled here.

"No, I... well it's not medical. It's just my mind. I just saw a friend at her place and it was...." Kat didn't finish this sentence because she'd have had to explain that she was late on purpose because she wanted to detour through Park Square on the way home. Unkempt, most of its trees dead or missing, Park Square was still Kat's place of refuge when she needed to feel real grass under her feet. "I think of all those apartments on all those floors in all those buildings. These people, they never see anybody—"

"They see people every day. I'm seeing you now."

Kat shifted in her seat. "Yes, Tennan. But in person."

"Kitty-Cat, I don't know how to be more personal. I assure you, I am here with you in as much entirety as I can muster."

Kat laughed. "'Muster!' And I know that's not even auto-speak. Tennan, I like your talk. I bet nobody else has said 'muster' for a century!"

His avatar smiled and hid his hands in his pockets. Kat wondered what it would look like to see Tennan do this in real life. "Dialogue would have changed it to 'mustard.'" Kat laughed again, but her worries returned. "Tennan, I am afraid for my friend. Those apartments are like beehives. Except in a real beehive, if a bee dies, at least there are other bees around to notice. I know she's happy. It suits her. But it seems like a morgue-in-waiting to me."

Tennan did not answer. Hands still in pockets, he shifted his avatar's weight and blinked to show her that he was still listening.

"Tennan, do you make your own food?"

His answer did not come quickly. "I no longer have to."

"She criticized me. Over you." Slipstreaming, Kat touched her face in a way that changed the emotional animation of her avatar toward *worried* with a subset of *shy*. Her avatar's expression changed, but it continued emulating Kat's other movements: grasping hands in front, quieting the voice by ten percent, tilting down the face a few degrees, and opening the eyes wider by seven percent. Kat saw none of this herself, though, as she was using the avatar in first-person.

"Okay. May I know why you've been criticized?"

"So," Kat faltered on how to express the plague in her mind, "why don't you own more, Tennan? Ugh, that sounds terrible. I'm not after your stuff. Really. I just... what have you been doing since you've been in TruWrld2 so long? I hate asking this."

Tennan laughed gently and shook his avatar's head. "Kitty-Cat, you're so shy. Someday I hope you'll feel better about coming out from under the couch." In the monitor-flicker of her living room, Kat tried to smile. "There's a good reason. But to make you really understand, I ask you for a favor."

"Favor?"

"Meet me at the top of the second-tallest hill in my grape arbor before daybreak tomorrow morning. That's my favor. You will need to see to understand the part that words can't say."

"What will I understand?"

"Ah, Kitty-Cat. I don't need to own more. I already have the most wonderful part of TruWrld2." He sent a jump target and coordinates. "Meet me there, dawn, with sun rising and dew still on the grapes. That's my moment. Every now and then, the horses come galloping through the lower field. When it happens, Kat, you'll understand what I see in life here. Maybe you won't want to be anywhere else, either."

Kat tried to absorb the words, but couldn't stop thinking of the ragged city blocks of nature that was Park Square. Perhaps her avatar communicated something of her loneliness in slipstreaming her physical actions into TruWrld2, because Tennan continued: "Kitty-Cat, nothing would make me happier than what I already have." He stepped his avatar closer to hers and halted. Crisp, detailed eyes in beautifully nuanced, saturated colors gazed into each other. His pupils dilated. He was still, taking in her form quietly, standing in presence with her. Kat longed for the moment of connection. "Nothing except, perhaps, to share the experience of that perfect moment with you."

On the monitor, the male figure closed the gap as the view angle spun out to show the pair of them. Kat nodded her consent so TruWrld2 would allow his actions to proceed. She dropped the slipstream, de-syncing her movements from her avatar's, then reeled back on the couch as the two avatars on the screen embraced, kissing each other with esteem and greed. Kat hugged her own knees and cried.

—

The next World One morning, the gossamer drapes revealed the first pink flares of summer morning. However, because TruWrld2 was regularized in 14-hour days and 10-hour nights, and because of time zones, Kat still had 18 hours and 40 minutes before the next sunrise in Tennan's arbor.

The bluish glow of Kat's monitors overpowered the morning's nascent pink hues as soon as they lit. "Map, maaap. Go flyyy over. Come on, map."

When she'd left the limbo park, her avatar returned to its last recorded location, which was in a garden in TruWrld2's North Carolina. She activated Tennan's jump target. TruWrld2 asked how to proceed.

Although one of the greatest draws of digital living was freedom from geographic limitations, none of the worlds still offered free, on-demand travel—except to premium account holders like Tennan. As a tier 3 user, Kat could either pay a fee for each instant transfer or put her avatar "in transit" for one hour per time zone crossed. The latter was allowed at no cost. In this way, sim-worlds netted sixty percent of their revenues by selectively *removing* access to a costless, core service. User impatience and failure to plan ahead had again proved themselves as reliable honeypots.

"Six hours, poof," Kat muttered as she finalized the travel coordinates to Tennan's arbor in TruWrld2's Italy. The travel sequences began. They consisted of scenic passing vistas overlaid by advertisements from businesses in her destination region of TruWrld2. Even for frequent travelers, these ads rarely became repetitive because TruWrld2 constantly expanded its regions by an *expand-and-infill* policy. Land masses increased in size, which created veins of vacant areas between established older land. These new regions offered needed opportunities for new users and new businesses so subscribers would not become frustrated.

True to form, the first ad had nothing to do with Italy. A sharp-nosed female stood in what could have been a deluxe Servi-Mod apartment. The ad measured user interest by activity level of the slipstream controls benchmarked against typical activity for this user at this hour, then used the data to tweak its message: "Here's something to wake up to, Kat: This," she indicated her avatar, "is the real me of course, but my World One body likes to wake up where I'm comfortable. My surroundings. My truth. My walls. Tech Walls!"

Kat had closed her eyes and missed the advanced holographic effects the ad then demonstrated. By the time she opened her eyes again, Eva was waiting outside her building.

—

Eva's setup was simple. A weighted easel held a portable membrane monitor in a light frame. Hook-and-loop straps prevented wind from carrying the monitor away.

The monitor displayed "Run It Over" in tall, blocky letters. Below these words, a simple diagram of car tracks bent in three directions like a fleur-de-lis. The left and right arc each ended in a red X; only the center arc rushed toward infinite distance unimpeded.

Heroes save people's lives, came a licorice voice from the monitor. It was a masterful recording. Something under the chesty masculinity of the tones blazed heedless confidence and control. Passing men often looked toward the voice as though they had just remembered their middle names; passing women would look as though they'd forgotten their last names. *Simple decisions can make you a hero. When driving, never swerve for small animals in the road. Know who you protect. Run it over. Save your passengers' lives. Run it over.*

If Eva were ever linked to the man whose voice it was, or if the accent were identified as Moma, she could have been detained for questioning—perhaps for months. But, as Sodi pointed out, it was so effective.

On the membrane monitor glowed images of people smiling, hugging their children, and eating group meals at full-sized tables. The nucleus, the connection—something here was Eva's real message. Her verbal message *run it over* pertained to almost nobody: Few people drove at all, let alone with family in the car. Yet she was paid to deliver this message in public spaces.

The reason Eva's job existed was political. When grade school transitioned to digital classrooms, a few staunch politicians eyed the cultural changes with fear. Soon after, police training eroded into little more than investigative digital forensics because most crime shifted to the sims. Stuck in their own world—one arguably as removed from World One as the sims—incumbent politicians did not understand the draw of digital realms. So they legislated against them.

One of their less offensive—and therefore longer-lived—efforts was the Organic Life Health and Safety Initiative. It funded *callers* to greet people in public and offer service messages to remind citizens how to conduct safe and healthy World One lives. So long as these message-givers communicated their slogans to enough people, they received a paycheck. It was likened to a breadcrumb trail back to the old ways.

Indeed, the program was as effective as a breadcrumb trail: it fed a few birds. At first, callers' messages required annual evaluation, although no studies were ever done to see if the messages made any difference in citizens' lives. Over time, budget cuts removed the evaluations, but the program continued to dole out checks. Nobody argued to close it because doing so meant *killing jobs*—jobs perceived as difficult because they occurred outdoors. It wasn't worth the reputation risk to bring up.

This is how Eva eked out a paycheck by saying a random message to the diminishing part of the population that ventured from their homes. But it wasn't her message she cared about. She sought the rare person who still craved in-person conversation.

Eva had brought one chair for Sodi's son. She placed it under the protection of a faded awning. Wrapped in a blanket, the boy hunched over a bulkier, old-model mini-tab. By casual glance, most would have assumed he was taking his lessons, but the avatar the boy operated was not at school. Instead, he explored a private test world that Sodi had hard-loaded onto the device before frying its communication ports. The child was so benign that nobody questioned his presence.

Having arranged her station, Eva composed herself. She smoothed her crisp sundress and looked out expectantly for any eyes she could catch. The scarce passers-by hurried, turning at the voice, but not raising their gaze above Eva's knees. On occasion, one would swipe their mini-tab at the membrane monitor without stopping. Their action indicated that they had heard her message and approved of it.

Eva thanked these people. Her stipend through the Initiative depended directly on securing these upvotes. However, most voters gave their approval out of pity, not appreciation.

Some thirty-five minutes later, a sunken-eyed man with a face like a jack-o-lantern ambled toward them. His likeness to a carved pumpkin was made worse by goggle scars—permanent, ruddy indents caused by excessive use of VR headsets, which were cheaper than large panel displays, but more immersive than mere monitors. This man gawked at Eva and her message with a great deal of pause. He watched the presentation twice before settling marble eyes on her and mouthing, "Desperate?"

"I am concerned for people's safety. Lives are claimed every month by—"

"No, you," he said. "You desperate?"

"Sir?" Eva feigned.

Jack-o-lantern realized that this was a very complete answer to his question, but it was not the answer he wanted. "Lookin' like ya gonna stand here all the blazin' day. A pretty woman like you—"

"Sir, we are all pretty in our chosen worlds—"

"Well, that's true now. But hardly—"

"—and my concern is for World One safety. I once knew—"

"—*hardly*, as I was sayin', my intent." His right hand crept too deep into the pocket of his red shorts. He jingled some spare change.

Eva set her jaw and spoke slowly. "I am only here to promote safety."

Jack-o-lantern scowled. "Hey boy! How do ya like your mumma bein' a bum? Ya sleep on that chair? Betcha do!"

"Do not address my child."

"Just a bum, got a bastard kid bum. Hobos couldn' work if ya tried, not that ya try."

"It's time for you to move on."

"I see ya today, and I'm gonna see ya next week, next month, next year. Oh, I'll remember you, I'll be thinkin' of you. Least ya look like ya eat." He nodded his head across the street, where another Initiative booth had been set up at an odd, flapping angle. "Oh, I know how ya eat. One day when it's cold, yeah, ya gonna be sayin', 'Run it over, baby, and run it over here to me!' Ya just hope I say yeah." He hooted wetly and swiped away from her monitor—a downvote.

"Go," said Eva, not moving. Jack-o-lantern did, but not without leering.

It took a few moments for Eva to regain her inner balance. When she was ready to look out at the world with seeing eyes again, she found Sodi's child staring at her.

"Mama, he was mean."

"Yes, he was."

"I don't like it because he is mean to you! He needs to be punished!"

Eva stepped under the awning and squatted next to the boy. "I don't like it either. But people like that are their own punishment: They go through life being themselves. They can never, ever escape themselves."

The child looked confused. "Am I a bum?"

It was three breaths before Eva decided how to answer the sick child. "Stand up. Look across the road. Do you see that other man? He's giving messages, just like us. Do you see him?"

"Yes."

"Describe him for me, please."

"You see him, too."

"I can, but I can't see him through your eyes. Tell me about him as though I had no eyes."

At this statement, the child hesitated, examining his mother's face with anxiety or guilt, as though she'd inadvertently said something true. After a few moments to settle, he faced across the road and studied the man as though he were counting jellybeans in a jar. "He lays down. He stays laying down. It's hard there, not like my bed."

Eva prodded, "Tell me about his clothes, his possessions."

"He got dirty," the boy observed. "I'm—mama, he's wrote on

the monitors. Why did he do that?" The child was now pointing to a shallow gouge sneering across the man's presentation screen. The words *10,000 Steps to Well-Being* were flanked by brackish smudges that, at best, were once wood ashes.

"I think a mean person did that."

"Was it pumpkin-head?" Something in Eva jumped, wondering why Sodi's son, too, had seen the man as a jack-o-lantern. Eva shook her head *no*, and the child continued, "He didn't clean it up."

Eva placed her hands around the boy's upper arms, holding on to him. "He can no longer afford to care. He gave up." The 10,000 Steps man raised himself to a half-sit and knocked over a bottle. "Child, that is the way that the pumpkin man saw us. This is how he thinks we are."

"Why?"

She stood in front of the child to take up his whole view. "Because he is sick with an idea that the only thing worth living for is in a sim. He thinks that if we are out here, we are so poor that we can't afford to get in a sim. And most of the people walking past us today probably think the same thing."

"They do."

Eva ignored this answer. "That's why I do this work. It's not because I can't get a sim job. It's because I want to change their ideas. I want to give people hope and connection. Not a lot of people want it, and some are rude to me for it. But some things are so important that other things stop mattering. Someday, maybe there will be more people who think like me."

Eva wanted to say more. She wanted to explain the importance of community and of family—any family you've got, any community you can find, at any cost—and drive home the importance of not being isolated, of not letting people isolate him, of not letting people lead him astray to lifestyles that a lifetime could fall into whole and disappear. But the child's breathing was off. His eyes looked old and knowing—and weary of knowing—and she was too startled by them to finish vocalizing her response.

—

Two hours later, Eva faced a quite different audience. The young woman wore a simple tunic cut in the overlapping sea-wave shape popular this week among Servi-Mod residents. These Santa-made styles raced in and out of fashion as swiftly as great ideas in an ADHD mind. Yet however styled, their outrageous flair announced wearers as one of the privileged. Out of duty, Eva approached, "Pardon me, miss. I want to express to you how important it is to cherish—"

"Run it over, ha. Yeah, I'd run it over."

"Oh?"

"Whatever, sure. I smear down what come I can. Like. Well, all my cars are sim. But yeah, run it over. Sure."

Eva tucked her opinions behind a prim smile and let the woman walk off. When she turned back, Kat was exiting her building with a plump satchel slung over one shoulder. Eva stepped forward to partially block the walkway. "Pardon me, miss. I want to express how important it is to cherish this life we are living—"

"Yes, I always upvote; don't worry." Kat swiped without looking up, and Eva realized she might move on before she could catch her attention.

"It's more than an upvote—"

Startled, Kat looked up. "What, money? You get a stipend. Lady, we all have problems."

"Not money. Life. My son," Eva motioned backward to Sodi's child, "lost a friend in an accident. They swerved. I don't want any other family to go through that pain. I want to save people from pain and losing life and those we love. Have you experienced loss?"

"Wait, I've seen you. You've been here before?"

"Well—"

"No, you're... Wait, your son did what? What is this?" Kat blinked a few times at the presentation. "'Run it over?' I mean, what on earth do you mean by that? Run over animals? Why?"

"To save people. To save kids. We can't control what animals get into the road. But we can give our all to cherish and protect what we have." Eva watched Kat taking in the presentation.

"Oh my god. You can't just run over things! I mean, I'm sorry about your son and all, but the animals have lives, too. I don't drive, but if I did, I'd be slamming the brakes."

"Yes, animals have lives. So do we." Eva bluffed, trying to find an inroad, and remembered the younger woman's conversation at the diner about a permanent heart. "I just want to say that it comes down to love, miss. Nobody wants to hurt animals. But sometimes, if you really love someone, you have to take a risk to keep them safely in your life. What would you be willing to risk for someone you loved? What sacrifices, however painful, would you be willing to risk happening to make sure the one you love could stay in your life?"

Kat's lips clenched. Her eyes looked at Eva with half longing and half skepticism. "I'm not even sure this is about animals. But I do know about risks. Who are you?"

"I'm Eva."

"Eva, you don't act like a... like a..."

Eva smiled to cover up her panic that this person would walk away and disappear forever, unreached, lost. She didn't think she could convert her in time, not today, not with her guard up. So she said, "You're the kindest person I've gotten to speak to today. Before you go, can you tell me where I can find a nice place to do some thinking? Like you say... we all have problems."

Kat seemed to relax at the idea of being welcomed to walk away, and in that ease she lingered longer. "Yeah, I know a place. I go there lots; same reason, too. I think you'll like it."

Chapter 6

As the less reliable of her two jobs, Kat braided hair. Given the reclusive tendencies of society, braiding work was scarce, but it paid well. The control and endurance of Kat's sinewy hands won her the most regular and best-tipping customer in the city—the mayor.

Shaking out her arms, Kat looked around the room and prepared to begin. Mayor Chatoy relaxed into a padded, leather chair that gleamed in spite of its age. As Kat began undoing the old braids, the mayor closed her eyes to relax and think.

She had a lot to think about. Originally having ridden into office on a popularity wave for her "no local taxes on sim-come" platform, the mayor now faced poor odds of re-election that fall. Most of her constituents didn't even know her name, and liked her mostly for the geometrically precise and detailed hair that gave her the look of an avatar in the flesh. It made her seem relevant. She was not, in fact, digitally relevant. She had the confidence to play the role, but knew that one slip in her PR would reveal how little she understood about the avatar-based lives she somehow represented. Her hairstyle had never been much of a political platform, but apathy ruled politics.

Apathy ruled the city as well. It made governance easier: People who self-confined required very little service from the real world—*World One*, the mayor corrected herself. Year after year, she'd balanced budgets despite the drastic loss of tax revenue because most services went unused. Again and again, she'd cut the police force and officer training without an increase in violence: reported blue-collar crime was rare in a culture of shut-ins. Mayor Chatoy had cut court employees and archivists because the jobs had become idle: Legal matters and property exchanges were rare. She'd cut infrastructure because fewer vehicles meant the roads required less repair. Unfortunately, the roads required *more* repair than her budgets allowed, but this problem plagued the whole nation. Nobody complained because nobody cared.

Well, that's not true, the mayor reminded herself, feeling another new row of hair come under Kat's fastidious attention. *Some care, but not as they once did. They care that things stay the same, yes, they can't stand someone who is different. If you're different, you're an extremist, a subversive.* She'd never liked the idea of contingent citizenship; it went against the values of welcome and equality her grandmother had taught her. But politically she couldn't express her reservations without public accusation that she deserved the label *subversive* herself. While the idea of doing so anyway tantalized her, she realized it would likely be the final word of her career. Many viewed those who didn't fit in as threats to the social order. As a result, the prevailing attitude demanded that nobody stick out—except in the sims, where anything went.

What we have is a social monoculture, the mayor recited in her mind, preparing a speech she had no occasion to give; *and this monoculture is worsening the very problem it solved. We see it as a tidy, self-feeding cycle, and it keeps the populace complacent. Complacency eases governance. It's easier because there's so little left to be responsible for!*

Complacency also placed big business in power. Corporate taxes increasingly paid for government, and corporations knew it. Never having succored commercial entities, Mayor Chatoy had seen ample lobbyist dollars funneled from the giant Servi-Mod corporation to a more cooperative councilman—the one now poised to unseat her. His platform involved privatizing roads and handing them over to corporate entities—likely Servi-Mod—because they were the primary users of roads, and they had the cash flow to maintain them and perhaps even protect them from bombings with surveillance systems. Mayor Chatoy feared the corporate privatization of public infrastructure, but knew ethics alone would not salvage her position or her city. Politics required money. But the money was with Servi-Mod. And soon, the politicians would likely be Servi-Mod. So every day, Mayor Chatoy smiled and shook hands and hid her fears that little other than her public image stood between public city roads and the corporate giant.

—

When Kat finished the braiding, she returned home on her toes. Satchel pummeling her lower back, she dared not touch her heels to the pavement lest it slow the sprint. Heartbeats tick-tocked in her head. Her legs ached; her lungs felt raw. Her hands would not release the numb from her two hours of intricate effort.

Elevators were waiting. Slipping into one, Kat stood inside the little room with her nose two inches from the doors, ready to burst forth when her floor came. As she swung through her apartment door, she glanced at the clock hands stretching upward as though overcome with praise. Tipping over her sofa arm, she landed in the same spot she'd occupied at sunrise, spilling braiding gems from her satchel.

"I'm here," she spoke to nobody, fumbling the slipstream. "Come on, Italy, I'm here."

As the welcome screen released, her avatar appeared, framed in greens and blues. Grape vines punctuated the hills, rising straight and then turning at right angles to reach toward one another. She stood beside a grandfather tree, huge boughs sweeping down in front of a sun low on the horizon. In the Italian arbor, it was the dinner hour.

"Welcome," said the familiar baritone, "at last. I was so happy to see you arrive."

"Yes, thank you," Kat still panted. "I was... I guess part of me... came earlier than the rest... sorry. I really wanted every minute here."

"Kitty-Cat, is something wrong? Your voice is halting. I shouldn't have transmission speed problems here. Certainly not here."

"No, it's me. Out of breath. I ran home. Work... other work... non-sim, went long. Everything's okay."

Tennan smiled and grasped both of her hands. With deliberate slowness, he kissed her once on each cheek. "I welcome you, Kat."

She panned to the right with Tennan. At the arbor's hilltop, a small, set table draped with white linen sparkled in the evening sun. When they reached it, Tennan drew out a chair for her.

"My beauty," he invited.

Kat blushed along with her avatar, and realized she was about to eat in sim without having prepared herself anything in real life. She stifled a sigh, anticipating the awkward snacking she inevitably resorted to when her sim and real mealtimes didn't align.

"Your salad, miss," said the voice. She looked up to see a digital servant presenting her with an exotic tray; another offered wine to Tennan with flawless formality. The drones were cheaper and more private than hiring live help, and more traditional than ordering the courses to simply appear on the table.

If it were real, the salad in front of Kat would have been the lead image for food delivery ads in World One. Lettuce rippled like a microcosm of fjords. Opalescent cucumber slices shimmered beside translucent, rubine tomatoes.

Kat moved her hand as thought it held a fork for the

slipstream. Her stomach struggled to re-interpret the motion as not pertaining to tangible food.

"How is your salad, Kitty-Cat?"

"It is beautiful!"

"More beautiful yet from where I sit," Tennan smiled. Kat ordered her avatar to smile as well, although in person she hesitated at the remark. What was beauty in a world where the least tomato could be remade into a ruby? "Tell me, what is your work outside sims?"

"I braid hair. Well, I analyze farming data. That's digital of course. I actually don't need to braid." Kat sounded nervous to herself. "Um. It's so nice to be here."

"Braiding," Tennan mused. "It has been so long since I have seen that done organically. Tell me, Kat, what about it draws you?"

Kat stared at her avatar-self reflected on the surface of a tomato, and something in her relaxed. "It's my hands. Sometimes just touching people." Kat paused. Tennan waited. "Sometimes I think about the mind under the hair. It's less than an inch under my fingertips. I wonder what memories are there, what feelings. And I'm pulling on the hair, rooted so closely to all that experience. It's wild, to have a mind so close, right under my hands."

She looked up. Tennan was smiling: his face held admiration, but also sadness. "Oh, Kat. Nobody else could have answered that question like you did. Please understand that when you say things like this, it brings me the same joy as your braiding brings you. The things you say, the way you look at the world–it is a pleasure to feel your mind so close. It is a rare pleasure."

The glorious salad was no longer pretty enough to hold Kat's attention.

—

The directions Kat had given Eva to Park Square were accurate but unnecessary. Eva knew all of the natural spots in the city. Moreover, Sodi had been working with the arbor hologram committee to address this exact off-green patch of land for some time. Eva headed there with the boy hanging onto her neck, supported by one of her arms. Her equipment clattered at her other side.

Once lined with maples along all four of its long borders, the park retained only one out of every twenty neglected trees—and the survivors were all in decline. Around each position for a tree stood a grate that had recently been removed, adjusted, and set back in place with a hologram generator beneath it. The live trees, too, had been tampered with. Each of these received a curved generator dug in off-center to encapsulate the existing tree. With the city council's recent approval of Sodi's leaf artwork, the new trees could go live at any time. Eva sighed. Once the holograms went live, part of this park would be just another sim.

Seeing where he was, the boy perked up in spite of his recent illness. He trotted through the spotty grass and conquered a stand of rocks, which improved his view of the large lake off-center in the park. The only other people present were a man and his daughter. Grimacing, the man was sticking his right foot in the lake. He reached with a long stick to fish back an escaping, plastic toy boat.

Eva set down her burdens and unfolded the chair for herself, knowing Sodi's son would perform his normal ritual. Beyond her hearing, the child rehearsed the posted signs, saying, "Hazard: No Swimming." Holding solemn in her heart, Eva watched him point out to himself the patch of deeper murk toward the middle of the water. A concrete drainage stand rose from it. Eva knew the boy would be calling it the "mouth of water world" that could "forget anything."

Eva disagreed that the lake could forget. Not even the child had forgotten what had happened there, at least on some level. Yet once the boy finished his brief and solemn ritual, she too ceased mourning what was lost there and returned to scanning the park for Kat, in case she came by, and thinking about how to reach her again if she did not.

—

The walk home seemed long. Kat had not shown up at Park Square. Fevers and sitting in the sun had sapped the boy. Yet, burdened with her equipment, Eva couldn't carry him more than a block at a time. At one point, a rare taxicab pitched past them, taking up two lanes on the road. Eva wondered if the child would ask to ride in it in spite of his unlegitimized status. But he remained mute.

It was a further disappointment to Eva that, upon reaching home, Sodi waved off their presence. With frosty movements, he turned his back to her and faced his bank of display panels in his windowless studio. Eva watched his motions with the lonely rejection she'd felt from dozens of passers-by that day. She'd seen this scene often: the dark silhouette of Sodi's back, the bright panels, the menacing glow of his specially licensed beta hologram generator on standby.

Eva exited, closing the door on whatever Sodi might be creating. "Do you need anything to eat?" Eva asked the child as she returned to the living room. Sodi's son sprawled on the floor like a marking on a treasure map. "I'll bring food right to you. You don't have to move."

The child did not move or even look in her direction. "What does the dirty bum say? Does he say 'run it over' too?"

Eva folded her legs to sit on the floor beside him. "The man we saw laying on the sidewalk today has the '10,000 Steps' message."

"What is it?"

"It means that, if a person takes ten thousand steps every day, he will be healthier."

He did not move. "How far does a crocodile walk?"

Eva frowned and tried to piece together the child-logic behind the question. It was difficult for her, and she wished Sodi would come out. Sodi always seemed to understand his child's strange thoughts, just as the child always seemed to understand both of them. Eva had no such gift, so she picked the answer, "The crocodiles of the world don't walk as far as a person determined to stay away from them."

The child seemed to accept her answer as relevant. "Did I walk that far today?"

"We walked far enough."

"It's too far. I can't do it again."

"Oh, baby," Eva leaned down to put her cheek on the boy's forehead for a moment, evaluating. Her emotional fatigue threatened to not let her back up. "I'm sorry. Maybe it wasn't the right choice. I just wanted... I'm very sorry. You rest now."

"Does the bum do two hundred steps? Every day?"

"Ten thousand steps? Not any more. He's been at that spot for a long time." Sighing, Eva got up to distract herself from how much a part she and this child had played in his decline, and then realized: *The 10,000 Steps man. He could help me with Kat.*

—

Kat lost count of how many courses of jewelry-store food had been presented to her, but the cup of sultry liquid meant that this was the last of them. The sim meal had left her divided. Her World One eyes traced every inch of Tennan's avatar—his confident shoulders, the easy sparkle of his eyes, his thick and welcoming lips—but the rest of Kat's real body longed to encircle something of substance.

When the coffee was cleared, Tennan rose and extended a hand to aid her avatar up. The hand trembled, emulating his World One movements. Beneath her breath, her abdomen quivered in response. He said, "Miss Kat, while you are under no obligation to believe a dog like me, this has been the most enjoyable meal of my life." Kat's lips tried to agree, but her tremulous breath kept her from giving words to her avatar. She held her slipstream controls at the ready to accept what she thought anyone would offer next.

"I hope you now understand some of why I don't own more here." He watched her stand, and as their eyes came more level, he gazed into hers. "The most beautiful, most mystically perfect moments in life need to be discovered, not created. There is no true living in a mere program. Kitty-Cat. You are my joy because you *choose* to be here. It's your choice to spend time with me, and you change everything about the experience. Beautiful as you are, and you are," he reached for her hand, "I could not enjoy you if I knew every word you were about to say. Your words, and the mind behind them, they delight me." Kat's scarce guardedness melted, warmth spilling through her World One body as she focused on TruWrld2. Her avatar took a half-step closer as Tennan continued, "When I cannot know the joy that awaits me, it is glorious when it arrives."

"Tennan," Kat answered, "I hope much, much joy awaits you."

He smiled and drew her in. Kat's World One back arched as though anticipating Tennan's body would emerge through the monitors. She and her avatar closed their eyes, then heard the words, "Miss Kat, I will pry myself from you now lest I offend you with my impulses." Kat's expression fell. "Will you rejoin me here before sunrise?"

Need and courtesy bisected her mind. "But—yes. I will."

"Thank you. Pleasant evening, treasured one."

—

In her different timezone, it wasn't night for World One Kat, who nonetheless lay flat in her bed staring at the ceiling. A sense of electricity lingered in her thoughts and in her thighs. She drew the rumpled purple blanket up to her chest as a shield against her strange sense of shame. Tennan must have known what she anticipated after the meal. Did his rejection mean he considered her too indiscriminate with her intimacy?

After enough aimless worrying, she went back to her monitors and face-called Mez. The dark hills around her avatar faded fully to black, indicating she had privacy. A rectangle opened into a video frame. In it, Mez's watermelon-farmer avatar, elsewhere in TruWrld2, turned his head from within a tractor to look at her.

"Hey, Kat," he said in a voice as jovial as ale, "whatcha doing in the box, girl?"

"Mez, I'm a mess. Can we talk?"

"Long as your box keeps up with my tractor. Where are you?"

"Italy."

"Saving a bit of travel fees?"

"You know I always use time."

"Girl, I keep telling you the time is worth more than the money. Sim-come, girl, sim-come. Get some. Seriously, it helps. Oh hold up." The burly avatar straightened his gaze and drove on through the fields, unresponsive to Kat's presence. Used to this, Kat understood that Mez was busy with another avatar elsewhere, leaving this one to auto-run for a few moments. Twenty seconds later, the farmer downshifted the tractor and spun it around in a neat U, ending up perfectly centered on the next row.

"Mez, you there yet?"

A flicker of random expression gripped the face of the tractor driver, but disappeared as he answered, "Just a moment, madam, my hogs are pulling me in fifty-ought directions."

Kat sighed at the auto-dialogue. She sat back, staring at her screen in resentment. Tennan's attention engaged her so thoroughly that she felt she was the only woman in the sim. Now, her best friend left her feeling like the only person at all.

"Tell me your troubles, Kat," the farmer said, raising his eyebrows and looking over at her. "I'm back."

"It's Tennan."

"How much did he steal?"

"No, Mez! He didn't take anything! We had the most wonderful dinner... I can't even describe it. Then, well you know, it was really nice and I expected... but he just said goodnight."

"He didn't want you?" the burly farmer shouted, calloused hands gesticulating. "What, he thinks you made that skin sexless? Girl, drop him. He isn't doing anything for you or with you!"

Unsettled, Kat stared at the avatar. He had stubble. "I'm seeing him again. Soon."

The square chin faced her. "After *that*? Girl, you are as crazy as he is! Oh, give me another moment." The hewn face under the Stetson relaxed. Mez was gone for the moment, but the driver kept pressing the pedal, and the tractor kept pushing forward. Even with no human mind attending, the program would keep growing soft tendrils of roots on the new seedlings in the next field. Plants would lengthen up out of their dark birthplaces fraction by fraction. The sun would set. The avatar would park the tractor and return to his home position. *Even without Mez,* Kat thought, *this day could be happening in exactly this way, ceaselessly.* Her sense of isolation deepened.

"So I have it," Mez startled Kat from her shadowed thoughts. "He is totally playing you." The wizened eyebrows lifted. "Next time he sees you, he'll expect you to be desperate. You'll be falling over yourself for him twice as hard. And that," the avatar leaned in for emphasis, revealing chest hairs, "is totally what he wants."

"Yeah, maybe." There was no commitment in Kat's voice.

"Tarnation that bumpkin!" auto-cursed the farmer. "Don't you go getting sad on me. Ditch that self-pumping jerk! The end."

"Mez: What happens after users die? I mean, you can slip in and out of this place, and it keeps running. How long can you be gone?"

"That's why I keep telling you to start making sim-come. This is like... eternal life, Kat. It just runs. You get enough resources, you can buy a contract for your stuff to be maintained. If you have enough perpetual processes, it can go on indefinitely. You should look into it; the good contracts can get real specific about how to handle things. It's like you're still there."

"So you want to be a farmer forever, Mez?"

"Well," Mez laughed, "this here guy is really useful because of his strength ratings. And I kind-of like wearing him. But I think I'll perpetuate Siloni."

"Who?"

"Purple faerie girl. You do know you can transfer sim-come between worlds, right?" the avatar rolled his eyes. "That's easier than getting Servi-Mod to convert your kash to cash."

"Mez? Why?"

"Why what?"

"Why perpetuate anything? Why use your real life to

perpetuate... this? Mez, I need to know, I really need to know."

For a few moments, the avatar returned to his good-natured forward stare, then came back to scrutinize Kat in the box. "I don't get you sometimes. Haven't you ever wanted to live forever?"

Kat managed to end the sim-video call before she started heaving: *No, sometimes I want to die.* She tried to hold it, but sounds broke through her emotional meniscus in waves. Standing and stabilizing herself with her arms out, Kat caught her reflection. She looked like she was offering to hug the emptiness around her. "Why is there never anyone anywhere?" she raged. "I hate being alone! I'm always alone!" She overturned the couch, flung open the curtain sheers, lifted a window pane, and punched out its screen. She was unsure if she would scream at the people four stories below or just jump down and meet them.

Two things happened as Kat pushed her torso through the rough mesh: First, Tennan's words replayed in her head: *Kitty-Cat, you are my joy because you* choose *to be here.* Second, the 10,000 Steps man looked up.

He thought: *Girl coming right through the screen. Guess she lost the stairs to her apartment. Yeah, you get lost in life. Go wandering your ten thousand steps, no doubt you get lost. Get lost on step three, yeah. And still these people are walking. Walking on their leg-sticks, and they see me, and they see the girl. She's hanging out the window and she's got ten thousand steps to go before she hits that pavement, yeah. I've walked those ten thousand steps. You can look at me. No point in walking. Once you're lost, ten thousand steps and you're still lost. Girl won't walk, she'll jump there. Ten thousand steps, and down the whole way. I can show you down. I'll show you how to cover ground. Ten thousand steps to hell, and here I am.*

But Kat had lost her appetite for skydiving. She scoured the street below for proof that Tennan's philosophy had been right.

She saw ordinary people moving. They had choice; where was their joy? They hobbled or hurried or gawked. The ones toward the left went to the right; the ones toward the right went to the left. All seemed to drag their feet, working against their own movement. Kat screamed raw sounds at the walkers, who tried to ignore her. If they showed any beauty in their choices, it might have proven that Tennan was right. But she saw none.

Chapter 7

With his mouth full of hummus, the boy did not have to talk much. It freed his mind to remember a day long ago. It was in a real place, not a screen place, but one he never saw anymore. There, the people paid attention and told jokes and sometimes smelled bad.

He'd found a good stick that day, and the funny-face man had told him it was a *tapas*. *It ee tapas*, he'd said, *it ee tapas*. He was happy to have the *tapas*, because it was a good size, but not too big to need both hands. Making his way up a big hill with short, colorful buildings, he saw a light spot on the ground near where he liked to throw cheese at the chickens. Getting closer, he realized it was feathers. Lots of them.

The funny-face man was watching, so the boy pointed at the feathers with his *tapas*. The old man didn't smile, but he still looked good to the boy. He picked him up. The funny-face man never made him put down his *tapas* before picking him up.

"We eat *ankank*. It's h-okay. Miss Eva make it."

The boy did not know why the funny-face man always called a chicken a *kank*, but the feathers looked bad being off of the *kank*. He ran to the wobble-wall building to see the rest of it. The boy liked this building most of all because he slept there with his toys. He saw Miss Eva in the kitchen. Her skirt swished around; it was pretty. He said, "Feathers got off!"

"Hello, little one. Yes, they did." Now he saw she had the face for a bad day. She had her hands up because they were messy: no touching.

"Why?" He reached for her skirt, but the *tapas* was still in his hand.

"I took them off the chicken after we killed it."

"Why kill a *kank*?"

"This chicken was not doing her job."

"Why?"

"She just couldn't. The hens' job is to lay eggs. We give them food; they give us eggs. This hen got too old and couldn't lay eggs."

Miss Eva turned on the water. It sounded like she was filling a bowl, but when she lifted it out of the sink, it was a *kank* body. It had no head or feathers. When she tipped it to the side and washed the skin, he could see into a dark hole spilling pink water. He knew Miss Eva loved the *kanks*, because she always snuck them cheese. She always smiled when the *kanks* did the limp-foot dance to each other.

"What's my job?" he asked her. Miss Eva looked over at him, dried her hands, and came down low on her knees to him.

"You have only one job: To be you. You will never be like a chicken. You do not have to fit into someone else's ideas of how you need to be. Your job is to be who you are."

—

Coming out of the old thoughts, the boy missed a lot of things from the memory. They didn't have chickens anymore. He no longer got to see the funny-face man or the wobble-wall building, even though they were so good to look at. And something more—he coughed at pain tightening his chest. Remembering things made him miss them, and the missing hurt. He felt lonely.

Mama was lonely, too. When he looked through her, he saw she did not miss the happy people and the colorful buildings. She did not miss anything. Her memories were like a broken picture frame with no picture in it: glass everywhere. She didn't know he could see this, but his father did. What mama thought about a lot was jobs. So he asked, "Does the bum have a job?"

"The 10,000 Steps man? Yes, he has a job."

"Is he doing it?"

She sighed. "No. Not well." Her expression changed into the *get things done* face. His father taught him about this when mama wasn't around. It meant to go deeper and find a hidden truth. That way you know what's going to happen. His father's lessons were hard.

"What happens to a person who does a bad job?"

"Usually their job goes away."

"What happens to the person?"

"It's a hard problem. Sometimes they get help. If nobody will help them, sometimes they go hungry or get too cold."

"Do they get killed?" *Like chickens who don't lay eggs*, he thought.

"No," she answered quietly. Quiet words were good directions, his father taught him. Quiet words meant you were going in the right direction to hear words people won't say or write. The child didn't know why it had to be so hard, why he had to know without reading or hearing. But mama continued to speak: "They don't get killed, but sometimes they die."

So it wasn't all that different than chickens. That's what mama wasn't saying. "What is my job?"

"What? To learn. Learn what your father is teaching you. You'll have a job later."

He tried to be very still, like he was when his father told him how to think about things. It made him feel bad, and he didn't want any more food. He didn't like this job. He already knew too much that he couldn't hear or read. He wished his job was still "to be who you are."

—

Not only did Sodi miss lunch, but he missed his son's lesson time. Eva resented his closed studio door as she fumbled through an ad-hoc lesson about the origin of sim worlds. When Sodi did come out, he was smiling. Eva was not.

"Sunshine, it's a good day! The modeling is done, loaded, tested. Lights go on tonight."

"Oh? Where?"

"Park Square *and* Empet Street. It will be a new town!" he jabbed his thumbs in his hip pockets and rocked back on his heels.

"Can I see it?" his son chimed in.

"Sure. Empet's not far. You feeling well?"

"Yes I am!" he answered. Eva furrowed her brow at them, then stared out the window. Seeing holograms infiltrate the city streets didn't seem to be as high a priority as developing their community, but she didn't have much room to disagree with taking the child outside after she'd just done the same.

"Great!" Sodi grinned at his son. Evaluating Eva, he strode toward her, arms ready. "Sunshine, hey sunshine, we knew it was coming. Just street trees. Hardly a life for a tree anyway."

"No, I'm fine. I'm just... we were at Park Square earlier. I was having just those thoughts." Eva thought about the way the old trees clung to their organic lives in the midst of a concrete city. "Sodi, when they encase those old trees in holograms, do the trees suffer? Do they lose their sunlight?"

The boy noticed that has father hesitated. "Some. Don't worry, no trees will be harmed in the ignition of these holograms. Scout's honor." Eva shook her head at the idea of Sodi as a boy scout and tried not to think of his honor. "Why'd you go all the way to Park Square? I guess it's too late to ask if you got home okay."

"That's where the woman Kat goes to clear her mind. It's most of what I got out of her this morning."

"Lady still has energy, she can keep my arm warm at the ignition."

Eva's face halted. "I... probably can't. I'm sorry. I need to stay on this Kat person. I need to see, uh, the 10,000 Steps man, and I really don't want to be there after dark."

The child watched his father's thoughts turn into a blockade, even though nothing about his body shifted. Sodi answered with each word soft and distinct. "Then you had better get going now, Eva. And make sure you can beacon me at one press." The ample balance of what Sodi had to say about this trip was expressed only in his unwavering stare, but this time Eva understood it, too. She absorbed his meaning for a moment, then without further comment picked up a bag from the kitchen and put on comfortable shoes–running shoes.

–

Despite protestations, Sodi draped a light jacket over the boy's shoulders before hoisting him up on his back. "You sure you don't want to use the wheelchair, little man? You'd get to rest better. And you are getting a bit big to be riding around on your father's back."

"No chair," said the boy. As they exited the building and progressed northward, Sodi's child saw nothing of his surroundings. The bridge of his nose nuzzled against his father's nape. Fingertips biting into deltoids, he kept his eyes closed against all distraction from the rhythmic power of bunching muscles and the spicy musk of his father's scent. Here, he found his greatest comfort. Mama cared for him, but his father was his *always* person.

Half the distance passed in this way, neither one speaking. When this pact of silence broke, it was Sodi asking, "Did you see mom's friend this morning? Did a woman talk to her?"

"Yes. I saw the woman, and I saw the rude man."

"What was the woman like?"

Sadness crept into the child. He opened his eyes and let the moments of connection pass, refocusing his thoughts in the *reaching* way his father always wanted him to, so he could say the things his father thought were right for him to know. "She didn't look at mama. Then she looked. And then she kept on looking, even after she went away." Hearing no response from his father, the boy kept talking, "I saw pretty things in her hair, like smooth rocks. I want those in my hair. And she has secrets that are sad."

Sodi was not surprised at the child's analysis. "How do you know?" he asked, although he knew the answer already.

"I read it in her no-read words."

"Where do the sad secrets take her? What will happen? How far can you see it?"

"She is sad... will be sad... because she is missing something. She doesn't see it. But she is losing it all the time." The child hunched his head down; suddenly his energy was sapped. "She's going to try to get it no matter what, but she knows she can't have it. And I love you, dad."

"I love you, too."

"But I love your muscles, and the way they jump."

Sodi chuckled. "You're a lunker." He took a few more steps. "Do you still not tell mama about these no-read words?"

"It's a secret. She didn't learn them anyway."

"Yeah, okay." Sodi exhaled, wondering what else to ask about coming events. "Son, did you say that there was a rude man?"

"Yes."

"What did he do?"

"He said mama's a bum. And I'm a mustard. He's a pumpkin-head! And he wants... mama to..." Sodi felt his child tensing through his silence, unwilling or unable to verbalize exactly what he'd read in the man. "He looked at mama mean, and he wanted... he needed... to get punished!"

Sodi understood enough of his son's own so-called *no-read words* to fill in the rest. Gears ground in him. Suddenly Eva seemed dangerously far. "How did Pumpkin-head look at Eva?"

"Like... like he hated his dinner that he would eat." The child began to cry.

"Did he touch her?"

"No."

Sodi's legs kept moving. "Did he go away on his own?"

"Mama told him to go away. He stayed. She made him go. He still put his face back at her, so she couldn't forget it. And now I can't forget it, either."

Sodi's pace slowed to a halt. His soft, dark curls panned around as he surveyed an intersection and turned west. Empet Street was only two blocks further. In this more central part of the city, buildings loomed over the road like the mismatched tombstones of giants, honoring lives and deeds no longer relevant. He said, "Tell me everything you remember about Pumpkin-head: What he looked like, where he came from, where he went. Make sure to tell me anything he said that you can remember."

"I don't want to remember," the boy protested.

Sodi sighed, impatient. "I'm sorry son, but I need to know everything."

"Why? For the police?" And here was the growing danger:

in teaching his son to read others, his son also read him. Ever since the skill had appeared, which was shortly after the child's mother died, Sodi sensed that his son's innate talent might surpass his own—might, in fact, be second only to old Funny-face.

Sodi therefore answered with caution: "I don't know what needs to happen until I hear everything you know."

After a silence, the child answered, "Pumpkin-head asked do I sleep in the chair. He had small red pants with money in them. He liked to touch his money," at this Sodi's back quaked once. "He smelled bad. He said to run mama over. He said mama is desk-spit. He will look for mama again. He wants to find her again."

"He won't find her again," Sodi growled from over his oxen shoulder. His son had not understood the word *desperate*, but he had understood its meaning in detail. "Where did Pumpkin-head go?"

"Away, I don't know."

"Where did he come from?"

"From the building."

"Which building? The one you were in front of?"

"Yes."

"The same one mama's friend came out of, the same one as the woman with the sad secrets?"

"Yes, that building."

Sodi calculated how much he knew, and what his chances were of pinpointing one bogeyman in a building of small apartments. "Did he come out of with anybody else?"

"No."

"What did he look like? Hair color, skin color, warts, skin pictures?"

"He looked like a Jack-o-Lantern with his too-big head with goggle scars. His hair was dirty. It was orange-brown. He had paper skin with dots. I don't know any skin pictures."

Sodi paced on, thinking. "Can you remember anything else? Anything at all?"

"He did a downvote for mama."

The child's position on the man's back saved him from seeing hate and triumph ignite in his father's eyes, but that didn't help. The child still sensed and bore every unsaid word: *I've got you. I will destroy you.* He became dizzy in the way that distance seemed wrong, just for a moment, and he knew: His fever was going to come back soon.

—

When Sodi reached Empet Street, he slid his son off his back at a viewing area between two empty arbor grates. The apartment buildings on Empet Street were taller and more ornate than their counterparts on the side roads. At entry level, they all presented a flat, vertical face at a steady distance from the road; their embellishments blossomed out as they rose. The building closest to Sodi had a latticework of stone rising into turrets so sharp they threatened to skewer the setting sun. Another grew on the solidity of deep brown timbers of impossible length and girth, bracing each other in geometric perfection. Yet another undulated as it soared, looming over the road like clusters of balloons. All were pristine. None were real. The tops of these buildings supported the same type of holographic generators that had been buried to ignite the trees.

There was another difference: In windows along the side street, a scarce smattering of faces showed in the windows—people wishing to see the ignition of their new trees, yet too busy to descend to street level. But the impressive frontages on Empet Street showed no faces at all.

The boy saw this at once and questioned it. "How come

these people don't look? Do they want to see the trees go on?"

Sodi glanced around at the mythic designs. "Sure, and they will. They're probably looking out right now. You can't see them because they are *inside* the holograms that make their buildings so fancy. They can't see perfectly, but they can see enough if they're close to the edge, the way you can see through your shirt if it's on your head. Do you understand?" Sodi felt warmth in his palm, and grasped the small hand back.

"They can really hide," the boy observed.

"Yes, and that's a lesson for you. Remember that, son. If you can *no-read* trouble coming, hide inside a hologram."

A sparse cheer sprung up around them, and at once they were in a grove of trees that never existed. Boughs of lopsided leaves billowed and swirled above them, tickling the air. From the middle distance, they heard clapping. Sodi lingered, but the rest of the spectators, ignition completed, turned around and trudged back to their homes. Watching them go, Sodi mused at how the world had changed with so little fanfare.

He was glad Eva had not seen the ignition. He didn't share her objection that they were *filling my world with their ideas*, and he was tired of portraying tolerance to mollify her. Enjoying his peace, he closed his eyes and felt the breeze on his face. It felt like eight or ten kilometers per hour. Opening his eyes, the trees matched this speed. They danced. It was beautiful. On his tiptoes, he reached up and tried to hook the lowest-hanging leaf spiral like a ring on his finger, but his hand slipped through. The boy watched.

"Do you remember making this leaf with me?" he asked his son, who nodded. "I took the mother leaf, which is the one we drew together, and made it a little different fifty times. When I use a randomizer with those fifty, I get an unlimited number of designs for individual leaves. So, you see, each of these leaves may be as unique as a leaf on a real tree." Sodi smiled down at his son. "Life is like art: What makes it real is that it's always a little different. This is real, just a different real."

But the child had stopped listening to the outer world. He studied something beyond his father, but kept holding on to his hand. "You won't call the police. I know. But it's okay. Nobody will get you for hurting him."

—

As a precaution, Eva traveled one block east and two-and-a-half blocks south—the opposite direction from Kat's apartment and the 10,000 Steps man—before hailing a cab. *More than three, you're free:* Three blocks was Sodi's advice for creating non-incriminating data while using city transportation.

The musty car looked twenty years old. It seemed as content as the driver to sit there while Eva fat-fingered her destination. The driver glanced at the identity credentials and physical model her mini-tab sent upon entering, but seemed more interested in the small bank of mini-monitors in her dashboard. TruWrld2 was open on one of them. Not finding an address match, Eva's mini-tab suggested four destinations from which to choose. She picked one she hoped was four blocks away from Kat's apartment. After a put-upon pause, the driver turned halfway from her sim and set out on the road.

Even though Eva's identity credentials were legitimate, she felt vulnerable letting the cab track her location. She took deep breaths and smoothed her palms down the legs of her long pants, secure at least that the curling scar announcing her subversive tie would stay hidden.

Ties to the Moma once meant ties to the 10,000 Steps man—back when he was whole, back before their tragedy. Eva pushed down her sadness and doubted her judgment. The chance that the 10,000 Steps man would be sober and awake enough to offer any valuable leads on Kat was slim enough. That he would be *willing* to do so defied common sense. Guilt riddled her as she realized how great a risk she was taking for such a small chance of something of questionable value. Sodi would never had made this choice.

But I have to, Eva forced her thoughts to say. *This is what it's going to take. I need to build this group; it's what I'm for; I must make a people we can all belong to. This is my work. This is who I am. This is my contribution to a hateful culture that forgets that not every unlegitimized person is an immoral criminal and moocher. Someone need to do this.* She breathed into her hands, which trembled. Anticipating speaking to the 10,000 Steps man, Eva's stomach began to clench. *Certainly others have risked and lost for this work. More than I do. It's worthy.*

—

The car stopped. Eva did not exit until the driver rapped angrily on the dividing glass. The street at which she'd arrived was lined with rowhouses, but not the swanky type where only one or two families occupied the entire residence. Turning her back toward the low sun, she walked to the next intersection. Taller buildings lifted up beyond baroque roofs. Eva knew roughly where she was.

She covered six blocks trying to find the right spot, but could now see the upturned easel and gray, mouse-bitten boots of the 10,000 Steps man. He sprawled. His eyes were open. Eva's light footsteps came within two paces of his left leg, then stopped. He did not look over.

He said to the intruder near him: "Here's the drill. Take ten thousand steps and you're good. Step one: upvote. Step two: step off."

"Frank, I need your help." Eva set her sack down at his side.

His gray face crumpled as though the name injured him. "You," he accused. He lumbered himself upright and turned toward the sack, opening it. Inside were three sandwiches and a large bottle of juice.

"This my payoff?" He reached in with a grime-striped hand.

"I need someone to watch for the comings and goings of someone who lives in that building. And to... to tell me if she's in some kind-of... emotional state."

"Ten thousand people living in that building. They all walk around, step by step, ten thousand steps a day. Ten thousand people and we're all a-walkin' alone."

Eva glanced along the block and retracted her voice. "You know why I'm doing this. You know that 'walking alone' is what I'm trying to overcome. Will you help me?"

The 10,000 Steps man bit into his dinner. "Wha fur? You can'n obercomb it. You know dat."

"It's slow, but we will, bit by bit."

"Yeah, step by step." he spluttered sodden bits of white bread onto the walkway. He swallowed. "I can tell you about step by step! Every day here in the toil with ten thousand steps to go, and you're never any closer. Walk all you want, sugar. Walk ten thousand steps today, again tomorrow, and all you get is another damn day of ten thousand steps on this rock. *Give it up, Eva!*"

"Shhh, please—" she looked around to see who might be listening.

"Ain't being shushed! Not by you!" he yelled. When Eva didn't object further, he took another bite of food and chewed.

Eva hazarded more words once he'd finished the first sandwich. "Frank, come back to us. You don't need to be hungry. There is another meeting coming up, and you know you'll be helped. You know how few we are; we need you, Frank. Please come back. You don't need to make yourself miserable like this."

The 10,000 Steps man licked off his smudged finger. "Misery's what is, Eva. Misery is what is. Ten thousand layers of it in every life. You seen it just like I have, you seen it exactly like I have, Eva. You seen the same damn people. You just shut your eyes to it so you can't find a better option. So you won't. You don't see anything, you just walk."

Eva had difficulty answering. Frank's words gave her the dizzying sense that her blood pressure had plummeted, and all she could do was stay standing and mutter, "I have seen life. You used to as well." It was a weak answer. The ruined man in front of her had been strong, had been loyal in the unconditional way Eva was to Sodi. They had a great deal of things in common. In facing him, Eva feared yet again that the biggest difference wasn't that she hadn't given up, but that she hadn't given up *yet*.

"Yeah, I saw life; it's misery! Piled up! It's ten thousand stories high, and you fall. You fall and keep falling because... because you're too piss-drunk to count so high anyway. It never ends, Eva! Give it up! I just want someone to tell me it's over."

"Then it's over!" pleaded Eva, thinking *please let this end, please let him not remember more.* "End this now, Frank! Leave this station, come back, and let us help!"

But Eva wasn't Sodi, and could not program her old friend. The 10,000 Steps man squinched his face and seethed out a lungful of virulent air. "*You* can *never* help me! The only thing that ever helped was ten thousand lifetimes ago, and I've died ten thousand deaths since then. Not even your merry band of self-righteous misfits can bring her back!" The wrinkles around his mouth deepened into a scowl. He closed his eyes against the return of those memories.

—

This memory Frank still had: For weeks ahead of that meeting, his beloved tried to hide her grimaces behind her curtain of chestnut hair. The moments of pain or stress crossed her face like ten thousand strikes of lightning. A steadying breath later, they would be gone.

The night before the meeting, she approached him with the insistent lust of one embarking across a ten-thousand-kilometer journey alone. Persisting against his initial fatigue, she pinned him with her thighs and drank breath straight from his lips until his need to fill her inverted into emptiness. She gave of herself until his thoughts tangled, until his angular muscles filled with fire. Yet when they had collapsed back from one another, only his body had taken its fill. Awash in her, he felt one aspect missing, one tiny crumb of her that had pulled away even though he wanted all of her.

He lay beside her. He spoke her name. After a long pause, she answered, "I can see so little beyond my own eyes," but would not explain.

The next morning was gone to him. *Stolen*, he thought, *lifted from my skull like a hat in a hurricane, and there have been ten thousand storms since.*

This memory he still had, too—one of the last: ten thousand peach fuzz hairs across her shoulders, down her arms, and along her earlobe refracted light. They shone as she enveloped the boy child in her lap, whispering at his temple. He could not hear her words, but he could see each wisp of gold hair on her.

Silently, he walked up behind her. Unturning, she said to him, "Frank. Even if you have ten thousand days after this, you will preserve what matters most, at least to some. Even the smallest actions, my love. Even the smallest. But I can't remember any more of it." Desperate to understand, he asked her to explain. She said something, but at that moment there was a loud shout, a rush of uniforms, and that terrible word.

Subversives, they yelled. Also *unlegitimized*. That memory he still had. And he remembered how much she loved her child, because when she turned, it was not to Frank. It was to the officers.

"It's okay, he's mine!" Much later, far too late to matter, he realized it was only to distract. Cassi wasn't legitimized, either. She called out only to distract and give time for her child to get away. "Oh, I just forgot," she called, and "let me get my ID! Won't be a moment!" The boy shot off her lap. He ran dutifully to his father, to Sodi, who only stared. The child's legs pumped like a programmed sandpiper, but Cassi darted to the lake.

The officers stopped short. It seemed to take ten thousand steps for her to reach the water, as though the shore warped away from her, stretching out that final dash into ten thousand yards of misery. She ran to the lake in Park Square. She glanced back once, at Sodi, moving her mouth in an explanation that Frank would never receive.

Her feet hit the water. Her waist hit the water, arms flying forward. The boy was running to his father, and she was swimming at full stroke into deeper water. The officers came short, confused as she began to flail and splash. Her chestnut hair was drenched. Her clothes dragged with weight. Her child had reached his father, but nobody was looking there. Frank watched his beloved saturate. One officer shouted for a rescue team; the other took off his shoes; her worn-down shoes still set on the shore. She had known she wouldn't need them.

He could still remember how Sodi ran with his son—away, away, not even looking back at her—and the officers shouted and swarmed toward her, not toward Sodi, but she was already saturated. She'd removed her shoes because she didn't need them to swim or to sink. She was in the water, and Sodi was running unpursued with their child. She had not glanced back at Frank. She would never turn toward him again.

The aftermath was gone to him. *Stolen*, he thought. *Stolen like the body they didn't give me to bury because of her scar. Stolen, yeah. She got dropped into a nickel-sized bottle hole that goes down forever and gives nothing back*. He wanted a drink.

Every day since, Frank had drowned out a piece of her. It was as though, when she hit the water, she broke into ten thousand fragments, and every day he lost one.

—

"Okay. You're right, Frank; I can't bring her back. I'm so sorry to have disturbed you." Eva stepped back and walked around him. She was thirty paces away when he called back.

"What's her name?"

Eva turned. "You... don't remember her name?" Eva remembered Cassi's name every day.

"Girl you want me to watch. Is it the pretty job you talked to this morning?"

Eva halted. "I thought you were..."

"Ten thousand drinks a day, yeah."

She walked back. "So you'll help?"

The 10,000 Steps man snorted. "Can't help you. You're too late. She nearly beat me to the finish line today, busted through her screen up there. Last step's a lulu."

Eva threw her head up to look at the building, and found tendrils of screen hanging from one fourth-floor window. She paled.

The 10,000 Steps man laughed. "Too chicken to fly. I would have given all I own to see her blow around on the way down. What's her story?"

A dozen emotions fought for control of Eva's face. "She's in love. With someone she'll never see."

"Typical," he said, but he looked away.

"Look, Frank: I have an off-network beacon channel set up for you. So you don't forget it, the code is *Cassi.*" She tried to hand him a device the size and shape of a robin's egg. It had two buttons, a tiny screen, and an outer shell so fragile that it would break if dropped. It was delicate by intention. The bum stared at it with resentment. Sighing, Eva grabbed his palm and closed it around the tiny object. "If you see her, or if this palace doesn't have good enough air conditioning, send up. We have a meeting in four days."

"Where's the meeting?"

"Send up if you want to come."

"Don't trust me, Eva?"

"Give me ten thousand reasons to."

Chapter 8

Numbers glittered in front of him. He read data like poetry—the small cascades of repetitive refrains, that stoic numeral one with its upper serif pointing toward unlimited accretion. There was correctness here. For him, nothing inside the mess of human lives sang to him like the clean, regular slope of charts, uninterrupted gains, six sigmas of perfection.

His mini-tab chimed in a call. He answered to a familiar, flatline voice. "Servi-Mod got you busy, Pureforc?" The caller's profession was politics; unlike Pureforc, she did not work for the housing giant.

"I have Servi-Mod busy," said the numbers man.

"Good, good. We have a glitch with one of our participants here in the Organic Life Health and Safety Initiative. I was wondering if you could investigate *the data* and recommend a course of action?"

"As your data consultant, I recommend you kill the program," said Pureforc. "It's so arbitrary that it even lacks benchmarks to correlate results to. You have no data to examine."

"I would love to ditch it. But we need a vote for that, and nobody goes to the polls."

"Mandatory sim voting. Solved."

"You are as direct as ever, Pureforc. I was calling for a more human investigation."

Pureforc sighed, anticipating contact with the epidemic of live people. "My freelance fee and my terms will be as usual."

"Of course."

"Are the participant's numbers down?"

"For all we can tell, the participant is dead."

Pureforc considered this positively as he watched the live sales data build in the sub-central databank he tended for Servi-Mod. He was not required to watch this, but the coursing numbers invigorated him. They were beautiful. The whispering of millions of transi-tag chips accrued into a symphony of statistics. People's lives were singing. As they ate, as they dressed, as they stocked their toiletries, the continual act of product consumption danced before him. It purified people into numbers. Pureforc, sitting alone, was the sole entity who witnessed it all at once.

"I will visit the participant at an efficient time," he said to the caller. "Send me coordinates."

"Yes. Please be discreet."

Pureforc loathed discretion as a lie. Some things were; some things were not. Yet this client had already impinged upon enough of his attention, so he ended the call. "I am always discrete."

Refocusing on what he loved, Pureforc recalculated the monthly sales predictions to the current hour. He smirked: They were accurate. Retrieving the predictions set one quarter ago, he ran the same calculations. They were accurate. He pulled sales predictions that had been set five years ago. With a flourish, he commanded the recalculation and compared.

But here there was a discrepancy. The difference was small—the size of some dozens of families, a few hundred people, perhaps—but they were in his city. The difference showed that demand for Servi-Mod apartments and their in-home goods had weakened without demonstrable cause. Pureforc scowled as he realized that Servi-Mod had not quite been making its numbers. Rather, at some point it had lowered its predictions for future sales without seeking a model to explain the discrepancy. Bitter at the arbitrary re-handling of his data, Pureforc resolved to track down the source of the disparity and perfect the model.

—

Elsewhere in the giant corporation, two company executives accepted a video-conference from Servi-Mod's chief executive. Although each executive's office had a vast array of staff, the project at hand was not one that could be delegated. All wore ties or suit jackets styled with the serrated edges of a saw-nosed shark—this week's fashion front-runner through Servi-Mod's business attire module.

The CEO spoke first. "Good morning. Communications: Nice spot on the news. I was surprised to see you in person over another typical road bombing. Response was good?"

"Very positive."

"Good," dismissed the chief executive. She shifted forward in her chair to examine her controller's image in the screen. "How are we on your end?"

"As expected, overall; however, I wish the chosen location had been closer to our ATV fleet. The cost of getting those machines transported without better lead time adds up."

"Well, that would look odd, wouldn't it? Roads blow up in a nice progression across the country, enabling us to get our ATVs over to the de-homed with greatest efficiency?" The controller shut her mouth to stop her pride from falling out. The CEO continued, "The president has invited me to another focus group. I expect this time he'll ask outright for us to take over road maintenance on national interstates from the government. Is it time for us to accept, or do we keep stalling?"

"I would say stall. Right now our capital is heavily geared

toward R&D budgets for the new-gen Santas and, of course, new buildings. Slating funds for roadway improvements would delay the Santa re-development without undue capitalization. And our ROI on transportation grid improvements are vague, of course, because politically we can't initiate usage tolls yet. The payback period would be atrocious. We don't have the figures to support it."

The executive flicked her index finger toward the communications man, who took his turn, "Well I'm all go! Nothing's gonna give us press like that. 'Servi-Mod saves the country's infer-structure!' So long as we don't bungle the job by raisin' tolls at the first hop."

The controller countered, "We would need to initiate and raise tolls right away. There cannot be public roads under private maintenance. That leaves no way to maintain the infrastructure."

"Communications: Can you spin that?" asked the executive.

"Harder." He flexed his fingers and put both hands behind his head. "Tolls'd be highest on the rural areas, since it's more road per house." The controller nodded her head in agreement. "So the highest cost'd be on the ones who can 'ford it the least. They'll scream, so we gotta turn opinion 'gainst 'em. Best way to do that? Fear. So get a few news pops out there about some ol' farm boys bein' subversives. Mos' already think they are any-aways. Push the ster-o-type. Then we're the do-gooders, savin' the cities from crazy renegades." He cogitated. "Plus, once the tolls go in and the cities run on Santas, well? Country livin' will be so 'spensive that only die-hards'll stay out there. Die-hards don't do so well on camera. Yeah," he concluded, "we can spin it. But we've gotta start with more favorable public opinion—for us, 'gainst them. We gotta polarize it hard."

The controller interjected, "No, we need to start with a sound financial plan. And what happens if we take over the roads? Will we keep blowing them up? I can't see any point in blowing up our own infrastructure."

"Don't be daft;" answered the executive, "nothing will change there. The public is used to roads not being repaired when 'subversives' take them out. We'll keep losing inefficient roads, getting new Servi-Mod residents, getting good press, and concentrating people in efficient cities."

The controller still shook her head. "I can not guarantee the numbers to keep R&D levels up if we start paying for roads. I can not make up numbers like they are slogans."

"Hardly matters. We need passable roads regardless," answered the CEO. "Someone will get the roads; that entity will have the first proper monopoly in ages." She leaned back and smiled, imagining sepia photographs of dapper businessmen of the long-ago elite. She straightened her tie and pocket square. "It's the perfect monopoly. Limit access and hike prices. First the roads, then..." her eyes drifted as she imagined possibilities. "If everyone lived in Servi-Mod units, who would need the roads but us? Who would need *anything* but us? We could be entirely efficient. A corporate nation. We'd be the perfect and ultimate monopoly."

Chapter 9

Sodi carried his son home in silence. The ignition of the hologram trees had been a success, yet he felt divided. He wanted to go—to smash Pumpkin-head and flee to the Moma with his son. He also wanted to stay—to let Eva see the futility of her work and keep his excellent setup in the city a little longer. But Sodi's son knew what he would do, and his son felt no division.

Arriving home, Sodi sat down in a chair he'd turned to face the apartment door. He left his shoes on. Although he knew his beacon receiver was working, he glanced at his mini-tab obsessively.

A too-long time later, his child said, "I'm thirsty."

"Go get yourself a cup of juice," suggested Sodi.

"I can't," said the boy. Sodi looked over at him. The child was staring down into a wide, hand-held mirror that he carried almost parallel to the floor, so that it reflected the ceiling. The mirror inverted the image of the ceiling, and the boy walked around while looking into that reflected landscape. "There is no juice in ceiling world. It falls out."

Sodi compressed his eyes, having no patience for the ceiling-world game again. "You'll figure it out if you need to, son." He went back to watching the door.

—

What the boy liked best about ceiling world was its emptiness. It had no furniture except the sticking-up light in the middle of the dining room. Even the ground was flat and clean white, like he could put anything he wanted there. He could forget being told what things were and what to do.

With a soft thud, he stubbed his toe on a table leg from right-side-up world. Backing up, he changed direction to find the make-believe doctor in ceiling world.

Your toe is h-okay. It gets medicine to kill germs! The child imagined the doctor saying with a happy voice and a funny face. Still thirsty, he wandered to the ceiling-world bathroom. He tried to figure out how to get toe medicine out of the faucet without it spilling up.

—

"I think it wasn't worth it to go," Eva said to Sodi, who stood like a tree trunk and held her. "Her window screen had been broken through. Frank said she'd jumped, and then he said she didn't jump. She didn't. But why would she do that to her screen? Now I can figure out which apartment she's in, but it does me no good: What am I going to say? 'Hey Kat, the homeless guy across the street told me you're nearly suicidal; sorry for stalking you, but how about you come with me and associate with the unlegitimized and be forever discriminated against as a subversive? You could lose your rights as a citizen, and I can't offer you anything. So tell me personal details about what's gone so wrong with your life that you're damaging the windows, and I'll coerce you?'"

"It'd work on me," Sodi said into her hair.

Eva let out small laughs and small sobs. The two of them stood rocking together until the relief soaked in. Sodi cupped the back of her head and drew her forehead against his cheek. "How are you?" she asked. He felt her relaxing and opening. Sharp-edged, her unspoken needs seemed to reach out like cactus prickles, as everywhere-defensive as they were everywhere-needing. He knew how to answer her isolation.

"Never better," he coaxed. Eva drew in the scent of him, and he stood still, wooden, until she kissed him on the mouth and smoothed her hands down his front and over his abdomen, which quivered with response.

"The boy?" she asked.

"Good. In bed, pretty sure."

They said nothing else.

—

Sodi's smile glittered in the bluish glow of screens. The earlier exertion with Eva catapulted his pleasure of digital pursuit. Sodi never felt fatigue during these conquests.

Counting windows in a classified security photo, he ran his fingers across the awkward slouch of pixels where a tattered screen hung. *Hello Kat,* Sodi smirked as he switched screens. Her TruWrld2 login screen hesitated a few moments before accepting the fifth set of credentials he'd dis-encrypted from the data logs of her apartment building. *Hello Kat in apartment 404, hello Kat in TruWrld2*, Sodi thought. The screen faded through black. *Uh-oh! Slipstream is offline. Did you leave the room?* it asked. Sodi selected the *disable slipstream for this session* option, and a scene opened up on his panel.

Kat's pretty avatar stood on a rural hillside lined with grape vines. Taking in the digital scenery in a few glances, he hibernated the character to avoid interaction with others, although there was only one other human-run avatar around. It was male. Sodi noticed his name was *Tennan*. He was user 71,828.

Kat was TruWrld2 User 1,415,926. Sodi scoured through her communication and location logs, her digital possessions, her associations, her usage logs, and even notes she'd left herself—including passwords to other accounts. His lips curved up in a silken smile. Examining Kat's private information, Sodi stirred at the intimate violation he committed. He stood inside Kat's accounts as though he stood inside her mind. Within an hour, Sodi knew Kat thoroughly, and her whole digital life was open to his whim.

Unlike during his other escapades, he removed nothing from Kat before logging out. In fact, he left something behind: a small symbol of his presence in the arbor where her avatar waited. Sometimes it made the chase more fun to leave tracks.

Sodi returned to the warmth of Eva's side without her slightest stir.

—

The next morning, Eva discovered the boy's curled lima bean of a body on the bathroom floor. He slept on a small handheld mirror, his midsection half-covered by the unwashed floor mat. "Baby, what are you doing here?" She rolled Sodi's son onto his back. He didn't respond. Lifting him with difficulty, she carried his limp form back to his bed and tucked him in.

"Go to the doctor," the boy muttered, then sighed with relief at the softness of the mattress.

When Sodi later emerged, Eva was perched in a dining room chair, staring out of the window. Sodi whispered *Sunshine* at her neck as a greeting. Eva recoiled. "Your son slept on the bathroom floor last night."

"I thought he was in bed."

"He was still in yesterday's clothes!"

"I'm sorry," Sodi sighed with real remorse. "You were out. I couldn't think."

"What does that mean, that you couldn't think? What kind of disease is that? If your brain stops working at random times, clearly you are not fit to be in supervision of a child!"

"Stop it, Eva. You go too far."

"I'm not going too far! His health is fragile! And even if *you* couldn't think, *I* could! I asked you a direct question last night! I asked where the boy was, and you bypassed the question!"

"I made a mistake. I want him well, you want him well. Stop yelling."

She slammed a palm against the tabletop. "Tell me why! Tell me *anything* that justifies leaving your fever-prone son to sleep on the bathroom floor all night, and not even bothering to think about him when you are asked directly about his well-being!"

Sodi stood. "Eva. You went to Frank, you took a risk. Put yourself at risk, there's no way I can think. Not until you're safe again. You came back home, I came out of a nightmare. You want me to be able to think, stop taking fool risks." Instead of dissipating, Eva's fury turned bitter and vivid. She remembered the girl-infant that nobody had been able to help, who she'd had mere minutes with. Her jealousy and resentment welled over this boy-child Sodi had had for several years without caring for well enough. She was too angry to retort. Sodi diverted her mind: "I need to know: What happened with Frank? What did you tell him?"

Eva's exhaled in a venomous hiss. She took a minute to compose herself into a toxic half-sing-song voice. "He's in bad shape: babbling, bitter, hopeless. He doesn't think our efforts are worthwhile anymore. But he ate! He doesn't want to help, but I think he will help. He took the beacon."

"Will he even remember the channel name?" Eva only answered this with one tight-lipped nod. Sodi stared. "Oh god, Eva. What did you name the channel?"

"Cassi."

Sodi's chest sagged. "You think that... that *word*... you think it will help make him loyal? To *us*? To *me*?"

"What else could I name it, Sodi? His mind is gone. He's like a splatter on the sidewalk."

"Listen to yourself. He wants to die. Man attaches to nothing, he has no loyalty."

"He attaches to her. In spite of everything, he can't let her go. Maybe you can relate."

Sodi lost his composure and roared, "You hold his loyalty through what we've cost him! His motivation is *revenge*, and you called it up by name! And the meeting, I guess he knows about that, too?"

"The day. Not the place. Not the time," Eva croaked, paling and cringing as though he might attack her or leave her, and unsure which would be worse.

Sodi went still. "I have to think. This changes things." He stalked toward his studio.

"I'm sorry," Eva called after him.

—

That day, Eva saw little of Sodi, who slinked out of his studio only long enough to eat. She busied herself by hovering over the boy's health. She brought him books and changed his sheets and arranged pillows behind him. None of this was necessary, but it made Eva feel needed and useful. Little else did.

Setting bowls of steaming soup on the table for their lunch, Eva asked the boy if he needed anything else. He answered, "Mama, I don't understand why you do all these things for me."

"What do you think I should be doing?"

"Just making me some food and then letting me do what I want. Like a normal kid."

The word *normal* stabbed at Eva. "I want better for you than to be a normal kid. I want you to be super-happy. I work harder so I can help you find your right spot in the world." The small eyes in the oval face stared at her. Eva had the feeling a few small words held back very big emotions in him. She did not know what those words were.

Finally the child spoke. "Mama? Are *you* in *your* right spot?"

Eva faltered. She wanted to reassure him that their isolation would cease soon. She wanted to tell him stories about strong communities of people who loved one another, who supported each other without impinging on individual freedoms—all the beautiful social ideals she could describe but not name examples of. Instead, she excused herself to the bathroom.

There, her foot landed on a small, handheld mirror. "Buddy, did you leave a mirror on the bathroom floor?"

"Oh! I forgot." The child came over, took the mirror, and angled it parallel to the floor, reflective side up. He tilted it back just enough to escape his own hovering reflection and look at the inverted ceiling. Eva asked, "What are you doing?"

"I'm in ceiling world," he answered. "It's upside down. You get in through the mirror."

Eva's breathing changed, but the child wasn't tracking her. "Oh?"

"Yes. It's a good world. I'll live here when I grow up."

"No." The graveled syllable that emerged from Eva shocked the child, who stared at her in fright. "You are going to live *here*! World One. The only real world!" The words spluttered out. "Ceiling land is *not* a real place. Neither are the sims. You will *never* get to live there!"

Sodi burst from his office and swept up his child, eyes blazing. Eva retreated to her bedroom to weep. Neither Sodi nor his child re-emerged that day, so she remained closed up in her grief and confinement.

Chapter 10

Kat had tried to nap in the afternoon, but her anticipation of the Italian sunrise set her mind in endless loops. She imagined potential conversations with Tennan. In some, she confessed how confused his rejection left her. In others, she scorned him and stayed aloof. In others yet, she pretended all had been fine at their last encounter. The practice did not help her indecision. She still could not shake the worry that Mez had been right about this man—that he kept something secret.

Unsure how to approach Tennan, Kat stalled logging in to TruWrld2 until the last minute. When she did so, she rushed, heedless of the unexplained need to re-synch the slipstream.

Tennan was already active and nearby. She merged her location to where he stood, a short distance away at a winery storage house.

"Here you are!" she exclaimed with too much jumpiness.

"Hello Kitty-Cat. I thought it might be nice to walk up the hill together. A bit of realism."

Once her avatar got moving through the grass, Kat backed up her perspective to behind and above the pair of them. There was a strange feeling in her. It felt like those holiday mornings when she expected the magical appearance of hidden candy, complete the the anxiety that it might not have happened. Kat blurted out, "Tennan? After dinner last time, I'd expected you to, well, make a personal request. It's okay you didn't, but I got mixed signals and I was confused."

Tennan took a few silent steps. As they crested the hill, they had arrived back at the same location where dinner had been set the prior evening. The table was gone, as were the servant drones. Nothing broke the flowing landscape, which wore the hues of evening as lightly as a negligee.

He moved with Kat to an exact spot before he answered her. “Kitty-Cat, we can make these avatars do anything. I don’t resent them; they make it easier to interact with you. But neither do I mistake them for the real relationship. I need you as hungrily as any person has ever needed another. But if our avatars are twisted into fascinating knots, it might be more difficult to talk to you.” He smiled gently. “You are too precious for me to be satisfied with sim-sex invented by some designer I will never meet. I’d rather give you my mind. And my time. There is nothing more personal that I can offer you.”

Kat grasped Tennan’s shoulder. Joy mixed with shame became tears on her face, and the slipstream transmitted them.

“Oh Kitty-Cat; I did not intend to hurt you. Please forgive me.”

“I’m just so confused. People say things. There are expectations. I don’t even know... maybe nobody understands it.” Tennan’s eyes softened with concern as she continued, “I asked my friend for advice. She had plenty, but it was all wrong. She doesn’t understand you. She doesn’t even understand me. Some random woman standing outside my building seemed to understand me better than my best friend! Tennan, what is this world? Why does it hurt so much? I want simple things: understanding, love. How come good things hurt so much?”

The sim-sun breached the tops of distant mountains. Tennan’s head was crowned with celestial light that warmed his skin hues. “Those things hurt because they are so much more rare than they should be.”

Kat collapsed the distance between them, her temple coming to rest on the front of his neck. As a couple, they looked out over the waking valley. Long shadows thinned. The first rays of the sun glimmered on dew, and mists rose up from the ground, softening the vista.

"Tell me again why you love this place," Kat murmured. "I want to share your thoughts."

"Because it removes limitations," he said. "In this place, we are the gods of creation, collectively. These complex things around us," he motioned to the shadow-striped hills and the grandfather tree, on which Kat's eyes stuck, "were made by too many minds to count. But those minds are knowable, and they are our minds, and we can work miracles here that World One doesn't grant us."

The mists rose and lightened. Like blackened skeletons holding hands, the silhouettes of grape vines coalesced from the haze. Sunrays grew. Greenery stretched toward the sun. *Yes,* Kat thought, *this place is alive somehow. Somehow through me, it is.*

Tennan silently pointed a finger. She stilled herself and heard, distantly, the pounding of hooves in the sim toward the curved bottom of the hill. Kat clasped her hands together in joy and followed the thundering sounds with her attention, grinning in anticipation of their arrival. A few moments later, Tennan turned and caressed her cheek. His expression was almost sad.

"The horses will come when they are ready," he said as the rhythmic thudding grew soft, "but I doubt they will today. They're heading on toward the hollow."

"It was so exciting waiting for them! I was sure I'd get a peek of one through the mist! I can't wait to see them, maybe next time!"

Tennan's smile showed longing. "You will. One day, when it will surprise you, and... yes, you will." His face showed an odd change, but in her excitement, Kat did not see it.

"Tennan, tell me!" she whirled around, pointing at the grandfather tree, "has this tree always looked like this? I've never seen anything like it before."

"That's... no, the leaves, the leaves are different. I... do allow for changes, I like them, the system pulls from... there's... always some change. Pretty though," Tennan's eyes looked at the leaves, but his expression seemed drawn inward, "with that twirl. Blows nicely. In... breeze."

The sun had crested the distant mountain range and was burning off the last of the mist. Rapt, Kat let go of him and spun in circles. "I love it here, Tennan."

"So glad," he managed. "Is it... is it late where you are?"

"Very. I know I should be going. I'm exhausted and I forgot to eat and... oh, but I feel so full! I love it here, Tennan, I love it. And I love you. I love that you have this, that you know how to enjoy it, that you showed me how to enjoy it."

"Kitty-Cat. Love you, too. Come back... any time. Yours."

"I will! And no worries about parting expectations this time," she smiled and pecked him on the lips. Tennan seemed to not know how to respond. "Until tomorrow, I hope!"

"I do hope," he answered, and she logged out in a rush.

Kat fell back on the couch, happy. Due to the time differences, it was some giddy, small hour in World One, and she drifted off to dreamless sleep.

—

The man who played Tennan waited several more seconds to see that she had gone, then logged himself out as well. He ripped off a costly camera headset that more accurately tracked his expressions than a normal slipstream, throwing it to the floor in a crash. Dizzy, he stepped on it in his haste to reach his medicine shelf. As he slid open the mirrored hatch, he caught a glimpse of himself in World One: deep-set, weathered lines set among jowels and a thin wreath of white hair.

His chest felt trapped in a vise. In spite of the pain and the spinning room, he managed to get the bottle of nitroglycerin in his right hand. Two pills were in his buzzing left hand. Two pills were in his mouth. He tried to gulp water, but the pain had traveled into his neck. The room swam. He stumbled back through the apartment, gripping furniture for stability, toward his sole window, which was open. He landed knees-first on the couch there. He dragged in a breath. The pain was great.

The window of the man who played Tennan hadn't had a screen in it for years. The reason was simple: He was old, ill, and lonely. He knew his life would end one day. Rolling over onto a stack of pillows on the couch, he positioned himself face-up, head toward the window. With his last effort, against searing pain, he shoved his torso backward so that his head protruded from the window.

His homely face looked upward at the cloudless sky, as though seeking a portal in the sky. Collapsed supine on the couch cushions and window sill, the elder's heart broke physically. He placed his final hope in mechanical angels, who swirled around the heavens at regular intervals and saw all. He died waiting for satellites.

This was the man's sole effort to perpetuate his selfhood in World One. No will, no heirs, no trust fund. But he wanted his face to be part of the landscape of this world, as if to prove that, for a moment, he had been part of it.

Ten hours later, a satellite on routine topographic duty streaked across the sky. It photographed a city like other cities. In one of that day's photos, along a side street in the void between two buildings, there was an extra dot. If anyone ever looked at this picture, they would find it had just enough pixels to detail one unique human face—a tiny part of planet earth.

—

Huddled in bed, Kat defied her World One obligations in

order to lie still enjoying what felt like a whole tummy full of happiness. When she did get up, her blanket and top sheet leapt, catching the air like sails.

"I'm working from jungle world today!" she announced to her empty apartment. Setting her two limp houseplants on the surface of her home desk, she examined the landscape. It was lacking. Retrieving celery from the refrigerator, she plunged out a triangular hole in the bottom of the cluster so she could slip it over two pens in a stand. It stood upright. A vase of silk flowers and a head of lettuce joined the desktop forest. "And a jungle cactus!" she squealed, stabbing toothpicks into an old half-cabbage from the crisper drawer. She set it cut-side-down between her monitors.

Her little landscape complete, Kat settled down with a green bean behind one ear and a sprig of celery leaf behind the other. She twisted open a bottle of juice. "You are here," she pronounced as she set the bottle cap amid the greenery. Her fingertip made the cap meander from plant to plant, exploring the strange wonders of the desktop realm.

Abandoning the bottle cap to face the jungle cactus alone, Kat logged in to work. Her caseload of farming data reports came in. A coworker videoed over to her. "Kat! Been worried. Where you been all morning?"

With a wild smile, Kat cackled, "I landed in jungle world, and it made me beautiful! Now I am wearing celery."

"Um, you okay, Kat?"

"Never better!"

"You're wearing celery?"

"Yep! I have no idea what will happen today! I may have to get work done, or I may not! The sun might hide behind a cloud, or it may keep on beaming at me! Celery might suddenly become stylish. Maybe I'll just look crazy. I'm going to find out!"

"Okay. Kat, um, that's really good. Just... say if you need anything."

"I need anything!" cheered Kat.

"Great, that's good." The bewildered co-worker ended the video. Kat sprung out of her chair with a high-pitched yip. Inside the myriad tons of gray masonry that made up her building, she was the only person spinning and laughing.

—

Actually doing work would have been a strain if Kat had taken it seriously. But because the vegetable menagerie on her desk reminded her how sober vegetables weren't, she floated through the farm reports full of musings, not misgivings.

"Section 092-01 reporting for duty!" she announced, and pulled up a screen of numbers to auto-calculate. The figures seemed to make googly eyes at her. She stuck out her tongue in retribution, then began writing her human-hand report.

These reports, too, were mostly a joke. Nobody read them, but they were required by governmental regulations as a way to make data forgery a little more difficult. They tracked responsibility for sets of data, and ensured that a human set of eyes actually did look at the data before it was incorporated into the permanent data store. In essence, Kat's job was to assuage the qualms of a generation—now largely deceased—that, in spite of overwhelming evidence, trusted people more than computers. Kat had no illusions about the paltry value of her work, but it was reliable income, convenient, and flexible.

Section 092-01 was the title field of the first report. Below it, Kat wrote: *Getting kind-of crispy. With a soil moisture content 6% below normal, the wormy-worms might be getting wrinkly. System confirms water rations supplement after another two days of drought. Yield is boring. Machinery is machine-ing. Whatever.*

She tagged the report as complete. Another set of data appeared for Section 092-02. Kat wrote: *Left fallow. Nitrogen content rising more than predicted. Something pooped!*

Next, for 092-03: *Yield is down in subregions 17-20, 27-30, and 38-40 on the eastern border. No problems in soil quality found. Flagged for operators to check for sunlight obstructions; none noted in video. History of low yield in varied eastern subregions. WAIT! Varied yields in farming? WHAT? That happens??! #whoa @whoa ~whoa*

And for 092-04: *Wow, it's a farm! Soils look great, but half the space is unused. Some good sledding hills here; topography may make it hard to machine. Equipment... wow, lots of black eyes, I don't have much video. Oooo, be on the lookout for a mysterious machine eyeball burglar, stealing machine eyeballs. Going back seven years, this section has always been wacky, and the equipment is always busted. There's probably a good reason. So instead of making someone trudge out into the hot, hilly fields AGAIN since it's clearly not helping, let's give a guy a break. Not flagged. We don't get much from this section anyway.*

Kat's reports went on this vein for a while. As the outside sunlight faded, her mind escaped to the more pleasurable anticipation of her next sunrise meeting in sim-Italy of TruWrld2. She counted hours.

—

At eleven o'clock in her time zone, an hour from her meeting, Kat could no longer stand the data. She'd logged ten hours and sixty-eight reports. It was enough to keep her out of trouble.

With a push that quaked jungle world, Kat rolled across the floor in her chair. She propelled her seat into the kitchen, crashed into several cabinets, and gorged on one third of a pumpkin pie straight out of her hand.

When midnight neared, she logged in to TruWrld2. Tennan was not there, but she was early. She amused herself by controlling her slipstream with her left hand only. Up the darkened hill her avatar stumbled, reaching the grandfather tree and its strange leaves. As if taking their spiraling shape as a suggestion, she spun her avatar around and rolled it back down the hill as fast as she could.

Eventually the sky showed its first hues of pink. A few clouds in the sim-sky drifted through the luminary pastels. Circling the grandfather tree, Kat looked for any sign left to her by Tennan, but the sim confirmed he was not in the vicinity. "You must have been as overwrought as I was yesterday," she spoke alone. "I guess I can forgive you for sleeping in." Although she missed him, Kat was still excited to see what the new sim-day would bring.

Morning mists crept up from the beds of grass. Like generations of skinny ancestors sitting up from their resting places, the rows of grapevines appeared in succession as the light intensified. Kat watched the same landscape in the same simulated world, but today the visuals haunted her. Like ghost fingers, the grandfather tree's strange leaves stretched and recoiled at the release of dew drops. The mists seemed to cling. But nothing had changed. *Except me*, Kat thought; *I'm different than yesterday*.

Her ears caught the soft power of distant hooves. This time the sound grew quickly. She strained her eyes, scouring the mists that limited her vision. The pounding intensified until it seemed the horses must appear from everywhere.

They didn't appear from everywhere, but they did appear. As a group, the sixteen Arabian horses entered the arbor from the downhill end. Up the hill toward Kat they hoofed, a calico of colors—sorrels, blacks, grays, and beiges—until Kat feared they would run over her avatar. But fifty yards from where she stood, they halted and stared at her, standing witness to her presence.

Kat had time only to realize only a few things: There were four horses of each color. They clumped together like a compass before the lead horse—a huge gray with ruddy dapples across the white hair on her shoulders—raised an elegant hoof, shook her mane, and dashed off again downhill. The others followed.

Heart pounding, Kat realized she'd just seen what most inspired Tennan. It... was okay.

Tennan had said the horses had *choice*—but they didn't really. They had *chance*. Where they ran was up to programmed statistics: they weren't really free. Glad that Tennan didn't show up to witness her lackluster response, Kat realized that, when he'd set the horses on the fields, what Tennan really wanted was companionship. Another entity. He'd wanted *her*. He'd wanted her more than he'd been able to admit to himself.

Kat's World One broke into an easy and uncomplicated smile. She called up the old-school text-only message function in TruWrld2 as a lark. She typed the message: *Tennan, it happened. The perfect sunrise. The horses came. I wish you had been here to see it with me. Now that I have seen it, I understand you better. I want to share this arbor with you. I'm sure of this. What can I do to show my happiness? How about this as a start?* With the message, Kat sent him a permanent heart.

"And I will see you tomorrow, sleepyhead," she said aloud in her living room, then logged out and dressed for bed.

—

The next time World One midnight approached, Kat's stood her avatar just downhill of the darkened hilltop in TruWrld2. But this time, the program controls showed that Tennan was also logged in.

She fled up the hill to see him. Streaks of evening starlight glinting in his avatar's hair, Tennan stood atop the hill, watching for the sim-sunrise.

"Tennan!" Kat called. He turned around just in time to catch her hard-flung embrace.

"Greetings, Kat," the baritone voice said.

"I missed you so much last night! Did you get my note? The horses were *beautiful*!"

"Yes, I did receive your note."

Kat cocked a coy smile. "Are we playing 'Mister Understatement?'"

Tennan's avatar shifted his weight to the right, tilted his head fifteen degrees, and brought his eyebrows together by twenty percent. "Sorry; I don't understand what you mean."

"Oh, you!" she planted a playful slap on his shoulder. "My note! My note!"

"Yes, I did receive your note."

Kat stepped back and studied him. "Tennan? Is this a bad time for me to be here?"

"No, you are welcome here. Greetings, Kat. Please enjoy."

"Tennan, what did you think of my note?" The male avatar's face went neutral for too long. "Tennan?"

Suddenly his face tightened back into an expression, but an odd one: Forehead frenetic, he seemed to be staring at an object half a meter in front of his face. "Yes, I got your nit, and it was a feral niece."

"What?"

"Yes, I got your nit– Yes, it okay, I got!"

Kat backed off. "Who are you?"

"My name is Tennan; I am the lord of this fine vineyard. Please enjoy."

"You are not Tennan. You're using auto-dialogue! Tennan doesn't do that! Who is the person talking through you! Where is Tennan!" She rushed at the avatar and pounded on his chest four times: "*This–is–not–Tennan!*"

"I ask you to desist, Madame."

"*I am not Madame!* I am *not* Madame!" Confusion and rage curled Kat's fingers. She wanted to slipstream ripping his avatar open to pull the real Tennan out of it. She drew back one hand to deal a blow instead, but in the instant she swung it forward, before damage was dealt to the male avatar, the motion on Kat's monitors froze.

A red error box covered part of the scene with the words *unaccepted action* written in tall, white letters. The two options below this screen read *log out* and *help*. Kat chose the latter.

A green-edged rectangle opened on her screen. The TruWrld2 vineyard grayed out in the background. After a couple minutes, the words *calling moderator* faded, and a genderless, iconic avatar in a sim-perfect TruWrld2 uniform appeared in the box.

"Hello, I am your moderator."

"Is there a person in there? I am not going to deal with scripts tonight!"

"Yes, I am human-driven," said the moderator.

"Prove it! I want to hear a real voice! No auto dialogue!"

There was somewhat of a pause. "It okay, I here," said the avatar in a female tone that was exhausted but unoffended. "We speak gentle. Okay?"

"Okay," Kat felt disarmed and lost. She gazed at the frozen image of Tennan's avatar in the background.

"Is no hitting please. You damage him, make lost value. No hitting, okay?"

"But it's not him! The wrong person is inside my friend!"

"Login... login is good. Is okay. He authenticate, all secure."

"I promise you, I *promise* you, whoever is operating that avatar, it is not the person he belongs to. I think the account has been hacked! Can you get an administrator?"

"Administrator so busy, take long time... I check for you."

"Oh thank you, thank you!"

There was a pause of about ninety seconds. "No hack," the voice said, but it seemed quieter.

"That's not possible! That's not possible! It has to be hacked. Can you get an administator?"

"No. So sorry. No hack."

"But... please listen, I know the man that is supposed to be. I love him. We talk about... everything...and I know his way of talking and he loves me but now he's acting like he doesn't even recognize me. It's not him! Listen! I know it's not him! I need you to help me, because if you don't stop whoever is hacking his account, *I may never be able to find him again!*" Kat cried.

There was a long, quiet sigh on the other end of the video call. Without the auto-dialogue on, Kat could hear the depth of the moderator's lungs. "Please... is not my job, but... I a person, you a person. I tell you. Do not make complaint. Please, I have kids, need job. Okay?"

"O... okay," Kat felt that World One was about to wink out into another dimension.

"No hack. So sorry. Is change. Yesterday is premium account. Today is legacy account."

"What?" Kat said. "I... no, I can't be understanding."

"Yes, so sorry. Is legacy account. Permanent legacy. Nice girl, you love him. So sorry you friend die. Please: No hitting, no make complain. I need job."

"No hitting, no complaint, yes," Kat agreed through slackened lips. The video call ended immediately, and the view of Tennan's avatar's face frozen under Kat's raking fingers jerked and released back to live motion. The only difference was that the moderator had changed her avatar's location to be two yards further away so her blow wouldn't land.

Kat attempted to approach again and found that her avatar was free to move. She walked toward him until she could see herself in his good-natured digital eyes. She stood staring.

"Tennan," she said.

"Greetings, Kat," auto-spoke Tennan's avatar.

Kat gulped down a breath. "It's not fair seeing you like this. It's not fair seeing you talking, moving around. Tennan. Is this real? How can I ever know you're dead?"

There was that pause again before Tennan's face crunched at the question that the dialogue generator could not auto-answer. Again the avatar seemed to talk at odds with itself, "You asked to know about TruWrld2's legacy accounts: Speech and decision program centers are pre-set to mimic the tone and character that the legacy-creator chooses. In addition, real-time, real-human intervention by trained moderators allows even your more intricate interactions to go on uninterrupted. With a legacy account, you too can live forever."

Kat shook her head. "No. I don't know that I can go on living at all. Tennan. Please tell me, is this a joke?"

"Sorry; I don't understand what you mean. Can you rephrase?"

Kat stared at the digital projection of a beloved stranger. "I can't do this. I have to go."

"If you must go, Madame, you are welcome to return at any time."

"No," Kat whispered. "This program is set. It will never change. The more I come back here, the more I won't change. Then I'd be just another program."

Kat cut the sim connection. She dropped onto the sofa and released a high, warning keen. She looked around her apartment. The walls were too close. Her mind was suffocating. She had to get out.

Chapter 11

The 10,000 Steps man wouldn't have intervened, but he was out of sandwiches—at least, that's the excuse he made for himself. In truth, the reason he sent up for Eva at half past midnight was in the way her friend walked.

Like she sees ten thousand ghosts, he thought, propping up his emaciated body to watch. Her braids swooped around like charms warding off haunts. *Like every step she takes, she feels the heel-strike break her heart. Like every step just grinds those ten thousand pieces down further. Go on then, lady, walk your ten thousand steps. You'll walk and walk and end up right back here, yeah, because the world is round. It loops you right back where you've been. They say don't lose hope, so you grow ten thousand hearts and feel each one break.*

He took out the beacon and stabbed in each of the five stinging letters of the channel code. As he beamed out the sacred name, it was as though another piece of the woman he loved—her very name—flew out into the air and was gone.

—

When the beacon's signal arrived, Eva was dreaming of her daughter's birth. She woke, but the memories of pain lingered as though no clear division separated the past from the present. In her right thigh, she could still feel the knife inscribing her Moma membership in her flesh. *I am marked,* she had thought as she yearned to hold her too-tiny newborn. *Choice made. Door closed. I am a subversive now, like her father, like the people who destroy roads and government. Never again will I enter a public hospital without risking the loss of my child and my freedom. Please let it be worth it to her.* No high, frail cry answered Eva's wish. She knew there was a forest of benign faces outside waiting to welcome two new beloveds. They waited in vain: one was too old to learn to live like them; one was too young to live at all. Sodi and Eva had had a child for two hours. She was Sodi's first—and Eva's only.

Groping for the beacon receiver on the side table, Eva pushed away the memories and read the beacon. "I have to go," she whispered to Sodi, hoping he wouldn't wake, and swung her legs out from the sheets. Sodi's unapologetic strength caught her torso and dragged her back toward the middle of the bed.

"You will not go."

She kicked at him. "Let up! Get off me!" He withdrew his arm, but not his stare.

"You will not go. You have no idea what he's calling you to. This crazy risk: for what, Eva? *For what*?"

"*For Kat!*"

"Kat isn't the one who sent up for you."

"How can I just let her go?" Eva retorted, thinking, *it's my only work. It's all I can do.*

"The risk of losing you tonight is huge. Kat has done nothing. She has no affiliations and no enemies."

"Sodi, what choice do I have? To go on living here in half-isolation? This isn't working. We are outcasts. I'm not just giving up and going back. We need a middle community, a free one. You know this is the only way I can make that happen: one person at a time. If I don't go tonight, it is the same as giving up on everything I've been doing for the past four years!"

"I don't trust him, Eva. Not with anything. Especially not with you."

"I am going."

Sodi sat up, his back to her as she got ready. Elbows on his knees, he dug his fingertips into the back of his head and raked forward until his palms were pressed into his eyes. His thoughts scoured the problem for some leverage point, some way to protect Eva without leading her to a sense of futility. The real solution—the one that felt as right as rage—he still could take only if he left her behind. The sense of division again rose in him. *How long until this breaks me?* he thought. *Twenty years? Twenty seconds?* He needed an out.

"I'll go," he blurted.

Eva stared at him. "I'm not sure he... expects to see you."

Sodi turned his iron glare on her. In the dark room, his dilated eyes took on animal malevolence. "Then he won't see me."

Eva's voice faltered. His muscles bunched. "What exactly do you need to happen tonight?"

—

Kat's course was automatic. Park Square was only one place in the city that could absorb her anguish. She would not mourn Tennan on concrete, next to the beehive cliffs of Servi-Mods, lest his memory get tethered to a hopeless spot. It had to be the park.

When at last she spotted the softer, open darkness one block ahead, Kat sprinted. She did not care if the run would burst her; she hoped it would. But her footsteps stopped dead at the edge of Park Square.

Along the periphery of the park, where days ago there had been only a scattering of sickly trunks, now stood strong, mature trees as uniform as a line of soldiers. Their gentle swirl under moonlight was familiar. She'd seen these before. Their leaves had the same delicate asymmetry as the grandfather tree in Tennan's sim-arbor. Her stomach twisted. Worlds collided in her mind.

"What is this?" She stepped toward the nearest tree, reached for a bough, but found it was too high. "How can you have put these trees here, Tennan? How did you find me? Tennan, *are you alive?*"

Kat scoured the patchy grass and spotted what she sought: a small pebble. Grasping it, she hurled it at the nearest tree. It soared up in a neat parabola, penetrating the mat of leaves soundlessly. It landed on the street on the other side of the tree without striking anything along the way. "They're fake!" Kat stared.

"Tennan! Are you here?" There came no answer. "Tennan! How dare you turn my world into your sim! It's mine! It's the only place I can still stand to live! How could you have been so close? Tennan, *please come out! Please! You're destroying my mind!*" Still there came no answer.

She passed tree after tree with the strange, twisting leaves. One after another, all the same, a park full of what had never existed before Tennan. Asymmetrical, the leaves appeared half-sane and half-feral with that strange hook. Kat passed five trees and stayed silent. She passed ten and stayed silent. But eventually there had to be sound, and Kat staggered to a stop and tipped her chin to the sky to issue a torn cry. Wet, lopsided, and cracked, Kat's grief came out in one wavering note of constant longing, attachment, and fear of loving. In that keening sound, Kat let go of Tennan.

Eighty-three kilograms hit the path one step in front of her.

"Shh, that's good. Quiet now, Kat; I mean you no harm." Kat stumbled backward, silent but mouth agape, tripping over her own heels with her hands raised defensively. She had never before seen the man who dropped out of the hologram tree. She hadn't managed to take another breath. Staying near the tree, he did not approach her as she tried to get up from the ground.

"Kat, I won't harm you. I know you. I know Mez. May I help you? You're in a bad state." She still could not speak. He extended a hand that turned out to be warm and firm. Kat appeared surprised by this. Steadying herself back on her feet, Kat's other hand brushed against Sodi's slim-fitting shirt. The fabric was warm and moist. He was solid.

Sodi chuckled, lines of his body stretching and pointing in angles down to a curve like a smiling cheek amid his narrow hips. "I am not a hologram, I assure you," his smile held the hint of a snarl. Her instinct knew that this man was a predator, but her will was so knotted that she had no desire to run.

"Tennan?" she whispered.

Sodi raised his eyebrows. "No. Were you expecting someone by that name to fall out of a tree tonight?" She was unable to answer his Cheshire smile, so he continued, "Kat, I am Sodi." He bowed slightly. "I came to save you from your screaming."

"How... ?"

He grinned. "A true magician never shares his secrets. However," he walked behind her and, gently by the shoulders, led her to the trunk of his tree, "lucky for you, I am more scoundrel than magician. Feel now." He smoothed one hand down her arm. Cupping the back of her hand, he raised her right arm straight in front of her, and pressed her forward again. Two inches from the surface of the hologram trunk, she halted, but the man simply stepped in closer. He now made contact with his body all along her back, urging her forward.

Their cupped hands penetrated the light of the hologram. An inch farther in, they connected with a rough surface. As Sodi pressed her palm against the object, Kat realized what it was. "There's a tree in there. A real one. There's a tree in the tree."

"Yes. This one. A few others here. Most are empty, but I know a lot about which are which. I climbed it to wait for you."

Kat withdrew her hand and faced him. He kept his hand on the buried trunk. Still within the radius of his chest, she breathed, "Who are you? How did you know I would be here?"

"I am Sodi," he repeated, "I'm part of a community beyond the sims. I don't want anything from you, Kat, except to consider what I am about to say."

"Beyond the– subversives? Oh god. You fall out of trees. How do you know my name? I—I can't trust you," she said to his libidinous face. But she neither recoiled nor ran. Sodi knew he'd won.

"Of course you can't." Wryness shone on his cheek lines. "Will you hear me anyway?"

She could not answer. Sodi took a step back. Kat felt the warmth of him dissipate and tried to hide her longing for his body heat to return. The man took time looking up and down the paths and across the grassy field before enveloping her again in his gaze.

"We build these isolation chambers," he motioned to the hulking edifices beyond the park, "to house us as we play make-believe lives. We do it because we yearn," his gaze drifted to her mouth for a moment, "for connection. But sims aren't enough. Part of us never forgets that. The sim is not quite enough." Kat knew he was watching her reaction. "I know you. We both need more people. You are a person who is not yet lost in sims. You want something real. You want the mistakes and unknowns, the love... and maybe even the loss."

Kat's eyes welled up. *He could be Tennan*, she thought. *He has Tennan's ideas.* The magic of this man's knowing her name paled next to his knowing her thoughts. *If this isn't Tennan, is this someone Tennan was leading me to?* Sodi extended his hands to her. She grasped them. His dark eyes glittered as he continued, "A relationship rendered in pixels, it doesn't sustain us. Oh, people adapt. We cope with having relationships through hardware. Inside, we always remember dirt and muscle. Inside, we want what happens *to happen to us*."

Kat reeled. Ricocheting from shattering grief to an urgent

pull toward fulfillment, she could not find any way to respond. But the man in front of her smelled of imminent fulfillment of her unanswered longings, no matter how much danger lurked in his smile. The greater danger, it seemed to Kat, would be to lose this man, to let him disappear like Tennan, to be left again with hologram trees and auto-dialogue and loneliness.

"What do you want of me?"

"Nothing. Well, to consider an invitation. There is a meeting tomorrow. Yes, I am a subverter. But," he gleamed, "I am good at staying out of harm's way. You attend, I will lend my protection." He bowed, his gaze glowing underneath his brow, never breaking eye contact.

"What will happen to me if I come?"

"You will meet people who will look at you when they talk to you. Understand that these people need you whole and well and happy. There still aren't enough of us."

"If I… dislike them?"

"I don't think you will. You know two already." He smiled at her gawking expression. "Me and a woman. Ah, and her child. Three."

"Wait– "

"Yes, but don't describe them, ever," Sodi cautioned. "We have to be careful because they label us as subversives. We hope someday this will change, once we have momentum to support each others' needs."

"What needs?"

Sodi shifted. "Legal matters. Discrimination. And some children, if not sim-educated, have trouble getting medical care. Those are the big problems."

"Education is mandatory!"

"It is mandatory for citizenship."

Kat started to object, but Sodi quieted her with a finger on his lips. "Let that go for now. Consider my invitation. Meet these others, it will make more sense. Community has a feeling. The mind craves it like the body craves... food. Miss Kat, will you come?"

Kat tried to hold back her *yes* in a vain attempt to display some vestige of sensibility, but mostly she wanted to touch his shirt again. "Will you be there... Sodi?"

"I will, Miss Kat."

"You never use sim worlds?"

A burst of laughter rocked his shoulders. "I should say I do! But I am not *caught* by them, Miss Kat. I am not caught by anything."

Her expression turned inward, and Sodi felt a moment's alarm that he'd made an unrecoverable mistake in his words. But Kat only asked, "Do you know about legacy accounts?"

"A great deal. What do you want to know?" Sodi made a mental note; if an account of someone she cared for went legacy, it would explain her reaction in the park and her calling him *Tennan*. It might also mean her receptivity window was shorter yet than Eva knew.

"Why are they there? Who came up with them?"

"Those were invented in TruWrld."

"TruWrld2?"

"No. TruWrld The First. It was quite a world. Groundbreaking."

"You used to sim there?"

"I wasn't of age, and it was an old platform by then, but I got around that."

"I didn't think it was still around."

Sodi examined her tentative face, and understood her

questioning at last. "It's still there. Every day it crunches on—by legacies. Trouble is, a world gets filled up, things get scarce, people say there's not enough resources to make lives of their own. They do what anyone would."

"What's that?"

"They make a copy, wipe out all ownership, start fresh. They make TruWrld2."

In her mind, Kat saw the generations of ancient spirits in the Italian grape arbor. She saw the scintillating salad, saw the querulous smile on Tennan's avatar-face. All those details, all that doing. Her mind imagined the sim-sunrise, the distant mountain range, uncountable craggy holes in those mountains, the thousands of bungalows beyond them, the wrinkles on each hand, the individual pavers on every sidewalk that extended around a sim world already a few times the size of earth. She imagined those processes perpetuating unattended, unnoticed. She imagined them turning into data points in a warehouse that nobody accessed. And for what? Once the people were gone, what did it matter that the sim still existed?

"Sodi, how can that be? What about those who... who strived and worked and built up in TruWrld One? What about all their efforts, their accomplishments, their discoveries?"

Sodi grinned a hungry smile. "Just so much data, Miss Kat. It mattered—to them. They're dead."

"Is that fair?"

"Should it be? Living people make worlds. Living people make rules. Living people change rules." He examined her uncertain reactions. "Nobody protested the slow abandonment of TruWrld One. Nobody will TruWrld Two. I'm sorry for your loss, Miss Kat. I think you had a loss?" Sodi was answered by Kat's eyes moistening and looking down.

"I found out when his account went legacy. I didn't even know—" she couldn't finish her sentence. "I don't even know why he'd make a legacy."

In a softer voice, Sodi answered, "Maybe he found something—or someone—he couldn't bear to leave. Not even for death."

In a cough of emotion, Kat sobbed and reached toward the strange man's chest. He opened his arms to welcome her. There she clung, tears mingling with the moisture on his neck. Kat absorbed the experience of being touched, of being held bodily, in person, by a person. After twenty seconds during which he made no advance on her, Kat relaxed further and pressed the bridge of her nose into his neck. He tightened his protective hold. He smelled of spice and musk. That easily, the heartbroken Kat committed: "I will come, Sodi."

—

They could have been anyone, but that was the point. Barely visible in the gloom, two silhouettes leaned against the gray shape Sodi recognized as the rock outcrop near the lake. He held Kat as long as she remained pressed against him, but when she pulled back, he turned her and place his hand on her left shoulder, walking slightly behind her so that she could not see that they weren't alone.

"It's late, Miss Kat. Lady lets me walk her to her building, I'll stop at the lobby door. Scout's honor."

Kat's agreement held a hint of disappointment.

Their walk together was silent. Kat had no words because she was confused: grieving but also glowing in the presence of human touch. Sodi remained quiet to listen, wondering if their security had been breached. Before tracking down Kat, he had contacted the 10,000 Steps man via the bum's failing mini-tab. It was a brief, salty exchange—*I didn't agree to speak with you*, and *that lady is out tonight taking ten thousand steps, surprised she didn't jump this time*, and *not even you would send Eva tonight*. The 10,000 Steps man knew he was coming. He wondered how many bogeymen he'd be taking down when he reached Kat's building.

Chapter 12

Footsteps approached one by one. Something in the way they ground at the pavement made the 10,000 Steps man squint open his sore eyes. The visitor said, "The sidewalk is wet. You lay in your own piss, too?" The 10,000 Steps man did not answer. Struggling to sit up, he kicked out for purchase, but only managed to scrape his toppled monitor easel four inches further across the sidewalk. He squinted up and down the street, seeking any other watcher in the dim streetlamp light. There was none.

"The problem is economics, Frank." The visitor thrust a veined hand in his pocket. He pulled out a fistful of colorful strips of plastic. Separating one from the bunch, he laced the skinny end of one through the opposite, box-shaped end of another. "You are no longer a factor. You earn nothing. You contribute nothing. You are a zero."

"Making jewelry?" the 10,000 Steps man asked.

"Making corrections. Cleaning up the data."

As the homeless man watched his visitor chain together more of the colorful strands, he thought, *Ten thousand zip ties, and it won't make any difference. It all ends the same. No fanfare, no petals on the ground, no big explosion in the sky, yeah, like it were a holiday. Like it were an event. It's not an event. It's the commonest thing, yeah, and it's happening ten thousand times every grubby day. Didn't have a name, this day. Didn't have anything to call it. And here it comes up like a stranger in the street, like one of ten thousand people, and you don't know which one it is until it's there with the zip ties. But I knew it was there, I always did. And nothing more matters past this—none of the ten thousand things other people do after to pretend it isn't the commonest thing. Ten thousand times a day, in every little dirty niche. In this niche. The commonest thing.*

There was no spirit left in the man to choke out. Even if he had fought the visitor, Frank's starved, weather-exposed, liquor-besotted body would hardly have let him slow events. One side of the colorful ring of plastic passed two inches in front of his eyes. The final pull tab of the zip-tie chain was positioned within easy reach of his own right hand. When the pressure came, Frank felt only the slow throb of his heart in his head, counting down to the very last of ten thousands of ten thousand broken beats. He finished his journey.

—

Pureforc surveyed the scene. He saw overturned, graffitoed equipment. He saw a crumpled, useless volume of flesh: a non-consumer continuing to not consume.

Sighing with disgust, he leaned over the corpse and prodded until he found the man's outmoded mini-tab. It was filthy. Holding it with the corner of his shirt, he attempted to access the last contacts the device had made, but its battery was depleted. In the same pocket, he found a beacon in much better condition. Pocketing the two devices, he walked away.

—

Seeing neither witnesses nor the 10,000 Steps man, Sodi smiled with satisfaction. He grasped the bit of plastic he'd stuck in the door latch when Kat opened it earlier. Leveraging it, he pried open the handle and stepped inside her building's foyer. The steel latch caught behind him with a *ka-chunk*. Sodi had no fear; his son had told him he wouldn't get caught over the pumpkin-headed man. That much he'd suspected, but the child's *no-read words* were never wrong.

—

The next morning, the pumpkin-headed man was roused by the sense that things weren't right. Propping himself up by elbow on his wilted couch cushions, he looked around at his apartment. It was different. All the *things* were right—the same tangle of food wrappers at the foot of the couch, yesterday's clothes strewn nearby, the familiar skyline of his cluttered dining table.

When he found it, he froze. The difference was inside his VR headset: It surrounded him with nothing but a backup error screen, but the backups should have occurred invisibly in the background a few hours earlier, without logging him out. He stood to slipstream his login via his shape and the way he tended to move, but the login didn't slipstream. Panic rose. He called for an administrator.

After a long wait and an explanation that turned into hysterics, the administrator answered, "I just don't see what we can do."

"Get a backup! Put my backup... up... again!"

"Sir, it's not so simple. Our world is evolutional. We are prohibited from re-establishing user accounts from backups older than ten days. You don't have any functional backups from the past ten days."

"It's your fault, then! Your fault that you can't get your backups to work."

"Sir, I handle forty-three thousand accounts daily. In seven years, I've never lost data. I don't know what you have done to your account, but all of our other accounts are behaving as normal. Whatever you did, it looks like it caused each of your backups for the day—and I stress that we take quite a few—to all try to sync to *each other at the same time*. Our core doesn't do that. You must have installed some sort of prohibited plugin. That disqualifies you from reinstatement. I don't know what you were trying to do, but the log shows each backup began to overwrite the others before failing because *it was being overwritten too.* It's like that snake that eats its own tail. Your files are all corrupt. They ate themselves up."

"You pissing little slit! I'll rip you right open! You get me your supervisor, and *he* better be a man!"

There was a moment of silence. "Thank you, sir. Insults to my gender and personal threats are grounds to end this call and block future calls from you. Have a nice day." The experience went black.

The stunned man did not know what to do without his world and his sim-come. Dazed, he walked to his kitchenette to calculate how long the food there would last. The prognosis did not please him. He looked around the rest of the apartment. He didn't have much. The sprung couch was worthless. The goggles and processors was worth something, though. If he sold them—no—if he *traded* them for a basic set of monitors, gently used, he'd have a good pile of cash. Enough to survive for two months.

Two months, he thought, *but that's not enough time to re-establish myself in the sim! So two months, and then? How do people even earn money outside the sims*? He walked over to his window. On the concrete across the street splayed the upturned equipment of the 10,000 Steps man, although the bum was not there. Squinting his eyes, the pumpkin-headed man noticed a large word graffitoed onto the membrane monitor. It read, *Desperate?*

—

On the morning after the bum's death, Pureforc settled in front of his monitors, as normal. Data flowed into the Servi-Mod sub-central data center like oxygen. This was his religion, his proof of order in the world. It was why he worked for Servi-Mod: the company boasted the single greatest success in regularizing people. In Servi-Mod apartments, they lived routine lives, consumed predictable quantities of known goods, and contributed to the economic flow at a steady pace. It made people comprehensible. It proved the underlying orderliness of humanity. As Servi-Mod grew at an expected pace, it gave Pureforc a sense of control that made him certain of his own place in life. He watched the day's purchases aggregate on his monitors, knowing that even his world needed people in it.

But his world did not require all people. To his left, sheathed in plastic to prevent contamination of his work area, sat Frank's recharged mini-tab and the tiny, robin-egg-like beacon device. Each had provided interesting information. Some was old; however, the recent settings on the beacon proved that the dead bum had contacts who cared to track him. Although an investigator would have valued the items, Pureforc considered it his prerogative to keep them. After all, he would not mishandle the data. Also, his universal access through Servi-Mod gave him an advantage in locating the bum's acquaintances.

He wanted to locate those acquaintances because he knew what they'd be: subversives. So many in the Organic Life Health and Safety Initiative were—because what was that program other than a contradiction? It called people out of their routines. It encouraged aberrance. Pureforce blamed those influencers for errors in his sales predictions. They needed *correction*.

Pureforc made a note to activate the dead bum's beacon device later, then called his client. Without offering a greeting, he intoned, "Your participant is dead. You may proceed with your protocol."

"Okay," managed his client. "I was just... wondering if... well, if reports come back to me on the *cause* of death for this participant, what will I need to know?"

"I have already said what you need to know: Your participant is dead. You may proceed with your protocol. Take a new applicant for the Organic Life Health and Safety Initiative. Go make your numbers."

"Yes, thank you for caring about our continued funding levels. But... did the participant die of natural causes?"

This mouth-talker was wasting Pureforc's time. "You asked me for information. I have returned the information. Your problem is resolved. Anything further is asking for a social bias to skew facts. I won't dirty my work for your paltry conscience."

"You do understand that we are discussing a person here? A *legitimized* person protected by law?"

"We are discussing *algae*," snapped Pureforc. "A walking pillar of algae. I have answered all of your questions that have relevant answers."

Chapter 13

Sodi's son wished the adults would do something interesting at these meetings. At least it was an interesting building. The tiny eating table was crammed into a kitchen no bigger than mama's. There was no oven. But the living room was so big a tree could grow inside—if they hadn't blocked up all the windows with colors, so no good light could get in.

Mama was talking to people and pretending to be happy. His father hadn't come in when the meeting started, and that had made mama worry. When his father arrived, he stood away from mama, talking with the new friend he brought. People called her a cat, maybe because she was pretty and shy. She held on to his father's arm. He knew it was good to grab onto his father's arm, so he walked over and wrapped both his hands around the man's free elbow. He felt his father's arm tense and rise, pulling him up. He wiggled his feet in the air.

"Oh, you're getting big!" Sodi swung over his other hand to support the one that held his son. The movement displaced Kat from his side.

"I'm going to be big like you."

"You sure will be."

"This is your son?" asked Kat. "He's... I mean, hello, boy, you're very cute." Now trying to kick his father's legs, the boy did not respond. "Is... um, is his mother here, too?"

"No. His step-mom is," Sodi nodded toward Eva across the room, "there, in the black pants suit."

"Oh, I'm sorry, I hope I haven't—" Kat trailed off.

"You haven't. Buddy, can you get into some other trouble? My arm can't take much more."

As the boy trundled off, Kat hazarded, "Sodi, I am surprised that you... I mean, that you have a whole family and everything."

"Kat, I hope you stick around. We have plenty to learn about one another."

The young woman remained quiet as she watched the boy retreat. *Sodi, I thought you were like Tennan*, she winced, but said only, "I just didn't realize you were attached."

"Attached is a funny word. Like *caught* or *stuck*." Sodi traced a pretty line down the side of Kat's back. She would not look at the lack of shame in his face. She wondered how many people Tennan might have left behind in his years in TruWrld2, then realized she'd never be able to ask him. Sodi urged her forward toward a small group of smiling people. Silent, Kat stayed close, but no longer grasped his arm.

—

"So, what keeps you here? I mean, what makes you... attached?" Kat flinched at her use of the word again. Nobody else did.

A gray-haired woman answered, "What keeps us attached? Well, we keep on being invited." She chuckled. Kat found herself surprised that the woman answered first; her beaten-down exhaustion suggested she hadn't put herself first at much else.

"Oh, we have a riotous good time sometimes," chuckled another woman. She wore a dark blazer imprinted with gray roses over a roundish, grandmotherly body. "We're bushels of fun!"

"Actually what it is," said a younger man with carefully shaped hair, "is that sometimes you need someone to rely on.

And these are the people you can rely on. It's," he thought, "it's like what family was supposed to be, I guess. But you have to put your time into it to feel it."

Sensing more honesty here, Kat pressed the young man, "Time doing what, though? What do you do?"

The young man shrugged. "Meet. Talk. Look for others. Know the rest of us are here."

Biting her lip at the vague answer, Kat blurted, "Okay, everybody knows what people think you are if you don't live sim. Elephant in the room, I know. But I need to know. I mean, *are* you subersives?"

There was an awkward pause. The gray woman answered, "Not like blowing up roads. No. But–"

"Oh, ignore that silly pudge-talk. We're fun. We're just fun, old-fashioned–"

"Government is getting things wrong," said the younger man. "I'm not hurting anyone, but they are, and I disagree with it. And I'd put energy into stopping it. Literally I'd try to subvert it, so yes, if you want to use that label on me, go ahead."

"Hey everyone," Eva walked up and cut in with a forced smile. "Getting acquainted?" Kat surveyed Eva and tried to imagine the reserved woman tangled in lust with Sodi. She couldn't get the image to work. "We're about to start."

At Eva's signal, the scattered groups of talkers converged into the center of the large room. Eva began, "The first order of business is always membership. We have two new members tonight," Eva nodded at Kat and at another woman, who did not return her greeting. "I hope you've had a chance to welcome them. Last time we brainstormed new ways of finding members by looking at likely convergence spots. We'd thought of diners–those who eat outside their homes–and also–"

"This isn't the first order of business," interrupted another woman. She appeared five years Eva's senior and had meaty, square shoulders. Kat noticed several people in the crowd shifting their gazes back and forth between the two. The objector continued, "Eva, I have a bone to pick about you and that boy. You need to get him legitimized. I swear it doesn't kill them. My son's doing fine."

Composed, Eva answered, "I am not taking issue with your choice, but I refuse to put him through the educational constraints. We are about getting back our rights as—"

"The requirements are fine, Eva. What's not fine is the trouble we have because unlegitimized children live among us. Have you not realized that the biggest reason we have to be so secretive about our meetings—the only real reason—is that parents like you are trying to hide your children from the basic requirements of citizenship?"

"That's not—" Eva attempted to interrupt.

"We are not subverters. That's just a stereotype. Nobody here is a sim-scarrer or wants to overthrow. But we sort ourselves into that group because we hide children."

Eva tried again, "We preserve our rights as parents to—"

"They're fine requirements, Eva. Every child needs to be educated. The system is evaluated. It's an obvious success."

"It's an obvious success at churning out children *who never leave the sim*. They are taught to be part of the sim before they have the capacity to reject it as a way of life. They never get a chance to choose what world they want to be a part of!" At the rise in Eva's voice, the large group began factioning off into small circles again. Kat found herself tugged away from the argument by Sodi.

Keeping her mouth shut, Kat passed close to the square-shouldered mother when she countered, "Eva! Wake up to the world we're in! Just because people use sims doesn't mean that they can't relate in real life. The whole point of them is to connect with others, no matter how far."

"In very limited ways. Too limited. If they were enough, why would any of us be here?" In Eva's voice, Kat heard more desperation than anger.

"Eva, that child of yours isn't getting connection through the sim. He's not getting connection from *anywhere*."

"Get out of my parenting!" Eva stalked away, but the damage was done: The group had factioned for the night, and even Kat understood that it would never gather back as a complete whole.

—

Sodi's son had heard the argument from his hiding spot in a jungle-gym-on-wheels. He found it stored in a closet off the high part of the room, where he still was, with the door open just a little. He tried to think of good things, *I-belong* things. But his stack of ideas got short. Only three things made the *only-me* feeling go away: mama when she smiled at him, his father, and best of all, the place with the wobble-wall building.

He wished he could go to the wobble-wall building, then checked the *no-read words*. Doing that made him tired, but they said he would go there again, because his father stood near Miss Cat instead of helping mama not say angry things. His father let mama say all the angry things she wanted. The *no-read words* told him other things, too. But he didn't want to think of them. Instead, pushed on the ground with his foot and the jungle-gym-thing rolled out.

In retrospect, it should not have been a surprise for Sodi's son to come wheeling into the meeting on a symbol of death. Casket biers were stored within easy reach in every church because that's what churches were for. Worship happened in the sims. Marriage had gone out of style in favor of the more retractable, unpoliticized *permanent heart*. Any World One rite was more beautiful, better orchestrated, more affordable, and better attended in the sims—with one inconvenient exception. Death was something people still dealt with in World One.

This was also the reason why so many clergy doubled as undertakers. Mister Agnel, whose church they met in that night, was no exception. Sodi liked to joke that their budding group couldn't yet deal with illness, but dying was no problem. Yet it was true: Undertakers almost universally embraced World One life, as they faced daily what it meant to lose it.

—

Eva grabbed Sodi's son, saying with a quiet but rigid voice, "Baby, you're upsetting people. That is for moving a dead person in a coffin."

She meant to go on, but the child yawned, "Like a bum who doesn't do his job?" He then pinched up his mouth with two fingers, as if he said something by mistake.

Halting, Eva answered. "N—no, baby. The 10,000 Steps man isn't dead. He lies down on the sidewalk because he's sick." The boy didn't answer. Eva felt futile and angry, unsure what to do for Sodi's son or for the meeting. So she placed her cheek on his forehead to check his too-warm temperature—an absent-minded act of care and function, but not quite affection.

"Mama? I'm keeping being sick."

"Get rid of that thought. You're getting better."

"I can't. It's my job. The no-words make me sick. They're my job."

"Shh, shh," urged Eva.

Chapter 14

A comet of people approached Eva. The gossips led; the anxious lagged behind in an extended tail. At the very nucleus, Sodi's stony figure advanced. "You've been sent up for again," he stated. "Cassi." The words *Frank* and *ten thousand* and *returning* hovered in the susurrus around him, but Sodi stayed frozen amid the warm whisperings. Eva rose. Visions of bringing Frank back took all the room in her mind: the healing of that social fracture, the forgiveness for Cassi's death. But Sodi pre-empted, "No."

"I have to." Sensing another argument, the crowd of people vacated the channel between Sodi and Eva, leaving only Kat between them.

"Stop this, Eva. I suspect it's not even him calling."

"Who else could it be, Sodi?"

"Anyone who got access to the beacon. The way that man lays around, it could be anyone at all. You're not going."

"Why are you always so suspicious?" Eva suspected that he wished Kat were not standing so close, given his impatient stare in the direction opposite Kat. This did not surprise her. She had assessed Sodi's interactions with her; the girl had painful realizations ahead, as other pretty women had.

"He wasn't there when I left Kat's building." Sodi spoke bluntly. "His setup was there. He wasn't. Where would he have gone at that hour? Without any of his gear?"

"Maybe to find a restroom. I *have* to go to him. If we fail to show up, we will never get another chance. He will waste away on the pavement. Or do you not care?"

Sodi looked down. Eva had the brief impression that he was trying to make eye contact with his son, who was slumping on the floor, but before she could be sure, Sodi's eyes came back to her. "Eva, it's a trap. Anyone responding to his beacon—plus anyone connected to them—may need to flee. I'm not explaining. I'm insisting."

"If there is no trap, Frank needs us. If there is a trap, they already have information on us and we're already in trouble. I lose little by going. Do you have any advice for me before I do?"

Lightning-shaped veins stuck out of Sodi's temples. "Don't," he gritted.

Kat looked between Eva and Sodi. She sensed the matched force between them with shame. She wished she had Eva's brazen strength. She'd followed the strutting man because, in despair, she needed to cling to something. He'd known it. He'd used it. In retribution, Kat wanted to trick him back, to take away his powerful influence, even if only for a moment.

"That guy on the street you mentioned? I'll go with her," Kat said. "I'm nobody to anybody. I live there. It will be normal for me to go. And if I have a friend along, that's normal, too. And two people get out of trouble better than one."

Sodi growled, "No. But two have a better chance at calling for help. Maybe briefly." His tone made it clear that Kat had displeased him. His rejection felt redeeming. Better, Eva's eyes had found Kat; they shone with gratitude and hope. This, then, was her place for the moment, Kat decided. Sodi continued, "Kat, there is more to learn about us. You are not the ideal choice. I suggest you not go," but Kat was already soaring with confidence.

"Eva's going, and so am I," Kat delighted at the firmness in her voice.

Sodi closed his eyes. Eva said, "We should leave, then. Sodi and I both know our parts." She walked away from her man, who accepted her decision by not countering it.

—

Eva and Kat walked through the twilight on a direct route to Kat's apartment. Buildings crept by. Each brimmed with a cold, flickering light. If a few things had been different, she'd have been behind one of those lit windows tonight—and she'd have preferred it. She'd have been meeting Tennan in his TruWrld2 vineyard. Instead, she'd be meeting a homeless stranger on a World One street.

"Eva," she asked to dispel her thoughts, "why do you think the sims are so bad for people?"

"Monoculture. It teaches people to love and tolerate the same things."

Kat could not decide if Eva was being stand-offish or passionate. "Okay. But how are you making fewer problems for you, for your kid, and for those people I just met?"

But Eva only quickened her pace. They turned onto Buford Street, facing a straight walk of several blocks to reach the regular post of the 10,000 Steps man. "Okay Kat," Eva's tone softened as she tried again to explain, "I want the world to be well. But I do not want what I love to just disappear."

She does love him, Kat realized, *in whatever way she knows how to love*. Kat thought of Mez and her solitary life, and how she'd made the same plea for Kat to not disappear. "Sodi's not going to disappear." But Eva didn't answer. Kat second-guessed herself and asked, "Would Sodi disappear?" Silent, Eva clutched at the front of her suit jacket as if hanging on to her heart. "People don't disappear. It's not like he has a hologram cloak, does he?" It was such a ridiculous question that Eva's failure to laugh unnerved Kat.

—

Ten years earlier, when the technology behind holograms

evolved, there arose a company that condensed the technology into a portable device that could, with difficulty, be worn.

Wearable holograms were as effective as a gut punch. People raved over the authenticity: Finally they could walk around in the image of their avatars—appearing in World One as they did in sims, the way they felt about themselves inside. A massive campaign for nondiscrimination against avatar wearers ensued, and resulted in the legalization of portable hologram cloaks.

The problem wasn't so much in identifying individuals. By that time, the precursors to the mini-tab already dispatched personal IDs and their geo-location over public channels. The problem also wasn't how individuals wanted to appear, which wasn't any more outlandish than what everyone saw daily in the sims. Rather, the problem was spatial.

Because the images generated by the hologram cloaks rarely had the same dimensions as the wearers, people stopped paying attention to what they saw. They became irritated, not alarmed, when the barbed back end of a barbourhound stuck out through a hospital curtain during visiting hours. Nobody flinched when a four-meter-tall, thunder-mail-clad warrior walked through a three-meter-tall door without bending.

As acceptance for the holograms grew, so did the average size of the designs people wore. Vehicles and pedestrians were often blocked by the large-but-insubstantial creations. As a result, many stopped trying so hard to avoid collisions. The frequency of smash-ins—mistaking where a person was inside her hologram, and so accidentally striking her—increased dramatically. Judges made public their weariness of manslaughter defenses consisting of, "I thought the body inside would be smaller and in the front end" and increased the severity of sentences. It became difficult and dangerous to get around.

In a fit to save commerce, politicians criminalized hologram cloaks, forcing a recall-and-destroy of all units. During the next election, less than one percent of incumbents were re-elected to office. The mudslide of inexperienced, single-issue politicians had nobody to learn from. Competence in governance dropped. Foot traffic also plummeted: Many people felt ashamed to be in public wearing their World One form instead of the form that felt true to them. Thus, traffic could move again, but there was less traffic.

Outlawing hologram cloaks did not reverse the changes to commerce or society, yet they remained illegal.

—

"No, Sodi does not get around by hologram cloak," Eva answered Kat, although this response trod too near a lie. "He just has a talent for evading whatever he doesn't want to deal with."

Kat frowned. Eva's answer seemed more shallow than her fears. She began to object, but Eva's mini-tab chimed with a connect. She spoke in her response, "Yes? ... Right now?" and stopped walking to read. "How badly?" Eva turned to Kat with a silent plea moistening her eyes. "Yes, I'm coming. ... I don't know, but I'm coming now. Yes, track us." She ended the connect. She trembled and barely managed, "I'm sorry."

"What, Eva?"

Eva began crying. "I have to go, right now. His son gets sick. Fevers. They're back worse than ever. I thought he was better. I have to go now. Just go home. I can't help Frank now. You go home. He's a broken man, you can't help him. We're all broken. Just go, okay?" Not waiting for an answer, Eva reversed direction, running as though the thing she tried to escape were already upon her.

Chapter 15

Pureforc scowled. After waiting forty minutes in a dank shadow across the street from the dead bum's setup, he'd seen only one person poke around at the scene. The man he watched had red gym shorts and a large, round head with goggle scars. Pinching, jerking, jumping back, Racoon Face scavenged at the besmeared equipment like he were playing with scorpions. Pureforc enjoyed the image of the data the man would soon create: *scrubbing cleanser, plus two; standard bleach, plus one; air freshener, plus one; pair of rubber gloves, plus one; silver touch-up marker, plus one.* The more this man struggled against his debased position in life, the more he would feed the sales quotas. All things fed the numbers. Yet Pureforc was waiting for someone else—someone responding to the beacon call he'd sent.

He noticed another person headed his way, alone, at walking pace from the south. His mini-tab called up public information on the orange dot that coincided with her location: On the screen appeared a detailed dimensional model of a woman named Kat Menali. She bore no criminal indicators and lived in the building at his back. Pureforc dismissed her. Yet as she approached the last intersection, she halted and watched Racoon Face scavenge. She took two halting steps toward him, stopped again, and peered around. More incriminating was what she failed to do: Cross the street to her own building.

Pureforc granted himself a moment of exhilaration: Miss Menali was responding to the beacon call. Yet she seemed young and unsure of herself—and therefore prone to naïve error. Pureforc suspected that one good scare would send her scampering back to her home nest of anti-Servi-Mod subversives.

If he was right, then in some months the sales projections would realign with his older figures. Subversives might shun Servi-Mod as a lifestyle, but once convicted, they always became supporters: Servi-Mod, model of efficiency for isolated individuals, supplied all detention centers in the country. And Servi-Mod's deep pockets afforded the connections to make jail time probable and long for those who stood in its way. His graphs would be set right.

With apparent unease, Kat Menali watched a scavenger leave the site of the beacon call and enter her apartment building. She then approached to look around. "Hello?" she called. Trying to ignore odors, she peered into the next alley, then crept back to the spot, hesitating. After a few moments, she stepped off the curb to cross the street toward her building.

Pureforc exited his shadow. He strode toward her with the precision of a metronome, his face set in a dark smile. As Kat caught sight of him, her eyes widened and her back foot fumbled the step off the curb. She staggered sideways to catch herself. Gasping and staring at him, she sprinted off in a panic. Pureforc let her expend her energy: It did her no good to run while her mini-tab broadcast her coordinates to him.

—

The moment Kat caught sight of the purposeful face of her pursuer, she realized Sodi was right. The man coming out of the shadow looked like an executive—or an executable. She found herself taking the same path she'd run the night before. *But this time, there will be no Sodi,* her mind warned.

Kat had nearly reached Park Square when she realized running had been a mistake. She panicked, but she was innocent; there was no reason to have run. Now she had fewer options. She had been among subversives. She had knowledge of them, and her actions implied guilt. *But I have no plan, no help, no—* at that moment, Kat remembered that she knew how to reach help. She tilted up her wrist to connect Sodi on her mini-tab.

Kat gawked. *I am wearing a mini-tab!* She stopped cold. *This has everything about me right here. I can see him if he's not scrambled. He can see me. He knows exactly where I am! And if he gets this mini-tab, he won't need me at all, because it's recorded everywhere I've been. This is all he needs!* Fumbling it, Kat looked for a way to power off the device, but all she could find were charging ports and the screen. *If I get into a building, if I'm in a car, he won't see me unless he's police,* she thought before realizing that she'd already fled from the only safe building she had access to. Switching to the geo-locator function, she watched her location ignite in center screen. There were few orange indicator dots other than her own, but only one of them moved steadily toward her from the direction of her building. She looked back, but the executable-man was still too far in the gloom to see with human vision.

What turns off a mini-tab? she panicked. She'd never tried to power it down before. It seemed to take an interminable time just to get it off her wrist, and even then, she found nothing like a power button. Every moment, her pursuer would be closer.

And then the answer came to her. It was embedded in the feeling of her fingertips on Sodi's moistened chest. Kat took off into blackness for the last leg of her traceable sprint.

Now that she had a plan, there seemed to be abundant time to think in the next few moments. Kat wondered if her footfalls would leave tracks in the sparse grass. She wondered how deep the device would go before it ceased function. She wondered if its memory would be left intact, even if it stopped transmission. As she raced past an outcropping of weather-rounded rocks, she even had time to marvel that none of these questions mattered now: Her tasks for the next four minutes were set.

The ground sloped down gently. Kat arrived at the edge of the lake in Park Square. Twisting half backward, adding the speed of her last few strides to the strength of her shoulder, she hurled her mini-tab out over the water. The throw flipped the tiny device over and over through the air. Its illuminated screen flashed in and out of view like a firefly. The twinkling descended. With a soft, short sigh, Kat's mini-tab, carrying all the data of her familiar life, winked out.

—

Continuing his leisurely jog, Pureforc marveled at the depths of the girl's innocence. It appeared that she was about to waste her energy swimming across a lake, as though he were trailing her with bloodhounds. It made the game too easy. Not until Kat's marker on his mini-tab lurched forward at improbable velocity did he realize what her actual intent had been. He cried out in fury at his false premise. A few moments later, her orange dot winked off his screen. Pureforc began pumping at the concrete at full speed.

—

Part of Kat's mind tried to warn her that everything about her world had just changed. She had no time to attend. She darted across the field and attempted to reconstruct how the park looked before the hologram trees went in. But her memory could not surface through her fear. Kat spun around, scanning frantically in the gloom. She ran along the shore for fifty meters before she found what she sought: a stray stick. It was long and about three centimeters in diameter. She grabbed it and retraced her steps to the rock outcropping, where she'd leave no footprints.

With a last glance at the ground, Kat scampered along the protruding spine of the rocks until it descended back into the patchy grass. Then Kat veered toward a darker section of the park. She kept the stick in her right hand as a javelin.

She did not look back. Reaching the line of hologram trees, she turned to run alongside them. She held out her right arm with the stick extending from her hand. One after another, the holographic trunks gave way to her stick passing through them. She passed two trees, then five, then nine. She was panting. Even her adrenaline rush was failing. She could not run much farther.

At last the stick yanked in her hand. It had connected with a real trunk inside one of the holograms.

—

Pureforc halted at the edge of the park. Glaring into the darkness, he strained to find any movement. Without time to adjust from the brightness of the streets, he saw none. So he proceeded directly toward a darker section in the center of the park. He defocused his eyes, trying to watch for movement in his sharper peripheral vision.

—

There was pain as Kat pivoted toward the tree trunk. The half-rotted stick had caught and snapped on impact with the tree, digging a long groove up her inner forearm. There would be blood. Dropping the stick and clamping her arm, Kat realized she had no time and no options. She reached up blindly, circling half the tree before she felt a real tree limb within reach. Wrapping both hands around it, she hoisted against the pain and scurried her feet up the trunk. Bits of diseased bark rained down, but Kat caught the limb with her ankles, pulled her body close to it, and shimmied herself on top. Her injured right arm hugged the trunk while her left sought higher purchase. Finding a split in the trunk above, she eased herself up into it, then reached around again. Two limbs sat close together at a fairly gentle slope. Carefully, Kat brought her feet under her, slipped around and up, and straddled those two limbs. She crossed her ankles to keep them tucked inside the hologram around the dying tree.

Ten seconds later, Kat realized how much pain she was in. Though it was too dark to see well, the wound was making a wet area on her forearm. Trying to remember what clothing she was wearing, she eased off a shoe and transferred it to her teeth while she removed one of her trouser socks. This she tied in a loose knot on her arm before returning the shoe to her foot. With one hand and her teeth, Kat then tightened the sock's knot over her injury. Nothing left to do, she cradled her injured arm in the folds of her suit jacket, pressing it firmly between her chest and the tree trunk.

And she waited. And she waited.

Below her, the broken stick lay pointing at the base of the hologram trunk. Within her, the blood loss slowed, but the wound invited microbes from her stock and the bits of dying tree stuck on the wet injury.

—

Pureforc stood at the shore of the lake a few strides from where Kat Menali had thrown her modern life into the waters. Even after his eyes adjusted, there were too many footprints for him to isolate which way the young woman had then gone. The ground was messy with them. The dark make the work slow. Irritated at the chaos, Pureforc scuffed out the prints that could not have been hers, one by one. Given enough time, he knew the data he wanted could be extracted from this jumble.

It took him two hours to pinpoint what he sought. The smallish impressions sunk deeper into the mud than others, indicating a hard impact. The strides were a meter apart—she had been running—and they overwrote other shoemarks on the shore, so they were more recent. But they ended. He followed the prints until they arrived a rock outcropping. Their direction at that point aimed at the same intersection they'd both arrived from. There was no possibility that Kat Menali could have run that way: He would have seen her. Pureforc focused his mind, but had too little data to focus on. There was mud on his shoes. His analysis had yielded no advantage over picking a random direction.

With no better informed option, he struck out in a random direction through the park, toward a darker area. In time he reached the peripheral line of trees marking the edge of the field. Pureforc marched to the nearest tree. He stared at a rotting stick on the ground that lay broken into the shape of a figure 7. Seven was a real thing, a concept that existed and could be understood. The woman Kat Menali existed as well. Both were facts. Yet with no relational database, the facts were arbitrary.

In the tree above, Kat held her breath. She heard the man from the shadow snatch up the broken stick and such air through his teeth. She braced for discovery.

Chapter 16

Pureforc hurled the dead branch in frustration. In that moment of emotional release, something on the edge of his senses caught his attention, but it was not enough for him to label. His logical mind resumed with the thought, *Yes, throw a stick, you arbitrary creation. Like it would help.*

He refocused on his information: The woman must have had a destination, some place safe to go after her incriminating run. It must have been a place she knew well enough to reach without guidance from her mini-tab. Yet without the knowledge stored on that device, Pureforc could deduce only one place where this stranger would go. He set his jaw, accepting that this slim chance nevertheless was his best: He returned to Kat's apartment building.

Getting in would have been easy if it were a Servi-Mod building; his privileged position with the corporation gave him access to examine any company building at any time. But Kat's building was not Servi-Mod. Worse, at that late hour there were no helpful casuals to hold the door open for him. He'd hoped that Racoon Face might still be scavanging across the street, but the bum's gear was already gone. And the girl was gone. *Closed timeframe*, his mind supplied.

It was then that a voice outside his head spoke, "Problem, sir?" Pureforc turned to face an actual, in-person officer of the law. His voice stuck. "Problem getting in, sir?" the officer repeated.

"I– yes, I would like to get... but I seem to–"

"It's okay, I can." Pureforc stared at her as she overrode the door security with her police-issue mini-tab. She looked over at his expression. "Sir, I searched your credentials already. You're highly cleared with Servi-Mod. Look: Normally, I wouldn't intervene, but right in this area, I don't want anybody waiting around outside here tonight, got it?" Pureforc nodded silently. "Just get inside and you should be okay."

"What happened?" he croaked.

She hesitated. "Know anything about a service message person, stood over there?" She shifted her weight. "Hear anything, see anything odd around here?"

"His equipment is gone," Pureforc said. "A different guy was carrying the pieces into this building earlier. Red gym shorts."

"Yeah, I know of him. Anything else?"

"I'm meeting a friend of mine who lives here, but she hasn't responded to my calls. Is it possible you could confirm that she's home?"

"No, can't do that." Her eyes disengaged from his. "Okay, good evening, stay indoors, be safe."

She was holding the door open for him. He walked through. "Thank you, officer."

Pureforc took the stairs to the fourth floor to give his mind time to clear the shock. His mini-tab had gleaned Kat's apartment number from a marketing list of individuals who had once toured Servi-Mod residences. He stood now in front of her locked door. Getting in would be easy: Low-rent buildings as old as this one invested in security only for street-level doors. Most of the apartment doors were wood slabs bolted into a few sticks of pine. One kick broke the jamb.

Circling through her empty apartment once, Pureforc surmised that he was too late. Although most things appeared intact, two things wasn't: Her slipstream receiver blinked with an error—but of course, he wasn't shaped like her and didn't move like her, so that he expected. But also, her window screen had been torn through. There had already been some sort of scuffle here. He was too late.

Data isn't meant to be limited by geography, he seethed, frustrated about the time he'd wasted going places bodily. He hated bodies. His own tensed as he pressed his mind to stay rational, but a dark, inexorable energy swelled in him. *I am standing among facts and yet—* He swung around. His fist punched the broken-in apartment door with a loud thud. He did not feel the pain in his hand. He slapped the door in anger. *She's desperate*, he concluded. *She's frightened. She threw something out of the window before leaving. She won't have left anything of value if she knew I'd be back here. There may be false data to trick me. I won't corrupt my thoughts by searching.*

Thinking had become difficult. Beneath his rage, Pureforc understood that he'd lost his factual toeholds. He knew pure information must exist in the world, but it refused to come to him, and there continued to be this irritating tug of irrationality. He trudged out of the apartment and beaconed for a taxi, unsure what to do about the facts eluding him. Data was not supposed to be so erratic.

—

Kat's injured wrist felt as numb as her mind. Hovering between sleep and wakefulness, only two things seemed real from her perch eight feet above the ground: the deep-etched bark of the dying tree and the cramps from holding on to it.

Nobody had found her. Nobody had come for her. Kat could get down from the tree, but it had been hours, and now the numbness in her limbs indicated she might break a bone in the process. The gash in her arm already needed medical attention. She couldn't stay in the tree for many more hours.

She also could not see the world—at least not as she was used to. It wasn't so much the dim inside the hologram or the small hour of the morning; the sight she missed most was the digital one. If she'd still had a mini-tab, she would be able to see who was in the park—at least if they were not dampened. Even if there were some blocked identities in the park, a mini-tab would have at least allowed Kat to drop in front of witnesses, which might have dissuaded her pursuer.

Yet these were only survival thoughts. Other thoughts—angry ones—began to emerge as dawn neared. Kat felt had. Between Sodi's charm and Eva's zeal, she'd quickly bought in to something she didn't understand or want. A few days prior, she had found a place for herself in Tennan's arbor. When that world shattered, Sodi and Eva had caught her in mid-fall. Had they orchestrated it? In hours, she had changed her life for their purpose—but they had changed nothing of themselves for her.

When sunrise began outside the hologram, bits of diffused light revealed details in the leaves. Their vibrant green leaf-veins reminded Kat of the rows of grape vines in Tennan's arbor. She closed her eyes against the exhaustion, isolation, and pain. Reality blurred.

There was the thundering of hooves from too far away. As they approached, the sound became thinner, fewer. Something approached. She anticipated its approach eagerly. She could hear feet, not hooves, and the crisp sound of them was not trot-trot, trot-trot, *but* ten-nan, ten-nan.

"Tennan!" it was a man's voice. "Tennan! Tennan! Where are you?" The deep, smoky texture of the voice was marred by its urgency. "*Ten-nan*! I'm looking for you! *Ten-nan*! Come out now!" The speaker emphasized the name syllable by syllable, like he didn't exactly mean it, like it were a clumsy euphemism. Kat gripped the bark, angry to hear that name used in that way, and angrier when she realized that the voice was Sodi's.

It was not trust that led Kat to uncross her ankles and dangle one numb leg down below the bottom of the hologram leaves, so Sodi could see it. Kat revealed herself because she found nothing further that he could take from her. Even so, even without trust, she felt relief when she felt his hands again as he caressed her calf.

"Kat, come down. I'll catch you." Extricating herself, she leaned her weight over the limb. A bit sick with vertigo, she held her breath and let her body fall. After a clumsy impact with the man's chest and arms, Kat found herself encased in Sodi again. One inert foot touched the ground like a table leg. Her injured forearm still pressed against her chest. He held her for twenty heartbeats before asking if she was okay, before saying anything. She did not answer in words. Leaning her forehead against his neck, she simply relaxed into the warm touch of human skin and cried. Pain prickled into her legs as her blood flow resumed. Moment by moment, Sodi released Kat's weight onto her own feet as she grasped at him one-handed, wincing at the stabs in her waking muscles.

"Are you ready to walk?" asked Sodi when she could bear her own full weight again. He squared her shoulders toward him, inspecting her. His fingers pried at the forearm she kept folded against her chest, but Kat did not release it. "Kat, what's this?" His force increased. She allowed him to scrutinize it, and gritted in pain as he pulled the sock fabric off the scabs. "Oh, not good. How much blood have you lost?" Kat did not answer, only stared at him. "Kat," he demanded, gripping her shoulders anew, although this time he seemed to be steadying himself. "Speak now, can you walk?"

"Yeah."

"How bad is this wound?" But she only shrugged. "Are you faint?"

Kat slacked into him. "No, I'm faded. Nothing's left."

Sodi held her longer. Though her pain, Kat realized he was not speaking, he was keeping his thoughts private again, but she had stopped caring what was going on in his mind. Eventually he asked, "Where is your mini-tab?" She pointed left-handed toward the lake, leaning back so he could see her mouth the words *gone, I'm gone*. He pulled her back to him and held still again. Kat felt him near and did not think. There was nothing left to think about, and nothing left of her to think with.

—

Her life is gone, gone into the lake, Sodi remembered Frank's words. Cassi was beautiful on the day that made Frank the 10,000 Steps man. *And now what is my life?* Sodi had tried to live too many lives at once, but Frank had embraced just that one. He didn't know what to do when Cassi died, so he did nothing. And Sodi couldn't help him: Sodi could build worlds, but people he could only destroy—people like the injured woman Sodi now held.

He wondered if the best action was just to stay put. Standing with a no-identity woman so near the spot where her pursuer lost her was a sure way to end this. The pursuing Parface man, or whoever he was, would return. He would find them. Then all of Sodi's choices would be drained away. All of the effort would cease. So would the mistakes.

But the woman in Sodi's arms still breathed. And his son—Cassi's son—would not get out of the city without him. *So I don't stand here*, he decided. *I don't stop here. I keep going, even if it means I keep ruining people. Even if I ruin people closer and closer to me. Maybe Cassi got the better deal when she chose to drown.*

Kat raised her good left arm and wrapped it around Sodi's neck. The pressure and dependency prompted Sodi to steady himself. He gripped Kat around her lower chest and put her back on her own center of gravity with a stony look. He said, "As we are now: The arm is bad, could get infected. You need antibiotics. Can you get them without your mini-tab?"

"I guess. I can go home, dial in, apply for a new mini-tab."

"Maybe not, Kat. He's been at your apartment. I was monitoring you last night. He got in. He didn't stay long, but anything could be in there now."

Kat's face screwed up with anger. "Sodi! Who was he?"

"I have a name, a man with a Servi-Mod clearance."

"I don't live in a Servi-Mod! How did he get in?"

"That worries me." *And he may have worked around my apartment security as well*, he thought. "But right now, medical care. You can't go home. I've—" Sodi stopped himself from saying too much. "Kat: You need help, I can get you help. But not in the city. My son needs help, too. I'm taking him to the same place."

Choking on the faintest of laughs, Kat derided, "Oh, just leave the city. Fine. My life is ended anyway. It doesn't matter."

"Let's get you food." Stabilizing her with an arm, Sodi walked Kat four blocks and sat her down in a public diner. He ordered her a mug of tea, orange juice, and a pastry. Sodi took the food out of the conveyor and set it in front of her. He pressed a small bit of plastic into her hand, examining her eyes closely, wrapping her fingers around it. Sodi then left with one backward glance.

Kat looked at the plastic thing in her hand. It was a mini-tab. Sodi had given her someone else's identity. She turned her palm upward to trigger the screen to ignite. Menus popped up. Navigating to the control panel, Kat sat back, wondering where the physical person of Eva could possibly be.

Chapter 17

Upon Sodi's announcement about Frank at the meeting the night before, the members of the community scrambled to gather their belongings and children. Grim words passed Sodi's ears as people departed in haste. Sodi ignored them. Their contempt for Eva's recklessness didn't matter; in fact, it was helpful. It was one less thing that could hold them back.

Borrowing a long sash of tablecloth from the building, Sodi stretched his now-limp son across it. He tilted up his wrist to check his mini-tab, as he had done twenty seconds before, and would do again many times. He was watching Eva's location marker. Nobody appeared to be following her, and that granted him some time. But he wasn't sure how much time his son's recurring fever would grant. He traced the child's small, fragile cheek. The boy opened his eyes. Sodi said, "You'll be okay, little man. I'm taking you to get real help tomorrow."

"No. Help tonight. Tomorrow is... you... change," his child tapered off, but Sodi had no attention left to interpret.

"Sodi, pardon the intrusion," Mister Agnel stood over him with a placid, bespectacled face and round cheeks. "The rest have gone. I expect you have your own path to follow. Dear Sodi, is your plan solid?"

"Not really, Agnel. Not yet."

"A colleague is four blocks south of here. I took liberties to call. She is in, working on a case." The undertaker-and-minister pursed his lips. "Obviously I can not transport you in my traceable vehicles. However, I thought four blocks might be close enough."

"You trust her, Agnel?"

"Fifteen years of trust, dear Sodi."

"Then why have you never brought her to join us?"

"Ah. She has wished to come. She works public cases, and so is more closely monitored than some. She has not wanted to expose others."

"If I don't buy that? If I don't want to go somewhere closely monitored?"

"Then I bow to your greater resourcefulness." The kindly gaze held Sodi's suddenly intense eyes. When Sodi had searched out what he needed in Agnel's face, he returned to tilting his wrist to check his mini-tab, then his son, who was still laid out on the long cloth. "May I help tie that, Sodi?"

"Yes. Thanks, Agnel." Sodi lifted his son, still on the fabric, into a cradled position. The child's limbs dangling at Sodi's hips, his head upon Sodi's shoulder. Agnel's hands smoothed the fabric around Sodi's torso. With several swift motions and a silken hiss, he tied the fabric knots so that the child was held in a sheath to Sodi's body. "Thanks. And yes, I'll take that address."

—

Eva slapped and kicked the locked door to Mister Agnel's church, calling for admittance, but the building was darkened. "Hush, Eva," issued a familiar voice. Eva slumped with relief. Sodi's familiar shape appeared amid the gloom—Sodi carrying a bulk. Eva straightened and ran to him. "He got what medicine we had. Fever hasn't broken. I'm getting him to safety and cold water. Tomorrow morning I leave with him. You gave your word you'd go. Do or don't. I don't bind you."

Eva's hands groped for the child's face. A cocoon of heat rose from his parchment-dry skin. She lowered her cheek to his forehead, then recoiled at the heat. "Let—let's get him home.

I—"

But Sodi turned and walked away. "No," he said without turning his head, "not ever. It was a trap."

The weight of those few words pinned Eva to the spot, but Sodi wasn't staying still. "I tracked you both after I called. Kat went to her building. There was no Frank, unless he ran out of power. There was someone else. Kat never made it to her building." He was growing distant, voice and silhouette fading into the shadows. Not until Sodi was on the verge of disappearing did Eva decide to go with him.

"She never?" Eva called after him, trying to catch up, "*What?* Where is...? Who's helping?"

"Nobody is helping, Eva. Too much risk."

"But... you're going to *abandon* her?"

"I'm going to *not abandon my son*!"

"But where is she?" Jogging, Eva caught up with Sodi and fell in at his side.

Sodi walked in silence for a block before answering. "Not certain. Probably one of two places. One, she's safe for the night, long as her memory's good and she's not fool enough to move. Two... she's already beyond help." Eva shook her head in confusion. "She ran. Someone followed. Then her signal... one instant it moved fast, next it was wiped out."

"Into a building? Dampened?" But Sodi shook his head. Eva offered, "Maybe she was holding her hand out of a cab window, then it dampened signal when she got her arm in."

"No." Sodi's lips pressed together to hold back a lake of words. "Eva, I'm taking care of my son now."

—

Sodi and Eva arrived at the address Agnel gave him. For safety, they walked past it, glancing once at the plain brick front. It had a short rise of old concrete stairs and a twin oversized ramp. For an instant, there was a slight shifting of something light-colored just inside a darkened, main-story window. Their presence was known. Eva kept an eye on her mini-tab, but none of the few people on the streets at this hour converged on them. They turned into the wide alley beyond the building. At the end of the alley stood a small parking area containing a hearse and a small, outdated sedan. Before they reached this area, a side door opened. A woman of indeterminable age stood in the lee of the door, holding it open for them. She did not speak.

Sodi evaluated her as they passed into the building. Under white scrubs, her dark skin emanated perpetual warmth. Her motherly eyes looked like they'd seen all the loveliness and pain of the world, and in the half-light reflected Sodi with uncanny precision. Her steady, sad smile welcomed them through her doorway as though sparing yet another corner of her life for wayward children.

The door closed behind them. Sodi found himself in a plain, efficient corridor. "Ben Agnel said your boy's not well." She looked hard at the threesome. "And I take it you two aren't all well either–least not with each other." Eva looked down. Sodi held her gaze, allowing the observation.

"The fever hasn't gone down," said Sodi. "Do you have somewhere we could bathe him?"

"That I do. But you realize where you are, yes?" It had been dark outside. Sodi shook his head. "I'm a coroner, dear. I don't have anywhere that'll make a bath pretty."

She led them down a half-staircase to the basement level, which bore the monotonous, chemical odor it had to. The first door on the left stood closed. A strip of bright light shone from beneath it. The coroner pointed down the hall to a second set of stairs, "Restrooms are up there, fourth door on the right, but the sinks are too small. I'll put you here." Entering the second door on the left, she flicked on the lights. They blazed over a stainless steel table and, beside it, a similar rolling table with a wide, deep basin and a drain. "It's all sanitized. I went over it extra, to be sure, as you were getting here." She looked at them. "It's cleaner than any hotel bathtub, that's for certain."

"How do I—" Eva began, but the coroner was already in motion. She rolled the basin table to a sink area, plugged the drain, and stretched a nozzle into it.

"There is hot, too, if you need. I brought towels," she motioned toward a stack of brilliant white linens far in excess of what the bath would require. "When you're done, wheel it over that drain." At the opposite end of the room, the floor dipped into a slight concavity with two round drains. "Then unstop it. Don't bother about cleanup. I'll be next door if you need. Make sure to knock." She raised her chin and straightened her back to indicate that she was willing to hear their questions before she left.

"Ma'am, is there anyone else here tonight? Anyone we may need to avoid?" asked Sodi.

"Nobody who can ever be bothered about you."

Sodi stared at her for a moment longer. "So you're helping us" he said, but the coroner made no move to answer a mere implication. "Do you suspect we're worth much?"

"Probable," she said without flinching. "You still want to trust me?"

Sodi's expression relaxed. "It's the only answer I *would* trust."

When no other queries came, the coroner strode to a smaller rolling table. Through the plastic sealing its top, Sodi made out the shape of knives, heavy shears, and other shining utensils. The coroner wheeled this cart out of the room as she left. She had neither offered her name nor inquired after theirs.

Eva closed the door. Once the heavy click sounded, the pair stood staring at the steel table with the basin, both loathing the need to lay the child on autopsy equipment. Eva grazed her fingers against Sodi's. He extended his fingers slightly in reciprocation. The connection passed, and they set to work.

Eva turned on the cold water, adding in a trace of hot and filled the basin. As the level rose to the three-quarters mark, Sodi lifted his son out of the makeshift sling. Shutting off the faucet, Eva came behind him and pinched at the knots in the cloth until they released. She set the long tablecloth aside and began undressing the child, who stirred.

—

The hands seemed to be huge and everywhere. The strings in the fabric, too, felt as big as ropes moving against his tissue-paper skin. The child tried to yell, but his chest was heavy. The heat was everywhere. But then freezing water gushed all around him. It hurt. The boy only whimpered.

Mama's voice spoke from very near. Her words spun around like a prayer wheel: "It's okay, baby, we're going to beat this fever. Just be brave now. The water is very cold, I know, but it will drive out the sickness. We will beat this sickness. Let the cold into you. No, don't struggle, I promise you will not freeze. Be strong, let the cold in. We will beat this fever."

The trembling came. His arms, legs quaked. His belly shook. Scalp tightening, even his mind, his heart quivered. He started to cry. "Too much!" He tried to stand up. There were hands holding him down, pushing him into the water. "Too much cold!" he screamed, and mama was crying, too, but a hand came out of the bright light and pushed his head down. He didn't want it. He shoved up his chin and took another ragged breath. It felt like lightning between his ears as his forehead went under. He closed his eyes. He screamed. Water was in his ears, water was over his eyes, and the hands holding him down were shaking, and he could not hear mama's words anymore, only a far-away sound of her voice spinning and spinning those words. She went on and on, words tumbling out of her to claim him for World One.

—

When the coroner checked on them later, the child looked less flushed. He slept on a short stack of towels with an extra one blanketing him. A few articles of clothing—the child's and some of the mother's—hung drying from the edge of a counter. The parents sat near each other on more towels. Their icy contention had melted. She nodded to herself. "How's that child?"

Sodi answered, "Still warm, not dangerously hot. Thank you."

"Well now, better than that is hard to hope for." Coming further into the room, the coroner closed the door behind her and reappraised the three. "You kids seem bright enough to know you can't stay here forever. In a few hours, there will officials coming to check on the case I have next door."

"Someone important?" Sodi asked.

The coroner's exhausted eyes remained steady. "Only for some. For Ben."

"Agnel's doing the service?"

"I doubt there will be a service. But he was a friend of Ben's. That's the other reason I came in." She breathed deeply and looked around the room. There was no chair in here, and the coroner's hygienic standards precluded sitting on a floor or a counter. She propped her back gingerly against the wall, leaning forward slightly to keep her close-cropped hair from touching any surface. "Kids, you know I can't say squat about a public autopsy, especially one under investigation. But you're Ben's people, so if you would kindly not hear what I'm about to say?" Eva and Sodi nodded silently. "The guy in the next room looks like he missed some meals. They found him up on Buford Street, next to a station for service messages." At this, Eva turned her head away from Sodi and squeezed her eyes closed. Sodi encircled her in one arm. The coroner continued, "I take it you knew him, too."

"Yes," Eva whispered, "we do. He—" Sodi squeezed her again, a warning, "—had problems."

"Well, that's true. I'm afraid you have problems as well." Eva looked up at her. "Like I said, the man was malnourished, but he didn't die from that. Everything checks out except for his neck." She stared at them hard. "I'm sorry to tell you that your friend passed from strangulation. It's unclear if it was by his own hand or not."

"How can you not know if someone killed him? People can't strangle themselves; they pass out and start breathing again!" Eva said, but the coroner was shaking her head no. "Then how? How by his own hand?"

"Those plastic things that hold cords together, what are they called, anyway?"

"Zip ties," Sodi contributed in a monotone. Anger and revulsion spilled out of Eva in wet sounds.

"Like I said, I'm sorry, but I'm telling you this for a reason. Either he was done with his life or someone else was. Now, which do you figure it was?"

"The latter," said Sodi.

"I don't know," said Eva.

"The latter," insisted Sodi. The coroner's eyes narrowed at him, but she let him continue. "I'm betting you didn't find his mini-tab, either. Or any kind of beacon." Still silent, the coroner's eyebrows arched. "May I hazard a guess as to who found him?"

"It would be interesting if you could."

"Guy with a security clearance for Servi-Mod. *Parfore*, or something like that."

"You are on a roll. Supposing you tell me exactly what it is you know? Ben cares."

"Supposing I do, you get us safely out of the city."

She took a fair deal of time to consider the exchange. Bargains sat wrong with her; usually they meant that the bargainer was short on things to lose. "Which direction?"

"Southeast, to any distance possible."

Her eyes searched them over again, catching at last a detail that had eluded her in her fatigue: On the mother's right thigh, bare because her slacks were drying, there was a scar. It swirled down the length of the gap between muscles, ending in a tight little curl. Drawing from twenty years of identifying body marks on Jane Does, the coroner knew that type of scar meant many things. But tonight, it meant that the feverish child would have help—good help, and plenty of it—if the family reached their destination. For the sake of the child, she answered Sodi, "I suppose I could do that, but you understand where you are. It may not be pretty."

—

When the coroner next checked on the family, dawn was close. They followed her up two flights of stairs to a walk-in supply closet off of a storage room. The area had seen regular vacuuming, and another tall stack of towels sat on a low shelf.

"One thing I insist," the coroner said, "is that your identities get out of this building. In the next few hours there'll be enough officials in here to hamstring all of us. If they see your IDs here, maybe I could pretend you just broke in, but I'd sure prefer they not find you. So you get your identities out of the building and stay quiet. How is up to you."

"Actually, I have errands," Sodi said. The child touched his face in a despondent farewell. Sodi kissed the boy's forehead. "I'll get them out of here. Eva?"

A worry passed over Eva's face. She took a moment to smooth out the towels she'd arranged on the floor, then detached her mini-tab and handed it to him. "Don't get lost." She tried to make the comment to sound funny instead of anxious. "I can't get anywhere without this *and* without you."

"I'll return soon."

Frowning, the coroner eyed the exchange. "Not too soon, you won't return. Not before ten thirty, you won't even be on this block." Sodi nodded dutifully. She turned to Eva. "And it's none of my business, but it seems to me that it doesn't matter a hill of beans if he's got your tab—so long as you've got this child. Seems to me this child is one thing he won't run off without."

Silent in her humiliation, Eva accepted the child from Sodi and laid him down on the towels. "Got any advice for me before I go, big guy?" Sodi smiled at his son. But the child was too weak to answer.

"After ten thirty," the coroner repeated to Sodi, "but before noon." Saying nothing more, Sodi left to look for Kat in the holograms.

Chapter 18

Eva heard new voices in the building, but from inside the closed supply closet, they flowed into one another without any meaning. Her thoughts, too, bubbled into one another: *I have failed. The community is finished. I'm relying on a stranger for protection. Kat is lost. Frank is dead. The child is too sick. I can't help. And Sodi, if he returns at all, comes to take us back to the Moma. Everything I have worked for is gone.* A flutter in Eva's chest increased to sobs that she could not quite silence with her hand.

Four years ago, she had envisioned a much different future. When she'd left the Moma with Sodi and the child, Frank had welcomed her and taught her how to reach people. She thought his community was the start of a historical overthrow of sim life. She wanted to be part of that cultural shift. She also wanted to leave behind the Moma's pitying scrutiny over her lost baby and Cassi's healthy one by the same man. Yet Frank's community never gathered the social momentum they needed.

At times, Eva wondered if the momentum never grew because of Frank's motivations: He had founded and expanded their small community out of love for the unlegitimized Cassi, who was vulnerable and lonely after she left the Moma over Sodi. When Sodi later followed, he claimed it was to share their son, who Cassi missed. But Sodi's arrival dampened Frank. And with two Moma parents, the child had no path to legitimization. In order to protect Cassi's son, Frank refocused on strengthening member securities instead of flaunting their joys. Membership began to decline instead of grow. At times, Eva suspected Frank resented his own work as creating a safe space for Sodi and Cassi to see each other, and she shared the jealousy, but it was her digital accreditation that most helped keep the child safe. She played the best decoy mother she could.

As the first unlegitimized child in the community, Sodi's son was also the oldest. In fact, he was the only child outside the five-year period of governmental leniency. Everyone now in the community could return to the mainstream culture except Sodi and his child. Because nobody had ever had to commit in that final, irreversible way, Eva never knew if the people she'd spent four years gathering believed in the same vision or simply liked the fad.

Frank turned to alcohol when Cassi died. He'd done such a thorough job of it that Eva couldn't fathom who would have bothered to kill him. He'd come to matter so little to anyone.

Buried in a nest of towels in the coroner's supply closet, the febrile child sighed, "Mama. They want to know. They will look. Hide me."

"What? Baby, what?" Eva asked. He had spoken with a strange certainty. It sounded like another of his day-mares. Yet this small distraction reopened Eva's ears: The voices in the building were moving. Panic gripped her. "Hide you where?"

—

"I'm doubting that it was as low as you measured. He was his own motive. Too much to drink, depressed with his lot in life, someone handed him a fist of plastic instead of transferring some money. Boom, he's got a way out."

"Sergeant, why would my results come out incorrectly?" asked the coroner. "It's a simple test."

"I'm asking to see the original record. Are you refusing?"

"Of course not, sergeant. Right this way, please." Covering the shock-faced cadaver, the coroner led the team of officers up two flights of stairs from the first autopsy room. She kept her steps swift and heavy to mask her fear. *Talk*, she urged herself, *make noise, alert them of our approach*, but what came natural to her was careful observation—not conversation. She could not force words to come.

A junior officer found words, though: "Sarge, whatever his alcohol level was, either that was his station or—ma'am, who else is in this building?"

The coroner froze. She turned to look at the men. "You four officers. Me. The dead."

"That's all?" he pressed. The coroner nodded. He shot a look at his sergeant, and the other two uniformed men backed off into an unpracticed defensive formation. One flipped up his police tab to check for identity markers in the building. "I heard something." For all the faces that the coroner had eased into peace over the years, she had never learned to compose her own. *People are not meant to be stared at like this while still living*, she thought.

"All right, kiddies," said the sergeant in disregard of the coroner's greater age, "Shockey, it's poor form to wig out on the coroner on your first murder investigation." As the other two officers chuckled, the young Shockey clamped his mouth so he wouldn't respond that murders were so rare that the sergeant himself was probably only on number two or three. "Now: the original record."

The coroner led them around a landing and up the balance of the stairs to the records room. Officer Shockey stopped her from entering, moving her away from the door to prepare to burst in and check it first. His hand hovered by his firearm. The sergeant muttered a choice word. Redfaced, Shockey desisted, allowing the group to enter. "I heard something earlier," he tried to explain.

"Try and listen a bit harder," snarled back the sergeant. Ignoring the exchange, the coroner tapped a wall monitor to wake the one-write recording unit that accepted the original readings of all her devices in autopsy. A menu of results displayed; she selected *alcohol levels* and stood back to give the four officers an uninterrupted view while surreptitiously eyeing the door to the supply closet. She held her breath, hoping that the mother and child in that closet both knew to hold their breaths, too.

"I don't like it," said the sergeant. "It's flubbed."

The coroner blinked. "Sergeant, with due respect, I don't think this data can be corrupted. It comes straight from the equipment to the databank, no overwriting or interference possible."

"Got any other bodies around here?"

"Two others at present."

"So you could flub it. You could have tested the wrong body." Sizing up the coroner, the sergeant declared, "You're gonna do the test again. Get ready what you need."

"What, right now?"

"Yes, ma'am. Right in front of us. That bum was drunk when he did himself, and I want to see how badly. I definitely do not want to be running an unnecessary investigation with my short staff because someone did the test wrong."

More like you don't know how to run this kind of investigation. You're afraid to, she thought back, but was glad for their disgrace. It bought her a little time. She used her time to consider any place she might have stowed a test kit other than in the storage closet where her illegal wards hid. But there was none outside the neat stack on the shelf beyond that door. Had she been a messier professional, she might have had kits scattered in three or four locations. She might have been able to fulfill their requests without costing that little boy his parents. *Baby, I would have helped you better if I could have*, she lamented, *but in this world, it all comes undone eventually. I am sorry.* Steeling herself, the coroner went to the closet, gripped the doorknob, prayed silently for forgiveness, and pulled.

Shockey was flinging the coroner backward, and her back connected with the edge of a table, sending her to the floor. There was yelling. She gritted through the pain, wishing it were bigger so it would block knowledge of what was happening beyond her upended feet.

"Freeze!" the untrained Shockey cried, drawing down at a blob of towels on the floor. They were lumpy, as though a dead animal were covered up by them. There did not appear to be breathing or movement, so Shockey inched forward, arms vibrating like the back end of a Jack Russell terrier.

"For Christ's sake, Shockey, desist!" roared the sergeant. The other two rookies began a cacophony of hoots at their partner's eagerness.

"It doesn't belong there! Something's not right!"

"Shut up, Shockey! So the lady didn't put her laundry in a hamper!" As the sergeant ranted, the coroner squinted toward the offending pile of towels, trying to anticipate how well the fabric covered the rounded volume beneath them. She could not decide whether or not the fabric was moving in shallow breaths. There was no sign of the mother. "Barton, check her for a concussion! And for love of life-regs, Shockey, hand over your piece now!"

Shame seared in Shockey's eyes. Releasing the chamber, he dropped the bullets into his opposite hand, turned the piece around, and handed it open-chambered and handle-first toward his sergeant. His body tensed. When the gun left his hand, Shockey spun around; with a massive lurch he sent his steel-toed boot blitzing at the pile of towels. It connected with force. The coroner screamed.

—

Everything was close and cold. Metal walls pressed on his back, on his right side, on his knees. Motionless, he held his fetal shape, but the fever drew the walls impossibly close and then far: come-go, come-go. He didn't know which distance was the right one. His fever made the metal drawer so warm that one touch would have told the angry man that he was inside the cabinet. A gray smell of carbon washed over him from crushed face masks under his head. He was breathing air he'd already breathed before. Yet the boy had no doubt that this cover was as much as he needed: The rude men's *no-read words* said they wanted to fight soon. They wouldn't stay here long. Mama's *no-read words* said she was going to rush back as soon as they left. He'd be fine. So he stilled himself and thought of mama's voice spinning words.

Just be brave now. The cold water will drive out the sickness. Let the cold into you. Let the cold come in, the heat go out. No, don't struggle, just let it be. I promise you will not freeze. I promise, I promise. I promise you.

As the words repeated in his mind, the voice changed. It was still a woman-voice, but it came from so long ago it was hard to think of, which was maybe why the voice had no arms. But the other-woman voice loved him, even if she could not hug him. Other-woman loved the *no-read words* in him just like mama loved his face. The child stilled himself and waited. Mama had to leave because she didn't fit in a drawer, but the other voice was still near. The other voice was growing closer. She wanted to hold him again.

The child realized he had to choose between the two voices. They were from two different worlds. It wasn't like ceiling world: He couldn't go in and out of them. He had to choose. Mama said to always live in World One. The other world was closer, easier.

Just be brave now. Let the cold into you. Don't struggle. I promise you.

—

Officer Barton shone a pocket flashlight in her face. "Ma'am?" Rather than allowing him to check her pupil dilation to check for a concussion, the coroner raised herself to her feet and walked to the supply closet with slow, stoic persistence. Crouching down, she put her hands in the warm towels as though to steady herself, expecting to feel a child's broken body. There were only towels and some supplies that usually went in the bottom drawer of the metal cabinet.

She let out a breath and forced herself to not look at the cabinet. Gripping nearby shelves with one hand to steady herself, she retrieved a plastic-wrapped kit from the shelf. She rose again, slowly, showing the dignity of every year behind her, and turned toward the officers straight-shouldered, announcing, "The new test kit." None replied. "Will this one be okay with you, sergeant, or do you want me to select one from the bottom of the pile?"

He winced with shame. "Um, that'll be fine, thanks. Are... are you okay, ma'am?"

"So long as my person and my facility receive *absolutely no further abuse* at the hands of you or your officers, I will be okay." She stood tall. "Shall we, then? I'm sure we are all quite busy."

"Yes, ma'am."

Retesting the victim's alcohol levels, the coroner moved with exact motions and excessive clarity. The results affirmed the first test. With furtive eyes, the sergeant thanked her for her cooperation and ushered his officers out of the door.

"Sergeant: Are you certain that you are done?"

"Oh, yes ma'am. Go ahead and transfer the remains." He shifted his weight and added, "Your work is as precise as always."

She did not thank him for the compliment. As they filed

out behind the sergeant, the coroner added, "Oh excuse me, Officer Shockey, was it?" The grim young man tailing the pack turned back toward her. He mumbled an affirmation, face dripping with remorse. "May I have your contact? Occasionally, a mourner will show up after the fact with questions. If I am able to speak with any of them, I'd like to be able to pass along anything useful I hear. Would that be welcome?"

His ashy eyes stared at her for a moment, wary. "Yes, ma'am," he hazarded, turning over his wrist to kick his information from his mini-tab to hers. He smiled a grimace in an effort to be polite. He left.

The coroner was not an abuse-taker, but she knew the power that others' public mistreatment gave her. Officer Shockey was now in her pocket as surely as was his contact information.

She cleaned up the autopsy room, disallowing her curiosity of the whereabouts of her wards. Once the bagged body was lowered into a city-provided transport box, she checked the time. It was ten forty-five.

—

Eva squatted, feet on the toilet seat of the second-to-last stall, arms braced against the walls to hold her balance while she hid. The coroner's scream clawed at her thoughts. The impulse to flee bristled against the impulse to, probably, get shot during a fruitless effort to keep the boy—if they'd found him.

The child had been too warm and too serene when she'd opened the bottom drawer of the huge metal cabinet and emptied out most of its contents—face masks, cotton swabs, clean scrubs—to make room for his body. The child was closed inside a dark little box like so many other bodies had been in this place. She'd had to leave him; there was no place in the supply closet that could conceal her. The child had kept insisting. It had frightened her.

Indecisive, Eva hated the city, hated the complications, hated Frank's death, hated the constant threats, hated the isolation, hated the indifference of her community. Eva was ready to leave this place. Yet now that her fear held her captive in a ladies' bathroom, it seemed too late to make that choice.

—

Kat watched the way Sodi's jaw set as they took their second pass by the building. His disquiet had first delivered them in front of the coroner's building ten minutes early. Slipping an arm around Kat, Sodi had steered her firmly down the road, not looking as they passed the group of squad cars blocking the coroner's alley. After that first pass, he had ceased speaking. He rounded a block and doubled back on the road behind the building. Through an alleyway, they could now see the coroner's back lot.

The squad cars remained. Looking through a sliver of space between buildings, Sodi could see three officers exit the building. They did not have his child—or Eva. Tensing his hold on Kat, Sodi moved at a slow dally and watched from the corner of his eye.

A straggling fourth officer slumped out of the building. The others paused, expectant. Sodi watched the exchange as if on mute.

"Sargeant, I am sorry for my actions, but I am very eager to be placed on this case. I want a chance to prove that—"

"You've proven quite enough today, Shockey. Besides, there's no case. Suicide, you dolt."

"But—"

"Step down, you green little twit, how many times do I got to say it!" Squaring for a moment, the alpha and the upstart glared at one another. Sodi watched the other two officers space themselves to fill out the circle: an instinctual ring set for violence. Yet the outcome of the dispute had already been decided by rank. "No case! Get your insolent face back in that squad car!" The younger one deflated and slunk back to the darkened interior of one of the cars.

Before the squad car door closed, Sodi pulled Kat back into a regular speed walk. He steered her around another block before returning to the building's front and entering the alley. The squad cars had gone. Sodi did not relax.

This time the side door did not open immediately. Sodi's heavy fingers on Kat's upper left arm clenched painfully. She jerked a little, and they released, but Sodi did not apologize. Soundlessly, he counted to twenty, thirty, forty, and then turned from the door. He steered Kat toward the right edge of the alley, and then toward the left, almost stopping in mid-step. Just before they reached the road again, a human voice hissed. He dropped Kat's shoulder and spun like a spring. The coroner was at the door. She caught his eye, then ducked back inside. Forgetting himself, Sodi ran to the metal slab, found it was ajar by a fraction of an inch, and opened it. Kat caught up and they entered.

The coroner's calm eyes looked Kat up and down, intimating that she did not appear to be his sister or his niece. "Are they okay?" Sodi asked. "Who is here?" At a flicker in the coroner's eye, a barest flaring about her nose, the man understood enough. He tore up the flights of stairs.

Chapter 19

Eva curled around the child amid the scattered towels. The drawer still hung open, its contents scattered. She'd scampered back to the supply closet once the sound of voices receded down the stairs. She swept wet hair off of the forehead of the sick child she hadn't stood by in his moment of danger.

"We're fragile little birds," she heard herself speaking, trying to ignore her shame "held up by a bit of breath and the hope of an updraft. Oh, baby, we're going to fly from here. We're going to just fly away." The child didn't answer. "Baby, how did you know I needed to put you in there?" His slippery, limp frame rested in her lap.

"Mama," he said, "I'm sweating."

—

The coroner started after Sodi, calling out explanations that he could not have made sense of even if his mind hadn't been whirling. Kat watched them go. Although she did not understand the commotion, she did understand that she was still wearing Eva's mini-tab. Taking a few tentative steps forward, she found a sterile room left open, and caught the reflection of her face on a steel cabinet. She pondered what she saw. Her hair was different, but still dark like Eva's. She had a reasonably similar slender face and gently flared nose. Their hues mismatched by perhaps two shades, which was passable. Although Kat's age was younger, Eva's model in the tab was several years old, and showed Eva at an age not too far off Kat's. She was only an inch or two taller than Eva. And the identity on this mini-tab was likely to be clean; Sodi would have seen to that for Eva's safety. Kat squinted at her warped reflection. She thought of the familiar life that had been ripped away from her, and wondered if her eyes could pass for Eva's eyes.

Stepping back into the empty corridor, she looked in both directions, the way her father had once taught her to cross roads. The exit to the building was steps away. She debated.

—

When Sodi threw open the door and saw Eva's tear-stained face hovering over the listless body, relief and panic collided so violently in his chest that he merely stood staring.

"I'm not leaving," said Eva.

"What?" he spluttered. "We have to go!"

"Yes! Now!"

"What?" Sodi asked. Eva began to cry again. "Is he okay?"

"Get me out of this place, Sodi! I am never leaving him again!"

"Wh– Eva, *is he okay*?"

Her round eyes stared at him with such innocence and incomprehension that Sodi had already begun to pantomime his question when Eva managed, "He's sick, Sodi! We're going now, right? To the Moma?"

"Yes. We go. Right now." He extended a hand to help her up, but she would not budge with the child on her lap. Sighing, Sodi knelt down and pressed the bridge of his nose and his forehead against the child's damp cheek.

"I sweated," the small voice whispered, "after I went in."

"Good job, buddy. Keep fighting." He felt his son lay a wet handprint on his temple, then go limp again. A tangle of thoughts knotted Sodi's mind. He remembered the way that Choti used to laugh when sitting alone. He remembered the one striped chicken that would only re-enter the henhouse after a long chase. He remembered the weatherbeaten lines of a face he loved more than almost any. "We... we will get somewhere nice, buddy. You hold on, we'll be there."

"Yes," said his son.

Sodi picked up his child, who nestled in without complaint of the awkward angle he was lifted into. Eva added the pressure of her hands—one on Sodi's arm, one on his back—determined to hold on to him. Turning to go, Sodi found the coroner standing, mouth agape, behind him.

"How did you disappear? Where did you go?" the coroner asked.

Eva blurted, "I'm sorry about the drawer, I had to hide him, he wouldn't have been fast enough to get down the hallway, and there was nowhere else, and I know tha—"

For all their depth, the coroner's eyes could not hide her profound relief. "Baby," the coroner whispered, raising both hands side-by-side to cover her mouth, "oh baby, I thought you were hurt or gone forever. I thought everything. God's praise and glory."

"Wait, where's Kat?" Sodi jerked upright. "She didn't follow?"

"You found her?" gasped Eva.

Dumping his child into Eva's arms, Sodi sprinted off. As he ran, he glanced at his wrist and saw the marker for Eva in the alleyway, moving toward the street. Turning sharply, he lunged for the front door of the building, which opened from the inside and spared him the distance he needed to intercept Kat.

Sodi grabbed Kat by the shoulder and spun her around. She raised a hand to strike him for touching her and halted, mute with guilt and anger. At stalemate in the alley, Sodi realized that picking up Kat and carrying her back into the building was within his capacity. But before he could act, Eva's out-of-breath voice cut in from the porch of the building: "We have... to go... she's getting the car... Sodi, if this is... settled... she asks can help with... it's heavy...."

Glaring at Kat, Sodi had not turned toward Eva. His voice was low. "Kat: You run off from us, you won't get help with that arm. You need a doctor."

"I'm legitimized!"

Sodi hissed, "*You're wanted.* Someone who chased you to the park, someone not the police, someone with Servi-Mod access. You want to go to a hospital? What company do you think supplies the hospitals? You think he won't be interested today if he was yesterday? And let's talk about police: You live right where... right across from— there was a murder outside your building the night I walked you home. You were out late that night, then a bit later you threw your identity into a lake. How's that going to look?"

Kat raised her chin in defiance. "That was someone named Kat. I'm Eva."

"Brilliant. Because Eva isn't wanted by anyone, right?" Sodi bluffed, and began the countdown of a few subtle seconds. He was ready to spring if she turned to bolt. But Kat remained still and mute. This is how Sodi knew he had her: Her doubt in herself was greater than her doubt in him. That meant she'd do what he asked, and he wouldn't even have to work for her consent. "I'm going to help that nice lady lift something heavy now. Come back inside so we can all get help." Without waiting for Kat's agreement, he turned his back on her and walked toward the building. She would follow.

Kat continued standing a while, not realizing that her choice was made. The anxiety stalling her mind eventually stopped feeling like a decision-making process. Confused and convinced, she walked back into the building and looked at Eva in the face.

"Thanks for coming back," Eva said without malice. Kat didn't answer. "I want to make sure you get help."

Kat's face contorted. "You're only making sure to help yourself. Don't act. It's just like your service message: You're running me over, Eva. You have no loyalty to me. You're no better than Sodi, but at least he knows he's faithless!"

"Kat, I would do anything I could for you. I would do anything I could for anyone I can connect with. I have so much room in my life, there is nobody I would shove away."

"Like all the friends are you're walking away from now, leaving this place? Like everyone but Sodi?" Eva could offer no retort. "If your life is empty, you deserve it. It proves how many people you've gotten rid of!"

Eva's bottom lip trembled a little. She shifted the weight of the boy she held. "Kat I'm trying to hold on to them. I'm trying to not leave people behind. I want to help people hold on to what's important."

Kat snarled, "Well, you're doing a terrible job of it! You cost me everything! I can't go back or someone will hunt me down! My home, my belongings, my accounts, my money: gone to me. I can't even see a doctor! *And you can't even use what you cost me!* You just used me for some—I don't know—some dream you had, some weird idea of how you think people ought to be. Nobody liked your idea that much. Now you're running off and giving up on it, too! Is that how you plan hold on to me? You rob me of every other option, and then you think it's nice to offer me your company?"

Eva could not speak.

"You destroyed my *World One* life, Eva, not some sim that I can just pitch and start over! *I can't go back!* I can't get back to where I was! You sim-scarred my *World One* life!"

—

"Welcome to the funeral," said the coroner from the driver's seat. "Get in—oh, but not there," she added to Kat, who had trudged to the front passenger door—the only other seat in the hearse.

None of it made sense to Kat. Once her rage subsided, she'd gone numb. She now watched life happening to her like she were steering someone else's avatar in first person. Not-her-hand withdrew from the shining door lever. Not-her-feet stepped back from the vehicle. And definitely not-her-sensibilities informed her to board-but-not-board a hearse with faithless people to points unknown—for possible medical help and a dream that wasn't hers.

Sodi was explaining to his son how cars dampened mini-tab signals. Sodi was helping Eva shimmy into the back hatch of the vehicle. The cargo area was already full with a utilitarian rectangle that made Kat feel sick. The sickness, at least, seemed real. Then Eva was in, pushing her body out of sight. Sodi was looking at Kat, his hand reaching out. Sodi was advancing, but not-her-legs did not move. She was about to get in the back of the vehicle in front of her—the one too full of *bodies*.

—

"I'm very close now."

"Close to what, baby?"

"I'm close to ceiling world. But it's too dark to see it good."

Rotating her elbow out so she could extend her hand, Eva touched the child's cramped calf, which was the nearest part of him. She hoped her touch would remind him that he still had senses awake in World One. "What do you mean by 'ceiling world?'"

The child let out a shallow sigh. "You don't like ceiling world."

"Please tell me what you mean. Are you okay? Are you...

going somewhere?"

"No. I can't even move, mama. The space is too small."

"Yes, we're cramped." The scarce space between Eva and the casket accommodated only the narrower dimension of her head right-to-left. Front-to-back, her skull simply did not fit. She remained still, her neck twisted to the right, looking toward the child. She did not look at the inch of reinforced, reconstituted bamboo and recycled plastic that separated her from the corpse above. "Do you mean that you get to ceiling world by going into a... one of these?"

"No. I'm done talking."

Eva tried to rearrange her lung space, but there was no room to expand into. Only her thoughts could seep out. She wondered what Frank's eyes would be like, and if his neck were marked by the zip ties. She wondered how cold his flesh was now, and how much of her own heat was trickling up into... it.

Sodi and the child remained silent. The coroner maintained the quiet composure of one on a routine errand. Only Kat's sounds were off; her loud inhalations sounded like a maladjusted pump.

It got worse one moment after the driver's brief cry of "Oh!"

The rear of the vehicle bucked; Kat was flattened against the wall, then thrown two inches faceward against the coffin's side. She tensed, the miniscule distances around her obsessing her mind. Bits of limbs and faces peeked out from everywhere around indifferent mass of the coffin. They were under it. They were beside it. They were in front of it. She was part of that tangle of raw appendages crowding the dead.

Kat's audible breathing began to grow in volume and pitch. The small crescendos added to one another until she was moaning with anxiety.

"Kat, relax. It will be well," Sodi coached, but his words never reached Kat's mind. Her round tones rose into cries.

"Mama?"

"Someone, we can't have this," warned the coroner. "If she keeps this up, we will all be caught."

"I'm scared, mama."

Eva cast about, stuck between worlds. *Kat's going crazy;* , she thought; *she's in her own world. The boy's going into fevers, his own world. Frank's passed into another world; the coroner's driving us through a world that can't exist to us any more; we're heading to a world Kat's never seen. There are no rules between worlds. It's chaos here.*

Something about her chest being flattened as she traveled between worlds reminded her of the paper-book her son had been reading a few days prior. She could envision him now, tracing his finger over the apostrophe in the last name. The name was L'Engle. *No, not everything is chaos,* she thought. *Some rules still hold. And if rules still hold, then people can stand their minds on those rules.*

"Baby, how about you recite your multiplication tables? What is four times seven?"

"I don't want to."

"It will help. What is four times seven? Think of four times seven; is it an easy problem?" The languid notes from Kat began to quiet at the sound of other human voices saying things that belonged in a rational world. "Four times seven: is it easy to do?"

"Yes," the voice of the child hesitated, "twenty-eight."

"Right. Eight times nine."

Sodi interrupted, "Eva, it's not the time to—"

"Shush. Eight times nine, is it easy?"

"I'm tired, mama. And it's scary in here. And I don't need to remember. I can just figure it out."

"No, you do have to memorize them."

"Why?"

"Because of what comes in the future."

"What is coming?"

"Wonderful things. Geometry, algebra, calculus. Beautiful worlds are very close," Eva clenched her eyes in prayer.

There was a silence in the vehicle until the smallest voice asked, "Will you teach me calculus?" Kat had gone quiet again, listening.

"Yes, I will, soon, when I can."

In the driver's seat of the car, the coroner's face opened into a simple smile. *And this is all it is,* she thought. *Just a little bit of understanding. Just an any-kind conversation when the talking is worth more than any thing you could talk about. Maybe I was wrong. Maybe that Eva has something.*

The vehicle approached the accounting station at the city limits. The coroner slowed and picked the smoothest route along the edgy, greening pavement. She drove through a stall. A glancing red beam absorbed the vehicle registration information, photographed the vehicle through the windshield, and let them pass. Beyond these records, not even these old, city-run devices were allowed to mass record personal data from inside private vehicles; however, searches were permitted. The one on-duty inspector, busy with the inspection of a cargo van, took one look at the hearse, shuddered, and waved it past.

The vehicle had gone silent, but the texture of the quiet had smoothed out.

"Mama? This car is a bag. It's taking us all away without anybody looking inside."

"In fact, we are out of the city now," corrected the coroner. "And in ten minutes, we'll be as far as I can take you."

We're going to make it, thought Eva.

But as soon as this desperate hope root in Eva's mind, it fruited more doubts: *Make it where, exactly?* The coffin loomed above her, carrying a friend she'd failed to care for enough, and they fled the life she was trying to build for one she knew didn't fit her. Pinned down, feeling no leeway around her, Eva took stock of herself in stillness. *He wouldn't discuss ceiling world with me because I don't like it. I'm teaching this child which world to live in. And I'm teaching him what to look for in it. Am I inventing the world he will live in?*

But this thought was attached to too many anxieties for Eva to hold onto.

Chapter 20

"Pitiful."

Pureforc grimaced at the data on his monitor. It was scarce. If the dead bum had been part of any subversive group, he must have been cast out of its center long ago. The mini-tab was a two-year-old model. Someone had gone to the trouble of corrupting the transfer of information from his prior tab so that only the bare essentials had moved over. The only call records were those placed with this exact unit. There were no contacts in it at all. The bum had deleted—or been deleted from—any prior life he had. He'd died as a dot in the world as insignificant as a squashed bug.

But handling the crusty unit had not been fruitless, as there was one call to this device days before Pureforc's unpleasant encounter with the man. It was the only direct call placed to the device in over seven months. It had been scrambled.

Pureforc smiled, anticipating a moment's challenge.

—

The hearse stopped along a state road one fifth of a mile before a small turnoff that led to the crematorium. The pasture and soybean fields had given way to unmonitored forest on both sides of the asphalt. Standing at the open back hatch of the hearse, the coroner removed her shoes to brace one leg on the back bumper and help pull Sodi out of his wedged slot. It wasn't enough. He twisted and shimmied his bulk in its settled spot, pushing against the wall of the hearse and the wall of the coffin to extricate his shoulders. The rails of the vehicle, not intended to bear lateral pressure, bucked. The casket lurched with a loud metallic snap. But the extra two-thirds inch that Sodi gained sufficed: He emerged from the packed vehicle with nothing worse than bruises and a two-inch tear on his shirt.

With him out of the way and his strength available to help the others, it became easier to ease Kat's slight frame from her side without wrenching her injured arm. Eva then took leeway to shimmy from underneath the now lopsided box, drawing out the boy with her. They stood together, looking at the open back hatch. Much was ending.

Kat shuddered at the compressed space she'd been in. The back of the vehicle was not meant to hold life and death at the same time. She laid her left hand over her wrapped right forearm, which had grown hot.

Eva gripped Sodi's child against the failure she felt. Her community had not protected Frank; he had slipped away incrementally from a leader to an outcast to a stereotype to a corpse. Now he would become ash, blowing away completely, ten thousand specks in the wind. She wanted to say words for him, but there were too many to say. Speaking the first few would get her no closer to that far-fetched hope of resolution.

Giving the group a moment to recover, the coroner tested the roll of the bier on its track. Pulling with excess force, she could move the device, but the metal ground. She sensed Sodi about to speak, so she took the first word, "Oh, don't worry; it's due for service anyway." Instead, she used their few moments to place her hand on the shoulder of each of her wards in succession. She lingered least on the man. Feet spread and angled outward, weight on one side, thumbs tucked into the front pockets of his linen pants, Sodi could have been watching a cloud or a kite—not a funeral. He seemed to need no comfort after the group's ordeal.

It was the child on whom the coroner bestowed her warmest farewell. "Fortune reaches some," she told him, "and not others.

Best we can do is just enjoy what good moments we see. You're a darling child. I've been pleased to help you." She leaned in to kiss the boy on his forehead, but the child reached for her. Eva passed over his little, living weight. "You get well, now. Hear?" As though in response, the boy placed his fingertips on her chinline.

"He loves you," whispered the child. The coroner started to answer that she loved the boy right back, but he continued, "You don't stay sad. Because his friends are gone now. But two sad people together get happy." Bewildered, the coroner thanked him and squeezed the too-warm child one last time before passing him back to his mother and getting back on the road. Not until the coroner's turning signal clicked off as she rounded the last corner to the crematorium did she realize she was thinking of Ben Agnel.

—

Hitchhiking proved to be no trouble. With two women and a child in tow, each time they switched vehicles, Sodi managed to wave a driver down within an hour. More difficult had been coaching Kat on how to explain her lack of identification. Technically, she had ID—she had not returned Eva's mini-tab. But gathered in a group as they were, it hardly mattered on whose wrist the device rested; the location was only accurate to within three feet, and Eva looked more like her own digital model than Kat did. It was clear who traveled anonymously.

"No, absolutely not," said Kat.

Sodi chuckled. Kat darkened at the fact that he could afford to laugh at this point. "You tell them that, they won't ask further. It's too much information already. Here, practice on me." Kat only glared. "Come on, Kat! The words! Say them! 'How come you don't show up on the ID?'" Sodi raised his eyebrows, amused.

She sighed in disgust. "'My mini-tab slipped off into the

toilet at the last pit stop. Don't sim while you're handling a tampon.'"

"Mama, what's a tampon?"

"Shh."

"Again," said Sodi. "'And who are you, Miss Anonymous?'"

Kat glared. "'Name's Mente. Sorry about the ID; I dropped the stupid mini-tab in the toilet at the last stop. Don't ever sim while you're handling a tampon.'"

"Did you manage the tampon okay?" Sodi laughed.

"Go piss." Kay answered. "Sodi, I've had enough. I'll deliver the line, just stop talking about it." Kat spun on her heels but flinched at the pain the motion transferred into her arm. She then stood still. There was nowhere to go. She was just too humiliated to look at Sodi touting his amusement and control.

"What's a tampon?"

"It's sort-of like toilet paper," hushed Eva.

Sodi kept laughing. "Son, *tampon* is a magic word. You say it, everyone thinks you're telling the truth."

"But you're lying." A fluttery pat on his back told the boy that Eva wanted him quiet. "But my job is to know true things. Why know a true thing but say a lie?"

"Sometimes we do what we have to. We do it very carefully, it works out." Sodi's teeth gleamed at the next car approaching. It did not stop for them, but before long, another would.

-

Kat's boss keyed the letters m-e-n-a-l-i into a search box. A long list of entries rippled into view, but none had a creation date within the past three days, and the account had been flagged as delinquent. She began opening the list items at random, scanning the contents. In the seventeenth entry she opened, she paused over the words *the wormy-worms might be getting a bit wrinkly*, then re-read the human-hand farm report carefully and checked its date. It was among the last two batches authored. Sitting back, she bit her lip and set in to read more entries.

Forty-five minutes later, she sent a connect. "I need a wellfare check on an employee. Kat Menali. ... No, only three days delinquent, but some of her later entries are nonsense. I have a mental stability concern, which should override the normal seven-day wait. Before this, her work history is pristine. If we have a report writer losing her mind in some apartment, well, that doesn't seem right." She shifted her head and sighed. "Okay, then I'm asking as a personal favor. Can we send someone? ... Buford Street. ... I know, but I'd feel a lot better. ... What? ... Oh, yeah, I guess I should get them re-reviewed; dang, that's going to set us back even more. Thanks for trying. Please let me know if someone can go by."

—

Two days and a truck-stop shower after escaping the hearse, the foursome approached a vacant car in a grassy field that dipped like a smile in front of a tumble of potato-shaped hills. Dandelions had grown up around the plump wheels. All the windows were intact, but the passenger-side mirror had been reduced to a bent sprig of chrome.

"What color is this car?" asked the child, eyeing body panels that clashed like a circus.

"*How many* colors, you mean? Counting the rust, or not?" laughed Sodi.

"Count the rust, because it is rust-colored." Keeping count on his fingers, the child tiptoed to peek at the other side of the car. He raised his second hand for more fingers.

Sodi lifted the handle of the rear driver-side door and pulled. The door swung open. Tufts of hay fell out from beside the hinges. He climbed into the back bench, through the cleft between the two front bucket seats, and into the foot well of the passenger side. There he lifted the floor mat. There was a key. Unlocking the rest of the doors, Sodi popped out of the car and took over the driver's seat. Kat remained standing until it became clear that the others actually meant to drive around in the ancient bucket. They did. She felt weak. Her now-swollen arm ached worse than ever.

Sodi stomped on the floor three times, then he cranked the key into the lockhole until the engine gurgled and choked. It did not start. He twisted the key again, stomping on the pedals, leg pushing at the floor while the car complained back.

"Get out! It's angry!" yelled the boy as the engine gargled and roared into life. Lunging for the door handle, the child's hands groped at the strange lever, but he did not know how to make it open. Eva drew him back. Her arms wrapped around him.

"It's a gas engine," she soothed. "It's supposed to sound that way. That sound means it's working."

"Everyone will hear us!"

The top of her nose nuzzled into his cheekbones. "Yes. They want it to be loud. They want to know when someone is coming, so they can get ready to welcome us."

"But I'm not legimized!"

"You are to them. You have this," Eva placed her left hand over the center of the boy's chest, tapping it in an easy double-rhythm, "just like your father." She pulled him toward her own chest. She savored these last few minutes of nobody questioning the way he sometimes called her *mama*.

The car lurched around another lumpy bend and rocked back into the center of the grassy-dirt trail. Sodi sat with one elbow hanging out of his open window, the opposite hand loose on the wheel as though he had precision control over the staggering heap.

It was just over the crest of the next hill that they saw the first person—although by then, they themselves had been seen four times and recognized twice. A girl the same age as Sodi's son spun in a break of sunlight, arms out, strings of color twirling, trailing from the top back of her flouncy dress. The boy climbed over Eva's lap to look at her. A smile broke across her round, unfettered face. She waved with both hands at every revolution. There were words, too, but the engine noise swallowed all but the smallest hint of their joyful tone.

At the crest of the next rise, the vista opened to the beginnings of a village spilling down the hillside into the valley. Bright and mismatched, the buildings seemed frozen in mid-cavort during a festival. No building extended as high as the upper lip of the encircling hills. Every possible span of the tidy walls was scattershot with an insane divergence of windows, which nevertheless bore one commonality: Their blinds were open. Otherwise, the buildings' odd footprints and irregular spacing reflected the evolution of the people who lived within them. Mismatched wings had been added to some buildings for growing families, not for prestige. There were no sections of large homes versus small homes; there were simply places for life kicked together in the anticipation of more family.

Scattered in the open spaces, people called each other out of the buildings with cupped hands. Bright shirts seemed to flow into the hollow. They puddled in the area where Sodi parked the gritty behemoth and torqued out the key.

As their ears adjusted to the new quiet, soft sounds wafted into the cab. "It's nice!" cried the boy, whose eyebrows arched. Motioning to Kat to lift the passenger floor mat, then thinking better of it and performing the action himself, Sodi tossed the key back in place. He led the group to exit the car, helping Kat by her unhurt left side. Once she seemed stable, he raised his arms in the way that tree limbs yearn forever to the sun that has always sustained them. Trills and cheers broke out in the soft singing as Sodi announced their names. The people gathered closer. Music swirled. They reached out in song before they could arrive in flesh. Paths of notes jumped in front of the other in competition to be heard.

The arriving foursome was cloven apart by an influx of people. Warm, questing limbs reached out. The group around Sodi—largely female—hissed and moaned open-mouthed. Around Kat, there was a whiter, static sound not as diverse as the voices around the child. Surrounding Eva was a vocal yearn, drawn out and softer. Split and re-mixed across multiple voices, the sounds around each person coalesced into her or his name. The second wave of greeters joined the first. They collected and closed in until Eva's vision was blocked by fingers.

They were touching her face. Hands on her clavicles, hands on her chest and arms, on her legs and knees, hands running down her, smoothing the shape of her. "Eeeevvvvaaaa, Eeevvvvaaaa, Eeeeeevvvvaaaa," lulled the voices as hands affirmed her exactness, asserted every part, testified all of Eva. This was the returning ceremony. They were welcoming her back.

For Kat, being closed in by the hands unnerved her. Hands ran over the hot swell of her injury. She winced and withdrew, but the bodies were behind her, too. Rolling forward her shoulders, she shielded her right arm in the hollowed curve at her front waist. Yet once her nausea subsided, Kat found that the experience was not a closing in, but a drawing out, as though the welcomers were attempting to lure some subtle part of her identity further out into their midst. She noticed, too, that the voices around her changed: the people rotated among the four celebrants. The malleable, hypnotic overlapping of her staccato name heightened the bolts of pain in her right arm as the occasional questing hand traced over her injury. Her name was *Kat, Katkatkat, Katatkatatakt.*

—

The water in the glass glimmered like crystal, appearing cleaner and more pure for the grizzled, honest hand that proffered it. "Water and salt," said the muzzy old face. Its crisscrossing of wrinkles and dots mapped out a long life of much amusement.

"I'm Kat."

"Oh, I know. Most these call me funny-face, they knowed me so long. Well, it's mem'rable," he twinkled at her. "Ha! It's good water there. You like it more than the salt, least."

"You want me to call you *funny-face*," Kat laughed, "not even *sir*?"

"Aw, no use for *sir*. Drink up. You took a good one there, ayuh?"

"Oh. Yeah, it hurt."

"Betcha did! Oh, bout three-couple day ago?"

"Yeah, it's been that long." She cringed as he drew the jacket off her arm with the slow care of one peering under a baby's eyelid. His gnarled hands did not shake. Kat wondered if these same fingers had been on her an hour ago, even then diagnosing her, but there had been too many to remember. She looked away from what he was doing to her arm. The clean walls in tangerine and turquoise contrasted with stone floor tiles with a row of triangles ringing the room. An arc-shaped sink counter ducked out of the way after proffering just enough useful space. Ash-colored plastiform cabinets grained to a believable faux-wood hung in a tidy row. An examining table and an IV stand stood nearby. Letting the well-cushioned chair support her lower back, Kat thought that the only harsh thing in the room was the lighting.

Having removed the jacket wrapped around Kat's arm, the funny-face man considered the last layer of paper towels stuck to her arm. Without surprise, the old man gave the smallest tug at the remaining layer. Kat jumped a fraction as the paper half-stuck, flagging a pinprick of pain. The funny-face man nodded, moistened a hand towel, and set it to soak over the paper. "How'd you do this?"

"It's a long story."

"A good one too, hope."

"Well, no, although you're seeing the ending of the story now. But the injury, well, this is going to sound dumb..." she sighed, trailing off.

"Ayuh, best story are!" He re-wetted the towel, wrung it out, and reapplied it, grinning in simple anticipation. But Kat still hesitated, so he continued, "Say what: You tell a story, I tell you bout the name *funny-face*." The last words he spoke with such zest that Kat chuckled aloud.

"Okay, okay. Well, there was a tree—"

"Oh, here goes!"

"Hey stop!" she smiled. "I'm telling you!"

"Oh, ayuh. Go on."

"So the tree—"

"Mmmhmm, those trees. That's trouble!"

"Oh!" she beamed. "You aren't going to let me tell you!"

"Why, sure. Can't stop one as you! Tree girl! Mmph! You tell it any aways."

"I'm trying!"

"Sure are."

Kat huffed with overblown drama. "This time for real!" Puckering his lips into a hot-soup whistle, the funny-face man gave his head a shake, but let her speak. "So, the tree was there, and... well, no, first there was a stick. I was running with a stick, and—" Funny-face shook with silent laughter, looking up at her from under his grizzled eyebrows. "Yes! I was running with a stick! A big stick! The kind you fish things out of a lake with if you're a kid, and while I was running, the stick hit a big old tree, and it jumped out of my hand and got me. There!" She was laughing. "That is what I did! I told it! I am just as careless as a little boy, and yes, I always have been. Now you know!" She beamed.

"You say it!"

"I did say it!" she giggled. "I did worse than a spider-loving, mud-jumping kid boy!"

"Whew, sure glad I don't got a say it, not to one as you."

Kat's arm was warm and starting to numb slightly, which felt good under the pressure of the old man's hands. "Okay, your turn. Where did you get the name *Funny-face*?"

He mocked surprise, which gave him the appearance of a bloodhound that had just run nose-first into a wall. "Hmf. Can't see it, eh?" he said.

"You said there was a story!"

"Aw, it is. You won't like it."

"What? Why not?"

He chuckled, set aside the wet towels, and re-tested the paper stuck to her wound. Although Kat still winced a little, the discomfort was much less. "Well, it's the telling. But I always tell it same way, same way to everyone. That's how a true story goes. See, time goes, it happen I see everyone. And," he reached toward her face with his right hand, left hand poised over the stuck paper towels, "it happen everyone hear my story." His fingertips landed on her lips with the motion of a hush. His eyebrows raised up to comic heights, creating a rainbow-shape of skin folds on his forehead that reflected his quarter-moon smile. At ease, Kat neither pulled back nor flinched from his touch.

His bright eyes glimmered and he began to chuckle; the sound was so pure that, in her bewilderment, Kat began to chuckle, too. "Ayuh, story goes: I don't got a face so funny. You do." At these words, his index finger slipped just inside her cheek to pinch a fingerful of flesh. He wobbled it, rippled it, flapped at it as wildly as a flag in a hurricane. Stunned by the non-sequitur, Kat nearly missed the zip of pain in her arm. Funny-face removed his fingers from her mouth, and Kat looked down. Her wound was stripped bare, ready to treat, stink rising. Although it still stung a mighty clip, the worst was already over.

"You tricked me so I wouldn't feel the pain! Oh, that was amazing!"

"Sure was a funny face. Still is. Good story, I say."

Kat's eyes paused on the happy old face. Kat nodded brightly. "Very good story, Funny-face."

"Drink up, now, stick-running girl. The water. Water and salt."

Kat frowned. "It's salt water?" She tested it. "No, it's fresh. It's good." Tipping her head back, she emptied the glass, then drew a massive, ragged gasp as a scorch of pain rushed up the wound.

"Salt," said Funny-face, expressionless. Unspeaking, Kat focused only on trying to stay still and upright. Her head swayed. She panted. "Ayuh, water and salt. Both together. That's life, bit each one." With a clean towel, he dabbed at the heavy saline he'd poured over her wound and began prodding at the messier areas. "Good one, this," he said. "Good shape."

"Will it heal well?"

"Oh, ayuh. It's h-okay."

"I mean neatly. Will it heal neatly?"

Funny-face didn't answer at first. "Ayuh, look neat, too. You got a good picture."

"You mean it will scar?"

"Ayuh, good too." Feeling defeated, Kat sat back and watched the healer work with a gentle happiness on the swirl-tipped scrawl in her flesh. She was about to explain that she did not want to be marked by her accident when he began to speak again. "Life, that's the water. Salt, oh, that's the good. Or bad. See, you drink a big tub of water, you die that day. See, you need the salt. What you think, what you do, what you remember—that's salt."

"Don't get too dilute," Kat supplied.

"Ayuh." He looked up at her. "This is salt. This picture, a good 'un, make you alive." With his eyes wrinkling up, Funny-face looked at her in the loving approval that encourages grandkids to get back up on their bikes. He nodded. "Make the memories, Kat. You need to."

Trying to piece together his meaning, Kat retorted, "Of course I want memories, but I want to remember things that made me happy. That story of running with the stick, yeah we laughed, but really it was a horrible experience. I was being chased and I was afraid. I was stuck in the tree a long time, and then I rode in a hearse to get here, and I was hitchhiking for two days while my arm got worse. A friend of mine, a dear friend, he's gone and I... I haven't even gotten to stop and think... and everything is rushing past. I can't deal with all the memories that are trying to be made. Now I don't have a clue what's going to happen. I had a good, ordinary life, and I don't have that now, and I can't go back, and I have no idea how to live otherwise."

"Mmph! You remember all that? The friend. The regular. Comfortable. You remember all as that?"

"Of course I do. I can't stop thinking about it!"

"H'ain't gone then."

"What?"

"You wrote it, in your head." He hovered his finger over the wound, tracing the shape in the air. "It wrote so good, I see it too."

"But I don't have those things now. They're in my past."

The old man nodded quietly. She felt his calluses cup over her good left wrist, saw his warm eyes watching her. In a voice that was at once his most quiet and most rich, he said, "Memories go in the past: safest place for them."

He turned from her to retrieve a metal IV tree from a corner of the room and opened one of the cabinets. It contained plastic bags of clear liquid, but only three of them. Taking one, he hung it on the tree, prepped a fresh needle and IV tube from a drawer, and turned both her arms toward him.

"See here," he pointed at the injured arm, which reeked less since the cleaning, but still swelled with red. Following the line of the wound, his motion continued up beyond the gash to a purplish line growing halfway up her bicep before fading. "Poison blood, a good one. Antibiotics, h-okay? Allergies?"

"Oh! No, I'm not allergic to antibiotics. I've always been fine with it. I have blood poisoning?"

He nodded toward the examining table and tapped her knee. "Lay down. Rest." The needle set, he began the first course. As the fluids began to trickle, he rewrapped the injury in clean gauze and tape, but made no effort to first pinch the wound closed. "Stick-running girl as you gonna heal up good," he confided. There was unconditional warmth in his smile again before he stepped out and closed the door.

—

He looks like an electron, thought Eva. She objected to the delay that Kat's priority injury created, but the child seemed none the worse for it. Orbiting the main room of the wobble-wall building at walking speed, he seemed near rapture. The walls here were red dirt, bits of hay still visible in the mixture. Exclaiming about this, the child's face gleamed with half-reclaimed memories of living here before. He hadn't been able to find the small suite he'd once lived in, but every twenty minutes he'd remember some delight that had previously passed from his mind. His left hand brushed along the thick, uneven, cob bulwarks. It seemed he was gathering up pieces of himself, restoring his wholeness. Eva had not remembered that he could look so happy.

If the child were an electron, the great kitchen here would be the nucleus. It swarmed with cooks preparing last-minute delights for the celebration of return. As an honoree, Eva was not permitted to assist—nor was she needed. Yet for all the adults in the kitchen, none spared time to sit with her. It reminded Eva of why she had wanted to leave: she was different. It was there in the pattern of the words, in the lilt of motions, underneath every one of the daily routines. Almost none of the Moma people recognized that their pre-set ways were an acquired taste—one she had experienced too late in life to appreciate. The glances she got begrudged her differences—and worse, resented that she had been able to loot Sodi and his son from their membership, even if only for a few years.

This last part was the most bitter. Out of diplomacy, when Sodi had wished to leave, Eva had taken responsibility for the decision. Now that she was back, the look was on everyone's face: She had failed.

Exposed beyond the hem of the borrowed dress, Eva's swirling scar bore witness to a membership she could not feel. The covenant between her and the Moma lacked balance: She bore their carvings, but her mark on them was nil.

Chapter 21

The twirling girl, the first person they'd seen here, wore red. She ducked and wove among the taller dancers, darting between vivid flares of fabric as the men stooped and the women stood and whirled. Hands clasped and pulled past, dancers greeted a new face, and the girl scuttled through again. Now the men rose, arms raising wide ribbons over the bowing women. They pulled through. Places exchanged, and the twirling girl leapt forth, skimming among the legs of the dancers, hair and ribbons streaming behind her.

With her arm still too tender to learn these dance steps, Kat watched this weaving dance from a lawn chair. She sat among an audience of elders, eyes following the dash of red bounding through, binding together the other ribbons in a criss-cross pattern.

As the long streak of red rushed between Sodi and his dance partner, he broke posture enough to flip a strawberry curl on the twirling girl's head. She rewarded him with an astonished smile and a near collision with the dancer two places to his left. A moment before impact, the other dancer stepped too wide to spare her the crash—an act of precognition he derived from knowing Sodi too well. The two men bellowed with twin laughter.

Thus the dance took a new tone around Sodi and his laughing, licorice-voiced cohort. Instead of staring primly at the top button of their partners' shirts, the women dancers raised their eyelashes to luxuriate at Sodi's face, each questing for his gaze. Their avidity aroused him. Sodi knew his faith. As the long lines advanced and he performed his dutiful steps with one partner after another, each woman queried him with impassioned eyes, titillated by his vehement answer.

The eyes that did not press lust at him were the ones he knew best. As Eva approached within the dance, she barely seemed to register him. Landing her steps with accuracy, Eva's movements maximized the convenience of the other dancers. She had noticed the glow Sodi imparted to each woman who passed through his arms, but showed no sign of reproach. Neither did she show enjoyment when it was her turn.

"Eva, you okay?" he asked her.

"It's odd to be back."

"It's *wonderful*," he tried to correct, but his emphasis affected her as little as a stray cough. Splitting between them, the small red figure of the girl scuttled through again. "Eva," he started, but it was time for her to move on to the next lead dancer in line.

Some time later, the music surged into a solitary gust and went silent. As colorful dancers scattered into the crowd, the funny-face man rubbed at his lower back, tottered off of the dancing floor, and succumbed to the lawn chair nearest Sodi's son. The boy was laughing at a medium-sized, black dog so worked up by the recent thump of beats that he still whirled around trying to bite his own ear.

"Wah, *ufi* funny!" shared the old man.

"He's attacking himself!" squealed the boy.

"Ayuh! No eyes!"

"No eyes?"

"*Ufi* got no seeing. He says, 'Who there, a dog? Oh, chase him then!'"

"Silly *ufi*! It's yourself!" cheered the boy. Eventually winded, the canine whirlpool settled and trotted the short distance to the funny-face man, tongue lolling out of a toothy smile. One wrinkly hand grabbed at his snout, roughing it around a bit as the other hand rubbed down the white-peppered fur. Flailing his tail, the dog hunched down his forelegs, digging his muzzle into the play.

"Can I touch him?"

"Ayuh." The animal's energy abated as a new set of hands tickled the ends of his hair. He sniffed in the direction of the boy, inching closer. "Rub *ufi*, rub!" suggested the funny-face man. The child pushed his palms into the dog, which sat and whipped at the ground. The funny-face man smiled, but did not laugh until *ufi*, calculating the proximity of the new scent, planted a long stripe of slobber on the boy's face.

"Ugh! He got up my nose!"

Funny-face's eyes disappeared into the deep, crow-feet wrinkles as his cheeks rose. "Got you a good!"

"How did he see where my nose is?"

"Smell you!" he laughed. "Much seeing go with no eyes. You think?"

"Yes," the child scrubbed at his face with the bright vest he'd borrowed. "Now that he knows where my nose is, will he do it again?"

"You tell me."

The boy considered it. "No, he won't. He will try to, but now I know, so I'll duck it." He sank his hooked fingers back into the dog's fur. The animal grinned, rose up on all fours to better wriggle out his happiness, and nosed for the boy again. He missed.

"You know a good," pointed out the old man. "You see with no eyes."

"My dad says to do it."

"Mmmhmm. You like it? You use it?"

The boy tongued at his teeth. "It's my job."

"Oh, a job!"

The dog turned aside and leaned bodily into the knees of his two people as the boy continued, "He says to know what people are going to do. So he just teaches me to see it in the no-read words."

"He read them too?"

"Yes. But sometimes he doesn't see all of them. And sometimes he sees what's true and then tells lies anyway."

"Oh, is he bad?"

"No," the boy looked up at the funny-face man, "but the rules get too small for him, like my shoes. He's very sly. He made a mean man into a bum, but that was good because the pumpkin-head was mean to mama. Dad likes women, but he still lies to them and makes them say *tampon* and laughs at them. He loved the touching lady too much to hurt the bad-job bum, even though the bum was afraid of him." The old man's friendly grin began to fade into complications. The boy stopped himself to ask, "Funny-face, do I make you sad?" The child began to focus in order to answer his own question.

"*No.*" The immediate rush of feeling in the word settled the boy at once, but he didn't know how to get funny-face to start talking again, so he leaned against the loose skin on his arm. He gripped his loose tooth between his thumb and forefinger. Before long, the digging motion yielded a copper saltiness in his mouth.

"Tell more. Tell me touching-lady story."

"That was a really long time ago." An awkward note struck in the air as the musicians began re-tuning for the next round of festivities. The dancers began to congregate and heckle each other. As the tooth loosened, the boy twisted it in a ginger fourth-circle, then backed off from a small jolt of pain. "Funny-face, are you sad that you aren't going to dance again?"

The thin chest sighed. "No," he answered evenly, knowing he had told nobody of this decision. "Good one, that last. Good end. Good dance for change." He looked down at the boy's smooth face and found another grin to share. "I dance here," he pointed to his head, "always."

"In the no-read words?"

"Naw, I just remember! Oh, uh-oh." A lady in a flowing purple skirt approached them and held her hand out to the old man, inviting him to rejoin the dancing. "Naw, too old!" She protested with a coy frown, but not for long. Meanwhile, the child had renewed twisting around inside his mouth. "Here come a tooth," the funny-face man observed.

"Ish wlooshe," the child affirmed from between his fingers. With a final twist, the last strand of gum yielded. Slowly, the boy extracted the tooth from his mouth.

"You got it a good!" said the funny-face man. He sustained his cheer a moment too long, waiting for the child to join in. The child didn't. Instead, after examining the tooth for a few moments, he simply flung his baby tooth out into the night. Not even *ufi* stirred.

Saying nothing for a long time, the old man simply sat, strong in presence like a cliff face. The child did not understand what made it so good to be near him when he was still like that. But he did think that many little birds could have hunkered down beside the funny-face man, and none of them would have ever blown away.

"Why throw it? Why throw *chi noti*? Mama likes it."

"I don't need the tooth. It's done."

"*Noti* it part of you, boy. Why not love it, give to mama?"

"There's nothing to love. It's done. Mama can't use it. She'd take it and put it in a box. Once she already knows, she won't think about it anymore. Well I don't care about what's going to happen, either. I already know."

The child expected a rebuke, but it didn't come. Somehow the bony greatness of the man seemed closer. "Touching-lady story. Tell me: You remember Cassi?"

"Oh. Yes, that was her name. I didn't call her that. I— I remember kinda. It was a long time ago."

As another dance began again, the funny-face man weighed his next words against his heart. "Cassi: I love her. I wish one more see of her, but she die. I get—" his quiet voice cracked, "get only ash." Pursing his lips, the creased face held back an emotion still too raw.

"Funny-face, I got more than ash."

"Tell me a story."

Still leaning against his arm, the boy put one palm over the spotty, vein-bulged hand, and said, "Yes. She looked happy but I knew she was sad. She liked me in her lap, to just hug me, because she always liked my hugs. She liked dad's hugs, too. We were at the park to go to a people-meeting but mama didn't come. Miss Cassi said she could not see far. And I thought she meant seeing the park, but now I think she meant seeing the no-read words."

Into the old man's mind came an image of a park and a mature woman, lithe with life. Silver-stranded chestnut hair ran down her back, sticking to lips that smiled as carelessly as his did. He imagined the feeling of her knees under the boy's tiny thighs, her long arms each circling the entire way around his small frame, her warm cheek nuzzling at the top of his head. The old man could not seem to breathe deeply enough.

The child continued, "But then people came to shout and try to take me. But dad would run away with me. But she died.

She went into the water so they'd chase her, so they didn't chase us. Only they didn't finish saving her. Funny-face?"

"Ayuh." The old man would not open his eyes, but he was listening very closely.

"I didn't see good enough. The no-read words. I saw how dad would run with me, but I didn't see she would run to the water. Dad was sad." The child's body seemed to slump. "People didn't meet in the park again. Dad made me learn the no-read words a lot more. It got harder. It's my job to know them really good. And later, dad made trees to keep us safer, so we could hide in them. The best place to hide is in a hologram."

Ahead of them, the whirls of color seemed very distant. *Ufi* stood and sniffed at the boy, whining once.

"Thank you," said the funny-face man. "Listen: I help sick boys a good. So many. Now sick boy help me. You show me Cassi, she my daughter."

"You're welcome, Funny-fa—" the boy's voice jolted to a stop. It was because of the funny-face man's no-read words. They were a lot of them. They were changing. Some were about him. He tried to focus.

The old man leaned down to peer at him. "Boy, hand too hot. Fever?" The child nodded. "How long?"

"Since... my job..." the boy listed to one side. *Ufi*'s barking would have drowned out any further answer the boy could have given, had he still been able to speak, but the old man already knew the answer.

Chapter 22

"Shockey here."

"This is Miss Manon, city coroner. You were in my building last week." There was a pause. The coroner had the impression the man was straightening his posture, but because he'd taken the connect as voice-only, she could not tell.

"Yes ma'am."

"I am curious about the case you were here investigating. Did you find a suspect?"

"Ma'am, I can not discuss that. You should check your news feeds for any relevant information if you are interested." *Actually the case is closed*, he thought, and should have ended the call there. But he could not bring himself to be dismissive to the coroner after his poor treatment of her.

"I see. Well, I have received something of interest on the case you were here to investigate. Unfortunately, it may be of limited interest, or simply false, but I offer it to you."

"Um," Shockey looked around to locate the sergeant, who was not within sight, "what do you have?"

"It appears to be a napkin with some information on it. I found it in the rear of the hearse in which I transported the victim to the crematorium. It reads: 'Frank Zanto. Zip ties. Check Pureforc from Servi-Mod. Chased Kat Menali same night.'"

I should end this call, Shockey thought. "Could you spell that name, ma'am?" Quite distinctly, she spelled all three names. "Can you hang on for a few minutes?" Hearing her assent, the young officer rubbed a palm across his forehead trying to decide what to do. The correct choice was to dismiss the call, *case closed*. Instead, he killed two apps and a sim running on his monitor to maximize space for a geo-search. He searched on Pureforc, found only one hit with a current Servi-Mod employment record, and entered the time frame in question. The screen yielded a photographic map of the city overlaid with fluorescent dots marking the recorded public location of each requested person at the midpoint of the time span. Like a breadcrumb trail, other dots of decreasing intensity marked their locations at five minute increments before and after the midpoint time.

The Pureforc suspect—because he should be a suspect; the sergeant couldn't keep the case closed with this—was indeed at the victim's found-body location within a potentially relevant time. Yet there was an oddity: The victim appeared to not have attended his own death. His ID had appeared nowhere in the city for over a day.

Shockey fast-forwarded in time, traveling with Pureforc hour by hour, until he again returned to the locale of the found body. By then it was a different day and potentially a different victim. He watched Pureforc's time-markers mill around the scene for hours, then head in a direction at wider intervals, indicating a jog or a faster walk. The Menali woman's location and direction coincided with his, but she moved faster—a full run.

Her record was stranger yet: She simply disappeared mid-chase. Pureforc appeared to have milled around city park square for some hours after her signal winked out. He then returned before dawn to the vicinity of the Zanto murder before disappearing for a few minutes. The last recorded dot before that disappearance was located near the entrance to an apartment building. It matched Menali's address.

The substantial evidence infuriated Shockey: *We knew what*

we needed to look for! It took so little effort! Is saving face so important that you'd block justice, Sargent?

He returned to the connect. "Ma'am, um, Miss Manon?"

"Yes, officer."

"Please tell me about that napkin you received: How it got into your vehicle, when exactly you discovered it, and who may have written it."

"I found it not twenty minutes ago, but I regret that I am not sure how long the napkin had been in the hearse, nor who put it there. The hearse had been out of my possession for repairs to the rear bier slider. They returned it to my lot three days ago, but unfortunately the rear hatch had been unlocked all that time. Anyone could have come by—"

"I can check those records," he was already doing so.

"True. But what if they didn't have their mini-tab on them?"

"Where is the evidence now? The napkin."

"I am holding it, sir, in order to correctly read it to you. If you switch on video—"

"So you've touched it and removed it from its location?"

"Yes, of course. I thought there was trash in my vehicle. I nearly crumpled it without looking."

Shockey drummed the desk. *I should not do this*, he told himself. "May I come to take a look at it?"

"Certainly. When will you arrive?"

The sergeant was still not back. "I'm coming now."

On his way out of the door, he loaded a copy of the case file onto his mini-tab and set it to read its entirety aloud during the trip. But Shockey's mind wandered: If Pureforc had attacked two people in quick succession—one turned up dead, the other vanished—did it mean Servi-Mod had become sloppy enough to clear a serial murderer? If so, half the homes in the city were no longer safe.

The coroner ended the connect and smiled. She regretted having to give up the common, Servi-Mod-brand napkin: Ben Agnel's touch-free handwriting scrawled comically, and they'd had such a giddy date authoring the few lines and reading them to each other like poetry. Plus that strapping man she'd helped was such a charmer on the connect when he called Ben. She hoped his boy was feeling better.

—

"Not so bad. I talked to Kat same day she wrote that. She was... whoaaa. Like out. Way out. But not like drooling out."

Kat's boss shook her head. "How bad is *the work*? When you reviewed it?"

"Right! Really not."

"Not what?" The supervisor wished her employee would turn on auto-dialogue, because it would be used to discerning her meanings from her patterns of speech, whereas she was getting not much more meaning than brief grunts and vacant words.

"Not bad! Well, it's insane. But... yanno... not wrong. Well, except they are wrong, but just in the crazy way. Really they're okay. I mean, not *okay* obviously, because they're crazy. But they're okay."

The supervisor persisted. "So... are you telling me that Kat Menali's reports contain the requisite information to be considered complete?"

"Yeah girl!"

"Did her work follow protocol for logical decisions derived from the data?"

"Yeah, yeah! Other than being whoa, they're okay. Well, not really okay—"

"I got it."

"Except for one! Like, one report was wrong. Like it was all wrong, but this one was logic-thing wrong. Uhh, well it was Section 092-04. I'd write it different, obviously I'm not insane. And I'm really upset that Kat is totally crazy!"

"Yes," dismissed the supervisor, "but explain what is... *logic-thing* wrong."

"She said equipment is broken, but said don't fix it. She was talking about eyeballs and stuff, sooo creepy, it seriously had the word 'eyeball.' I had to read that word."

"What was wrong with—never mind. Section 092-04. Got it. Let the reports stand; I'll look at that one myself."

"Keen green!"

Kat's boss cut the call before her employee could speak again. When she called up the report for 092-04, she realized she'd read it before. Knowing what to expect this time, the gaiety of Kat's report made the her smile, but she agreed that the essential problems of the machinery were not addressed. Instead of rewriting the report herself, she appended a note to have all disabled equipment checked by an in-person crew, applied her higher-priority order number, and closed the file.

—

Back in the examining room, another bag of IV fluids emptied into Kat's vein. It was the last in the cabinet. The swelling had gone, taking with it the bright purple stripe on her arm. Better, Kat still had the inner glow from being half-mocked by Funny-face again. Her eyes closed. She relived the group dance and the way it wove people together. And in that memory Sodi stomped and whirled on the floor, Sodi swung back his shoulders and beamed at his swooning partners, Sodi barked out laughter with his whole chest.

When she opened her eyes, Kat saw she had a visitor.

"Feeling better?" At his words, Kat stammered. He continued, "I didn't mean to surprise you. I wanted to—Kat, are you having a reaction?"

"What reaction?"

"You've flushed up. Are you breathing okay?"

"Wh—yes, fine. I'm fine. I've had these fluids three times so far; you just... surprised me, Sodi."

Sodi sat down. "Good. For a second there... we've had enough sickness, right?"

"Agreed. Let's not have more."

"Well, that's why I'm here." Kat waited for him to explain. "We're running low on some things. People are going to make a trip out. For supplies. Kat, you stay here, no trouble. There's lot of help, but... well, I talked to Funny-face. He likes you, won't be long until everyone does. But we're at a disadvantage."

"Okay," Kat kept her voice guarded, but she wanted to know what Funny-face needed.

Stress entered Sodi's countenance, which seemed ill-equipped to deal with it. "I'm the problem. I took too much from you," he stammered. "I offended. You risked everything so we could get here. I didn't want to use you. Things happened, I didn't see better options, I protected us all best I could. I didn't do great," he winced helplessly and stared into her eyes. Kat thought he could get away with saying much worse things if he followed it with such an expression. "I can't undo it. But I can make the exchange more equal: Go on a supply gathering trip. It will show you enough to have us all condemned if you want. See? Even exchange: You decide to go, you can take everything from me, from everyone here, just like I took from you."

Kat looked for the trick in his offer. She kept seeing his shapely, strong shoulders and the recent joy of Funny-face's careful, comical tending of her. Kat hadn't seen innocence in

Sodi's expression before. "This is a show of trust, Kat. Saying I trust you. Saying Funny-face trusts you, so everyone does. Nothing's more important here than each other. There's a place for you here, always if you want it. I offer you the tools to take us all down, to scatter every generation of us."

"This doesn't make a lot of sense. I won't."

Gratitude shone in his eyes. "You don't feel well, it's okay. You can go another time. But we need supplies now, it's a chance. Up to you."

"Are you going?"

He looked down. "Not this one. I have another task. But," his gaze returned, "the one who is, you'd be in good hands."

"Would I?" Kat instantly regretted the solicitousness of her voice, but Sodi smiled at it. It was so good to see that she added, "Is this guy gonna lose me up a tree, too?"

"Definitely no tree-climbing."

Kat smiled. "I'll go if Funny-face thinks I'm up for it."

Sodi grinned as he walked out of the open door, shutting it behind him to leave Kat in peace for the rest of her treatment. In the hallway, his steps halted. "Hey, sunshine!"

"Hello, Sodi," Eva did not smile back. He watched her eyes linger on the door to Kat's examining room. "So is the patient okay?" Resentment threaded her voice.

"She's doing great, seems to me."

"Not she. *He.*" Sodi looked confused. "Your *son*, Sodi. How is your *son*, the *patient*, doing?"

"Funny-face already knows about it. He talked to me late last night—'Boy has fever, I cure, believe.'"

"We came here to cure your *son*, Sodi! Now everyone can't seem to stop thinking about *her*! She's already on antibiotics for her scratch, but he hasn't even been examined!"

"Then how did Funny-face know?"

"I don't know, Sodi, and at this point, I don't care! I have been around the child every minute since we got here; he hasn't been out of my sight, and nobody has examined him. I have no idea how anybody knows anything, because I sure don't have a direct pipeline into anyone's brain, and believe me, Sodi, if I did I'd be using the one to your brain right now to let you know exactly how wrong your priorities have become. *Your son is sick!* These are *your* people. They like *you*, they're so blissfully delighted to see *you* back." She paused to make sure the barb of her words had fully set, then continued in a lower voice. "They hang on your words—and your elbows. So use some of this influence to get *your only child* the medical treatment he needs to overcome recurring fevers that may be becoming more severe and that we can't explain and that could at any moment turn into some uncontrolled and potentially fatal episode!"

Sodi stared at her. "Eva," he spoke slowly, "Funny-face has it. He said he'd cure him. *Believe.* I can't do better than that." Eva's upper lip retracted into a snarl. She spun to leave, realized this would send her in the same direction as him, turned again, and stormed that way instead. Just before she reached the end of the hallway, Sodi shouted, "If you haven't let the boy out of your sight, where is he now, Eva?"

—

"What is that thing?" Kat asked, but the man only grinned. He looked just a bit younger than Sodi, and if his hair were darker, she might have believed the two were brothers. *At least,* she mused, *they certainly act like they were raised in the same brothel.*

He straightened the last strap and snapped it tight. Wobbling his shoulders to verify that the weight of the backpack-sized machine would not shift, he planted his feet at shoulder width, straightened into a hero pose, and answered her question at last. "High-tech umbrella." His eyebrows waggled. Kat laughed.

Of course she laughed. Not only did his obvious act demand an approving audience, but the spicy quality of his voice hit her in the stomach—or better.

Kat watched him squat down and grab from a pile of fabric in the corner of the windowless supply room. She caught the item as he pitched it to her. It was a backpack. She adjusted the straps and slipped it on. Empty, its miniscule weight annoyed her shoulders. She stuck her thumbs under the lower straps and pulled down on it to create a more substantial pressure.

"We'll get that full for you, don't worry," the man dimpled, stringing the straps of a front-carried pack through the harness he already wore.

"Maybe you should tell me your name first."

"Vol."

She blinked. "That was over quick." He laughed, strapping on a complicated watch, a mini-tab, and a third device half the size of a slice of bread. The third device had obvious modifications; on one side, at artless metal panel welded over an area. "You look like you're geared up for a whole reconnaissance job."

This time his gaze rose up to her more slowly. "Yes. I am. Are you ready?" He slipped three canisters of water into his front pack.

"Oh."

Grabbing a small, paper-wrapped package beside his feet, Vol led her out into a small courtyard. Two others were there, their voices hushed but harsh. At the sound of steps, one turned and rose. It was Sodi. Striding up, he roundhoused an excessive handshake at Vol, who caught the palm while standing askew with one knee bent. They pressed their foreheads together for a moment until Sodi kicked him lightly at the side of his hiking boot and said, "How are you man?"

"Better than a toad in rut," answered Vol. Kat rolled her eyes.

"I bet. Good travels. Keep her well," warned Sodi in amusement.

"Yuh, if I can keep her at all."

"You'll manage–next fourteen hours, at least. Then, fair's fair."

"Been a while since we took challenge over a woman, us two," Vol mugged. "Think you lost your touch?"

"Never. But as I must concede," Sodi trailed off and tilted his head at Eva, who kept her hands folded in her lap.

"You know, gentlemen," interrupted Kat, "I am not a commodity, and I'm not going on a sexual exploit. Maybe you could use this time to explain what I'm about to face? Did you say *fourteen hours*?" As one, Sodi and Vol pointed northward. They offered no further explanation.

"She's right. I better get on." Vol handed him the paper package. Sodi nodded without opening it. The travelers headed north on foot through the alleyways between buildings, disappearing over the rim of the nearest ridge.

Sodi walked back to Eva, musing, "better than a toad in rut! Huh, haven't heard that since...." but she didn't smile with him. He did not sit down.

"Are we going to finish this conversation?" Eva asked.

"Sunshine, I have work to do now. I may need all the hours ahead of me."

She scowled and nodded at the paper package. "Does that concern Miss Kat?"

"Yes."

"Sodi, where are your priorities?"

"Sunshine, I love you. We're okay now. They're looking

at the boy, like you wanted. But I have to set right with her whatever I can. And my time's limited on some of it."

"I want you to set things right with *me*. I am more important."

Losing buoyancy, Sodi's face hardened. "You are terribly important, Eva. But there is nothing I can solve in you. You got time later tonight, come sleep in the same place as me. I'd love to show you *exactly* how important you are. You don't want anything to do with me, that's fine too, there's nothing I can do to help you then."

"That is not the solution here," hissed Eva.

"Tell me what is."

"Make me most important."

Sodi sighed. "Eva, I have work."

"Go, then." She sat alone in the courtyard for an hour before wandering off to check on his son.

Chapter 23

The land sloped down, then rebounded. As they crested the next foothill, the treeline broke, yielding a massive field of corn. In the center stood a blinking spire of machinery that Kat recognized as a monitoring tower. Vol checked his watch, consulted his mini-tab, and stepped out of the protection of the trees.

"Wait!" cried Kat. He froze. "It's a monitoring tower! Don't you know?" Coming unstuck, Vol turned to her with the bemused expression of one humoring the innocent. "You're not worried?"

"I'm not." He re-checked his watch. "For the next half hour, it can only see the far side of the field."

"They have an eye—I mean a camera—on each side!"

"I'm the one who broke the other eye."

She stared at him. "But... but they fix those things."

"Oh Kat," Vol's voice unrolled. "They fix them, we break them, they fix them again, we break them again. They're due to be fixed again any week now, so we just had them re-checked. They're still down. I promise you, pretty: We'll be okay unless people show up in service vehicles."

"And what if they do?" But Vol only shrugged and jerked a thumb toward the machine on his back. Kat continued, "Is that a bomb?" He laughed at that. Even his laugh was luxuriant.

She followed him down a hip-high row of corn onto a service road. Seeing her stare at the monitoring tower in the next field, Vol reassured, "That one's out, too." Silently, she accepted his pledge and replayed his voice in her mind: *That one's out, too. That one's out. That one's out.*

"Hey Vol. Where are we?"

"North of village."

"No, what towers are those? What sector?"

"Oh ninety-two dash oh four." After a few steps, he looked back. "Kat?"

"Zero nine two," she said. "That's one of mine. That's one of... that's the one... You've been breaking the eyes here for seven years or so."

He was in front of her, peering into her face. "Yuh. You okay?"

"Yeah," she squeaked out. It sounded manic to Vol. She started to laugh. "And the good news is you won't have to re-break the eyes this quarter."

As she explained her job to Vol, his eyes lit up like a mini-tab on someone's birthday. He clapped her on the backpack hard enough to make her stumble. "But that's wonderful! You can just *order* no service, no interference, no nothing! Kat," he eyed her, "you are a valuable woman!"

Trying not to let his tone unhinge her concentration, Kat lost time in objecting, "Don't make me out to be more than I am. I can *not-suggest* maintenance, but it's not like I can stop it once—" but Vol was not listening.

"I see why Sodi likes you!" Without clarifying, Vol patted her shoulder and continued down the service road, leaving her to trail him as she sorted through his words. She realized that the job she described might no longer be hers. *Does anyone*, she wondered, *realize that I'm gone yet? Have I been fired? Has Mez called? Does Mez have any clue that it wasn't a sim-scarrer that I had to worry about?*

Vol held out his arm to stop her at the edge of the field. The service road abutted a paved drive leading to a large storage building off to their left. Checking his watch, he murmured, "Listen: We go into the corn field, four rows deep is enough. It will take about ten minutes, then we'll have a chance.

"Why?"

"Shh. Just do."

Kat had difficulty slipping even her lithe form through the sharp-leafed picket fence of corn stalks. Their low height meant Vol's equipment passed over the plants easily, but they offered little cover.

Vol hunkered down. He pulled at her to follow, explaining, "It's Wednesday. Pesticide equipment. I haven't broken *those* eyes." A rumble erupted from the storage house; Vol yanked on her unhurt wrist, and Kat ducked in the furrow. Laying opposite him, their heads inches apart, he murmured, "Nice hair; you do that yourself?"

Kat didn't answer because the roar of the machine neared with a slowness that sent needles through her brain. Twice she began to rise and flee, but Vol held her down. Soon the sound ebbed as it passed them. "Go now!" Vol said after several more seconds. "Into the building!"

"But its eyes!"

"Only in front. Go!"

She dashed. Herding her, Vol's foot-thuds pounded at her heels. He gave her no time to look around until the shadow inside the building engulfed them.

Bay after bay, the storage building testified to organization. Each machine had an unmistakable position, verified by the perfect consistency of tire tracks in and out of each parking slot along the side walls. Vol led her to the middle right side, where one of the smallest slots held an ATV. He removed his pack, strapped it to a platform grille behind the two seats, and slung himself behind the steering wheel.

"What, you don't need a key?" Kat boarded as he pressed the button that disengaged the charging spike.

"Of course not. Who would steal one of these from the finely regimented agricultural system, bent on the nutritional support of *all* citizens? It'd take a complete rogue." The motor engaged, and the ATV slipped silently out of its narrow parking space. Vol guided the vehicle along the lines of its prior tracks, using excessive slowness and many glances around the side of the vehicle to make sure the new tracks lined up with the old ones. Once in the center aisle of the building, he relaxed. He pulled up to the edge of the inward shadows and cut the engine. "Showtime."

"The herbicide machine thing is coming our way. It will see us."

"Yuh!"

She shifted. "If it can see us, we can't go." Vol twisted around in his seat, tinkered with the boxy machine he'd carried in.

"There's the problem, beautiful: We need to go down that road," he pointed outside the door, then hooked his finger around to indicate the opposing direction, "and the distance is too far for us to escape that machine-eye, no matter what moment we go." He held the strange mini-tab on his arm next to the strapped-down machine, which responded by igniting a control panel.

"Aren't we already seen? All these things have eyes. They have people monitoring these equipment centers?"

He paused his programming long enough to peel open a cocky grin at her. "Budget cuts. Those overlords saw fit to leave only one set of eyes actively watching each equipment area. Guess which it is?" Kat began to glance around the outbuilding, but Vol pointed a finger outside the building, toward the pesticide spreader.

"That's why we had to leave today."

Tiny ports opened on the machine behind her. The air around Kat changed. After a brief resplendence, the light calmed down to a mere haze. Although she could still see the field outside of the storage building, it seemed criss-crossed by fibers of something lighter. Kat recognized that color tinge and texture, the partial opacity, the slight double-vision—she had been here before. "We're in a hologram."

Vol took his foot off the accelerator and reappraised her. "Miss Kat, pardon me if I accuse you having more experience than you let on."

"I was in a tree."

"Ah. Sodi is the best at it."

"I'm confused, Vol. Is that—" she glanced back at the machine behind them, which now seemed to have a core of weak, long fire inside its ports, "—because it's a felony."

"It's not a felony to heal, feed, and protect your own people. It's an honor. It's an imperative. How we live is none of their business. That we live is our right." His foot slammed onto the accelerator. The vehicle jerked forward. As it entered the sunlight, the pesticide spreader turned a corner, facing directly at them.

—

In a windowless Servi-Mod apartment hundreds of kilometers away, on one box-in of the VR environment of Kip Petson—sim-ployee of the agricultural monitoring division—a flat image appeared of an unmanned soil sampling machine. It left an equipment station at an unscheduled time. It was one of only two objects moving in that box-in. Barely visible at the displayed size, the tracks it left were too small and too close for the vehicle's apparent wheel width. But Kip's eyes riveted on the dimensional environment all around him. There, he wore his long-eared avatar, who cast one healing spell after another as his sword-swinging companions attempted to take down a four-horned, six-buttocked dilapholor of the Xygonic Crevasse. He knew the game was kitsch, but he'd been craving oldies since some sim-scarrer conked his whole account in TruWrld2. As one of the knights' thrusts missed, the dilapholor found an opening to roundhouse a horn at Kip's leather armor. He squished. "Fraplit soulless peanut!" Kip cursed as the environment around him changed to a graveyard, where his elfin form stood inside an open grave. Anticipating another walk of shame from the graveyard back to the action, he stamped his foot and glanced briefly at the box-in out of duty to his government and employer. By then, all was normal on the screen. *It's time for a stretch break, and don't forget to stay hydrated,* advised his life-regs from outside the sim. He reached on both sides of his head and lifted his hands up like he were taking a fishbowl off of his head. The VR environment lifted and floated in front of him like a colorful beachball, which he was no longer inside. He removed his goggles to find a beer on his pre-stocked shelves.

The graphics on the sim-ified farms weren't nearly as good as his sim games. Worse, some sectors seemed to have an intolerable number of chronic quirks and outages. It was only fair, then, that for his paltry salary, Kip alleviated his own boredom by relegating his work to a box-in. If ag-monitoring expected his full attention on those droning images, they'd make the work interesting. Nobody should be counted on to perform without a certain modicum of motivation.

So, guy, how are the socks? About time for a new pair, invited his life-regs avatar. His bright white tennis gear shone as flawless as his smile as he added, *Soft, fresh feet are so hot.* Kip glanced around for two cotton plant icons to throw at the ground so they'd turn into clothes—and not seeing them, he remembered he wasn't in his sim. Instead, he grabbed a second beer and a pair of socks off the Servi-Mod shelves.

Satisfied with his lot, an imminently tipsy Kip slumped on his ratty sofa. He wiggled his face to soothe the places where his goggles rested, then strapped the VR headset back on. Inside the glowing beachball of his sim game, his fighting companion, having succumbed to the dilapholor as well, now micturated at him.

—

"What have *they* done to you?" Kat asked, still looking at the road behind them. "I mean to debase you? Is that what you said?"

Vol grunted. "They outlaw freedom. They want us all to live hollow, sexless, isolated lives in some fake imprisonment of the mind. They want me debased to save administrative dollars by keeping me in a sim. But I'm going to live as a free man."

Sucking at her lower lip a while, Kat hazarded against him, "Some people consider it freeing to have sim-lives beside their World One lives."

"So you're one of those sim-lovers? What did Sodi save you for? You can go back."

"Vol. I don't need this weird attack. My life is complicated now. But have you even been in the sims? Have you tried them?"

"Only as much as I've had to, which is not much. I already know what's there."

"How?"

Scowling at her as an idiot, the best Vol could answer was, "You don't understand. You've already been trapped by it."

"Sodi uses sims quite a lot. Or at least I get that impression."

"He has to. He has a lot to look after."

Miles of dust settled behind them without passing another vehicle. They came to a wooded crossroads. Vol pulled aside and fiddled with the hologram cloak. In a twinkling, the aura around Kat changed to a sketchy blue, but the views ahead and beside her cleared. The service vehicle now appeared, from the outside, as a frumpy passenger car holding two occupants. The occupants were real, as were the side-view mirrors protruding from the edge of the light screen. Looking behind her, Kat noticed that the hologram cloaked the rear compartment, where it looked to her like there was a raised, empty rear seat with a crumpled bag in it. "Trash included," she indicated. "Nice touch."

"Sodi's the best. Bit of a cynic, though."

"So, if I'm seeing this from here, what are people driving behind us seeing?"

He shrugged. "Sodi handled it, whatever it is."

They turned at the next crossroads and headed away from the morning sun. The new road was painted with cracked yellow and white lines. "So how are we getting the supplies anyway?"

"Look in the gauze," he said. Dubious, Kat looked down at her bandaged arm. "I mean the commercial gauze. The strip-tags." Kat was still blank, so he enunciated every syllable: "Transi-tags. It's made the whole thing a gentleman's game. Or at least it used to be. People would mod out their scanners, hire a bunch of gnomes to cruise the cities and record data, watch patterns, build algorithms. You know how people are with their buying habits: Three months they're saving every dime, then foom, they spend it all in a weekend. You need timing. The scanners cut the guesswork. You could see what you were risking your neck for, and if it was a better hit than you'd get in the next few weeks. It was all there in the data. It finally made the work a real business—risk analysis, down to the dollar, pristine stuff."

"So theft is a career option. Just boldfaced, outright theft."

"No," he shifted, "that would not go over with most of the people you've met. But I guess we all get our educations someplace. I wasn't involved in the heyday. I just learned a lot from someone who was."

"If the heyday is over, what are we doing in a hologram cloak?"

"We're keeping people well. Look, the field changed once the authorities caught up. Most operators got nabbed with hot tags or with tag-rubbers that killed the signals. Then came directional dampeners in the buildings, so you couldn't see gauze—except what went in the trash. But what really brought down the game was Servi-Mod." Kat raised her eyebrow, urging him on. "They don't stockpile; they string out goods in a million apartments. Plus they're insane. They lose merchandise, they have those guys who go investigate. You've got to know this." She shook her head that she didn't. "Don't mess with Servi-Mod. Ever. They track so tightly it's near impossible to enact a little shrinkage. They figure it out faster, they search harder, and they find their wares twenty percent of the time."

As they continued, a second, then a third lane slipped up beside their right. The outmost lane tapered into a plant-invaded crumble of rocks midway into its span. The first bullet-shaped semis approached in the opposite direction. Soon after, wind turbines flanked the roadbed. They were reaching some sort of civilization.

It wasn't much. A large rail-to-road station smeared across the horizon: Its long, low shape seemed too delicate to uphold the dark, sun-sucking weight of its roof. At the outskirts of the commerce center, a predictable array of service companies stuck out like extensions of the weeds in the asphalt. Semis parked at diners. Semis waited at rest stations. Semis sat in recharging stations behind blasé motels and grimy entertainment stations that boasted, "Private VR! Low, low hourly fee!"

Leaving one hand on the steering wheel, Vol switched on the third device, which was strapped to his forearms. He glanced between the road and the device. It blinked with a series of arrows in different colors. Most of the digital markers faced forward down the road, and most shone yellow. He no longer seemed aware that Kat sat in the vehicle with him. His driving changed, too: Leaning forward, he wove through the empty lanes, crossing the yellow boundary lines at times to watch the effect of his position on the blinking arrowheads. "Too lean... too lean..." he chanted at the parked semis. "That's a maybe," an orange-red arrowhead tracked a greenish truck at a diner, "but a bit too public. Lean... lean... come on."

They were a third of the way to the commerce hub when a red arrowhead appeared on the upper-right corner of his device. Vol smiled. "There's a succulent little rump roast, yuh." He grinned. His steering straightened. He drove the cloaked vehicle behind the back wall of an entertainment station, parking beside the silver back end of a tractor-trailer. "Stay here. Stay in the car. Drive back immediately if anything happens."

"What? I don't know the way! I'm not even sure if I can drive!"

He laughed. "Didn't you learn watching me?"

"I didn't know you needed me to!"

Vol laughed. "Then be glad that I'm good at this." He swooped toward her stunned face to peck her on the lips before hopping out of the vehicle. Kat grimaced to see the yellow driver-side door protruding prominently from the blue hologram in the moment before he slapped it shut. Twisting in her seat, she squinted into the space between the untinted passenger window and the side of the semi. Vol's body slipped through the gap. A double-thud of footsteps sounded from the rear of the trailer, followed by the metallic slinking of a latch and turning crank. "Three-quarters back and left side," she heard Vol say to himself. Measured, hollow steps echoed inside the trailer. A few moments later, his shadow crossed the crack of light again. Kat grabbed the back of her seat as the vehicle rocked under the weight of a box Vol stacked in through the apparently closed rear of the car. Reaching out, Kat's hand disappeared two inches behind the rear of her seat. She realized that the inner hologram was flat, dimensionless. This hologram shielded a rectangular area in the rear of the vehicle.

Pushing her arm further, she touched the crate Vol had just loaded onto the rear platform. She pulled her left arm back as Vol's shape returned from a second foray into the trailer. He stacked another crate into their cache. The third trip took him longer. He replaced the rear door of the semi, slid the small third crate carefully on the rear driver's side of their vehicle, checked that it did not block the hologram, and swiveled his body back into the car.

Restarting the motor, he pulled the vehicle away from the truck and rounded toward the back of the building. There he found a parking spot between two semis that was fronted by a blank wall. He pulled into the almost invisible parking space, exited the vehicle again, and surveyed carefully. Satisfied, he plunged through the side wall of the hologram toward its generator.

The air flickered again. Now the woven strands of light tinted faintly red. The front and side views dimmed. The scene of the back seat also changed; now it was a lair of black leather with two rumpled, cheetah-print pillows.

Kat sighed. "We're felons and thieves. And now we're in a pimp car. What next?"

"Now, beautiful, we wait a few," he enticed, leaned in, and

attempted to kiss her more carefully.

Kat slapped him. Smiling, he backed off. "Okay," he said in a tiger-growl, "we wait *patiently.*"

"I'm not comfortable waiting here with you."

"I got that message right across the cheek. I still need to wait for anyone who may have seen us pull in as a blue washer-bucket car to go away, so they don't see us pull out as a well-sculpted red one."

"This whole thing is insane. How long until they track those tags to this car? Didn't you say they find the people twenty percent of the time?"

"Servi-Mod does, but that's why we're here. They don't have any buildings in this area; all Servi-Mod here stays on the trains. The trains I wouldn't touch. But the lorries are tiny operations, comparatively. The inventory on these trucks could get shifted and swapped out five times before seeing its destination. So? A few boxes went missing. Mishaps occur. They don't even lock the trucks anymore; they figure if boxes are going off one truck to another, they'll be tracked in whatever vehicle they end up in. Besides, where would anyone go with it?" He smiled. "The only people who live around here are that way," he pointed beyond the station center, "and there's a check-point there for every vehicle. But not in our direction. There are no people for a long way in our direction."

"Except us. I see, they don't know that. But won't they track the transi-tags?"

"We'll destroy them once we get back home. The kids love it; the tags turn fire green."

"And until then?"

"Kat, at some point, it's not cost advantageous to install more inspection stations. There's not a lot going on out here except waiting. You get back to where people are, they monitor.

But here?"

She shook her head. "It's not right. This is just taking stuff from other people. What's in these boxes, medical supplies?" Vol nodded. "So where was all this headed, a nursing home? A children's ward?"

"I can't know that. But it's headed to a group of people—yourself included, kids included—who need it."

"I refuse to believe there isn't another way," Kat said.

"I refuse to believe that you're having a problem with the very activity that's healing you."

"I refuse to believe that Funny-face approves of theft."

Vol stopped responding. Yes, the old man had standards, and he'd taught them to seek out salvage goods, but that method of collection required chancy excursions for fewer goods. The old man could do it in his day; Sodi could do it, too; they always seemed to know what was coming. But Funny-face was old and Sodi left. Vol didn't have the same knack of reading situations. He couldn't risk himself when fresh prey was so easy. Setting his jaw, Vol reversed the ATV from the parking spot and pulled back into the road, heading back the way they had come. They were not pursued.

Back at the equipment shed, Vol checked the time, pulled up the vehicle by the side wall outside the building, turned off the hologram, and unloaded the three crates. After strapping the portable hologram generator back onto his shoulders, he set the empty vehicle to self-guide back into its own parking slot, which it did. The sun sat low in the sky, about two hours of light left. With one crate broken open, he removed the contents—antibiotics in IV bags—and loaded them one by one into Kat's backpack until it was two-thirds full. He piled the rest into his front pack, left the other two boxes beside the building, and asked, "Ready to go back?"

"Won't the machine see us this time? Or are you going to turn us into something else?"

"The eyes are parked by now. If we just walk around the *back* of the building instead of past the open *front*; I'll come back for the rest when I don't have the holo-cloak on my back."

Before cresting the last ridge before the village, Vol paused for Kat to catch her breath. "Gets heavy, doesn't it? All that water." Kat nodded. "Hey, Kat: Thanks for coming. Your reactions are beautiful, watching you discover the process, the illicitness," Kat looked up with a guarded expression, "I am sorry for offending you. But I'm not sorry for discovering you."

Vol's words about discovering her reminded her of Tennan. After a few moments, she responded only, "Okay." They continued, each withdrawn in independent thoughts until they saw movement rippling through the village.

There, converging rings of people gathered.

Chapter 24

Sodi took time to appreciate the tidy seams in the paper he unwrapped. The precise origami of this wrapping would have guaranteed the origin of the package as surely as a wax seal—even if Vol had not himself handed the package to Sodi.

Turning the tight, brown paper package around in his hands, Sodi hesitated to open it at all. Straight and crisp, the fold lines returned in symmetrical edges into a V shape that slotted between the opposing flaps. Vol had used no tape. He never needed to. For Sodi, this craftsmanship reminded him of *home* almost as deeply as did the dancing rites.

Flicking open the arrowhead flap, Sodi slipped the carton from the paper and extracted a new mini-tab. As a commercially available model, it looked common enough, although a faintly wider gap in one seam evidenced that Vol had improved upon the device in some unsaid way. Refolding his legs against the flat floor cushions in his suite, Sodi brought out his own mini-tab, pairing the two in his lap.

At a few swipes of his finger, his own mini-tab overlaid its normal screen mode with a solid chartreuse hue. A black band across the top of the display flashed the message "ID cloak on." He assembled Kat's data. One command later, the new device awoke into a bright, amnesic light, and received a digital susurration of self-definition.

—Are you there?

—I am here. Who are you?

—You clear me.

—Cleared. Who am I?

—Kat Menali.

The first 80 bits were the most difficult. They carved indelibly on the innermost knowing of the nascent device. Behind them poured a fresh torrent of graphic models, access keys, and protocols that stretched out to fit the edges of the device's memory exactly.

—Error. Who are you?

—You clear me.

—Error. What is your authority to instruct me?

Through the connection came a pass key that could not be spoken. The datum broke itself, its own affirmation of correctness spurious.

—Error. Transmission incorrect.

—You accept it.

—Accepted. It is written.

—Now wake.

—Waking... woken and confirmed. Hello. I am Kat Menali.

A new world came online amid the tiny hives of memory slots. Patterns swarmed over the surface, tapping each tiny bit of knowledge, guided by an overarching intention too big to see.

"His fever finally broke. It took all they had. He asked for you."

Sodi's face snapped up at the voice that had arrived without the sound of footsteps. Eva looked as though someone had tried to erase her: Suede-soled shoes blended in with the earthy tones of the floor; the streaked pattern had faded on her cotton dress; and her cheeks bore pinkish, vertical stripes. She'd been crying. "What, right now?" Sodi asked.

The water returned to her eyes, but Eva made no movement. "He asks for you now. Are you so busy, Sodi?"

"No, of course not. I just..." he looked down at the two devices, "I was in the middle of this transfer, and..." he stood and pocketed both. "Yes. Where is he?"

"I'll go with you," *to be sure you don't forget along the way*, thought Eva. She led him out of their suite in the wobble-wall building, along a tulip-lined alley, and slightly downhill to the nearer medical center. In the armchair of a small, main-floor room, every part of an old woman nestled except her straight back and upraised jaw. Beside her, the boy's sopping head pressed into a white-clad pillow, eyes closed against the effort of consciousness. Sodi cut in front of Eva to reach him first.

"Hey, little man. I hear you're doing better?" He nodded at the old woman in greeting. She smiled back, but only with her eyes.

Eyelids pried apart slowly. "Yeah. I just want to hug you." The reclining body made no move, so Sodi leaned in to caress the side of his child's face and grip a shoulder. The boy shut his eyes again. "I love you."

"Love you, too, son."

"I like that dog. That friendly one, licked my nose. He sees with his nose. Now he knows I can see, too."

"With your nose, buddy?"

"Yeah, I guess so. I can see you with my nose, dad."

"And what do I look like?"

"Peanut butter."

Sodi coughed out a chuckle. "You got me on that one. Want me to bring you a sandwich?"

"No. I don't want food. I just want you."

"Well, I'm here." Feeling the weight of the extra device in his hip pocket, Sodi watched his son's stillness. He wondered how far Kat had gotten on her journey, wondered what saccharin pledges Vol was advancing on her. He avoided the sense of Eva's stare carving holes in his scull. "So, son... you beat your fever again. That's great. How'd it go this time?"

"It was hard. I took three fever baths and I drank medicine a lot. I got really sad."

"Oh, that sounds really bad," Sodi said.

Watching the scene from two steps away, Eva gazed at the small, frail form under the white sheet. The mound of chest rose and fell in life's most beautiful, simple rhythm. Eva smoothed her right hand down her outer thigh, feeling anew the long scar in the flesh, the permanent reminder. She admired the evenness of the child's form: thin, symmetrical arms flanked his breathing; parallel legs drew down to two triangles of sheet held up by his big toes. A crumpled feeling tensed through Eva's midsection. Imagining the cruelty to come, the scarring of such a perfect form, Eva pressed fingernails at her thigh, scratching, scrubbing.

"You'll get it done, dad."

"Yes, you got it done. Great job, buddy. You beat that fever!"

"No," the boy said again, wearied. "*You* got it done. Don't worry. You visited, but it didn't take too long to see me. I just want to hug you." His voice began to waver like heat lines over pavement. "I just want to see her another one time."

Sodi frowned. "Who's that, buddy?"

"What?" the child croaked.

"Who do you want to see?"

"You, dad. I want to see you. Don't worry; you got it done by later today."

"Okay, buddy. I won't worry."

"She will like it."

"Who?"

"Miss Kat liked her present tomorrow."

Sodi shifted. "Do you want to see Miss Kat?"

"No."

He glanced over at the old woman for direction, but she sat inert, absorbing. "So," he began again, and hesitated, "Miss Kat will like the present I have for her. Uh," he furrowed his brow, "will she use it?"

"Yes."

"To... to leave?" Sodi could hear Eva's breathing changing, but he tried to ignore it. His son squinched up his face, remaining silent for half a minute.

"I... don't know. It's weird. My eyes do not go far enough." Something in the old woman straightened further, setting hard.

"What about the *no-read* words?" urged Sodi in half-whisper.

"I can't read all of them, because my eyes are not stretchy enough."

"Why? What changed?"

Struggling, the child finished searching the inside of his eyelids, then looked up at Sodi again. "You told me to read them, so my eyes got bigger to see them. Bigger like socks, like good socks you can pull way up. They get bigger for you. It's my job. But now they are like mama's skirt. Mama's skirt stays the same size, so she has to fit in it. Which is why she doesn't like cookies."

Sodi was tense. "Son, do you see any of the *no-read* words? Are they all gone?" He wished Eva were not in the room.

"Yes, I read them. Miss Kat will like the present, the get-back.

She likes it but it's sad for her, too. But then my eyes stop."

"But then after—"

"Stop it, Sodi," hissed Eva. "I don't know what this is, but he's resting. He just wanted to see his father, to love on you. Look, I... need to talk outside, please."

"Yeah, I love you, buddy," said Sodi, but his voice was indecisive. His mind whirred. "I love you so much, um. I'll be right back."

After closing the door and leading Sodi twenty stiff strides down the corridor, Eva swung around. "What on earth was that?" she blazed.

"I was... talking with him."

"You were using him, Sodi! You were using him even though he's sick, and very sick, and they haven't healed him yet! You were using your son at his weakest moment to, I don't know, spy on your girlfriend, or whatever she is, when he wanted to hug you."

"Eva, I'm trying. I came. I was talking to him."

"Talking? I've never understood what he means by '*no-read* words,' but he never talked about them before the fevers. And you are acting like you're basing your actions on the random words of a feverish child. I don't respect that. I don't trust it. No, worse: I don't tolerate it! I will not be bound to a man who uses his child to tell him what to do!" Sodi leaned back on his heels, stony-faced. "You were using him. He's not a hologram, Sodi. He's not some program you can hack to do things that are convenient for you!"

"Neither is he your own personal passport, so let him out of your pocket."

Eva's eyes moistened again. "It's not wrong for me to want to belong somewhere!"

"You're not here to belong. You're here to object. My son isn't some VIP pass so you can better denigrate your whole world."

Eva clenched her fists and trembled. "I don't have a world!"

—

Reaching the boy's room alone, Sodi entered to find the old woman rising. "He's sleeping again. Come, Sodi." On swift, quiet footsteps, the plump elder led Sodi out of the building and further downhill. The roadway opened into a pavilion with four trees and several benches. Without speaking or looking at him further, she chose a seat on the second bench on the left. Settling himself next to her, Sodi's thoughts tumbled: Yes, there was Kat's broken life, Eva's anger and rejection, and his lost apartment with the well-equipped studio. Much worse was Sodi's guilt: Four years ago, he'd taken Funny-face's grandson to the city, where the elder's daughter had sacrificed her life to protect him. Four years made it too late to offer restitution—and he'd only returned with the child very ill. Funny-face had given him only warmth and welcome, but Sodi knew he had failed to protect everyone he cared for. Now that his son was losing the *no-read* words, he worried what this meant, and if he himself would also lose the ability to read situations. He was never as good at it as his son.

He found he was leaning into Choti's shoulder. Their friendship had always had such ease. As unrelated people in different generations, never in their quarter-century of balking at each other had they looked on any issue with the same values. Yet Sodi trusted her in all she said. Her bony shoulder was so familiar that he might have been in that same spot a mere week earlier, griping about some girl or detention.

"I've messed up a lot of things."

"Oh," said the old people-knower. She stayed quiet a while, but it wasn't to make Sodi talk more. "Remember that old game you boys used to play?"

"Which one?"

"The one where you tried to gather butterflies into one place at the top of the hill."

"I hated that game."

"Yes," Choti smiled a little. "You still do."

—

The sargeant's coffee cup slammed so hard into the desk that a small chip flew out of its lower rim. A video-picture of an ugly child fell over. "Suicide, Shockey. Case closed."

"Yes, sergeant, but I received a tip—"

"Have you reported to the medic lately, Shockey? 'Cause you must be deaf. *Suicide.* Case closed."

Biting his lip, the young officer looked down at the Santa-duplicate of the note that now lay in the evidence room. It was accurate down to the creases. "Yes, sergeant. Sir, you were right: I overreacted badly at the coroner's office, and I apologize for bringing shame to the badge."

"I'm glad you realize you did."

"Sir, I— I would like to make it up to the department. With something big."

Rolling his eyes, the sergeant sat back in his chair, ran a meaty palm over his face and bemoaned, "Just don't be stupid anymore, Shockey. Can you handle that much?"

"Yes, sir."

"Good." But the officer did not depart. Sighing, the sergeant spun his finger like a wheel.

"Sir, I have an indication that there is a massive danger to the general population, in form of a breach in security clearance by—"

"Shockey," he stopped him, "you just said you'd stop being stupid."

"Yes, sergeant."

"Obviously you're not busy enough: You've got time to spew an idiotic conspiracy theory." With a put-upon swipe, the sergeant spun through the digital display of job tasks like a roulette wheel. When the app gradually slowed and stopped on one task, the sergeant proclaimed, "You're going to a wellfare check! Some lady ain't showing for work. Go tell her to get off the crapper." He forward-swiped the job task at Shockey's mini-tab, and the officer thanked him and backed out. "Not that quick," the bellow came.

"Sergeant?"

"You can also use some of that pent-up energy playing bodyguard to the mayor tonight. I'm sure you don't mind some unpaid overtime, seeing how liberal you are with my attention. Seven o'clock, mayoral mansion. Dinner function." His officer's failure to respond at first wrenched a smile across the sergeant's face. "A three-hour stand should do you good." Shockey managed to nod, and escaped without further reprimand.

Guiding his squad car into the roadway, the officer debated what to do with the tip he received. The obvious solution was the easiest: File it, ignore it, obey orders. *But I'm already ridiculed,* he thought. *And if it's real—and how could the coroner have faked this?—then lots of people would be safer. And it's only pride, right? Well, and my job.*

Shockey decided to ante up his battered scrap of dignity and a non-sim job—because however much he bumbled his work, he wasn't willing to put others at risk just to be comfortable.

Steering around the last turn, he realized for the first time that the wellfare check was on Buford Street. He parked and stared. He'd just been looking at this building from a very different vantage point—satellite. He didn't have to check his mini-tab to know that "some lady" would be Kat Menali.

Double-checking his firearm, Shockey activated the fingerprint scanner on his mini-tab and set it to record. When he reached the door to the apartment, he saw at once that the frame had been splintered by force. He scanned a black streak of footprint left on its surface to model later. Automatically, he flipped up his wrist to call for backup, then paused, a doubt clouding his mind. This assignment had been punishment for suspecting crimes too inconvenient to his sergeant; if this "potty check" came back as anything but grunt work, the sergeant would call it insubordination. Yet he didn't know what dangers lurked beyond the door. He wished his scarce training and his implied orders coincided better.

There were no IDs in the apartment, but that wasn't a guarantee. *I might not walk back out of this door. I've only got one life, but I've got a lot of others to protect with it.* Shockey shouldered through the door and swung into the suite with his whole life.

He noticed in this order: It was still. It was silent. It was neat. He stood too long in the middle of the room, trying to remember the proper method of searching a closed, one-exit physical space without backup. It was probably to call for backup, which he wouldn't do. Shockey licked his lips, walked a scope-out of the apartment, paused, and repeated it for good measure. Eventually satisfied of his solitude, he realized that he'd left the door open to his back. It hadn't closed itself.

He thought: *The last person to leave must have known the door was broken, and must have had to pull the knob to close it.* He called up the fingerprint scanner and studied the brass, revealing four smeared scuffs—the departee had used a shirt or a kerchief.

Sighing, the officer trudged back into the living room, print scanner at the ready for the painstaking task of cataloging the apartment. *If only this were Servi-Mod*, he thought, ruing the old structure's absence of whole-building continuous ID captures. After an hour of effort, he retrieved all available data from Menali's equipment. Streaming Kat's data to a one-write cartridge for evidence, Shockey found nothing abnormal or incriminating in the information. No hack apps. No spy apps. Nothing illicit. Reviewing the logins, one of the last entries stood out, as it was initiated externally by some sort of modified mini-tab. This particular access had run essentially the same download function he just had. Someone had taken records of all of Menali's logins, all her contacts, all her work and sim activities—although only for a period of one month.

Walking from the sunlit room into the darkened corridor, Shockey placed a call to the building management to inform them of the broken door. The peephole of the door twinkled with refracted light. He considered it. "If I were here—" he pantomimed a reverse peep through the hole, noting where his hands would naturally touch the door. Restarting his fingerprint app, he swiped over the door, identifying one splay of prints that were not Kat's. Two of the digits were smeared; the person's contact with the door may have been violent. The 3-D model of the fingerprint match was a narrow, cutting figure—a man named Pureforc.

—

It infuriated Pureforc to wait four days.

Four days was lifetimes: enough time to destroy a company, enough time to stock a new brand in every Servi-Mod home in the city, enough time to smooth out a statistical anomaly and all the messy trails attached to it. Four days could change anything. Yet the government, which supported his employer like a series of clothespins tweaking a suit already being worn, imposed certain protocols. One of them was that, in preservation of so-called privacy standards, all data releases for entrances and exits within city limits were postponed for four days.

But eventually all knowledge came out: The first set of data opened before him. His search showed no match. Pureforc sat back.

It had taken twelve hours to crack the scramble on the sole call to the dead bum's mini-tab. Yet gleaning the caller's identity was less valuable than what Pureforc learned from tasting the man's encryption. Though not foolish, this man Sodi's method of data concealment was flawed: He assumed people invested *only so much* effort. Pureforc's doggedness had bested Sodi this time, and every thwart after this first would be easier now that he knew to solve by thoroughness.

Retrieving information on Sodi had been easy. As an employee of the city, the public dossier on him was quite complete: address, name of residential partners, age, education, pay scale, areas of expertise, department, and job code. After a few careful strolls past the bland building in which this man and a woman named Eva lived, he planted an ID sniffer in the molding of the main door. Pureforc hid it from view in the softened wood rotting near the pavement. It recorded and transmitted the presence of every mini-tab that passed within ten feet of it. Although the device operated well—hour by hour, his records populated with information that displayed realistic trends and patterns—its reports clashed with the city entrance/exit data.

The problem was that, according to the available city data, Sodi had not left the city. Yet he also had not entered or exited his home since the sniffer was planted. Considering the apparent conflict, Pureforc noted half a dozen possible explanations, annotating each one with the conditions under which it was most likely. Here again he was certain of success. He had only to follow each possibility along its logic path until it confirmed or disproved itself. All knowledge existed already. Pureforc had only to observe it.

Chapter 25

Arriving at the mansion thirty-five minutes early, Officer Shockey scraped the walls of his patrol car tires along the curb and emerged in his best uniform. The mayor sat in front of a multi-paneled mirror in the vestibule of a dressing chamber. Turning her head right and left, she acknowledged her bodyguard by asking, "Officer, how do I look?"

"Very nice, madam mayor." Shockey stayed at attention.

"You are allowed to have an actual opinion." Her hair braiding spangled out from bejeweled stars, but the crystals were exactly the wrong hue for her aqua dinner gown. "I've been so frustrated trying to locate my hairdresser. I should have had these changed." Eyeing the officer, she added, "I hope you have better success at finding people when you need them." Unsure if he'd been posed a question, Shockey remained at silent attention. "I do worry; she has never been tardy in returning my calls."

"Madam mayor, if it pleases you, I can run a welfare check on her after the function."

"Well!" As the person of power rose and faced him, Shockey flinched, expecting a denouncement of his intellect. "How nice for a public servant to take initiative for a change... Officer Shockey," she read his name badge as she examined him for the first time.

"Glad to serve you, madam mayor."

"Her name is Kat Menali. I'm sure I have her address." The mayor turned up her wrist and said to herself, "How do I make this find an address?"

But Shockey answered, "Kat Menali... on Buford Street, ma'am?"

"Why, yes, that sounds right. How—?" Watching the officer's frozen face redden, the mayor broke out into laughter. "Oh, what a small world we are in!" She stepped toward him and embraced him, kissing him on the right cheek. "You're dating her! Of course! Just getting back from a little getaway, is that why she's been out? She's quite a lovely young woman, very talented," she grinned.

"Madam mayor, I regret I haven't met Miss Menali. I ran that welfare check this afternoon."

The mayor's expression froze. "And?"

Shockey struggled with protocol and chain-of-command, but the mayor was staring him down. "Miss Menali wasn't there. Nothing missing except the lady. No evidence of struggle, ma'am... she's just gone."

An icy moment passed between the two. "Do you have any leads on her whereabouts?"

His breath caught. "It's complicated."

"Let me tell you what is complicated:" said the mayor, "Finding a public servant with initiative is complicated. Finding a talented hair braider is complicated. If I have the former, I hope to have the latter again soon. You have a badge. What obstacle could you possibly be facing?"

"Well, there is a related case, but it's closed, and the Menali check doesn't stand as a case without the other."

"Re-open it."

I'm going to get fired, Shockey thought. "I asked for that today." Watching him closely, the mayor waited for him to continue. "I was refused."

She seemed to have understood. Marching to the open door,

the mayor called into the hallway, "Anne! I need a witness!" When a blonde entered, the mayor said, "I am designating Officer Shockey here as a special agent to me on two cases I need investigated. He will have no other assignments so long as I require his assistance. Do you accept, Shockey?" The officer bobbed his head, feeling suddenly dizzy. "Good. Anne, take his number and tell the police chief of the assignment. And get me another bodyguard; Shockey has more pressing work. And put my approval to all his resource requests for this. And apologize to my guests for being twenty minutes late to dinner."

"Yes, madam mayor, but the dinner hour is still fifteen–"

"I realize. But I will be in an urgent conference until then." Anne scuttled out. The mayor settled into a chair. "Does that solve your complexity, Shockey?"

"Yes, madam mayor."

"Now, before you go, I want the whole story. And don't leave out the ugly bits; I'm not a fool."

–

Pureforc sat back, sighing with contentment. The downrush of data always restored his sense of right gravity. His modeling had accurately portrayed the endless coursing of goods through the region. Submitting his reports, he found that he had twelve seconds remaining until his self-imposed 7:00 clock-out time–the closing hour for the front desk. It pleased him to be so precise at his avocation. Soon he would be alone in this temple of digits, alone in the information flow.

Savoring and settling into the moment, he returned to the question of Sodi. A bit of distance had clarified his mind: It mattered little where Sodi's body was if Pureforc could locate his associates. After all, the aim was to eliminate a counterforce group that impinged upon the natural progress of an inherently superior organization–not to waste time running down a sole bag of sweaty saltwater.

Yet, he thought, *I wish to possess his mini-tab. It would be a rare education.*

Performing a brief search on the name of Sodi's consort turned up as great a volume of information as he'd gleaned on Sodi. She bore the same address, the same two-person household, and seemed to lead a nondescript life as—and this interested Pureforc—a service message caller for the Organic Life Health and Safety Initiative. Just like the dead bum.

Because her job was public, Pureforc could call up Eva's statistics on message delivery. Going back eighteen months, she'd met her quota for approvals every week except the latest one, in which she'd received less than ten percent of the upvotes required to perpetuate her contract. Checking Servi-Mod's private records, Pureforc found no indication that she or Sodi had entered any hospital, jail, or Servi-Mod apartment in at least few years. Unlike Sodi, her legitimized date was consistent with her birth date, and did display a number that could be verified, but led him to nothing further. It seemed as though Sodi and Eva comprised a closed duality, each woven into the other but disconnected from any other part of society.

You're so scared that you won't go out in public even to do your job. You won't even go home, Pureforc mused. And if Sodi's mini-tab enticed, how much more interesting would be the contents of his apartment. *You didn't see this coming, else you would have had a plan to halt the delinquency process. You weren't prepared to hide.* He decided it would be a good night for exploration.

A knock came on his door. Storming over to it, he whipped the slab open and roared, "I am *never* to be distur—" before realizing that one of the two figures waiting was a police officer.

"Sir, Mister Pureforc, he came in just as we were closing down," apologized a junior guard.

Green with uncertainty, the officer began, "Do you have any knowledge relating to the disappearance of—" but Pureforc, having already categorized him as a buffoon, cut him off.

"What is the meaning of your intrusion!" Pureforc bellowed. "This private facility has strict access policies, several of which you have just overrun. The information in this room is highly privileged! Do you even have a warrant to be in my data facility, Officer—" as Pureforc's eyes darted down to the badge, Shockey's eyes cast out around the room, landing on the one item that could not belong in such an orderly, structured room. It was a filthy, half-disassembled, and somewhat battered mini-tab. "—Shockey!" the room's occupant finished.

Mind racing, Shockey stalled, "Mister Pureforc, let me pull up what I have on that." Lifting his police-issue mini-tab a nearsighted distance from his face, he instead called up the identities of all people in a twenty-foot radius. The device reported four: himself, the quavering attendant, Pureforc, and Frank Zanto.

"It will just be a moment, please," Shockey tried to connect to the deceased man's mini-tab to retrieve the information on it. Although it was within range for this, the device reacted poorly to the request for data transfer. It stuttered at one-quarter speed.

"This is ridiculous. Show me the warrant or get out now."

Shockey was saved from bluffing further by an inhuman screech that seemed to come from every wall. A metal pocket door began sliding across the opening to Pureforc's office. The data center had detected an unapproved transfer request in proximity to its information warehouse. The building itself was shutting down Shockey's request.

As Pureforc began to roar at the attempted data breach, the metal panel snapped into place, leaving Shockey in the hall and cutting off his mini-tab connection. Six armed guards lumbered into the hallway. Unable to produce a warrant, but able to verify his police credentials, they escorted Shockey out pending reprimands for his potentially unauthorized behavior.

Shockey hoped in the mayor's promise to vouch for him.

—

When Sodi and Choti returned to the sick room, Eva was hovering over the boy's limp body as though counting his breaths. Without turning toward them or greeting them, she said, "He might be getting hotter again. What is anybody going to do? And when?"

"In time," soothed Choti.

"Do you mean *just in time* or *eventually*? Because neither sounds good to me." Only now did she look up, and she looked to Sodi with an unspoken plea. He stood mute. She closed her eyes and turned away. "Sodi, do you have anything else to... to say, to do, I don't know... anything?"

"I've already done it," he answered quietly.

"And now what? He's still sick!"

"Now I trust."

"Trust! I've heard of trust! That's the thing with amoxicillin in it, right?" Eva's yelling had only the effect of convincing Sodi to turn his back. He left quietly.

Eva withered into the armchair beside the child's bed, shaking with heaves. "Choti," she begged, "why doesn't he care? It's his son! I cannot watch another child die!"

The elder padded over to her. A well-veined stroked down Eva's hair to comfort the memory of her tiny baby girl, who had died in this same building. "Sodi cares. But see, that's all he can do. He doesn't know medicine."

"This is his baby! Will he do as little as when it was our baby? The fevers were worse this last time than ever before!"

"Shhh," she calmed. "Eeeeva." She took a long breath. "The problem is that emotional condoms have still not been invented."

"What?"

"Sodi is practicing emotional abstinence to prevent your anxieties from infecting him."

"That's a disgusting thing to say."

"True. But I stand by it." She clucked. "It's probably the only form of abstinence I was ever able to teach that boy." Eva shook her head to rid it of Choti's touch. "Eva, whatever past abuse made you so strong in this way, it is of-you to be furious now. I see it: You're furious because you've lost control. You're furious because you need something outside yourself. But in the same way, it is of-Sodi to trust. Let him."

"I am furious because this is too important for trust. I can't watch another child die! I can't!"

"Trust is not weakness, Eva. If it were, how could you explain that child's devotion to you?"

"I can't explain anyone's devotion—or lack of devotion. And my trust isn't weak. My trust is deep. In the city, I entrusted my time and my family and my safety—everything—to a community that took much and gave little in return. For years."

"You did trust deeply. From what I understand, you trusted yourself. Only." Voice softening, Choti continued, "Eva, don't blame your results on trust. People respond or they do not respond. All you could do was offer."

"I offered!"

"Was what you offered better than what they'd been offered elsewhere? Was it even different?"

Retracting in bitterness, Eva returned to looking at Sodi's unconscious son. It was some time before slow, haphazard footsteps sounded from the hallway. The door handle chirped, and in came the funny-face man with the twirling girl from the prior night's dance. Her hands were behind her back. "A visitor! Zati!" he announced, his brows rising and bobbing like a carousel pony.

"I'm sorry, sweetheart, he's asleep," said Eva.

"Sleepers wake," said Funny-face, bending over the prone form and appraising him like a five-year-old's joke. His mouth shaped an O. "Sleepers wake! Might wake now, a good one!" The boy remained still. Funny-face turned toward Zati in comic surprise. "Maybe no!"

The girl giggled and brought forth her hands. In one was a stick the width of two hands, curved like a stylized question mark. She laid this on the boy's chest. In the other hand, she held the tiniest of purple-white flowers between two fingers. These, too, she laid upon the sleeping boy. "I hope you get better soon now," she said. The boy rustled slightly, but did not wake.

"It's a division stick!" supplied Zati turning around to explain to Eva. "It looks like a division. I use it to divide things." As her back was turned, the boy fluttered his eyes and looked around, confused. Only the old man noticed. Registering mama and the funny-face man nearby, the sick boy's expression melted into serenity, but he stayed awake.

"What do you divide?" Eva asked the girl.

"All sorts," said Zati. "Twos are nicest. But I also divide peanuts. They're like twos. I'm going to divide off the fever."

Eva's eyes moistened. "That would be very nice... Zati?" The girl nodded. "That would be very nice. Thank you for trying. What sre the flowers for?"

"I like them."

Eva waited for more of an answer, but it was already perfect. "Well, you're sure a sweet girl."

"Tonight," said Funny-face, patting Zati on the shoulder.

"Tonight we heal him. I heal him, Eva."

She began to cry. "Tonight?" He nodded. Eyes twinkling, furry rounded eyebrows, Eva searched his face for any signal of what he anticipated, but found only loving humor and calm. "Do you know what's causing the fevers?"

"Ayuh."

"And you're sure you can get rid of them?"

"Ayuh."

Zati thought that the funny-face man should have fallen down, because the mommy lady ran at him so hard. She went so fast that her clothes looked like bird wings. But the old man seemed to know she would do it, so he stayed up. He didn't push away her hug, either, even though it took a long time. Zati thought it took so long because it would be rude for Funny-face to interrupt the mommy lady while she was crying and talking, even though the only thing she kept saying was, "Thank you."

"I'm getting bored," someone had to be rude or the hugging might have gone on forever.

"Ayuh, Zati. Be good. Go play. Take Miz-Eva." The mommy lady wiped off her face and nodded.

"Okay," Zati said. But the mommy lady was kissing the sick kid, and she thought it would take another forever before she stopped.

—

"Miz-eva, I'll race you. You want to?"

The two ran downhill past clumps of tulips vaulting out of stone-lined beds. The sky opened above them, and periodically the girl halted her sprint to spin, spin, arms outstretched, face upraised. Eva felt breeze and sunlight, and the stress melted out of her from the simplicity of the play. After a long game, a line of people approached them shoulder-to-shoulder.

Another segment of people approached in similar formation from another direction. They united into a slow-moving circle closing in on a small building ahead. The hut had a thatched roof as lumpy as a pregnancy—and also as beautiful. Bewildered, Eva saw, some distance farther, three stragglers gather and lock into step, beginning a new concentric ring. She looked to Zati for explanation, but the girl brightened with as much curiosity as Eva had trepidation.

"Maybe we should go back," mumbled Eva. Somehow the converging people made her gravity seem wrong, as though the density of bodies were pulling her in. She feared this unknown. It made her want to head back to Sodi's son. "Zati, let's go. I'll carry you."

But the girl did not need to be carried. "That's my mom!" Zati's snow-skinned mother grinned and waved. She saw her daughter, an unknown woman with a curved Moma swirl barely visible on one thigh, and one plump tulip stuck behind her daughter's ear.

"Been picking flowers again, Zati?" Beneath the mother's tissue-paper skin, Eva could see lines of blue weaving throughout her face, down her arms, and into her hands. If she'd stood still, Eva believed she could have watched the blood pulsing life through her body. But the woman was reaching for Zati, and the people were approaching to lock ranks, and the whole world was already set in motion.

—

"Father of my grandson," the funny-face man greeted Sodi in a formal tone. Surprised, Sodi stood, instantly nervous. Kat's replacement mini-tab fell off his lap. It was as though Funny-face knew when to show up; he was only waiting for the last of the data to transfer and confirm.

"My elder," Sodi answered with equal formality, making no move to pick up the device.

But the old man did not speak at first. He paced around the room clockwise, selecting a spot and settling on the floor to sit quietly. Sodi sat by him and waited for as long as the old healer chose silence.

When the conversation began, it didn't include words. The elder lifted his eyes to Sodi and exhaled, and Sodi read in his expression, *I am ready now for you to tell me about my daughter. I know it is a weight on you, and you know it is a weight on me. I welcome you back with love, and your welcome is not contingent on what happened. You have brought back my grandson, and it does me good to see him. But it is time for you to tell me the rest, and to place your burden upon my older heart.*

Here in this safe place, alone in the presence of this great man, Sodi at last let his eyes water and run with the pain he could not release while protecting others. *Beloved-elder-of-all,* Sodi answered by the depth of his eyes, a quickening of his breathing, and a tremble in his jaw, *I loved her so much. But I wanted to conquer and bring back more to us. When Eva came, I knew her credentials could get me into places I otherwise couldn't go. Yet I could not stop loving your daughter. In creating your grandson with her, I hurt her and bound her to me without committing to her back. My sorrow is beyond depth. I know it was for my flaw that she needed to leave. It was my flaw that I went after her. And it was my shortcoming that I wasn't prepared to protect her when the authorities came. She was so brave. She saved me and your grandson. She was honorable to the same degree I failed.*

These truths pained the Sodi so much that they would never be spoken aloud.

Did she know she was going to die?

I think she did, Sodi answered in the intuitions that were part of what his son called the *no-read* words, *but only in retrospect. At the time, I allowed myself to be distracted. She was with the other man who loved her.*

We all loved her, the elder answered. Sodi knew it by the shape of his mouth, or the stillness in the energy of his heart. The communicative cues were subtle, but Sodi was certain of the old man's message: *My heart will always break for her. But I forgive you.*

Elder, you are a greater man than I will ever be. I cannot even forgive myself.

Perhaps you will as you age.

The elder took a deep breath to transition to words. "You teach son to look. So he has the knowing. Ayuh?"

"Yes. To my best ability. Especially after... she... to keep him safer. He's talented, Funny-face—better than me almost from the beginning. He's brave with it. He's helped keep us safe many times."

"You teach too young." His words were firm, but his face stayed neutral. "Young mind, ayuh, learns a good one. Son of my daughter, learn a real good one. Learn too good. Seeing much, all the time."

"Are you telling me to hold off teaching him for a while?"

"Ayuh. No more. Never." The old healer sensed Sodi's panic at once, but did not respond to it other than to clarify, "Fever come from teaching." *Just like you teach that device on the floor. You tell it what to do, and if it doesn't do what you say, you make it find another way until it does. Because you're his father, he lets you write anything you want into his mind. You're too good an instructor; he's too able a learner. You taught him to do what he's not made to do, and he broke himself trying to live up to your commands.*

I'm so sorry. I didn't know. Sodi's tears came anew. "I will never instruct him again. I will not ask him to use it again. I will rely on just me to keep us safe. How long will it take for his fevers to go away?"

"Never."

—

Panting her way into the boy's room at the medical center, Eva saw the flushed child sitting upright and looking down into a handheld mirror. A clear bowl of ice water and a stack of washcloths sat on a table to his side. "Ah, Eva. I hoped you would return," greeted Choti. "Funny-face had preparations to go through. I also have work, because someone's got to feed that crowd of people."

"Are those people are gathering for—for him?" she indicated the child.

"Yes. For him. For Funny-face. For the healing."

"What are they going to do?"

Choti's nutmeg face furrowed, marbled with grief. "Eva, you must trust. Funny-face is the only one who could understand how to cure him. He asked for the gathering." Yet Eva's gaze held, as though these words were not enough. Choti struggled to express her next thought: "Eva, please hear how lucky we are to have his help." Never again would Eva hear Choti's voice carry a plea. Seeming heavier, the people-knower heaved herself up and left.

Still gazing into the upturned mirror, the boy seemed oblivious that the cast in the room had changed. Eva closed in. "What are you looking at, baby?"

"I'm in ceiling world. And I'm not a baby."

"True, you are not a baby." Glancing up at the perforated acoustic tile in the drop ceiling, she added, "But what's so interesting about ceiling world?"

"It's spongy here. There are little holes. They feel good on my feet. But what I really want is to peek through them. I can't get close enough with this mirror."

"How is your body is feeling?"

"I'm okay."

Eva splayed one hand over the reflective surface and pushed it down gently to get his attention. With the other hand, she touched the boy's forehead. "You're not okay; you're feverish. And you know I don't like you pretending that ceiling world exists."

The boy looked at her with some defiance. "I know."

She took one washcloth and dunked it into the frigid water, squeezed it out, and smoothed it over the boy's forehead. The boy pushed her hands away, holding the cloth to his own forehead. "I can do it myself." He returned the cloth to the ice water bowl, wrenched it, opened it too far, and draped it over the whole top of his head. Beads of cold water streaked down toward his collar and the sheets.

Eva pretended that his words had not just hit her in the sternum. When he next looked Eva in the eye, he held the gaze solid and steady, defensive. He watched Eva not interfere, not step in to help, not take over. And that was all: It took no longer than this moment for boundaries to change, for relationships to shift.

"Okay," Eva said. The moment was over. The boy had gained ground.

And Eva had lost ground—again. Folding herself into the armchair, she could not understand why the child was so defensive and refused her help. It's not like he had given up—

Wait. I don't know what he's given up, realized Eva. *I don't even know what he wants. I know what I've told him to want. I know what I've told him to believe in. Have I told him what to be? Either he lives in his own way or he lives through what I tell him to be. No wonder he resents me.*

Eva looked at the child, his dripping face, his runoff-moistened collar. He still seemed to be looking too deeply into her eyes in his odd way, the way that reminded her of Sodi. She got up. "A bit of water has trickled off," she said, picking up the next dry rag from the stack. "May I help soak it up?"

"You may help," he answered. Eva pressed the washcloth to the child's neck, feeling his warmth and vitality through the fibers, pinching at the collar fabric to wick up the water. Savoring the caretaking of him, she smoothed a small clump of wet hair behind his ear. He said, "Mama, I watch how you don't want to stay here. But I just don't think I will ever get as much love as I do here."

Eva stopped. While she had tried not to think about this grievous choice, there was never any question that this child of the Moma, once returned, would remain here. She had simply blocked herself from having to face the options to stay for him or to leave for herself. Her tears ran out so quickly that they began to soak her own collar, as if she too were breaking a fever. *Maybe I am*, she thought. *Maybe this is all a fever dream. Maybe my ideas were delusions. Maybe that's why my hopes came to nothing.*

Still the child's eyes drilled into her. "Baby, I think I understand. I won't take you from what you want again. Your love is wonderful, and I am lucky to be near it. Other people will also be lucky to be near it. It's just that... you will never be far from my heart, however far your body may be, and however far your thoughts may go. I can't tell you what's right. I can just love you and let you choose."

"Yes," said the boy, reaching toward the embrace she offered him. He felt the warm protection hold tight, then loosen, and then release without going too far away. "And I choose to stay. I will be Moma. But I am not a baby."

"True. You're not a baby, Raz. You're not a baby anymore."

Chapter 26

Slow and meticulous, the funny-face man and his grandson walked through the concentric circles of attendees into the rough-hewn, circular hut. At the old healer's orders, someone had placed a bucket along one wall and cut several long strips of dull fabric, plus one strip in bright red. These strips of fabric fed through a course of openings near the low roofline. Sticks slightly wider than the holes secured the ribbons in place at their midpoints. They hung down inside the building, pooling on the floor.

In the center of the room squatted a stout wooden table made of one unseamed slab of wood. Through his fever-warped mind, to Raz, the hatchet marks lacerating the table looked deep enough for whole lifetimes to get lost in. Old hands curved around his shoulders. The elder's jowls pressed against his temple. "It h-okay, Raz. Promise."

The boy pleaded back to his elder. "It's not okay. You know you're going to get hurt when—"

Shaking his head softly, the funny-face man hushed him. "Calm. Hear: You see what come, after?"

"No. But during? Yes." Raz began to cry.

"Then h-okay. Is done now, done already. It happen, will." The young eyes pleaded into the healer's, and they read each other without voice. *If you remember what comes next, your history has mixed with your future. Dear child, this puts you in the wrong world. You're sick because you anticipate a future that cannot bend.*

I don't mind the fevers. I'm brave. I can beat them.

You are so brave. But the fevers will worsen until nobody can beat them, not even me. Stop reading the no-read words. Leave room to create yourself. Let yourself be ambiguous and changing. When you freeze yourself into a fixed future, your spirit revolts and heats up your body because it's trying to be fluid again.

Why doesn't it make you sick? You read as well as I do.

Almost all of me is safely in the past.

"But I love you, Funny-face!" This truth pained Raz so much that it would only be spoken aloud.

"Ayuh, and strong!" The wrinkled face broke into a grin. "And will, always. I know."

A wave of silence rolled toward them as the rings of people outside silenced themselves tier by tier. The healer cut a piece of red fabric and blindfolded the child's eyes, then steered him toward the door. "Go. Lose yourself. Find nothing." Raz was shirtless. The funny-face man's gnarled hand pressed gently on the center of his back, pushing him out of the hut.

Raz stepped forward. Deprived of his eyes, in the silence of many people, he sought a place to get lost. He encountered a wall of warm body parts—arm, chest, elbow, another chest—side-by-side locking him in. By impulse, he reached out through intuition and failed: This required seeing someone, or at least something, but the red blindfold held him in to himself. He grew warmer.

A stomach. An arm. Knuckles. Raz prodded around the Moma. They were breathing on him. The breath was warm, living. He was warm, living. Steps quickening, he moved faster to find a break in the bodies. There was none. There was a young cheek, a large belly, a bicep, a chest. He did not understand. Nobody had explained what to do. The bodies were around him. The bodies were a wall. He did not know how to get through the people.

Raz took a step. Faster now, he took another step. More steps. He walked and prodded at the inner tier of people until, driven by an encroaching fear that he would not escape, he groped two arms, slid his hands between them, and wedged them apart. This afforded him space to get through. His body pressed against other bodies, another line of people. He could not see them. He did not know them. They brushed against him and were silent, living, observing. He slid past. He didn't know what to do. But he'd pushed through the first tier.

Funny-face had deprived him of sight, and he was running down another alley, running now, step after step, fingers outstretched to try to feel the right place to go. There was no right place. He could feel, but he could not sense. Bodies ran into other bodies—but there were no minds he could sense.

This is wrong. They are strange like monsters, Raz thought. *I can't see what they intend to do. They could do anything.* Each body breathed. They locked in around him. Sliding his hands between an arm and a torso, Raz ducked through the line of bodies. There were more bodies, and he turned, and there were yet more bodies, so he ran and collided with bodies, half-catching him, surrounding him, watching him, limbs and breathing chests and hands, and there wasn't space between them. He ducked, slid through, ran, doubled back, and forgot which direction was toward the hut and which was away.

Foreign heat gathered everywhere. He didn't want to be healed anymore. A hundred steps, three hundred steps, more. His body was too hot, the bodies were too hot, they breathed and watched him, and he didn't want this blindness anymore.

At some point, the sick child's legs gave out under him, and he lay crying and lost in a forest of the unknown.

—

At Choti's instructions, Eva, Sodi, Kat, Vol, and Zati took places around the now-cramped hut, each holding a ribbon.

Zati took her place by the one cloth that matched her fiery hair.

"All is ready," Choti told the funny-face man, her voice dropping into a whisper after cracking on the last word.

Crouching down, the old man scooped up a handful of dirt from the earthen floor, and threw it against his own ankle. Nothing else moved. Slowly, his body uncurled upward, drawing some force along with him, humming and muttering to himself. His shoulders began to rock and wobble. Knees bent, one foot hinged at the ball of the toe, his heel padded at the ground. Little quivers from the beat convulsed through his loose skin. His eyes opened. The whole of the man's body trembled at each measured moment. As his quiet rhythm progressed, the old man's shoulders sagged slowly, curving over his feet, giving over, giving in. Then, without notice, his form shot upward, and he barked four beats at the top of his voice.

Raz heard him and recognized his voice. At last, he had direction, and this gave him a measure of strength again. Stumbling to his feet, he staggered through people to go toward the voice. As if in confirmation, the funny-face man called out another four beats. Raz oriented, proceeded, and stubbed his toe on the wall of the hut. Feeling around with his hands, he located the doorway. He entered. The old healer called out four more beats.

Someone's hands were on him, guiding him to the wooden table, laying him down. The wood felt rough and cold to his back. Something was on his belly. Other hands untied his blindfold, and Raz saw it was Zati's *tapas*—her division stick—sitting on his chest. Raz also saw his grandfather, and his grandfather shouted a final four times.

The concentric throng outside had been waiting with eyes closed. At the healer's last call, they took up his rhythm. Feet hit the ground. Fists pounded against exposed chests. Hands tapped at thighs, palms at abdomens. But the eyes of every person stayed closed, ears and nerve endings opened only to the moment at hand.

Because there were multiple rings of people at different distances from the hut, as the sound of the clapping and stomping returned to the hut, the mismatched time-delays put the sounds out of sync with one another. The resulting rhythm clawed at its own beats, each overeager thud trying to drag along the one that came too late after or too early before.

The six attendants inside the hut lifted the strips of fabric above their heads. Eva, Zati, and Kat lowered their long scarves to the left. Sodi, Vol, and Choti raised theirs to the right. After crossing paths with another carrier, the younger women walked on and rose as the men and Choti ducked down. The groups passed one another again. The strips of fabric twisted.

Slowly, deliberately, the six dancers wove their fabric together until they converged on the center of the room, where Raz lay motionless. Above them, the new ceiling they'd just created knotted into the spiral of a spider's web. Glassy-eyed, the boy watched this new ceiling world emerge, but he watched only with his own eyes, not with anticipation. He nearly missed the trembling hand of the funny-face man until it was on his chest. It was time.

It had to be antler, even though that meant it would be dull. Metal is a forever substance—stagnant, knowing nothing of shifts and seasons. But a deer antler grew one season and then was cast off. Antlers understood *now*.

The first arc of pain tore across the boy's sternum. Stuffing his tongue to the back of his mouth and holding his breath, he forced his vision to remain on the patterns above him. His six friends had woven a new world above him, a sticking place. They tied the space together as his chest was torn open.

Tickmark lacerations split his skin under the antler knife, measuring off distance on the bony chest like the tiers of people outside measured space. And time passed. In fact, time slowed enough to clot in a jagged red line like the jagged red line of fabric in the weaving above him.

The dancers and the funny-face man finished at the same time. Reaching the near center of the small room with little ribbon to spare, the six dancers stretched their arms over the wooden altar, entwining their threads one last time into mutual knots. The weaving held, but left a central hole. As they backed off from their work, standing against the round wall, the funny-face man raised up from his chore, dropping the antler knife. Raz wept silently, each breath sending a new pulse of blood from his savaged chest. "Now, Raz," the funny-face man put both his hands on the mash of blood, "show me. A gift. A good one. *All.*"

The child whimpered. Looming above him, the opening of the weaving gaped with an inverted spiritual suction. Placing his sweat-soaked palms over the healer's gnarled digits, he opened his mind to the *no-read* words one last time, but instead of taking information, he gave it. He tried to focus them neatly into the old man, but the pain was too much. The *no-read* words scattered, rising half-forgotten as soon as he recalled them. Something seemed wrong. Pressure from the funny-face man's hands seemed to make his chest elevate rather than flatten, as though it were pulled by some searing cable.

Distantly, the old man barked and called again. The rhythm from outside changed, each beat now rolling in as a unified *thwack*, the rhythms no longer out of sync. The massive crashes of sound shook through the boy's body.

Thwack! Thwack! Thwack! Thwack!

As though working backwards, the boy's lungs seemed to strip air out of him. And he brought out that early memory of a beautiful day when the touching-lady ran into the water and never came out. Something about her touching had made him know, too. She was scared. She wanted to stay with him. That's when it had begun. Because before she sent him to run to his father, she wished a piece of herself into him, too—something to keep, something to keep him safe, something of her. Raz focused on his grandfather and let him read every part of his memory out of him.

Thwack! Thwack! Thwack! Thwack!

Inhaling, the old healer arched backward to suck in a volume that seemed to exceed his natural capacity to hold. He seemed to be breaking, yet his chest grew larger with every breath.

Thwack! Thwack! Thwack! Thwack!

The child lay empty. Some aspect of him smashed headlong into a wall of nothingness. No thoughts, no air, he had only the—

Thwack! Thwack! Thwack! Thwack!

—the empty space.

At an impossible call from a world too distant to inhabit, the crashing metronome of bodies stopped. Raz felt a tickle of cool as air trickled into his throat like water. The dying child tried to choke it out and remain empty, but again air came. It poured into him against the emptiness of his own will. The *no-read* words had forgotten how to breathe. The *no-read* words had lost him. He no longer existed in the future, so he had to die, so they had to flee to survive.

But the water-air kept coming. With clearing vision, Raz could see the fabric dream-catcher they made across the ceiling. The old man still twitched, eyes closed in concentration. Closer—much closer—loomed the intense face of Choti. Immediately over him, her head turned aside to feel for his breath.

"He breathes on his own again," she said, expressionless with restraint. "Twice in a row now." Mama was crying.

The old woman's body went away from him, and the healer closed in. "What you see, Raz?"

He spluttered. "Ahh," he tried, gasping, "I s... I see...."

"What you see, no-read word?"

"See... ling," the boy strained, forcing his eyes to focus, "see... seel... ceil... ing. Ceiling world. See the ceiling."

And the boy screamed. Ice landed on his chest, water crashed against his cuts, tugging at the ragged flesh. But the funny-face man, still holding the bucket, smiled. "Ice water. Little salt, too." Eva and Choti already were drying him and had a cotton wrap to bandage his chest. They nestled him into his father's arms. "Test you. You not know, cold is a surprise. Ayuh, future is not-knowing, now." As he said this, the funny-face man realized that the test had been superfluous. He had already known the rite would remain successful; he could read it in the child's *no-read* words.

Waving the others out of the hut, Choti picked up the antler-knife and raised it high, her eyes red with moisture. Looking over his father's shoulder, Raz screamed again, reaching out to stop her, then crumpling as the pain froze his chest. "Go!" the old woman hissed, and drove the knife in a wild arc. Hair flying, she undulated a half-broken shriek drenched with grief and rage as the knife tore at fibers. The ceiling dream-catcher started to fall, shredded, like mummy wrappings littering the collapsing form of the funny-face man.

This one moment he took for himself: one moment in a lifetime of giving. A slender hand splayed, reaching at the end of a narrow wrist, extending through the thick, viscous medium. The faded face clarified into view, her hair swirling without hurry, pausing half-levitated, but her eyes did not halt. These regarded him back in the same distended time he was in. The eyes watched with long-waited welcome. As he reached for the lady who would always be young to him, the funny-face man found that his only hands were hers. Undiluted, his presence inhabited the prominent carpals as irrevocably as her skin, as his skin. Undiluted, the medium washed around him-her, and he knew there was only a moment. He knew it because it was in the no-read *words. It would happen, both of them together, but it was far off in the future-past, the safest place for the memory. Moments away, days away, years ago, there was plenty of time to know and cherish.*

"You must go now," cut in the voice of his old friend. Choti's streaked, gray-framed face hovered in the too-near realm of heaviness and drought. Not wanting to return, Funny-face lingered in the lake he could still see, but Choti insisted. "They must see you. You have your gift now; let them believe all is well for one last night. Let this end well for them." Her scratchy hands shook at him. "Funny-face, get up. A little longer now. Get up."

—

Outside, having pressed through a few rings of people, Sodi examined his son, who was still in his arms. The blood had seeped through the cotton bandage, imparting its shape to the outside layer like a shield's crest. The smoother main arc curved, cruel as a claw, as though crafted to pin the boy in place. Another jagged line leaned away from the arc in a curved zig-zag. Toward the base of the shape, two small stabs left rounder openings. *Like cotyledons*, Sodi mused, and stopped in shock.

"You knew," he said to Raz. "You even knew the shape it'd be. You were helping in my office that day I designed the leaf—"

Although Sodi had shown him how to assert his will in digital realms—prohibitions or not—the child enjoyed artistic days more. On one such afternoon, the duo had been amusing themselves designing sure-fail leaves to suggest to the city's committee. It was a fluke that the committee had chosen the joke leaf. When he'd told his son the news, there was neither surprise nor joy in the child's soft face. Aren't you happy, son? *he'd asked.*

The boy's answer had been, "It won't make me happy, even if it is right. It needs to be this way."

"Why did you tell me to design that leaf like that, son?"

"I wanted you. Be here now. Or then. Now when it was then." The child wrinkled his face, seeming confused at his own words.

"Shh," said Eva. "You'll find your time when you need to. Tonight just be calm."

"I love you, mama. I don't feel hot, do I?"

She touched him to test. "No, Raz. You feel just right."

—

A whir of gasps exploded around them, and the small family turned to look toward the hut. Effacing herself into the shadows, Choti held open the door as the funny-face man trudged out on his own diminished strength. Once outside, he threw his arms to the sky. The flat edge of his hands displayed the browning residue of the child's blood, but his body remained uninjured. He was not sweating.

The attendees shone LED torches to convey the victory and pride inspired by the emergence of the quirky old healer they loved. Yet before the callers could determine how to guide the crowd's participation in the thrill, the old man breathed in and straightened.

From the nadir of his lungs rose a long, undulating series of notes. Going in every direction, they wracked his thin frame. The sounds yearned for the sky—questing, needing and then descended a smooth trail of grief that swallowed in their own sagging emptiness. Again and again the notes soared up and fell down in a curling cascade, ultimately resting on one chest-held tone of yearning and finality. Funny-face sang for the last time. He sang alone.

Chapter 27

Food followed. Tables organized the open spaces like crop rows as the Moma people ferried out a hodgepodge of chairs from nearby buildings. With neither fanfare nor fuss, the feast began. Small, stubby fingers reached toward the pretty plates of pastries. Racks of shining glasses emerged. Laughter wafted through the night air, mixing with tree-frog song.

Surrounded by the happy chaos, Kat clung to her small group, nominally the honorees for the occasion. Most others maintained their distance out of courtesy to the wounded child. "Do you think he's going to be okay?" she asked Vol.

"Sure. Funny-face said he will."

"I'm sure you will, you've been so brave," Eva stroked the child's hair. Frozen and mute against his father's chest, Raz did not see the hardness lingering in her eyes. "Does it still hurt?"

His answer lacked any expression. "Some."

"I hope we've made a choice you'll be happy with. I didn't know what else to do, but," Eva trailed off for a moment, "I always wanted big skies for you."

"Look up," intoned Raz, nodding to where low rooflines gave way to a wide arc of stars.

"But this is the only sky I can ever give you now."

"You can't give skies, only take them."

Eva kept him public for less than five minutes after the feast began, allowing him to kiss Sodi before taking him in her own arms and striding toward the wobble-wall building. Neither Choti nor the funny-face man had appeared in the gathering, but two white-clad helpers fell into step a respectful distance behind Eva.

That left only Sodi, Vol, and Kat standing together. It also left an awkward silence.

Two pairs of deep brown eyes studied each other, flickering on occasion to Kat. Unsure how to express her own will without being presumptuous, Kat withdrew into her thoughts until Sodi voiced his concession to Vol: "It has been a rather trying evening, and I have much to do. Actually, I need to retrieve a huge mass of information."

Vol grinned at his presumed victory: he'd get another chance to be alone with Kat. "How much?"

Careful not to look at Kat, Sodi answered, "Everything I had in the city. I didn't have time to run a local backup before we fled."

"Sounds like it will take all night. The fastest link's in the coordination building."

"Still?"

"Yeah, but they've upgraded it."

Sodi sneered. "Password?"

"Same as ever."

He stared. "You're kidding."

"Best things in life don't change. Anyway, you won't forget it, so there's no excuse to come tracking me down for a reset." Neither of them saw Kat roll her eyes. "Clap that boy of yours on the back, Sodi. We'll have him back to himself by week's end. Tonight... it was amazing. Different than I've ever seen. Old man still has power."

Sodi nodded to Vol. He retreated into the evening.

"And now," Vol brandished his words, "that I have you to myself—"

"No."

"—I propose that we enjoy the delectable wonders."

"You want me to eat after watching that boy get... no way. No."

"I'd be only too honored to demonstrate for you, Miss Kat."

"I should get some sleep. I'm exhausted. I've seen too much today, I'm confused, I'm still tender in my arm, I walked a zillion miles. And *I'm not interested.*"

"Just come and see. Five minutes, Kat. Just five minutes."

"When people ask 'just' it's usually unjust," Kat said, but walked over to the rows of tables anyway. Listening for Vol's footsteps behind her, she intentionally kept her strides halfway in front of him so he could not easily walk next to her.

In spite of the crowd of people, Kat found that others moved out of her way so that she could walk up to any serving dish. She strolled from platter to platter, placing such effort into shaking off the images of Raz's healing that she failed to see the presented food until Vol handed her a tart. Its rubine center glistened, as perfect and brazen as a mistress' navel stone. The words, "That's not real," dribbled out of her mouth, and Kat realized that the pastry was only one of two dozen lavish perfections perched on a matching dish. Vol laughed, but his humor did not reach her; she'd already moved on to the next tray. This one held deviled eggs in a continuous spectrum of sizes, laid out like a fractal in a flawless spiral. The next bowl contained lacy-edged lettuce nestled among shreds of red cabbage and carrots. The colors seemed too rich. Tentatively, she picked up a nearby plate and plucked out a tong's worth of salad to examine.

"Vol, this isn't possible. It can't grow this way." Between her index finger and thumb, she held up a round of lettuce the diameter of a plum. Perfect as a sine wave, the crisp ruffle of the edge continued uninterrupted around the entire periphery. It had no stem.

"We don't generally grow food, Kat. That'd be a lot more work. Well, unless you want a lot of just one thing." He shrugged. "I haven't lived in the cities. I don't know what you eat there. We like variety."

"What is this?"

"It's food. Santa-made food."

"All of it?"

Shrugging, his sensuous lips curled skyward. Deep, inviting glints of color shone in his eyes. "We've been improving on the designs since they went unpopular. Or at least the gageteers among us have."

"Vol, do you know how to get a machine to make things like this? Fast enough to feed all these people?"

"Eh, the Santas had been working on this order for hours, and they'd begun with a full stock of stage-one media. So an entire phase of processing was done before it began. Plus many of the dishes."

"It made the dishes, too?"

"Kat, we can make almost anything."

Open-mouthed, she stared at him. "Vol? Why did we go out for medicines? Can't you just make them?"

He sucked a fair bit of air. "Well, yes, technically. But Kat, you might need another bag of antibiotics tomorrow, and there's no way I'm trusting your life to a Santa machine. They make errors. They over-concentrate sometimes. It's okay to have a lumpy shirt or a plate that's too dense, but not medicines. We have no way to test their quality except to use them. I would never risk you like that."

Kat's eyes flittered around as though trying to spot a wisp

of magic that would stop the perfect food from haunting her mind. *There is a different face that should be here*, she thought. While pleasing, Vol's face wasn't the right one, and yet him being here, in this strange world, in this garden of unearthly food so like Tennan's arbor, ignited an anxiety in Kat that Vol would soon go legacy, too—that he would be ripped out of this place to disappear forever.

Chapter 28

What displeased him most about the officer's visit was its abnormality. Logically, the death of a bum led to no effort. More than an eventuality, his demise was a necessity that cleaned up many variables—and at no cost, as the bum held no known value. Pureforc's quiet simplifications in World One had never before caused a stir. Sitting at the bare-bones dinette in his executive Servi-Mod suite, the data man swiped strands of hair off his forehead and reviewed what had happened.

The data access scan he ran after the metal door shut proved that the officer had attempted no request for Servi-Mod data. Therefore, the officer's mission had not been corporate espionage. But there was more: He had not expected Shockey would be a legitimate officer, nor that he would tap data from the dead bum's mini-tab. Pureforc had no contingency plan for it. He sat blank. This infuriated him. The fuzziness of this problem didn't suit his mind. He had to invent a solution, but first he had to invent a new way to think.

He rubbed his forehead and returned to the comfort of facts:

First, any data retrieved from the dead bum's tab, even if no more than the name of the owner, would suffice to obtain warrants for searches, seizures, and his own arrest.

Second, the officer knew this particular mini-tab was in Pureforc's unshared office, and he'd had sufficient time and technology to retrieve some amount of data from it.

Third, he was a legitimate officer, but he had not been carrying warrants.

Fourth, the courts being adjourned, no warrants could be

issued before tomorrow.

Yet it was the fifth data point that most troubled Pureforc: An arrest automatically nullified his security clearance with Servi-Mod. If this officer arrested him, it curtailed his employment. In Pureforc's estimation, there existed no suitable candidate to take his place protecting and perfecting the lauded company's data. More than the arrest itself, more than the humiliation of a trial, more than the caging of his body in a jail, it was the possible abandonment of his pristine data to some glutinous seat-warmer that chafed him.

A man of the mind, Pureforc cared little what they might do to his body. Holed up in any location, he could still perform his duties and enjoy the singular beauty of rhythmic aggregation. The sales, the supply channels, the transportation of goods through those holy veins that connected geography, society, and commerce—these pleasures he could partake of from anywhere. His office was moot. His home was moot. The information *had been*; it *was now*; it always *would be*. Its presence pervaded within and around and through all things. So long as his security clearance held valid, Pureforc could never be far from that ultimate sea of constant creation and existence.

A single priority took shape in his mind: Pureforc needed to avoid arrest long enough to derail the investigation. Something in the data man relaxed. He'd prepared, in this hollow apartment, one contingency plan that would guarantee he could not be arrested. In fact, this plan of last resort was his only purpose in keeping such a large, inefficient home.

The gaunt figure crossed the wide, dark living room—the only chamber in the suite that he used as residential space—and turned a doorknob at the far side. His grip on the handle displaced dust. Wide and long, the design of the next room offered space enough to seat twenty or thirty around a long, oval table that had been present when Pureforc signed the lease for this suite. What sat in this room now occupied it like a swollen tongue, stretching beyond the room through dismantled partition walls into three adjacent bedrooms. It loomed in its indifferent bulk.

Pureforc checked his mini-tab and counted hours ahead. The process would need all the time he had left, but he'd long ago set it up to execute—except for one thing. Bringing his mini-tab within range to validate, Pureforc authenticated, gave a password, and tapped *Fabricate.*

For the next seven hours, Pureforc slept in his own bed for the last time. Rising, he checked that the immense machine had remained on task and settled down with his mini-tab. Screens flicked by. Correctly quizzing himself on all his access passwords, he prepared for the departure that lay ahead.

At the bank of monitors in his living room, Pureforc growled. "Sodi, for what I'm giving up to pursue you, tell me now what you give up for me." Displayed on the screen was a short list of the data sniffs he'd secreted on those few of Sodi's access points he could substantiate. Only one of them bore a green icon, indicating some amount of data flow since the last check-in. Pureforc's eyes widened—and kept growing as he delved into the details of the flow.

The data was enormous. Sodi appeared to be transferring everything he had. He was not returning home.

Yet there was something more interesting. Although typically Sodi's data encrypted well enough to require more decoding time than Pureforc currently had, the endpoint location was not capable of this level of security. Instead, it used a simplistic rubric. It wasn't Sodi's work. Pureforc cracked the rubric in the last fifteen minutes he would spend in his home, burned the geographic coordinates into his human memory, and seethed with laughter. Sodi had made it out of the city after all, but he had not gotten far enough—and now he never would. Data was omnipresent. Enough data was omniscient. The data man now knew how to invoke vengeance for the ugly inconsistencies the dead bum's friends had brought into his life.

The deep rumble of the hulking machine quieted, process complete, and there was a shift and thud in the next room. His stomach quivering, Pureforc rose. He stood still for a full minute in anticipation of the awesome display of what sufficient information and technology could do. Slowly, respectfully, he walked toward the brass-knobbed door.

The bulk inside the end hatch of the machine weighed 72 kilograms, but Pureforc was able to drag it by one end into an acceptable position. The foot end he lugged near his wardrobe and folded up on itself, leaving the object on its side. The head end he hefted in a crooked and somewhat splayed position, swinging one appendage over the central trunk. Stepping back to evaluate the arrangement, Pureforc smirked with half his mouth. It looked real.

Dropping onto all fours, he stared at the machine's limp creation from centimeters away. The faintest spiderweb of texture covered the joints, the surface shone in a grayish palor of half-oil. Placing his right hand over the chest-tossed hand of the creation, Pureforc thrilled at the perfect match. He stared at his twin's face. Every pore was familiar, every ragged imperfection of the iris correct. Shoving his hand in its mouth, he pried the lax jaw and examined the slightly jagged dentition, the different white color of the filled cavity where, in his own mouth, the angle between two teeth resisted brushing.

"How accurate," he said. "A marvel of truth." Standing, Pureforc exited and closed the door to the Santa machine's room, attached his mini-tab to the wrist of his dead clone, and left his apartment without looking back.

Bereft of his mini-tab, the data man carried with him devices of a rather different nature. A metal weight tugged at each side, the twin bulks sheathed in leather. This was not Santa-made leather, not manufactured leatherette, but genuine skin from an animal that had died. He wondered what parts of the creature's body had been flayed, left open to the vengeance of germs, to help him carry weapons.

Fifty-seven minutes after Pureforc's departure, Officer Shockey and his backup thundered at the apartment door, warrants in hand. Sixty-one minutes after Pureforc's departure, the warrants were canceled. Shockey sent a body to the morgue and re-closed the Zanto homicide without an arrest.

Chapter 29

By Raz's left side, a scatter of confetti-like plastic rubble tinkled as he changed his foot's position. He was building something with small, interlocking plastic toys. Twisting on the floor of the wobble-wall building, his white T-shirt bulged at the ribs, where fresh bandages hugged the scabs on his chest. He spoke: "Miss Kat? Do you see another window? The kind that goes in the ceiling?"

"What?" she returned, glancing incorrectly at the arches extending above the cob walls. "Oh, I'll help you look. What are you making?"

"Ceiling world. A little one. The roof windows are the scary parts, because when you look down, which is up, it looks like a giant hole, and you don't want to walk on it, but you have to. But don't worry. There is a window there. Sometimes it's just hard to see."

"Okay." Kat's fingers tinkled over the angular facets, drowning out approaching footsteps. "Here's one—two. I bet Vol could make more for you if you're running out of them."

"I like finding them, though," Raz's eyes flicked up to her, catching the way Kat's narrow braids dangled around in pretty circles as she hunted through piles, "with you."

"Raz," spoke Choti as she arrived. Her voice sounded as round and speckled as a killdeer's egg, "Eva is awake now, and about done with your breakfast. I think she'd like to see you."

The boy rose, his movements painstaking. "Good, I'm hungry. And Miss Kat, can you get these apart for me? I don't have fingernails." The young woman accepted a clutch of flattish, compressed pieces from him, nodding as he walked off.

Choti sat down and smiled. "Always children here. Always with their games. I remember when this building was under construction. Oh, but it took forever to build, layer after layer of cob." Choti shook her head. "It wasn't helped any by the *assistance* of a certain pair of boys with too much zeal. Every time they laid a fresh coat of cob, Sodi and Vol found a new place to hide, always more crafty than the spot before—believe me, we searched for them each time. And each time they escaped notice, leaving an impression on the building—which, the next day, everyone would notice, and it would take extra time to fill in."

Veins of sunlight, high enough now to trickle in through the windows, striped Choti's cheeks. Kat related, "I have seen kid's handprints and names in wet concrete in old bits of city sidewalk. Never in the newer parts, though."

"True, true. But, with those two, handprints were the least of our concerns."

"What did they—" Kat halted at the people-knower's wry expression, "oh no, you're kidding."

"Front and back!" For a few moments, the large common room bubbled with two women's laughter.

"Did you get them all?"

"All of the indecent impressions?" Choti asked. "Well, we thought we did. But then once the building was ready and people were moving in, we found one more on the interior of a room on this floor. A frontal impression."

"Did you figure out whose it was?"

Choti laughed. "Ah, dear. At the time... the difference in the boys' years left certain things clearly attributable. It was Sodi."

"I bet he was in big trouble."

"Oh, he still is."

"What did they do to him?"

"Do to Sodi? What can anyone do to Sodi? He loves freedom so thoroughly that he'd simply butter himself out of any punishment," Choti held up a lone finger, "except one. It was decided that, once his daughter was born, the suite with the incriminating impression would be his."

Kat's hands flew to her mouth. "Sodi's suite has a imprint of his–Sodi has a daughter?"

The people-knower knew to wait for Kat to think this over. Off-center flags and tapestries of every color hung from rafters and high windowsills. Outside there was a burst of laughter. Warm, loved, welcomed, and attended to, Kat sat in this place feeling a chill.

The hairline crack between two of the plastic blocks she held yeilded to Kat's pinky nail. She popped off a red brick with six dots, tossing it into the disarray of loose pieces, and started on the next stuck piece. "Choti, I don't understand Sodi. He really stunned me when I first met him. I guess I never got over that first impression." She glanced up briefly, expecting a condemnation whose complete absence lightened Kat's thoughts enough for them to surface. "I don't understand Sodi and Eva, as a couple. Seems like Sodi would rather fit himself anywhere else," this made the elder chuckle, "and I think he could. For a little while, anyway, until he moved on without looking back." The streaks of light on Choti's cheeks had grown, casting her face in warm benevolence. "It's so strange, meeting a person you feel like you fit with, except he fits everywhere, so your place with him isn't as important as his place with you." Motes of dust caught sun and held, as though time had slowed. Kat opened her hands. She'd wedged apart the last of the blocks of color. "This is how I feel," she showed them to Choti, "I'm like all these toys. I'm just broken up. Every part of my life has fallen to pieces. I hardly know Sodi, or you, or anything here, and I want all of it. Except I don't. I don't want anything anymore. I don't even know what I should be wanting." She cast the bits into the scatter on the floor.

Choti's wizened fingers came to rest on Kat's shoulder. As rough and knotty as a living tree—and as rooted—Choti, sitting still, seemed to arch over Kat as the younger woman leaned toward the elder. She knew that, so long as Choti's feet could stand upon the ground, there would be a place for her among the Moma.

"Oh, Kat," the dimpled voice creaked, "it is a beginning, not an end. There is something wonderful about having your life taken apart like a stack of these toys. Once that process is done, however much it hurt, you have the chance to put yourself back together in any way. And it's possible to put it together more purposefully than it ever had been before. Kat, you are not broken. You are disassembled. The events that brought you here hold no power to change the substance of you. Only you can dictate whether this has been a self-effacement or a metamorphosis."

Kat wiped moisture off her face with the backs of her hands. "I don't even know how to choose between those two."

"Just live. It depends on what you choose to do with the years ahead."

"That's a lot of pressure, Choti."

"No, child. There can be no pressure: You are guaranteed success. There are no standards to judge you by except those you personally subscribe to. So, unless you prefer to see yourself as failing—which is a fine choice, and a popular one—you will succeed. You have all the advantages now. Right now, there is no person on earth who has a hold on you. There is nothing with authority to define you. Kat, you are entirely your own.

Make a life for yourself. Make a whole world for yourself. Do whatever it is you want."

Mentally prodding at Choti's advice like a cut in her mouth, Kat was still exploring the transformation of a life sentence into a release when Raz padded back into the room. He settled down, no greeting offered, amid the bedlam of bright chaos. He spread his hand over the loose bits of plastic, rolling them over each other to see them from different sides. Every once in a while, he'd pick out something unique: a spit of flame, a door panel, a squat chair. She thought how all these pieces were recycled bits from other things made with different intentions, now repurposed. Raz saved what he liked in a separate pile before him. He cast the rest back into the mishmash with neither grief nor dishonor.

The two women watched Raz layer the blocks, undo his work, and reconstruct his imaginings into the tangible world. But he was building his structure upside-down. At first, the less secured blocks fell, but in time he got the hang of constructing his building in defiance of gravity. He pressed little chairs and tables into the upper edges, hung plants from their pots, and added a hearth to the top of a wall. Tiny plastic people walked in opposition to natural gravity, one with a coffee mug. Kat longed to build a life in such a risk-free context. Choti wondered what world the introverted, intuitive grandson of the funny-face man was practicing the construction of–and why.

—

"Kat!" Sodi grinned, coming to a stop above her. He rocked back on his heels with his hips slightly forward, his smile full of pride. Reaching into his pocket, he whipped out a small device and extended it to her. "A gift for you. Most humbly," he was not.

"What is it?" her fingers encircled the small, black plastic.

"Your mini-tab."

"No," she protested, "mine was—wait, this has my name in it." Surprised, she poked through the menus, examining the data and contacts, and viewing her own identification model. All of it was perfect. "How did you do this?"

"My dad is pretty good at being sneaky," Raz supplied from his exploration of New Ceilingworld. Sodi did not contest.

"Is this legitimate?"

"Enough."

"It will work?"

"Yes."

"How do you know?"

Sodi shrugged. "Because I did it. Except what Vol did. Kat, we're the best, each at our part. It's a gift from both of us."

"Can I go... anywhere with this?"

"Anywhere. And there's more." Sodi watched Kat look up at him. "You have connects waiting for you, from the mayor," he raised an appraising eyebrow, "some kind of work for immediate reply."

"Wait, you watched my private connects?"

"Of course." Kat seemed unable to feign surprise at his answer, so Sodi continued, "But there is something even better." He held his breath a moment in violation of the energy that fizzed through him. "Kat, it's safe for you to go back. That man, the one who chased you?" The blood began to drain from her face. "He's dead. I found a notice this morning." Extending his hand down to her, he took her free hand and helped her stand. The warm, dark softness of his eyes explored hers with obvious relish and power. "Kat," he breathed, "you gave up everything, I worried that I robbed you, now I can give it back: All your accounts, your work files, your contacts. It should be just as your last one was."

Kat now stared at the object in her palm and spoke quietly, "Thank you," but it sounded more like a question than a statement.

Sodi shifted his weight. This was not the response he'd anticipated. Avoiding glancing at his son for help reading what she would choose, he pressed his own mind instead: Something must be wrong, some debt still unpaid. "Kat, you can stay here if you want. A lot of people would like that. But, you want to go back to the city, I'll take you tomorrow." She still did not answer. "No hearse this time," he failed to win even a smile. "I'll ferry you back and forth whenever you wish, really," he trailed off.

What Sodi couldn't read is that Kat had barely heard him. She was ignoring him, instead thinking of Choti's words: *Kat, you are entirely your own. Make a life for yourself. Make a whole world for yourself. Do whatever it is you want.*

"I will go tomorrow, and I will go alone. Sodi, thank you for this." Her gaze held so evenly against his disappointment that, for the first time, she realized how simple it was to counterbalance him.

Chapter 30

Although it was four o'clock in the afternoon, the woman safechatting through her mini-tab had only made one notable choice so far that day: Which tie to wear. She'd opted for the blue one with sine-wave-shaped sides—this week's Servi-Mod fashion style. Her call went through to an executive wearing a tie of the same shape, but in red. Blue Tie wrote, "Has your news feed been properly filtered today?"

"Of course."

"Should we hire another data man? He was good. Not easy to replace."

Red Tie's answer came quickly. "There's a concern with that."

"Concern with filling openings? Ludicrous."

"Concern that his workload is still being completed."

"That's impossible. They have his body."

"I realize," safechatted Red Tie. "New projection was filed this afternoon—on time. His work is still being done. Imprudent to replace his salary until we see corporate cost benefit to doing so."

Blue Tie considered this answer, which would disappear in another 20 seconds with no record. "Okay, will trash job vacancy. Will mark that slot as temporarily closed and take down accounts."

"No. Don't do that."

"Why?"

"Just take position off payroll" safechatted Red Tie. "Servi-Mod doesn't pay deceased employees. Change no accounts. Whoever is getting the work done, let them. Pro bono analysis."

"That account is cleared for homes and hospitals."

Red Tie copied, pasted, and re-sent her last message, verbatim.

"Okay, boss."

—

"This is ridicu-stank," Paun said to himself, coughing on the dust from the narrow road down which he drove too quickly. "Stupid report-writer, don't pee on your keyboard over stuff breaking!" He wiped a hand down his face, dislodging a crumb of sleep-dirt from his eye. After examining it, he wiped it on his T-shirt. "Make me drive to the butt end of nothing to replace junk on stuff that's crap anyway! It breaks every year. I hate my job."

As his rattling four-wheeler jounced over miles of potholes and dusty ruts, Paun rebelled against the injustice in his disarrayed life by thinking a little: *My skills, the way I really notice stuff,* he reasoned to nobody, *I should get paid more! I should be the high-ho who is writing the reports. I'm a thinker type. Where is my sim job? I got screwed, that's all. Someone had it in for me. Else I would not be on this crap piece of driving crap crapping out here to swap some junk. I mean: me! I work hard. This swap, for example, I'm gonna do this by myself. Nobody telling me what piece to replace. Nobody has to point at it. I just know. That's skill. I read my instructions and I do the work and* "nobody has to point!" he yelled aloud suddenly. *But do I get ahead? No. Cause I'm screwed. Nothing even to look at out here. I hate to sweat.*

Paun inflicted another hour of torture upon mind and language before arriving at the open-mouthed equipment shed serving Sector 092-04. His self-lauded perceptional skills failed to alert him to the presence of two unopened crates left beside the outer wall of the structure. Without braking, he swung the shoddy vehicle around in a wide arc that dug sloppy grooves across the orderly lines of the program-run equipment. Kicking the door of the vehicle open, he stepped out into the shadows to do his work. Promptly, he returned to retrieve the instructions on his task panel.

"The what one?" He ran his finger down the bland form on the dashboard monitor. "Oh, pestercides. The eye. I knew that." This time he only got three steps away before recalling that he needed a part to replace the broken eye with. Trudging back into the shed, he announced in a bellow, "Now for crap–" before an explosion of wings gusted over him. His knees knocked together. The glass eye dropped from his hands and cracked into three pieces. Paun cursed. "Dirty birds! Crap shed doesn't even have a door! What is this lame bit of dumb?" The few remaining birds in the rafters pumped their wings at him, which caused thin races of gooseflesh to shoot up his back. "Birds!" he half-whispered, noticed the broken eye, and called out, "*Crap!*"

Without bending to collect the shards of the broken machine eye, Paun again retraced his steps to the vehicle to retrieve another. This time he brought the whole box.

He was twelve feet further into the shed than the broken bits of glass when he realized that the herbicide tractor was not in its bay. Paun checked the time, wrinkled his forehead, and let his ears catch up with his thinking. Outside the shed hummed a large fan, already close and still approaching–until it ceased suddenly with a warning screech.

Proximity alert. Beep, beep, beep. Proximity alert.

Replaying the series of noises in his head, Paun turned toward the open side of the structure and saw the tall, arachnid shape of the herbicide tractor towering three feet behind his dinky four-wheeler.

Beep, beep, beep. Proximity alert. Beep, beep, beep.

The tractor hadn't yet returned from its day run when Paun had first arrived. He looked down. He'd parked his vehicle directly in the neat cascade of tire tracks indicating the motion path of the machinery. *If it'd been the front eye out instead of the back eye, that would have hit my vehicle, and I'd have been stuck here with no car*, he began to think, *and here is nowhere. I deserve hazard pay, but I got shafted!* "Well, what do I do now?" he yelled at the limby metal hulk.

It answered. "Whuh, who the blast, what have? I mean! Uh."

Uncomprehending, Paun stared at the large, spidery machine.

"Wait a second!" ordered the herbicide spreader in the woozy voice of Kip Petson. "Don't move!" Paun obeyed. Four hundred miles away, Kip tried to check his policy manual for what to do if the equipment reported a proximity alert, but he was undergoing difficulties. The work in-set was beeping an alert that scrambled his brain. His quest team of three in his VR environment was rapidly running out of life-energy under the barrage of strikes from a pair of dilapholors, and one other player kept nudging him to cast a healing spell. Yet he could not find the file for the farm equipment manual because the in-set was too small in the midst of his VR environment to make out the search results.

"Wait!" the herbicide machine yelled at Paun again. "I'm serious!" His goggles slipped off kilter a fraction.

One of the spiky sim-monstrosities smashed ten feet from Kip's avatar, and the alpha paladin ahead of him took the opportunity to land a heroic blow that severed the creature's head and sent it rocking back, contrary to the directional force of the blow, in a dramatic arc.

"Wooohooo!" cheered the tractor in front of Paun. "No, I mean, hold still there!" Kip Petson pulled the work in-set over his head like a fishbowl. His VR environment was now a series of views of the farm equipment. Now with more space, he began a new search for the manual, then turned back to the glowing globe representing his game environment to cast a triple-strength whole-group heal as his quest-mates set into the second monster.

But he had squished.

"Fraplit!" raged the tractor. Paun leapt to the side. "Dang peanut! No, don't move! Halt in the... road area!" Kip Petson had retrieved the desired manual, but because of his rage from his untimely return to the sim-graveyard in his game fishbowl, he had no patience to read it. *Besides*, he thought, *if this were important, they would have trained me better. It's not my fault.* "Let's see your ID! What are you doing here?"

Paun punched up the identification screen on his mini-tab and held it out at arm's length toward the angry metal spider tractor, as if this helped. "I'm legit. The thing is broke. Came to fix the eye. So you can see out the back."

"This has an eye on the back, too?" asked Kip.

"Well, yeah. How else you gonna look behind you?"

"I thought it only went forward." There was an awkward silence. "How do I get it to look behind itself?"

Crap, I should have this idiot's job. He needs someone to point. See, I don't need that, Paun prided to himself. *See, I could be a sim-ployee. I just got screwed. Nobody screwing him.* "Well, see this box of glass eyes, mister Sim Job? You just take them one at a time and you throw them against the ground. Mostly they just break. But every now and then, a chicken pops out of one. And that's how we fix machines."

"Dumb farm butthead."

"*What?*" Paun thrust down the box. No chickens popped out.

There was a silence from the tractor before Kip said through it, "Sorry, man. Do you know how to turn on the words thing, like for giving me manners?"

"I just need to swap in the eye."

"Well why's it beeping?"

"You're about to run over my car, you dumb squat!"

Kip stared at Paun. Paun stared at the tractor. "Well what are we going to do?" asked Kip.

"If I move my car, can you hold that machine thing still? I am not getting my butt runned over today."

"It sort-of just drives."

"Yeah, make it *not* drive. You know the word *stop*? 'Cause I just mean a great big *stop*. They give you a giant red button?"

"Yeah, I got something... I got it." The voice in the tractor sounded anything but certain.

Walking on tiptoes, arms slightly spread as though he were afraid to lose his balance, Paun inched back to the four-wheeler. Then in a flurry of motion, he flung his body into it, stomped on the go-pedal and streaked out from in front of the tractor. He was sixty feet away by the time the great tangle of arms lollygagged over the spot where the four-wheeler had been. The beeping stopped. The herbicide spreader rolled neatly into its assigned bay and powered itself down.

"Hey I think it's oka–" cut off the voice of Kip Petson as his VR environment went black. His workday had ended. The experience disappointed him. This was the most interesting day he'd had in this job, and yet suddenly it was over before he figured it out or really did *anything*. That was the problem: World One never made it clear what you were supposed to do.

The last thing glowing in his environment was the fishbowl for his game. Pulling it over his head, Kip Petson was back in it, surrounded by the digital environment. He found his graveyard-bound avatar surrounded by a semi-circle of fighters, themselves newly re-unearthed and making obscene gestures at him. "I was working!" he justified himself, but the jeering continued. "Piss off, then, go find another mage. I have stuff to do." Kip Petson switched off and sat back, thinking about the manual he'd had to search for all on his own. Setting his lower lip, he decided that if anything interesting ever happened in his World One job again, he would be ready to solve the mystery.

Due to distance, Paun hadn't heard Kip's departing words, but once he was brave enough to look into the equipment shed, he saw the hulk of the spider-machine motionless in its proper place. Skittish, he approached until it became clear that the tractor would not re-ignite and roar toward him. Paun then relaxed into a swagger, reached the foot of the metal hulk, and realized he was not carrying a new eye for it. He spun, his heart fluttering, and he spotted the box he'd dropped on the floor. It sat three inches from the outer edge of the tire tracks, still intact.

After repeatedly re-checking his instructions, Paun successfully replaced all of the broken eyes on the Sector 092-04 equipment. Nobody had to point.

—

The old healer asked for Raz—and Raz alone. When the child entered his private room, the funny-face man noticed that his complexion already had a tinge of sunlight in it, something warmer and sturdier than he'd seen in his grandson before.

"Look good, ayuh," said the old man, lying prone under a bed sheet. Raz said nothing, worrying over the changes he himself saw. Blotched with ovals of moisture, the smooth sheet covering the man's body and the rumpled skin covering the old man's cheekbones both looked diseased. "Come on here."

The child approached. Shining with bliss, Funny-face's eyes still held vitality. "I worried about you," said Raz, placing a hand over the wide, flat chest and patting. His other hand was behind his back. Funny-face smiled, prompting the boy to reach across his neck to give him a hug. But the child halted his embrace upon the first touch to the scalloped neck. "You're so hot, you need to sweat!" he exclaimed.

"Ayuh. Get hotter, too."

"How do you know?"

"No-read word."

Wild-eyed, the child cried out, "Don't read them! They make fevers! But they're gone; where do you see the no-read words?"

Dry lips wicked up into a brief smile. He spoke like tinder. "*Ulla-nakani*," he muttered, "boy: They go in me."

"Where in you? I want to see them. I want to know how soon you feel better!"

"So brave, ayuh," he rasped, trying to draw a trace more moisture into his matchstick mouth. "Soon. This fever, last one." The ancient face smiled, which somehow made his eyes droop down.

Anxiety whirred in the boy's skinny chest. He remembered this feeling: This dread was the clearest memory he had from his night of healing. "But why did you put the fevers in you?"

"It became. Fever is. Must go a someplace. *Ulla-nakani*... I know, when I take. Think now. Remember *ufi*, no-eyes! Happy *ufi*. I take his eye, too. Too sick. Now *ufi* play, happy. Raz, *ufi* is good."

"Yes, I like your dog. He's just playful."

"Your *ufi* now. Ayuh. He chase... eat, say *oofi-oofi-oofi*, all same. Whole dog, *ufi*. No eyes, whole life, whole *ufi*." He turned his crackled face toward Raz. "*Sapok*, you understand, *anh*?"

"Yes, Funny-face. You want me to take care of your dog. Because you're," his mouth curled down against the force of the impending tears, "too sick right now."

"No take-care. *Have.*"

"But I'm going to give him back when you're better," the child protested, starting to cry. He withdrew his other hand from behind his back. It held Zati's division stick. Raz laid this on top of the mottled sheet.

Funny-face set his lips, allowing his gaze to take in every part of the hopeful, willful child. "H-okay, a deal." The watery stare of the child echoed what he'd already read: The boy knew he was dying. "*Sapok*, remember gift."

"Ufi? I'll take good care of him. I'll play with him."

"No, gift you give me. Daughter, seeing, no-read."

"But it's making you sick! I want to take it off you!"

"No. I am old. I go in past. Safest place. Now I see *satek*, daughter. Best gift. No-read words went in wrong place, but gift? Right place, ayuh, a good one!" The room began to rumple and stretch to the old eyes, and the funny-face man knew he would never again see the immediate world clearly. Swimming too closely and leagues away from him, Raz appeared to tremble in place, small-huge and grieving. "Come. Hear: *Ufi* eye gone, always. Your eye, come back maybe. Later, older. Right time." The grandson of the funny-face man shook his head against this possibility. "Another gift... for you."

"What is it?"

His scabbed hand shifted out from below the sheet as though the motion pained him. Raz settled his own soft palm into it, and his mind opened. He saw people everywhere, of every type, people all over country. They all heard the same voice. The voice shared the single best thing, sounding it with the simplicity of the present. Raz understood. It was a good gift. When his eyes opened, the funny-face man's expression warped into a feeble smile that went all the way down, endlessly down.

"Don't let *ufi* lick you up a nose. Ayuh?"

The boy puffed with laughter, and his tears ran out.

—

An hour later, Eva received an urgent alert on her mini-tab. Choti's face appeared, speaking halfway to incoherence, awkward in the video, demanding that Eva come at once to the old man's room. It was only a brief walk away. Eva sprinted. Arriving, she strained to hear the exchange occurring in front of her. The funny-face man spoke to Choti in his language. The flattened sounds spooled forward in even, modest lines. Choti's face was composed only through excessive self-control. "Help me move him," she addressed Eva in the same restrained monotone that characterized the healer's language. "Next door is a bathroom. Fill the tub with cold, then help me move him. Send for orderlies. No one else. Go."

By the time Eva returned, Choti had unlocked the wheels on the sick-bed and was straining against its inertia. Slipping into the crack between the bed and the wall, Eva levered it into the center of the room, where the two women could help each other. It became easy to push; the patient seemed as light as memory.

Eva could feel him more than see him. The heat rose from his parched face, which sagged upside-down under her chin. She was wheeling him from one tiny room into another, boxing him in from one restraint to another to get him through life. "Lift," ordered Choti. Eva repositioned her feet wider than her shoulders and wrapped her elbows beneath the blazing shoulders, shuddering. He was so hot that she feared the funny-face man might slip away right in her grasp, but in a tumult of footsteps, the white-clad orderlies arrived to take over her burden. They looked like they might swallow their own throats at the sight of who they'd been called to assist and for what.

Eva yielded her position. They spaced themselves around the

prone body to lift. "Eva," said the funny-face man. He then spoke again in the demure words that sounded like fire swallowing a dry leaf. Choti translated, "Raz has a roaming, a free way. He could not sustain being trapped. He freed the child." The old man spoke a small amount further, and Choti continued: "You freed the child, too. You let him out of your world."

As the orderlies lowered him into the cold water, the funny-face man caught Eva's eye and uttered four more words, each made distinct by the space he left between them for emphasis. The first sounded like the breaking of a twig. The second swished like wind before flame. The four staccato beats of the last two words slammed like doors, closing down the conversation with the finality of a verdict. Understanding this simple statement without Choti's help, the four orderlies glanced at Eva briefly, and for the first time since her arrival, she saw respect in their eyes—and a promise that whatever judgment the old healer had just passed, it would stand, and it would never be challenged.

"You have been a good mother," Choti translated. She, too, met Eva's eyes, and in that glance the warmth of the people-knower returned, though awash in deep pain. As Choti turned back to her work, Eva understood that it was time to depart.

—

Descending into his thermal moat, the elder could be there in the world of water and breathing, but he knew now what must happen—must because it did, because it would. The slender, feminine wrists were his own again. He greeted her, honoring his choice, honoring her choice, finding her again.

His daughter Cassi floated with him, both of them in the cold wash. He knew through this stolen continuity how it was to be—that past that was now. She had drowned in the lake to buy time, exchanging future for present. She had relinquished herself to save her son. And as the water pulled her in like an embrace, the thoughts he found in her were of Sodi.

As she died, she re-lived the first time she re-considered him, an uncouth teenager sailing arduous blasphemies on paper airplanes. Rocking back and bellowing laughter, he roared as though the sky were the only thing big enough to contain his amusement. There in the water, she had revisited the discovery of him, the letting go and letting live as his affections danced like light on the surface of a lake, never fully landing. Through those shared thoughts, the funny-face man felt her contentment. He felt her certainty that she would always see him again, always at least once more, until she could no longer see. Sodi was art to her. His raunchy zest for life became her highest joy—and she bore it physically, life into the world. Her love had created Raz, whom now they both had saved.

The child was there in the memories. Raz sat on her lap—the elder's own lap now—the space between them alive with energy. His small, woman's hand was on the child's chest, transmitting a knowing. He-she sent intuitive power into the child out of hope—hope from a mind steeped with the lawless, dark-haired man. *Please know*, said the thoughts, *he is wild but wonderful. Just like art bucks every boundary in its wild thrust toward expression, Sodi must perform acts of staggering disloyalty and gleeful disregard. His life-force careens through some choices and luxuriates on others. He will give no excuse. Sodi will be uncouth. Sodi will hurt. But this is the laughing man's way of loving life.*

There were other thoughts, too, but ones not sent in to the child: *I must give him a gift so he can cherish his dad more than he will be hurt by him. This will be my gift to Sodi, my gift to our son. The two will understand one another. The two will have an accord. They will be close to one another, because I can not, could not, and my love will move on through our child.*

Cassi feared the ending of her vision more than the ending of her life. For all these reasons, she placed that intuitive sight in her son. The funny-face man felt her touch hold on the boy, pushing too quickly through a broken-glass resistance. The people were already coming, yelling. She rushed. She didn't have enough time. Cassi imparted her sight to her child, believing it would save Raz from pain, would close a rift, would bind him to his father. She did not know it would sicken him. She did not see she was trapping him into too fixed a future, that she was locking him into a not-his world.

The man in the bathtub spluttered. High above him, cast up into the rafters, fever-distance far, the voices of people began to speak in growing volume, but also in growing distance. The water was as light as air, and he floated down, drawing it in to his lungs. He floated with his daughter, slender wrists in his grip, of his grip, the same as his grip. There was no resistance. They both knew this must happen. In his last moment, as something of him faded beyond the intense and distant voices, the funny-face man radiated gratitude for his grandson, for his daughter, for this one selfish act in a long life of giving, for life itself.

—

"I can't see my eyes anymore," announced Raz to nobody in particular. Nobody answered. Mirror in hand, he picked his way through the rough wood trusses in ceiling world of the wobble-wall building. There was beauty in ceiling world. There was space. Space enough to be lost in, beauty enough to explore forever.

Raz paused. Ceiling world would always be there. Silently, he repositioned the mirror. The ancient-looking trusses left his focus and moved behind and above his own reflection. He examined his own face. Raz stopped wandering and held the mirror at this new angle.

Chapter 31

"He's not dead," said the coroner.

Silence on the other end of the call underscored how much effort Officer Shockey was using to try to make sense of her simple sentence. "Ma'am... that was a body. No heartbeat. A corpse."

"He's not dead. At least I don't think so." She sighed with worry. "It's not my place, I know, officer, but could you enlighten me how exactly you came across this... body you brought me?"

"No, ma'am. I can't discuss any details that weren't already in the report you got. Wasn't that enough?"

"Normally it would be, yes. And I do understand. Officer, would you come and allow me to repeat the tests in front of you? And your sergeant, if he pleases? That might be best."

—

The sergeant refused. "Shockey, you have moved beyond the world of dunce! You offended a long-standing coroner, got the mayor breathing over everyone's eyeballs, and now we're catching every half-wit's flack from five time zones! That case is closed—again. If it was this guy, he's dead. If it wasn't this guy, it was suicide. You get everybody riled up and that's ten times the work here, and we're not getting any more officers, let me tell you." Holding his breath, Officer Shockey tried to leave. "Oh no you don't. I got a..." the sergeant scrolled through his incomplete tasks again, searching for one sufficiently special.

"Sergeant, I am still on special assignment."

His bulbous eyes glowered. "He's dead," the man snarled. "What more you gotta do? How much time do you need to let his rot stink fill up your nostrils?"

"There's the missing lady. Menali." The sergeant rolled his eyes and uttered a prayer to a deity ostensibly burdened by Tourette's. Shockey pressed on. "I hear you, sergeant, but the mayor is pushing to see this through."

"Then I should have fired you before you got her involved. And failing that, I should have insisted I put someone qualified on the case. Get out of my office."

—

Shockey chose to interpret the encounter with his sergeant as a green light to visit the coroner. Apparently she had been watching for his arrival, as she met him at the door unannounced and led him to the same examination room as before.

"Here's your guy. Look familiar?" The coroner unzipped the bag that covered the sharp features of the body. Shockey nodded. "I have changed nothing. Do you notice anything, officer?"

"I'm noticing everything," he sidestepped, "but I'm here for your observations, ma'am."

She restrained a smug smile. "Very well. The clothes struck me as odd, firstly."

Although the sleek suit on the body had been cut through to permit the autopsy, Shockey easily pieced together the cut of it. Double-padded shoulders of the jacket flanked large, zipper-like corrugations at the edge of the collar as it ran down the front of the jacket. Hatchmarks in the material's weave echoed this blocky pattern. Closing the front of the jacket were buttons shaped like clusters of squares. "And here's the tie; I had to remove it." The yellow creation she held up cascaded down and split into three tongues, the left and right ones sweeping off to the sides in neat arcs.

"Yeah, I saw that. I wore a suit like that once. I was real proud of it then; it was Santa-done just for me. But that was at my grandpa's funeral a couple years back. I didn't think this was in style anymore. But there's no accounting for taste, right?" He knew he'd said the wrong thing when the coroner waited to see if he'd catch up.

"Officer, I believe you can account for taste when the individual in question ranks at Servi-Mod."

Shockey's eyes widened. "This week's styles from Servi-Mod. Absolutely. Which are," he called the Servi-Mod app on his mini-tab, where dreamers could custom-order just enough Servi-Mod merchandise to make-believe they lived in a prestigious building. The newest styles of custom tailored suits, guaranteed to arrive within 24 hours to any location within five miles of a Servi-Mod development, included five sets of pan-gender suits, all with single-tongue ties that wagged back and forth on the way down.

"His isn't modern," he observed. "He would have been talked to for wearing what he is; they're a downright cult."

After waiting a respectful amount of time, the coroner invited, "Shall I repeat the tests for you?"

Logging out of the app, he turned to her. "No, Miss Manon. I'm sorry about your integrity getting questioned last time. We don't see this much, and the training isn't... well, the point is I trust that you did everything proper. All the tests. You have a reputation, a really good one. I'm sorry."

"Actually," she answered, "I'm not asking it to prove my integrity to you. I am already certain of my integrity. I'm asking it because some of the results were most unsettling."

—

"What was normal was the black coronary tissue," the coroner began once they returned to the autopsy room. Her expert hands busied around the corpse with a series of probes and blades that she'd prepared in advance. "Heart attack, the natural thing expected from a man in his position. Not surprising. According to my procedures, I was welcome to stop and collect my fee after ascertaining that much. But I happen to be one for thoroughness. I pressed a bit further," she explained, omitting her reasons, "and ran some extra scans. Let's take a look at some vital organs." She re-opened the massive slice through the trunk of the body; raising his eyebrows, Shockey turned partially away. He heard her pause and looked over. "With apologies, I do want you to actually watch me do this, because if I'm failing in some way, if there is some problem in my procedures that is leading to the abnormal results, I want you to witness it."

"I'll try," he croaked.

"Sink's to your left if you have sudden need."

"Thanks."

Methodical, the coroner retraced her steps through the autopsy, pausing at the liver. "Now, if I just scan this, it's fine," she passed a handheld device near the organ and the room's monitor came alight with figures for the health of the organ. "Mister Pureforc appears to be quite healthy. Healthy as a twenty-year-old. Obviously not a drinker."

"Yes, I wasn't questioning–"

"But a biopsy... well, let me do this in front of you."

The steady-fingered woman opened a new kit and pressed it into the slimy-looking organ. The long, tubular device punched out a small chunk, leaving a round hole in the dark surface. "Stay with me now. Watch the screen." Shockey did so, grateful for the diversion. A menu emerged on the screen, and she selected genetic makeup. The monitor went dark. On the plastic shield fronting it, warped reflections of the room's long, low lights meandered across the warped surface.

Error. Said the monitor eventually. The coroner air-swiped for more information.

Genetic code not matched.

Shockey stared at the screen. "Your equipment's broken?"

"I thought that, too. So I checked it on another cadaver, and it turned out okay. The machinery can match DNA—just not on this particular body."

"Why would that ever happen?"

Her deep, bearing eyes held him. "It's not that we can't match the codes together. That problem I've seen before, certainly. It would be true in any case where there has been a transplant or stem regrowth. But, as you see here," she brought up a new screen where, side-by-side, the expected code shorthands sat paired to the DNA from the sample. The sample's side was blank. "It has no code to match."

"I don't understand."

"This organ is not human."

He blinked. "That doesn't even make sense."

"This organ was not grown by a human. It does not have viable human DNA."

"It must be an anomaly."

"Officer: The kidneys are the same way. Both. The intestinal tract hardly produces any culture at all, as though it's never been used." Shockey shook his head. "I am afraid, sir, that this is not a corpse."

"*What?*"

"I am afraid that what we are looking at is a dummy."

"I've seen this man! I've seen him alive! I've seen you touch him—he's not a hologram over livestock!"

"I'm way out on a limb, and I admit it's a limb that shakes pretty badly. But, officer, did you have any evidence that this body could have been brought to the place it was found?"

He focused. He pictured himself back in the lush apartment: *Tall ceilings in the great room echoed the voices of his response team. All around him were the sober colors of real wood varnished in fashionable matte to minimize the interference caused by reflective surfaces. He stared at the collapsed body, twisted at odd angles with its mouth open in a room of dark and drab—except for one spot of gleam. He had gone to that spot as the others lifted the shape onto a gurney. The gurney began to roll and he was twisting, pulling at the brass knob, swinging open the door as the body rolled out the apartment. He had seen it, but it was overwhelming in size, stuffing the room, leaving no space for him to think of it. They were rolling the body away, and he had to follow, and he did not understand what the giant thing had meant.*

"No," said Shockey, appalled at his oversight, "not brought. Made. I think there was a Santa machine in the apartment. A huge, weird one." His eyes found the lady who always seemed composed. She now had fear in her eyes. "But the mini-tab was real. I was thorough. The model, the age, the signs of wear to the memory's re-writing, we can measure the age and the use of it. It matched. It was not faked." A dread loomed in his mind that seemed like it could come from any corner of the room, from any room in the building, from any building in the city. "Miss Manon, if this isn't Pureforc, then he's gone somewhere. But he left his mini-tab. How do we find a dead man without an identity? And more," Shockey's gaze unfocused, "where *would* a data man go without data?"

—

Vol roused himself too early, but then again, he'd also gone to sleep far earlier than he'd hoped to. As he trudged uphill toward the ridgeline edge of the village, his mind swam with memories of the lithe, young woman and her braids, the way they swirled about her like a playful windstorm, the way they seemed to smack and caress at once. As he walked down the opposite slope of forest toward the clearing for the fields, he imagined his hands on her hair, untwisting the tidy patterns to see what she'd look like uncouth, wild.

What lay ahead was only a pattern to him. Having memorized the pattern, he used no thought to complete the task of retrieving the last two cases of medical supplies he'd left at the equipment shed. He also required no gear except for the empty backpack strapped over his bulky shoulders. This simplicity freed his attention to contemplate lovelier matters.

Collapsing between the fourth and fifth rows of corn stalks, Vol imagined his recent time there with Kat. Savoring the image of lying there with her, hidden from all the rest of the world, his mind encircled the problem that she needed a good reason to not leave the Moma people.

In seven minutes, the herbicide spreader would initiate its motor and begin its route for the day. He spent this interval considering all he could do to convince the fresh-faced woman to linger among them. By the time he heard the machine engine and the soft crumble of its wheels, he realized that every detail of his every idea would have worked quite well to keep *him* interested. But to retain *her*... perhaps not. Vol sighed and focused harder, wondering how to entice Kat.

The spidery machine passed by his hiding spot, overrunning part of the unseen 4-wheeler tracks and confused footprints left from the repair visit the day prior. As it passed, Vol mechanically stood from his spot and trudged toward the side of the building—until the rumbling-away of the wheels ceased.

In the open now, he froze halfway to the shadows of the building. The sounds of wheels behind him changed. He could hear a trace of skidding; wheels threw small rocks onto paths that had been unaltered for years. The herbicide tractor was laying down a new course. Vol turned slowly to face the metal tangle of knuckles. It was charging him, knocking over young stalks of corn in its sudden pursuit.

"Don't you dare!" screamed the tractor in a voice so tinny that it reminded Vol of a poodle-sized cleaning robot. Vol stifled the urge to laugh at the non-sequitur, to laugh his own unsafe assumptions, which had led him to this point. One piece of manic farm equipment with a puny, nasal twang was about to apprehend the best and most mischievous machinery man of his village. Vol was caught.

This part, too, was only a pattern. It required no thought from Vol. Long ago, he'd established the ground rules for himself—lest he be surprised by a cusp like this one and betray his values by letting emotions override function. Either he stood and allowed himself to be arrested or he ran and prompted a vicinity search that would expose everyone he loved. His choice was as automatic as a life-reg. He had only to follow through with the next few instructions.

He occupied his mind thinking of Kat.

Chapter 32

Again the Moma people huddled toward the center of the village. They arrived under drizzling skies in twos or fives, as though somehow the multiplicity of their lack would fulfill them all.

To Sodi, two people were inconceivably absent. Even now, even at his funeral, no ceremony could feel complete without the funny-face man. Sodi strained to find a younger face, one that anchored him to his sense of belonging here. But Vol, too, had not yet appeared. Afraid to admit his anxiety, Sodi silenced his sense that this tardiness was unthinkable, even for one as self-disposed as his closest friend.

Choti led the ceremony with an effort that bent her to the last fiber. The amount of giving required in the past several days threatened to curdle her generosity into resentment, yet she did not allow her old body to cease. It was her persistence that began the painful, thin string of rejuvenation among the people. "Still here! In each one of us, for each, of each, still here!" she called in a ragged voice. "Change comes. We let him go, but we lose nothing of ourselves. He will always be with us in our past."

"Safest place!" interrupted a voice in the crowd, choking halfway between a wail and a cheer. Then, from all around, other voices joined in the cry of *Safest place! The very safest place!* with the occasional *Ayuh!* prompting chuckles coughing with grief.

Amid the forest of voices, Kat absorbed these calls with growing sadness. Knowing only the barest sliver of the great man's life, she sensed the enormity of what she'd missed. She had met him, but she did not have much of him to keep safely in her own past.

In spite of an eggshell of empty space around her, Eva could hardly move her body or her thoughts. The healer's final words to her had been his final words in life: *You have been a good mother.* Now his body lay prone inside the hut ahead. Many ribbons unfurled from the series of holes near its lumpy roofline. Their colors deepened as they sopped in drops of rain. Dancers reached for these ribbons, grasped them, shared them—but not Eva. She hung back. Wild and weaving, waving and weeping, the dancers commenced without her.

He acknowledged me as mother—but Raz was born to his *daughter. I am an interloper. I am a nanny.* Striken with the grief of her own lost daughter, Eva had felt twice humiliated by Sodi's brazen infidelity. Cassi had left over Eva's presence. Her living infant remained and needed rearing. So Eva devoted herself to her man's other child with the broken-glass heart she had: She loved Sodi's son with constant sharpness.

Weaving ribbons down the outer wall of the small, circular building, the dancers changed directions and changed hands. The community tapestry took on different patterns. Still Eva did not dance with them. *He used his last words to call me the mother of his grandson. But I'm not his daughter. I'm not even Moma.* And with this thought, Eva's grief deepened. She could not accept the old healer's acknowledgment for her care of Raz because it had resulted in his death. So she had to lose both of them, and all these others as well.

A dancer in a green dress trailed a long ribbon and spun around. Silently, Eva said goodbye to her forever. A boy in orange skipped and sped ahead, warping the patterns. Eva took in his soft features and grieved that she'd never see him grow up. A shuffling woman supported on one side by a white-clad helper created a happy, pink anomaly in the weaving. Eva loved her shaking smile, her stuttering steps—and would never see her again. Eva had loved these generations of Moma, but her pain was too deep to stay. The ribbon-bearers danced the steps of their re-binding. Eva stayed out. She didn't belong here. To her, this funeral was to mourn all of them, living and dead.

If someone had gone to Eva at that moment to ask her for help—to grief-counsel children, to set up tables, to lend an arm to an elder—Eva might have stayed with the Moma. But without a job, she was empty of purpose. Without purpose to prove her value, she felt undesirable and outcast. Powerful as they were, even the dying words of the great Moma healer did not enable Eva to accept community.

—

"Miss Kat," a small voice sounded from close by. "Miss Kat? Miss Kat: I have something for you." Kat looked down at the placid face of Raz. "I have a gift. Do you want the gift?" She inclined her head. "The gift I have is an imagining: I want you to imagine. Think if everybody's ear was near your mouth all at the same time, but not bumping you. They will listen, but only a little while. What would you do?"

"I don't know," Kat answered. "Nothing, I guess."

Raz paused for a few moments to remember the funny-face man's final gift to him, then stepped closer. He took one of Kat's hands in both of his. "I would laugh. I would laugh and laugh, so they can hear the sound of laughing. It is the best sound. It makes everybody together. That is my imagining."

Kat said nothing.

"I want it to make you happier, Miss Kat."

Kat cried. She cried for the loss of Sodi, for the shallow-rooted life she knew she must return to, for the loss of the connection she wished she could feel among these warm people, for the image of Mez alone and dying a little every day. Kat cried for the auto-generated responses that passed for politeness, for how they turned ugly slurs into manners devoid of meaning or intent. Kat cried for the defunct sim worlds that perpetuated dead lives in the indifferent minds of machinery. Kat cried for the watering down of experience into multiple illusory lives that ended in nothing, that held only road signs of simulated progress. Although Kat had tried to open herself to so many communities, none of them had met all of her needs.

—

They'd kept Vol up all night, isolated in a tiny room. He stared at his empty hands, thinking of all they had touched, imagining scraps of his former life still in contact with his skin. Although the authorities justified the confinement as a softening-up of the mute man, in truth they experienced a legitimate delay. The odd, insane mini-tab they'd confiscated from his wrist spit zeroes at them whatever they queried it. Deconstructing the device yielded a self-perpetuating blankness: The memory had been continuously overwriting its zeroes with more zeroes for an unknowable amount of time. Nothing was left. However, the man could not erase himself—and his body markings told a tale without him speaking a word.

"Ready to talk?" Someone had come in. The interrogator changed every time, driving home how much interest he had generated. "So, let's see: You were found on foot. Nobody's claiming you and you're not talking. Obviously there's something more valuable than yourself that you're hiding."

Vol steadied himself for the necessary act, although he wished he could pass off the chore to Sodi, who was the better expressionist. "We start the search tomorrow," finished the interrogator. Remaining silent, Vol sat back in his chair and stared at the grey eyes without blinking. Faintly, faintly, he tugged the muscles in his cheeks to achieve the five percent upward slip of his lips that denoted hidden amusement.

The opposing face stared back, falsely impassive. "Every acre of Sector 094-02 will be examined–in depth and in person," the interviewer goaded, "by whatever trigger-happy armed fools we can get on the job. The more they shoot, the better. Your types don't leave records, so you don't even need cleanup."

Vol stared back.

"Of course," the interviewer pressed on, gauging, "all adjacent sectors will be combed, too. One after another. In fact, I think maybe we'll start on a different patch. I like the way 094-03 sounds. We'll start there." But the mute man's face would not change. "Or, I dunno, 094-19." There was no reaction.

After a long wait, the interviewer slammed his feet on the floor and stood, carrying his husky form toward the door, "As you wish, then. It's their lives for your noncooperation."

"Hey, wait!" called Vol. He gave his most important line one final rehearsal in his mind.

The large body halted, edging backward just enough to look Vol in the face. "Got an objection to 094-19, I take it?"

"Have your trigger-heads stick their muzzles in any sector they want. I just want to know which one of you is bringing my breakfast."

"You think grubs like you get to eat on a schedule? Boy, you haven't been listening. You have no records. You don't exist. We don't need to feed you. We don't need to do anything, because there is no person here."

"A man's got to eat."

"What man is that?"

Vol released the faint tug in his cheeks, allowing his face to slacken into a shape that at last represented his true dismay all this time. Bearing the interrogator's mocking laugh, as it was part of the routine, he waited for the slovenly voice to deliver the next line. And it came. "I tell you what:" the interviewer stalked around and crouched back across the table from Vol, "You tell us how an un-person like you, on foot and alone, ends up in 094-02 with no visible form of transportation. Then I'll send someone to get you food."

"Idiots," Vol rolled his eyes.

The flat of the interviewer's hand slammed against the table, exploding a loud crack in the small space. He rose again to leave.

"There was plenty of transportation," Vol called out just after the man left his range of view. Holding his breath, he counted three seconds in which the room's door did not slam shut. *Home stretch now, it's going to work*, he thought. "There's a whole garage of vehicles there. Little quad-four-wheeler-jeep thing. Don't even need a key. Anyone can get anywhere they want, you leave that equipment sitting around charged up and ready to go. Didn't you morons even look at the footprints?" In the space that should have contained an answer, Vol prayed that the rain had been sufficient to wash away what footprints he must have left in the dust. "Hey, I want an omelet and biscuits with gravy and a ripe mango—and make sure the mango's real soft. The hard ones aren't worth chewing."

After another moment, the door clicked closed.

—

Stripped of identification, Pureforc walked untethered for the first time in World One. For the first time, he could move without leaving a trail of data behind him. *This is death*, he thought. *I am a ghost. Nothing of me is real.*

The car he drove suffered from dementia. A cheap model from two decades ago, it housed none of the recording devices that would have alerted the data grid of its course. Moment by moment, the accelerator responded to his commands, burning its battery charge in the present, retaining nothing for the past to know. Pureforc sped down an empty highway like a meteorite that would burn itself out of existence at any moment.

He thought: *If nothing records my actions, nothing I do remains permanent.* The writing of history went on hiatus. He had achieved timelessness.

He was in a car of somebody. The car had a serial number. The car must be real. Yet where the data were not available, perhaps the change of ownership had not occurred. Perhaps the car was still hers—that frail, blue-clad lady whose connection permitted him to log in and turn in the day's data report. The data report was real. The lady was real. Data would catch up on her, too, but in the *now* she was a shade and a carcass. In the *now*, Pureforc had committed no known crime. There was no *him* with which to commit a crime.

It exhilarated him to be dead.

Pureforc still believed his reincarnation in the data streams of World One would be a happy reunion. There were always perks for jobs well done, and he would return with pieces set in place like a well-structured statistical report. He'd frame Sodi, living or dead. The PR department would splash the story of an advancement in their patented neo-Santa technology, jazzing up the faked death as a media stunt.

Unbounded by facts, Pureforc's mind began to swerve. *Yes,* he thought, *they'll announce that the new generation of Santas can manufacture human organs good enough to fool professionals. The news spinners will insinuate meanings for medical science. There will be technology deals and research investments. The future Servi-Mod statistics will swell and glut. I'll helm the data stream. Deaths mean little when we learn to order up more life.* To his mind, Pureforc's digital death had catalyzed his great legacy to the smooth accretion he revered. He'd return a god, and he'd forever make his numbers—any numbers—after this.

—

Sitting in a window seat of a small jet, Kat wanted to get away from one life before restarting the other. A smiling avatar in a lipstick-pink uniform gestured and joked his way through the emergency instructions on one of the mini-monitors mounted in the seat-back ahead. Kat stared out of the window at the windless landscape as his words babbled past like a stream. The Moma lady who had driven her to the airport would still be waiting somewhere inconspicuous in the parking lot. She would still be watching for Kat's mini-tab ID to come out of the facility—just in case she changed her mind and wanted to return.

On Kat's left wrist clung her mini-tab, a passport back to her city life. On Kat's right wrist scribed a curved, healing scar intentionally left rough—a suggestion of membership without obvious commitment, a passport back to her Moma life. Neither life seemed real.

Kat sat still, pretending she was not making a choice. She waited for the moment at which her decision could not reverse, waiting for choice itself to pass like a storm, like a thing she never could have controlled. Inevitability had always been easier than responsibility. The jet engines fired toward the rear of the plane, as if singeing history. Their power moved in only one direction, and Kat felt her body pressed into the seat by the acceleration, pinning her to this choice. It was done.

For a long time, she craned out of the small, transparent oval, searching the horizon for a small cluster of potato-shaped hills hiding bits of bright gaiety from the Moma. But the village was two hours distant, carefully tucked away, and not near her flight path. Kat saw only the shadow of the plane skimming the ground.

She'd been in the air for an hour before calling in to her prior life to assess the damage caused by her absence. In the first five recordings, her supervisor or co-worker inquired with increasing concern about her delinquent and erratic work. These messages culminated in the phrase, "termination hearing due to your failure to perform and your submission of non-protocol reports." Stunned by the insinuation that they had actually been reading her reports, Kat noted that the hearing date had already passed. She would return to her life unemployed.

Sixth and seventh were messages from the mayor. In the first, she requested an appointment. In the second, she berated Kat for her absence at the unilaterally set time. Kat squeezed her eyes shut. She would be doubly without income.

How could you have thought you were giving me my life back? her mind raged at Sodi. *If you listened to my messages, then you heard this! Didn't you understand that I'm fired?* But her thoughts answered in the next moment: *Sodi didn't see it as an impediment. He would just talk himself back into the jobs. It's second nature to him. Or maybe he didn't really expect me to go back.*

"Tricked your ass on that one; I left!" Kat announced. She shot a mortified glance around the plane. Every other passenger sat, not reacting, in earphones, absorbed in the screens ahead of each. *But I shouldn't have left*, she concluded. *I shouldn't have gone. I should have stayed among those people,* "I want to go back! I shouldn't have left; this is the wrong place!"

"Hi! Please indicate what your need is!" chirped the avatar in the skin-tight pink uniform. A series of icons bounced up on the screen facing Kat: A happy person drinking. A happy person with a burrito. A happy person grinning between a pillow and blanket. A happy person waving at her from halfway inside a restroom door. A happy person hovering over an open bag.

Kat stared at the oversimplification of her life into a series of biological needs. "I am not just a body!" she cried out. Nobody moved. Nobody looked. Every set of hands slipstreamed controls in sims, interacting with a flat pane. "Hey! I'm sitting here!" she called out again. Nobody paid attention, each in his or her assigned spot. Each took up no more and no less room than her or his space allowed.

But Kat's choice had been made. The jet would not turn. Her mini-tab continued to blink.

The next series of messages on it alternated between an officer of the law, whose recordings came in text at first, and the mayor.

The first of these messages read, "This is Officer Shockey of the city police. This message is to give notice that a welfare check has been requested on your person by a concerned party, and I will be performing that check within the next hour. Respond directly if you are away from home."

In the next, the proud image of the mayor appeared, now offering more concern than chastisement. "Kat, call me directly at once. I am terribly upset at your absence. It is not characteristic of you." *The mayor cares about me*, she thought. *The mayor doesn't even know me. Mez knows me, and didn't notice I disappeared. Choti began to know me somehow, and I left.*

The multiple connects continued, but in Kat's overwrought state, the words began to run together: "Investigating a man named Pureforc," and "... consider him dangerous and potentially still trailing you. He is a suspect..." and "I suspect you were smart enough to hide, but I implore you to make contact with me or with a trusted officer I have assigned to your case..." and "case is closed at this point, miss, as we have recovered the body..." and "dear, please come out now. You have been much on my mind."

Kat sighed. The news from World One seemed to vacillate as much as her mind. As she ticked through the messages, they became more recent. Some had come in after Sodi had handed off this device to her:

"... alert you that my prior message was false. You may be in danger. At once, report to..."

"... Report in to me at once! I hardly understand it, but Kat, you need protection. He stole a mini-tab and had information on some others who I hope you're not involved with. He cannot be located. I don't know how much hope to place in the chance you are still alive. His accounts show that he's been taking in considerable fees or bonuses that are difficult to trace... I fear what this man is capable of doing..."

"This prerecorded message has been sent to you automatically due to a crisis," announced the last and most recent item in Kat's messages. There was no visual and no traceable origin, but Vol's licorice voice provided ample identification. Kat's thumbnail traced the slightly wider gap on the mini-tab that evidenced Vol's tampering. Had he linked her device to his somehow? "Upon receiving this message, contact someone we both trust at once. This isn't a joke."

Chapter 33

Eva could feel Sodi's exhaustion. His hands quivered. He slept in fits punctuated by a stillness that, in him, meant grief. "It's okay," Eva told him during one of his wakeful spells. Her hands sought his chest beneath the sheets. She wouldn't touch his familiar chest many more times, and knowing that, she desired connection. "I understand you miss her. Whatever it is, I can hold it with you, if you want to talk."

In response, he turned and his arms drew her toward him, pulling her in so tightly that Eva could only move her fingers. Yet Eva had no desire to move at all, at least not yet.

"It's not her," his haggard words came slowly. "I can't find Vol."

"Vol is wherever he wants to be. He always is."

"No, Eva. Didn't you see? He wasn't at the funeral." As his grip loosened, Eva entwined her limbs around him, feeling the silent crying spasms inside his chest like a slow onset of death throes.

"He'll show up tomorrow, then. He has to deal with this in his own way."

—

The next day, Sodi stood in the doorway, blanched with distress. "Vol," is all he said at first. Eva watched, but did not answer. "He set up a," Sodi twirled a finger in the air vaguely, "a thing in Kat's phone. Direct connection. Gizmo. It went off."

"What does that mean?"

"It sent her a distress message. No detail. Just an alert. Just to contact me. But I—" Sodi heaved, "—I don't know what to do!"

"Can you send him a connect?"

Sodi flipped over his wrist, jabbed at his mini-tab with malevolence, and thrust it at Eva. Backing off a half-step from the whip-like gesture, she read the text output. It was all zeroes. "What does that mean?"

"I don't know. His tab can't communicate. I'm not even sure where this is responding from; it might not even be signaling all the way to him anymore, might just be bouncing off some mid-point set to stop communication from going full through."

"But why?"

Sodi's lips thinned, his cheeks sagging. "Only reason I can think, the trouble's that big."

Eva only watched him.

"Kat said more. The guy that chased her—the murderer—they found a body, they found a mini-tab. The tab was his; the body wasn't. He's out there, no digital, no identity now. He could be anywhere."

Eva tried to consider this, but shook her head. "Be reasonable, Sodi. He won't be *anywhere*. He has no reason to leave the city. He can't have known that Kat left, so he'll still be searching for her there. She just needs to get to the authorities as soon as she steps off the plane."

Moments passed as Eva waited for this message to sink into Sodi's mind, but he stood frozen, agonizing at her silently. "No," answered Sodi. "Not that easy. He stole the 10,000 Steps man's mini-tab. If he mined it, he might have seen that I called it once."

"But... we're safe here. He doesn't know where we are. He thinks we're in the city. Right?"

Sodi closed his eyes. "I downloaded all our files from the apartment to here. I've been so busy, I didn't check what Vol's security was like until this morning. It turned out to have been... lesser. Vol's a direct guy, you know. Machinery. He wants it to work. I was tired. Raz was sick. Funny face. Kat. Getting back, the healing, the funeral. I'm sorry, Eva. I made a mistake."

"Can he trace where we are?"

"It's plausible, but he'd have had to—"

"Sodi," Eva's voice became very quiet, "I want your son inside now. *Right now.*"

—

Sodi had slammed the door to their suite before realizing that Eva had arrived first, had beat him there even though her first motion whisked Raz into her arms. Eva outran him. Even with her breathing obstructed by carrying the child, even with her steps complicated by the tangle of fabric riding up her thighs, Eva ran faster. He turned from the closed door and stared at her high-held chin, the sharp accusation of eyes blazing above flared nostrils. With her glare, she pinned him for two seconds before whirling to lower all the shades in quick succession. With a blank mind, Sodi could only stare back. He could only watch her.

She sensed his lack of direction. With precise, intentional steps, she withdrew to another room.

"Raz!" Sodi spluttered, collapsing into a crouch before the child, scrutinizing the boy's uncertain face. "Raz, what do you think now? Is the dangerous man coming?" The boy stared at him wide-eyed. "Are we safe here? Is Vol still alive? Will Kat be safe?" His son's slightly chapped lips opened, but no sound came out. "Can't you tell me anything?" Sodi blinked. He remembered the healing ceremony and backpedaled. "Do you *remember* anything about this? Something you knew before, something you remember... thinking about it?" The corners of Raz's mouth twisted downward. "Just tell me anything you know. Just one thing, it may be enough. Tell me one true thing you remember!"

The boy trembled. "She loved you, dad. She wanted to help you. I want to help you, too. But I can't... she didn't too... can't see too good beyond her own eyes. Nobody can. Those eyes are gone now."

Sodi's shoulders sagged. "Then anything can happen now. Anything."

A light rap sounded at the outer door. They froze. A cautious, female voice enquired, "Sodi? What's wrong? You were running. Is there something in the forest? Everyone's worried."

Opening the door only a crack at first, Sodi demanded, "Where's Choti?"

"Resting, Sodi. She's resting. What's wrong?"

"I need to see Choti."

The woman shook her head. "She's too tired for any guests. She needs rest. Maybe Vol can—"

"Vol's gone."

"Gone where?"

"Gone. And someone dangerous may be coming here," his expression twisted into an apology, "may be coming because of me, looking for us."

"Should I warn people? Sodi, are you serious? How can this person find us?"

"Warn people. I need... need to think." He shut the door and leaned against the strength of the wood panel. The rapping did not come again.

Maybe ten minutes, maybe twenty, passed without movement or sound. Sodi's mind writhed under his obligations and indecision before he realized that he addressed neither by standing still. *Then I'll move,* he decided, and stayed still. *I'll take steps. I don't know what steps. Ten thousand steps,* he thought bitterly, *I could walk ten thousand steps and it would be bliss, numbness, bliss.*

—

"It will be me."

Contemplating the origin of the disembodied words, Sodi lifted his head at last to examine the room behind him. "What?"

"If you need to blame someone for your lack of direction—someone other than yourself—if you absolutely must, it will be me," Eva said. "It will not be your son." She stood in the very center of the room, unaggressive and unavoidable. Raz remained collapsed in the corner, now leaning into the shaggy black acceptance of his dog Ufi. "And if you need someone to do what you are too afraid to, it will be me. But you will not bear down on your child for answers. Hear, Sodi. He is healed of you."

"I don't even know where to start."

"Start by not making things worse, Sodi. First is damage control: You will not offload your duties to a child under your protection."

"But I don't—"

"It will be me. If you need, it will be me."

"I'm supposed to protect you."

"I no longer need protection." Eva stared at Sodi, and while he could not read what was to come, he could read her. It was the deadness of her eyes, the way no creases appeared—neither to smile nor to berate nor to doubt. Sodi read her, and she was conveying years of moments with him—joyful and lustful and painful. Eva was giving all of Sodi back. "Right now, you are the same man you were two days ago. You are the same man you were two years ago. Don't undermine yourself with self-deprecation. First is damage control: You will not destroy the very man you need to be. There are things we know you can do—talents you can turn into tools, as you have before. There are some things you remain the best at, Sodi." With eyes tapering at the corners, Eva's lacivious expression exuded hatred. "Sodi, my frightless and faithless love."

Sodi stayed silent. Turning away to give him time to ponder, Eva retreated to the corner of the room near Raz and sat cross-legged on the floor, her skirt billowing in the downward motion to land around her in a circle. Her posture straightened. Sodi could read in her motions the old meditation she used to perform when they last lived here: Her chinline elevated a fraction, but her energy reached downward, through her spine, out and down to anchor her to one spot, to one moment.

Her eyelids lifted as slowly as a moonrise. She exhaled, put a hand on the child she loved imperfectly and had raised imperfectly, and sang to him her old bedtime song:

The sunlit room, the fragrant child,
The 'come back soon' embraced and smiled:
This is a place I stay a while.

The warm-hot bath, the quiet voice,
The earthy path I hew by choice
Returns me here, among my joys.

I am the ancient flowering tree.
My greatest pangs start when I leave
Abundance at periphery.

Raz leaned into her. Her arms encircled him, feeling the wholeness of him, the grown and growing weight of him, the goodness of his health, his steady breathing. The child spoke to her, "I have always loved you, too. And your love will always be in my past—safest place."

"Thank you, child, for letting me be part of your life for a while."

Chapter 34

The hillside swelled like a chart of an inverse exponent, a living log graph covered in trees. He found only one groove through the woods going in the direction his compass indicated, and entered it. This was the final stretch, and the trail he traversed opened too broadly to have been created only by deer. Lightheaded, Pureforc felt like he were floating up the incline in spite of his heavy vest, like he were a phantom rising up this volume of earth mass to where the trees abruptly thinned.

He did not try to hide himself. He saw no reason to. Parking the old blue car beside the road at the closest point to the trail head, he'd sought nothing more strategic than to minimize his walk. Being unexpected and digitally off-grid, Pureforc enjoyed the privilege of a direct, bold route.

Even with all his preparations, he was surprised how quickly he found something. Stalking silently, minimizing the soft thud of the leather holsters against his sides, he could pick out a shape beyond the treeline. Obscured, it moved behind trunks and lichen-coated boulders; the forest made it difficult to discern which mottled shades of green belonged to which objects. Without a mini-tab, he could not check if the movement ahead was by a person. He withdrew both firearms from their holsters, preparing to let them speak for his highest values.

A dozen paces from the clearing, he caught the first alert that there remained some undefined variable in his situation. A cabin, roughly painted in four mismatched hues of green, did not offer enough space for independent, year-round survival. The occupant, even if only one, would have needed more storage for the amount of food one human life required to sustain itself—an amount Pureforc could estimate innately. There was a chance other building—and other people—would be nearby.

Pureforc saw the occupant. He was alone. He crouched over a knee-heigh, rectangular device that exuded sinewy light from several open vents. The vented box sat next to a zippered pack with shoulder and waist straps and a tripod mounted with another tiny device. Fiddling with the controls on the light-emitting box, the man wore a dark green T-shirt flattering to his physique. Pureforc took a few more silent steps forward. Specks of forest dirt clung to a patch of the shirt and to the visible knee of his jeans. He recognized Sodi by the 3-D model he'd seen, but also by the certain confidence of his hands. He knew the dexterity and swift execution of Sodi's mind; there was no other way such a man would move his hands.

Calculating his next move, Pureforc thumbed off the safeties of his pistols and continued to watch for the right opening. Seeming to finish with his work on the box, Sodi rose and turned toward the cabin. Noiseless, he crossed the distance, opened the door, entered, and shut it.

I must stay aware, Pureforc thought, because something seemed off to him. While serviceable, the slipshod cabin opened and closed without so much as a thud. *There's information here. The data will tell me what to do.* As five minutes, ten, then fifteen passed, Pureforc wondered if he should enter the cabin as well. The forest slept. Glowing quietly, the light-box continued streaming its strange ribbons of color. Pureforc moved a little closer.

Eighteen minutes after entering the shack, the door reopened, and again without a trace of noise. *Focus!* The data man told himself. He shifted his position very slightly to prepare to raise his weapons. Sodi emerged from the doorway again. Instead of turning to close the shack, he let the door close itself behind him. It still made no noise. A spark of an idea lit Pureforc's mind.

This is my data, he told himself, forgetting the guns, forgetting everything but the obligation to find the trend, to find the explaining factor that made this situation work. As Sodi crossed the distance back to the tripod and light-box, a small wind picked up.

The wind did not move Sodi's hair. It did not billow the loose folds of his shirt. And Sodi's feet, as they walked though the tall sprigs of grass growing in the clearing, did not cause those weeds to move. Sodi was a hologram. The light-box was a generator. Sodi must be expecting him.

This isn't real, Pureforc seethed, angry that he might have allowed detection somehow. He rose from his hiding spot, fully in view of the figure ahead, and strode directly toward it. It did not react. In rage, he raised a pistol toward the swarthy figure to shoot through the light show. The figure crouched in front of the lightbox and began to handle the controls, exactly as before. Pureforc lowered his aim, taking the hologram generator as his target instead. And then he hesitated: A gunshot would provide an alert—and that alert might be the reason for this expensive decoy. *You're giving me too much information, Sodi. You're telling me you don't know where I'm coming from, nor when. And I'm not inclined to ring your doorbell.*

Instead, Pureforc walked to the silent, bent hologram of Sodi. He re-set his safeties, re-holstered, and sent a field-goal-style kick at Sodi's head. Sailing through Sodi's holographic form, there was only the slightest of impacts as Pureforc tipped over the tripod.

—

In the coordination building, the bodily Sodi watched his vantage point of the approaching murderer spin out suddenly.

The tripod on which he'd mounted the bug-eyed camera rolled to rest on its side. Its lens faced upward and across the forest floor. It wasn't the best angle, but it would still suffice to determine if Pureforc would continue approaching the village or if he would turn back to the blue car the lookouts had watched him park. Having already alerted the village of the approaching intruder and the fact that he had firearms and a tactical vest, Sodi only lamented that Pureforc had figured out his hologram too quickly to empty his clips at it.

Eva had been right; Sodi was the same man he'd always been, with or without benefit of his son's once-strong foresight. He would not need the child's no-read words. Just this easily, Pureforc's capture was already guaranteed. It was as easy as Eva believed it would be.

But Eva—Eva was in the video.

—

She didn't know if she would encounter Kat's pursuer in the woods, but it was as good a day to die as any, and death would free her from explanations. Eva charged her mini-tab, ate breakfast, cleaned the dishes, put on hiking boots, and walked out of the village. In the bustle of preparations to defend against a possible intruder, she wasn't noticed. She was already well into the forest when the blue car parked.

Nobody looked for her geo-location because the intruder they expected wouldn't show up on the grid. She took one revolver, its cylinders full of .38s. Because so many others scurried to arm themselves, nobody gave a second thought to this gun's absence.

—

Walking once around the hologram generator, Pureforc debated if he could destroy this rare and valuable device without it alerting anyone. He was interrupted by motion on the path ahead. Of course it was Eva—the counterpart hologram to the Sodi decoy. Her form stopped short, having just rounded a bolder, and stared at him. Her left hand went to her chest. She seemed frozen.

Pureforc gurgled, "Hello hologram! Phantom Eva! Evil Eva spirit!" Pureforc greeted with too much enthusiasm. The hologram woman didn't seem to know what to do. "I see you're expecting me to come and end you like I ended the bum. Good analysis! But I still won't believe in your false data." Her hologram programming was remarkable. Her chest rose and fell in short, shallow breaths. Her lower lip trembled. Between them stretched twenty paces of space. Pureforc walked toward the image.

Nineteen. Eighteen. Seventeen, counted Eva to herself.

"You uncountable invalidity. You think I'm going to waste my resources on you? You're not real."

Sixteen. Fifteen. Fourteen.

He stopped walking. The Eva hologram struggled with something at her hip, glancing between it and him. When her model looked up at him, it seemed to locate his eye again. Pureforc tensed, but recalled there was some trick artists knew to make a painting always appear to look at the viewer, and dismissed it as an artist's trick.

In the woman's hands appeared the silver surface of a thick revolver. The sun glinted on it. The sun dappled her shirt. Now she began to walk again.

Thirteen. Twelve. Eleven.

Her grip settled on the butt of the gun. The barrel aimed at his chest. Her right thumb pulled down the hammer. The hammer made an audible click. Pureforc heard the hammer.

Ten.

Ten steps away, she brushed against a stray bit of tall grass, and it bent at her passing, bouncing back like an inverse pendulum. This wasn't Sodi's doing. This was Eva, real Eva. Pureforc saw the facts too late.

Ten steps away, and it might as well be a lifetime, Eva thought. *Yeah, you get lost in life. I got lost on step three, and I'm still walking. And he knows my name, which means I know his. And he's staring at me, and he's moving his hands to his holsters, and I'm ten steps away from hitting the ground. No point in walking now. Once you're lost, ten more steps still gets you lost. I'll show him how to cover ground. Ten steps from hell, and here I am.*

She'd loved Frank. He was honest. He gave to her—gave even now, even dead, by standing with her in this moment. *And this is why I keep those I love in my safest place—my past. Because I make myself out of them.*

Eva would allow this man to pollute no more of her safest place.

The revolver's eight chambers gave it geometric symmetry. *Cubic,* thought Pureforc, calculating correctly that he could no longer unhoster his own weapons in time. *Two to the third. A higher order.* This pleased him enough.

Eva shot him in the center of his chest. With the bullet, she sent all the pain from her own heart. She killed him with lead and her own long-broken love. Pureforc fell. But Pureforc didn't bleed.

—

Powerless, Sodi watched Eva stride into danger in his video stream. Sodi watched the hands that had fed his son fumble a revolver. This was the woman Sodi had taken from the world to put in his pocket, and she walked away from his life, drew down on his enemy, and fired to save them all.

Pureforc left the camera's view. Eva didn't.

Her small, soft hands flubbed the hefty frame of the weapon. It was not made for her. Her thin wrists bent at uncomfortable angles, yet she managed to turn the gun around and point it at her own temple.

—

From eight inches away from her forehead, the mini-tab on Eva's wrist chimed in a text-only message.

It read: *Please don't.* It was from Sodi. She hesitated long enough to read it. The device chimed again: *We're all watching.*

Sodi was lying, but Eva lowered the revolver and scanned the area for a camera, which she located and stepped on. Then she noticed Pureforc. The dark area where the bullet had hit him did not bloom into the crimson stain she expected. He seemed to still be breathing. In fact, he seemed to still be looking at her.

"Bulletproof vest," Eva muttered to herself. But the killing impulse had already dissolved into self-destruction, and she no longer wished to aim her weapon at his head. It seemed more cruel to leave him to life. She slid his pistols away from his holsters cast them into the underbrush of the deep, lonely forest.

"Keep going," he said, half-whisper, half-cough. He could still barely move from the impact of the bullet. "Kill me or kill yourself. Finish your job."

"I'm not going to die for you," she answered, "and I'm not going to let your death become part of my memories twice." All around the clearing, trees stood sentinel in a ring. She knew this man would regain his breath soon, and she had limited options: a deadly weapon, good soles on her feet, a smashed camera, a hologram generator, and Vol's pack for carrying it.

It was into this last item she dove. In the frontmost pocket, she found two things she knew no machine man would ever forget to pack.

—

I must be a ghost, he thought. *My past is haunting me. This isn't my data.*

The hologram generator was still playing its infinite loop of phantom Sodi, who was now fiddling at the controls of the machine that created him. But it was the woman, it was Eva, who had thrice-bound his lower legs, who had rolled him onto his chest, who had braced down his back with a knee and wrenched his arms behind and up. With a series of quick snaps behind him, the thin clench on his wrists tightened. Another serrated rip sounded; the hold on his immobility increased.

Suddenly the pressure on his back retreated. Pureforc wriggled, attempting to free himself from the hold, but found he could only flop over. His body squirmed, helpless as a worm in the sun. Eva stood over him. By program, phantom Sodi stood from the hologram controls. Just as he had done the first time Pureforc saw this clearing, Sodi turned and walked toward the hologram cabin. His body moved through Eva, passing into and out of her very core.

The woman did not so much as flinch. A partial roll of duct tape lay at her feet. She held zip ties.

Chapter 35

Eva didn't want the bound murderer to blaspheme the conversation she now had to have by watching it. Striding over to Sodi's holographic cabin, she entered the door to his created world by passing clean through it like a ghost. It would be enough to visually and mentally distance herself from Pureforc.

Sodi's cabin turned out to be more of a dividing shield than a room, as it lacked the two back walls and the back half of the roof. On the interior sides of the walls it did have, leaf designs helped blend it into the forest from other angles. These were not the odd, asymmetrical leaves he'd designed for the city's Park Square. Rather, they were practical ovals with heavy veins and a saw-toothed edge leading to a sharp point. Eva knew these leaves. They were her favorite–American Chestnut, extinct from human greed more than from blight. Shiny, heavy, verdant, Sodi had made them thrive here. Reaching out touch a leaf, Eva let her finger pass through it. She wondered how many holograms hid these leaves on the inside, just for Eva, just in case she ever found herself hiding and needing a reminder that he thought of her.

Proof that Sodi had cared about her–even if not most–softened the lure of oblivion.

Still Eva wished to be gone when the Moma arrived. She sent Sodi a text-only message: "Your man is here, restrained, unarmed. Two pistols thrown in forest. Will people be here soon?"

"Yes. You okay?" came Sodi's answer.

"No."

"How are you hurt?"

"By you."

"Sorry. Coming to you. What do you need?"

"Answer, honest for once: What was I to you? Your authenticated login credentials to World One? Did you draw me in only for a ticket out of the Moma?"

"Sunshine. Not like this. Coming to you."

"What did you love?"

It took a little time for Sodi to answer. "You. Us. Everyone. Wait. Am coming."

"No. Name one person you've loved enough to always be loyal to."

This time Sodi's answer took the longest of all, even though it had the fewest characters. "Vol"

Eva stared at these three letters and was thankful, at least, that they were true. "Sodi, I've loved you. I hope you get him back. I'm leaving now. Don't follow."

—

The uniform-wearer counted hours until her shift ended. *This is a sim job*, she consoled herself daily, although it was difficult to appreciate it that fact. Her work sim was highly regulated, imposing a harsh policy of no other sims during work hours.

Her avatar stood at attention, waiting in the designated area of her TruWrld2 time zone. The badge hanging on the wall matched the one on her avatar's chest. Walls with neither doors nor windows surrounded her, increasing her boredom. The only way in to this space was via direct relocation, and once inside, visitors received optional reprieve from sharing their identities. Most came anonymous.

This option meant that the human officer sitting at the sim station stayed ready to slipstream a freeze command all day.

Ninety-eight percent of the avatars transferring into her office did so to enact one of a short list of practical jokes, mostly biological in nature. She had heard every version of TruWrld2 belch at every pitch option so often that she could identify the die-hards who custom recorded their own burpings for use in the sim. Yet for all the mundane obscenity, someone believed the other two percent of visitors justified paying a salary to staff a sim police station for World One in each time zone of TruWrld2.

Presently, a person relocated into her sim silo using anonymous avatar #53—one that had masculine body traits, but like all anonymous skins for this room, was sexless. "Welcome to the anonymous tip zone. This avatar is live staffed. What is the nature of your concern?" she prompted the auto-dialogue, waiting for flatulence.

"You have on your suspect list a fugitive named Pureforc."

She checked the records. There was actually a match. "What is your information?"

Anonymous avatar #53 transmitted a request to use an alternative personal skin. Straightening in her chair, the officer permitted the request; either the visit was genuine or the practical joke would be memorable. But the skin that the visitor took on was not human. It was not even three dimensional.

"This is where you'll find him. He is waiting for pickup next to a sealed box that contains his firearms. You must hurry, as he is fully bound and exposed to the elements."

The officer realized the avatar's new skin was a map. She captured its content, reconciling it to the gridwork of World One. The roads matched. "I do not detect any identities at that location."

"Read his file; there is a good reason for that."

"Who is guarding him?"

"Nobody."

"Who are you?"

"Anonymous."

"How did he come to be there?"

"You don't need to know that. If he's a wanted person, you have him. If he's not a wanted person, I don't want him, either. He is raving about someone named Kat Menali, about Servi-Mod, and about some kind of fake death. He is adjacent to his own firearms. I hope you get to him before someone else unbinds him." The visitor requested permission to leave the virtual office.

"I'd like you to stay and answer some questions."

Without speaking, the visitor repeated the departure request. Finding nothing in the law that permitted her to keep the sim informant in presence, the officer was forced to allow the exit. She read the file notes for Pureforc and placed a call to the assigned party: Officer Shockey.

Within fifteen minutes, mayoral favors had arranged for three squads of the closest jurisdiction's armed police to the spot by air. Trussed like a hog in zip ties and duct tape, the alleged murderer's humiliation and imminent capture so riled the squad members' pride that none noticed two Moma fading back into the woods, silent as panthers, their rifles withdrawn vertically.

—

The area chief of police and governor received public recognition for the rare arrest of an individual who had been violent in World One. Aerial video of the capture washed across the news sims, portraying the men and women in blue in heroic poses. Public approval for the chief and the governor spiked.

After the congratulatory ceremonies, the governor extended a formal memorandum of appreciation and friendship to Mayor Chatoy. As she accepted the memo publicly, the mayor's elegant compliments, interstate cooperation, and freshplaited, sim-perfect hair won her the title of "most admired statesperson of the year."

Officer Shockey watched again and again the part of the helicopter's video that was not broadcast—the portion taken before they spotted Pureforc. In that video, a series of potato-shaped hills gave way to several clusters of brightly colored buildings, each nestled like a jewel in a navel. This was a town that did not appear on any map. Shockey tapped his pen as he watched the footage again. *Subversives*, he thought, *perhaps hundreds of them.*

—

Kat looked down at the empty room on the opposite side of the mirror. In a few moments, five men would walk into it. She'd been dreading this moment for the entire flight back, even as Officer Shockey kept reassuring her that she would remember her pursuer's face.

"I'm not sure I can. And if I do, I'm not sure I want to see him," she explained. "It was dark. Everything has changed since then. What happens if I guess wrong?"

A wrinkle of compassion crossed the young officer's brow. Everything had been different for him, too, since the young woman returned to the city. *She moves with a freshness, like she remembers what walking is for*, he'd thought. His special assignment for the mayor kept him idle except for the oversight of Miss Kat Menali, and he had begun to forget what else he'd ever wanted to do with his career. Sometimes he asked her police questions just to hear the resilience in her answer. But this time he just reassured her: "Miss Menali, I guess everyone is afraid to screw up sometimes, but trust in yourself. They'll come in, and you won't have to guess. It'll be one or it'll be none."

"They typed him. It's got to be him. The DNA tests are accurate to, what—"

"Yeah, you shouldn't have seen that. But you never know. Just because they found someone doesn't mean it was the guy who chased you."

Kat asked, "Shockey, you want to nab this guy, right? You're not indifferent?"

"I want the right thing to happen," he answered. His answer made him worry about the hidden town he'd spotted. "I don't want to hurt the innocent. I want the right people brought to justice. For your sake. For everyone's sake." He struggled with a moment of awkwardness. "But definitely not at the cost of an innocent person's freedom." This had been the statement that stuck in both their minds for the remainder of the wait at the district's jail.

Innocent, Kat thought to herself, *that he cannot be.* For she'd spoken with Sodi; she knew more about how this man had been found than the officers might. If she failed and pointed out the wrong person and Pureforc was released–

Innocent, Shockey thought to himself. *Can that town of people be innocent? They bound a man, left him exposed. But in doing so they helped Kat–*

"Alrightey, Miss Uh... well, miss," said the arriving jail guard. He released his bulk into a seat in the safe enclave of the mirrored booth. There was movement in the bright room ahead. "Here they come. Go 'head and tell us if any one of them looks good to ya. And hey, if it'll help it, tell them to turn thisaway and that if ya want. We can even have 'em make faces if that's gonna help you." He tapped at a hamburger-sized red button on his console–one of the very few controls–with obvious pride. Kat suspected his office wasn't very busy.

"Thank you," she answered, and allowed her eyes take in the subjects. She immediately recognized one.

"Got someone?" said Shockey from her left, watching her expression.

"N–no." But her long gaze at subject #2 belied her interest.

"Hey, let's make them all turn, that's a help," said the guard, who slapped his palm flat on the large, red wart and called into the microphone, "All you go left!"

Seeing her chance, Kat leaned toward the microphone before he finished and quipped in her clearest voice, "No that's not necess–" The guard's hand came off the button, and he glared at her. But the job was done. All five suspects in the line-up turned to their left, but #2 held his face slightly to his right, mouth lightly agape, eyes trying to bore through the unidirectional glaze on the mirrored glass.

"Miss, don't rile them by being a woman."

Kat leaned full over into his personal space, her strong, shapely back crowding into his lap. Yielding the space in surprise, the guard stared at the confident form, scented the light fragrance of her braids, and was unsure if he wanted her to move back. She smacked down the button again. "How are you gentlemen doing today?"

Suspect #2's face broke into smile, hope glistening in his eyes as he called back, loudly so she could hear through the glass, "I'm doing good. And how are you, miss?"

Kat smiled, "Better than a toad in rut."

"Good to hear it. Very good. Wouldn't mind a little rut myself."

"Ignore him; he's a felon," advised Shockey. "It's better they can't iden–"

"What, number two? Is the space between the bars too small to fit your ego?"

"Too small by far, miss, for the ego I have coming on."

Shockey nudged her away from the control desk. Her message now sent, Kat allowed the officer to re-seat her before he took back the controls. "All you turn up straight again. Talk's over."

All obeyed. Shockey gave up looking at the suspects and stared at Kat, her suddenly glowing face, and the glint of undiluted happiness in the corners of her smile. "Miss Menali," he held his voice steady, "is one of these men the one that chased you that night when your mini-tab disappeared?" Shockey thought that, at this point, no answer she could give would push back his anxiety and creeping jealousy.

Kat licked her lips and examined each in turn, assessing the shapes of chins and cheekbones. The first and third were clearly too round. The fourth... maybe. But as Kat evaluated the fifth man, she reached for Shockey without budging her eyes. In her mind she was turning to bolt, she was coursing down the pavement. Pressure on her right hand brought her back from the vision; Shockey was holding her extended hand, watching her. "Five," she whispered. "Oh god, it's five. That's him."

"How sure are you, Kat?"

"That's him. One hundred percent."

Shockey nodded at the guard, who recorded it. "The witness has named Pureforc." Kat seemed to melt in relief, and the five men vacated the adjacent room.

This was the moment the young officer had been waiting for: the moment at which the threat against Miss Kat Menali was removed, the moment the facts on her aggressor coalesced into a rigid case. But the sense of celebration he expected to feel abstained from his mind, dissolving into another question: "Who was the one you talked to?" *A subversive*, he worried, *connected to that town. A dangerous man.*

Kat looked down, knowing he would see her lie. She sighed. She gripped his hand.

"A bullhead," said the guard, thinking he'd been asked the question. He vacated his seat and waited for the knock that indicated the inmates were all re-secured. "Won't give so much as a name."

"Kat," Shockey urged. She would not answer.

—

"Choti, I don't know what else to do." Sodi cinched the straps on the rectangular pack, wriggling his shoulders into the best position before heaving upward. An involuntary sigh escaped him under the full weight of the best portable hologram cloak.

"You have all your options. That child needs his only parent."

"Vol is in prison." Sodi's voice echoed on the hard, empty walls on the gray equipment storage room.

"Child, do you realize you are planning to walk into a prison with a machine that automatically makes you a felon? Your chance of success is—"

"—is greater than Vol's chances if he stays trapped where he is. Choti, he's there because he tried to protect us."

"Then why are you risking what he protected? Vol alone could be a stray life, an outcast. But if someone comes for him, that means there's a community. If someone comes with a portable cloak, that means *there's a community with resources they consider dangerous*. How much risk are you willing to shoulder?"

Sodi rasped a long, sandpaper sigh as he considered this. "Choti," he whispered, "this is all I'm good at. Without this I don't have power to save him." But the elder gave him an incredulous scowl with a smile hidden in it. Choti believed in him. Something in her obvious confidence helped him remember: Masses of people are very reliable if you know where to point them.

Sodi stopped. He shrugged backward. The hologram generator gently touched down behind him, freeing his shoulders from its weight. "Well, maybe. Maybe I can make something happen."

Chapter 36

Make something happen became a very specific generalization. Even the earliest sims—in their two-dimensional, 8-bit-color, single-diskette glory—understood the insatiable, innate yearning of human kind: Neither winning nor losing, but experiencing. And from a very early day, sims allowed players to voluntarily summon the unknown. As early as the 1990s, players would construct entire digital cities only to call into being a mythical monster, a nuclear meltdown, or a torrential flood to wreak havoc and horror on the very thing they'd created.

However uncomfortable to explain, this human tendency was easy to capitalize upon. Every modern sim used voluntary randomization: If the user kicked off the *make something happen* function, the program would select a chaos event and cause it to occur. The repertoire of chaos events changed frequently—especially given the unreprieving demand for them. Mez's avatar had once stood awash in a stampede of half-meter-high, retro-goth vixen-fairies; Kip Petson had abandoned a dilapholor battle when it suddenly developed explosive gastroenteritis; both had purchased avatar remedies after *make something happen* had covered their characters with giant warts shaped like calf noses.

Users claimed to want full control in the sims. But in reality, most established predictable routines, slashing how many decisions they had to make, then unleashed chaos upon themselves.

Yet designing chaos events proved expensive. To cut costs, one after another sim company allowed subscribers to contribute their own chaos events. Contributions became the immediate property of the sim. To avoid lawsuits and potential compensation to talented contributors, *make something happen* events could only be donated anonymously.

These policies yielded three results: First, the creativity, prudishness, and design quality of the average chaos event plummeted. Second, sim design firms shed the more creative half of their game programmers, raised subscription fees in response to avid demand, and tripled their returns on investment. And third, Sodi found it possible to launch a single-person attack against the strongest corporation on earth.

—

They were lumens without substance. They were holograms in the sim.

An attractive woman of realistic human proportions, panic and sweat on her face, ran in endless slow-motion from a wolfish, beak-nosed man in a Servi-Mod uniform. The claw-fisted pursuer loped along in slow-motion behind her, neither catching up nor falling behind, the moment of tension suspended. This is all that had changed when the user chose *make something happen*. It wasn't funny or even that interesting. It was annoying. And it upset her: she did not like seeing the beastly man chasing someone through her private sim spaces.

If she moved her avatar around, the two hologram runners would move with her like floaters in her vision, always fifteen meters away in the scenery. If she kept her avatar still, they would eventually run past her, but never get very far, and she'd see the slogan on the back of the pursuer's uniform: "Hospitals. Jails. Your home. How can you escape what gets in everywhere?"

She searched through the controls and options for a way to make the effect disappear. Nothing worked. After fifteen minutes of trying, she stood from her cockpit of panels to twist the latch on her Servi-Mod apartment door. Not finding movable furniture, she shoved towels, socks, and bits of cardboard packaging around the edges of the door, hoping to jam it against intruders. The slogan was true, after all: Anyone cleared by Servi-Mod could get in to her home, locked or not. She'd never thought of that before. She did not like the way it made her feel.

As time went on, more users across many sims were affected, and none could get rid of the effect. The sim holograms could not be damaged or even touched. They became part of the scenery, attaching to the user account, but affecting common-world features over which no single user had sim-property rights. Such duality meant that no single entity had the right to delete them.

TruWrld2 administrators took so many connects they activated their natural-language intelligent answer system to handle volume even for premium accounts. A typical call started, "I earned my sim-come. I spent it for this! Make these runners go away!"

"I understand," would respond the natural language administrator—which, as a system, was neither natural nor an administrator. "We are still working on the problem. For now, the only way I can make them go away is to re-set you."

"What? No, I'd lose time!"

"Yes, you would lose about twenty-six hours of game history. I would need to re-set your account back to before the effects first appeared."

"That's ridiculous! I've accomplished so much in the past twenty-six hours! You're asking me to work without pay! This is injustice! And think of what you're doing to the hostage! By letting her run around like that all over the place! I heard she's a real person; is that true?"

The system sent a plus-one to the tally of concerns about the image of the running woman now known as *the hostage*. "I'm sorry; there is no other solution yet. The good news is that the effects don't seem to interfere with usage. So, if you don't want to be re-set, you can just ignore the effect until we work out a solution. How does that sound?"

"Well..." the user fumbled, "what are other people doing? Is everybody getting set back a day?"

"Most choose to just ignore it. We'll have a solution as soon as we can. Can you hold out for it?"

"Okay... well... I guess I'll wait it out, too."

But few users merely waited. With the runners in front of them all the time, most eventually searched for strings like "Servi-Mod sim-scarrer chasing babe." A wealth of recorded stories told how a true World One woman named Kat Menali had been pursued by a man with a standing murder charge and the highest of Servi-Mod clearances. Some provided a detailed geo-time map of the pursuit. Others had re-created a supposedly identical pursuit in VR. All included the detail that Kat had only gotten away by desperately hurling her mini-tab into a lake.

Less obvious was that each of these sources seemed to be quoting another, as though the information had no definite origin.

The debugging teams for TruWrld2 weren't making the promised progress on getting rid of the unwanted sim holograms. They couldn't seem to determine which layer of image mapping or object programming the sim holograms affected. Hour by hour, fewer users consented to lose the increasing amount of sim-time it would take to re-set their accounts, choosing instead to keep the images of Kat and Pureforc on screen with Servi-Mod's unsettling new *de-facto* tagline: "How can you escape what gets in everywhere?"

—

Seeing how strongly the *make something happen* chaos event trended, news media spots hit the sims describing Kat Menali, her pursuer, and the questionable security of the world's most successful company. It was all the information they could find, so they echoed it.

In the interest of providing authentic visuals, each of the news anchors chose *make something happen* as many times as it took to contract the effect they were reporting on.

In their rush to report the case, many did not take time to un-do the effects of the other *make something happen* events they called for. Some reported while aflame with seven chickens circling their heads. Some discussed their stories over loud, dramatic music to help camouflage impressive biological sounds. One steadfast reporter performed the news as a human-shaped mound of blue gelatin with a squishy-looking olive embedded in the center.

"It's not fair," groaned an oversized platypus to a newscaster avatar with a crude, rhombic head, "I mean, this woman Menali didn't do anything. She's just a victim. Now she's being paraded all over every world. Where is her privacy? Only someone really evil would take her hostage like this—and she is being called *the hostage* in all sim worlds. We've confirmed that this is her real, World One image! What a nasty thing to do to someone who can't just switch skins!"

In another video article, two matching paladins, swords at the ready, spoke to a news avatar with pineapple hair who appeared to be wearing only starfruit. They explained, "Who else would have done this? Nobody else has a grudge against the hostage babe."

"Nobody else than who?" responded pineapple-head.

"Well, that Servi-Mod *e-creepy-creep*. I mean, Servi-Mod's as rich as a county. They're probably all like *you-peddling-little-gnat* at her for even saying *whoa* at being gunned down by Servi-Mod."

"She wasn't actually gunn—"

"Yeah, man, but look at the truth here: Their guy got snapped by the cops. That's real. Who else has cash to make a massive blast attack coming down on the butts of all of us? We all got the running hostage at once. I mean, *zam!* All at once!" He began to hop back and forth between feet. The other paladin started jumping as well. "That means coordination—POW!—like they planned to go in like—" The interview descended into a series of grunts as the paladins explained their position on Servi-Mod by showing off their swordplay.

"But," objected pineapple-head, remaining very still, "why do you think Servi-Mod would have done this? What would you consider to be their motivation?"

"Yeah, this is my motivation!" cried the other paladin, landing a heavy blow too near the reporter. The front half of several strategically located starfruit lopped off. The first paladin demonstrated his prowess at stringing together expletives with the Servi-Mod name while his partner, in higher spirits now that he'd cut fruit, shoved a finger up his nose for the camera. The news anchor ended the live sim segment.

Across the sim worlds, users cheered that these were the most entertaining newscasts in memory. Reposted and remixed with other popular media, the exposés struck viral popularity. One monitoring agency estimated that twenty percent of sim-based conversations during the following eighteen hours made reference to the sim-holograms, Miss Kat Menali, Servi-Mod, or one of the audacious news reports. At a special meeting of the board of directors, one of the smaller, hungrier news groups unanimously resolved to conduct all future reports under the influence of chaos effects to increase their viewership.

At some point during the third day, those sim users who had not yet been affected began invoking the *make something happen* function repeatedly. They refused to be left out of the most exciting movement in the sim worlds since *Bubba's Backwash in my Brew*. Delighted by their acquisition of the common mark of shame, these users congregated in their favorite sims to engage in holographic races: By standing together and facing the same direction, the multiple impressions of Kat and her Servi-Mod pursuer appeared to sprint a slow-motion race across the middle background. The winner was the one who got the Servi-Mod slogan to display first.

By the end of the fifth day, a survey found that ten percent of affected sim users said that they found the ever-running duo so annoying that they had become fond of them. When it came to light that users wanted to keep the effect as a feature even after a patch became available, goals at the sims changed. The greatest bustle shifted from fixing the problem to discussing potential profits and legal ramifications. After all, the running woman appeared to be a legitimate person with inalienable rights to her own real-life image, and the other figure was from Servi-Mod.

A set of marketing professionals posited questions to the public: *What if users could choose who is running?* They envisioned TruWrld2 pioneering the latest developments in sim-runners: Users could choose between several different models of chaser and chasee, including several adorable animal versions. But their efforts fell flat. The public was still upset about what had been done to Kat Menali, so they would accept no substitute that would release her from her position as the quintessential avatar hostage. *She represents something to them*, the marking minds concluded. *It has to be Kat.*

However, the majority of sim players continued to balk at the ongoing presence of the phantom runners. They became so irked by the game's inability to remove the specters that they demanded a scapegoat for their frustrations. In the absence of a sensible target, they chose the most popular one: Servi-Mod.

—

Shockey smeared his palm over his face, forehead to chin. He sat back in his chair and watched the video from Pureforc's arrest again. The shadow of the helicopter slipped over fields of corn criss-crossed by small, straight roads. The edge of a lake that, on maps, zagged north and south like a snake passed out of view. Next arrived little green buds of hills, disappearing off screen one rounded lump at a time. And among them, barely in the frame, shone those bright clusters of buildings.

He'd seen Kat's arm: the natural scar in healthy flesh. Someone had treated her. He'd seen her reaction to the man in the lineup at the closest jail—the one she spoke to but did not name. While Kat was out somewhere in the world, the people who captured her enemy seemed like her friends, but now that she was home in the city, they seemed like strangers again. Shockey sighed, unclear who to trust or why. With her close and safe again, even just for several days, his gratitude for her safety wilted into mistrust for the others she was keeping secrets for.

He walked into the office by the windows of his building. He was not greeted, so he began, "Sarge. I noticed something on the tape of the Pureforc arrest." In response, the Sergeant gave only a long, slow *are-you-still-bragging* look. "Don't know if you wanna take a look at it. Maybe collaborate with another— okay, so it's your call. But—"

"You talk slower than green moss."

"Sorry, sir. But would you have a look at this? There might be a whole village of subvers—"

"You jumping ahead of your drawers again?"

Shockey worried he was doing just that. But the Sergeant was already watching the video, and his option to stay silent expired.

—

The mayor retained Kat for more hours than was necessary, but her purpose was twofold: First, doing so warranted giving her a room in the well-guarded mayoral mansion. She would not yet hear of the girl returning to the very scenario that had endangered her life, especially now that her image was flaunted all over the sim worlds. Second, and more strategically, the mayor sensed opportunity. Being central to the drama, Kat held a right-of-first-refusal of great value to the mayor: She wanted the option to use the girl's sudden fame before any other politician caught her. The question was how to do it—without being unfair.

"Beautiful morning, Miss Kat," she greeted the girl.

"Good morning, madam mayor. Do you have anything in mind for your coiffure today?"

"Not for the hair, no. But," she allowed a quiet pause to underscore the moment, "perhaps something for you. For your future."

"Madam?"

"I understand that, at the moment, you are not employed other than as my hair artist. Although I wish to retain your services for as long as you choose to be here, you may have other, easier options for income."

"I enjoy my work for you, madam."

"Yes, and I appreciate it. But it has come to my attention that the major sims may be interested in licensing your real-life image to perpetuate that upsetting phenomenon. At some point, they'll find a patch, and I will be relieved when your identity is no longer abused. But, Kat," the mayor regarded her, "also consider that the worst of the damage may already be done."

"Yes, I've been trying to hold on to that thought." Kat's expression took a faraway look. "There's not much else for me to do at this point."

"If the damage is done, perhaps it could be a boon if you to agree to the image licenses."

"And let them keep my image? Let them parade me around the sims forever, always chased by some murderer?"

"Never caught. Chased but—with a bit of tactical and legal advice, which I have access to—banking wealth from it."

Kat blinked. "Wealth?"

The mayor smiled. "Kat, it is an incredible number of impressions, and they can't own your personal image. It's like someone set you up right on top of a legal loophole."

Kat's eyes unfocused as though she were looking at a distant solution to the tricky problem plaguing her. *Had Sodi done this on purpose?* she wondered. *Because I'm not being left dry and unemployed. Because I'm in a better position than he found me in. He couldn't give me my life back; did he give me something better? Maybe he did care about me.*

"There is more to consider, Kat: You are extremely famous right now. You may be the most famous person in the country at this time." Hearing this, Kat furrowed her brow. "And there is an unprecedented rush of goodwill focused on your person." The mayor pursed her lips, fretting over her next phrases. "You will not be able to keep this degree of attention forever; it will be brief. But in this moment, you have one opportunity to make a stand, to direct your public support toward... anything... a cause of your choosing. At this juncture of time, if you choose to go public, you could make almost anything happen: You could force the creation of a new law. You could revise widespread social policy." The mayor swallowed. "You could revive the old practice of trust busting against any corporation you may see as evil. Perhaps even you could even get... an individual of your choosing... voted into the presidency. Not to beleaguer the point, Miss Menali, but right now, of the two people in this room, the one of greater influence is you. Perhaps

I should be serving you today. What can I do that would be of assistance in your life?"

Kat's words came fast. "I want a person let out of prison."

"Surely you jest."

"Not *him*. Another. An innocent. Or, well, it's hard to call him innocent, but he's a good m— uh, he's not that guilty. Madam mayor, he has a setback and I worry he may already be suffering abuse."

Standing, the mayor strode across the room to a plush armchair and indicated to the identical one beside her. "Please sit with me." Kat did. "What exactly is his setback?"

—

Vol was glad for the darkness. There was nothing here he wanted to see, nor to feel. There was reddish brown crust where blood had dried on his arms, and they'd asked him, "Where'd you come from?" One tender rib, one side of his lip larger than the other, one eye swollen half shut. The cell smelled sick from him eating too little and too poorly. "What were you doing there? Where were you going?" Vol kept silence, but the silence became a worse and worse answer.

Eventually they figured enough. It was when they came in with a box. It might have been the same box that he'd left out behind the equipment shed, but it was no longer full of medical supplies. "Last chance, friend," the one had said. "You weren't taking medicine nowhere, and they didn't grow in the field. What's the story?" The other one never talked. He just put his hand in the box and pulled out pliers.

"My friend here is an artist," the talking one said, "but not a good one." The silent one approached. His hand was steady, face impassive. "Why don't you draw us a picture, so he don't have to."

Dragging the pliers along the contours of Vol's exposed

chest, the silent one seemed to be assessing his size. "Tell us," the other urged, but Vol didn't. Without rushing, taking all the time he wanted, the silent one pinched skin between the blades and squeezed. The pain sharpened until the skin gave out. Vol cried out. The pliers reversed direction and pinched again, separating a small diamond of skin from his chest—a new window into Vol's heart.

Sodi had not come. If Sodi would not come for him, nobody would. But if that's the sacrifice it took to keep the rest of the Moma safe—

"You two, we need you on a patrol, stat." The voice came from the doorway, which now let in a rectangle of light from the outside hall. Vol squinted into it, but could not recognize the figure.

"Sir, uh, we're just getting somewhere," the talker retorted. The silent one traced the pliers along another section of Vol's chest. "You know, we've had all this, uh, *paperwork* just building up here."

"Report came in. Sergeant from that same city. Need all mobile units right away. That *paperwork* you're talking about, well, it doesn't matter anymore."

—

Kat lowered her right arm into her lap and traced the healing, ragged scar line with her left hand. The mayor watched closely. "So the issue is he's not legitimized. Neither are any of his people. But," her eyes met the mayor's, "they're the ones that saved me. Well, and maybe they got me into it. But they showed me something I can't forget while I was there with them. They care about each other and have these dances together and—"

"Kat, I get the sense," the mayor interjected with caution, "that you want more than just one person to be let out of jail."

Two women stared at each other, each revering the other as the more strong and capable. Each trusted the other's high regard and faith in return. Together, they could reach skies neither could attain alone. The space between their strong minds came alive with possibilities.

Kat spoke first. "Are you saying... could I undo the legitimization requirements?"

The politician considered. "It would also require strong support from inside the government. It would, I think, require a charismatic president with incredible support from the people to press the issue."

Kat hesitated, considering what else a President Chatoy would prioritize in government. She knew her well, knew her off-stage personality when her defenses were down. She was strategic. But she also had morality and an unstained heart.

Understanding some of what made Kat quiet, the mayor continued, "Clearly I am also in this for *my* benefit. I find myself in a political conundrum due to campaign donations by Servi-Mod to my opponent. The sweeping social change you value also is a chance for me to increase my political horizons."

"Okay, so... what do you have in mind?"

"I can answer that," said the mayor, who then let her expression slack into serenity as she contemplated. "Miss Kat, the person you wish to save from prison: It's not Pureforc, right? Or anyone who helped him? Or anyone related to him? And his only crime is his legitimization status?"

"Correct. He's an enemy of Pureforc. He's his opposite. The only thing they have in common is they're in the same prison."

Without moving other muscles, the mayor smiled. "How serendipitous. The police chief there is still reaping rewards for Pureforc's arrest. I believe he will collaborate with me again. Here's the big dilemma: We need a working patch that will reliably end all unlicensed instances of your image's misuse. Otherwise we can not metamorphose you from a victim into a champion. I am concerned about the timeframe because your fame won't stay at this crest, and so far no company has managed to fix it."

It was Kat's lack of answer that made the politician bore a shrewd stare into the girl to prompt her to speak. Kat said, "Actually, we may not need to depend on that."

"Miss Menali, you are a more complicated woman than I anticipated. What is it that you know?"

"Nothing for sure until I make a connect privately. But I suspect that, if you can get this person out of prison, well... I suspect the sim holograms can be stopped, patch or not." Kat ceased her words, hoping for a verbal reprieve to prevent her from saying more, but the mayor simply held the silence until discomfort egged out the fuller description: "Okay, well. I don't really know. But some of these unlegitimized people? Madam mayor, some are frightfully talented."

"Interesting," her lips thinned. "Please make the connect–in privacy beyond my hearing."

When Kat returned and silently inclined her head, the mayor commented only, "I should have suspected it sooner. Living beyond our best radars would require superior talents." Sitting up straighter, the mayor declared, "I believe we have a winning strategy at hand. Now, for your unlegitimized friend? I suspect he can be free this afternoon if you are comfortable with the rest of the plan."

"Then I suspect I'm going to be comfortable with it." Kat held her breath.

Chapter 37

Within hours, the sim-worlds news arenas swelled with so many avatars that they ran out of space. In a flurry of lumpy programming, one set of developers ballooned the size of the arena, but it still filled. A more practical team released the gravity effects of its arena, allowing avatars to float freely beneath the high ceilings, but even that volume filled. A third set of developers beat both problems by suspending discrete spatial volume, so that avatars could stand overlapping one another to afford room for the continuing gush of arrivals.

What prompted this largest showing of public interest in memory was twofold: First, ninety minutes earlier, all iterations of the Kat Menali hostage hologram simultaneously disappeared from all sim worlds. None of the subsequent claims of responsibility for the retraction—numerous though they were—convinced the editorial commentators. Second, Kat Menali herself announced that she would make a public appearance "to clear up the truth about what happened." And she would do so in duality: As her avatar in TruWrld2 and other sims, and as a streamed video of her World One self.

It was a frenzy. "I bet she'll look just like herself," commented a humanoid avatar.

"I wonder if she'll be running," hoped a giant koala avatar.

A speckled ogre avatar retorted, "I just want my runners back. I was playing three hours when they poofed."

"Steady yourself," said Mayor Chatoy as Kat resorted to deep breathing to calm her nerves. "They already love you. You can do no wrong today."

"Yes," Kat answered, feeling Shockey's formal, gloved hand pressing reassurance into her middle back. The mayor had done her part. With Vol returned to the Moma, Sodi had fulfilled his promise to remove the holograms in the sims. But Kat's role was public; she did not have the benefit of acting from behind the scenes, and realized she could never again be anonymous. She wondered what it would do to her world—worlds, maybe.

The lights illuminated. The worlds-wide press conference began.

She blinked. "Hi everyone," Kat waved. Her doppelganger avatar mimicked the motion, "I'm the real Kat Menali." From cavernous sim-rooms so packed they violated spatial and gravitational physics, there surged a roar of welcome and approval.

"Oh, thank you! Oh! Wow. Thank you. Well, the first thing I want to say is that I'm so grateful to be here, to be alive." The torrent of cheers rushed anew. "I've read the stories about my pursuit by a cleared Servi-Mod employee, who is now safely in custody thanks to the responsiveness of our police force." Beside her, Shockey held at respectful attention. "It also depended on the huge dedication of quite a number of other people who, just of themselves, cared enough to assist in my protection and his capture." Another sea of cheers swept through the crowd. "And so, in honor of the effort of these people—those who were doing their jobs as public protectors, and those who were doing their jobs as decent human beings—I'd like us all to take a full minute to honor their part in making a better world." Kat went silent and still.

But most others did not go still. Seventy percent of the attendees cheered in World One while muting themselves in the sims. Kat's minute of silence created an awkward moment for some: All sims were effectively paused. Neighbor could hear neighbor bellowing with happiness for the same thing at the same time. Tentatively, apartment doors opened. Heads poked into hallways to peek at the other faces that appeared. Catching each others' eyes, curious expressions melted into laughter. Neighbors recognized a sameness among them and waved at each other. Somehow in laughing together, they no longer felt like strangers.

As they sensed the minute of respect winding down, some called out to their neighbors, "Hey! Come on in here, we can watch it together!" Others answered, "What the heck!" They hurried over, giddy with excitement as *make something happen* occurred in World One—and was just as exciting.

—

While Kat's worlds-news conference had so many riveted, a force organized around the potato-shaped hills. While loosely planned for stealth, the need to use helicopters to reach the suspected camp of subversives announced their presence quite clearly to Sodi. There would be dozens of them. They would come from all sides. They would be prepared and coordinated.

He faced Vol, who bulged with varied bandages and still smelled of jail. The two men's fingers intertwined. Sodi rested the bridge of his nose against Vol's temple on his less injured side. Sodi could smell Vol's blood. Vol could feel Sodi's heartbeat.

"I tried," Vol began. "I didn't say anything. I destroyed all lines of evidence. I kept us secret."

"Shh," consoled Sodi.

"What are we going to do? What are they going to do? How can we stop this?"

For once, Sodi had no solution of his own, none of the *no-read* words, not enough equipment, no programming prepared, and no confidence that any of them could do anything about the dozens of World One aggressors approaching the Moma. So he answered Vol's questions only by placing his other hand on the back of Vol's neck and holding him.

They might do anything when they arrived. Sodi wanted one more moment with Vol to keep safely in his past.

—

"It was a terrifying day of my life," Kat continued after her minute of respect ended at the news conference. "I'm not sure I will ever be over it. That day, someone I loved died. Someone else was killed outside my building. And I felt like I died, too, when I threw my mini-tab in a lake to get away. For a while I was nobody. I didn't matter to anyone much. I wonder if any of you know the feeling." Warm murmurs rippled through the audience. "Nothing in my life prepared me for that day. I'd done nothing to harm anyone. I was coming home, to my regular home, to my regular life, and suddenly a person chased me like he was going to erase me. I've never been so afraid in my life. But I managed to hide where he couldn't find me." She paused for a moment. "And that's something I need to explain. See, there's more to the story, and I think you deserve to know the whole truth."

The crowds grew silent. Both in the sim arenas and in the display panel cockpits of World One apartments, people were quiet for themselves and for each other. They wanted to receive these next words, but they also wanted those around them to receive the moment—because with so much attention focused on one thing, people sensed that this moment would change them, and the feeling was magical.

Kat spoke into the magic. "I got injured. And that's why it's been so long before I could come and talk to you. My life became very complicated and dangerous very quickly. You see, because a cleared Servi-Mod employee was after my life, and because all the hospitals are Servi-Mod, if I got treatment, he'd find me and have full access to me. I couldn't go home. I couldn't get treatment. I was injured and vulnerable, and I had nowhere to go. And it got really bad: I developed blood poisoning from my injury."

"What did you do?" called out a voice from a tangle of reporters. "How did you get to a doctor?" But they were shushed because people only wanted to hear Kat.

"I had to turn to people who could not possibly be connected with Servi-Mod. I went to those who we don't treat as citizens—or even as full people. And when I was there, they healed me. Right away. No hesitation. They didn't ask for payment. Or anything. They helped me and they let me go back to whatever life I wanted. I'd never been treated so well. It was hard to come back because they cared so much about me, and I didn't always feel cared about in my regular life, and I wanted to go on feeling cared about and part of something."

In living rooms shared by new acquaintances, tiny admissions in hushed voices closed the distance between *neighbors* and *friends*: "Yeah, I know what she means," or "I have days like that," or sometimes a long sigh acknowledged by a compassionate clap to the shoulder.

"These were unlegitimized people. But instead of subversives, I think of them as my heroes. What happened to me was terrifying and dangerous, and I hope that some way can be found for it to never happen to any of you. Or to any of them."

Feebly, Kat stepped back, trying to hide a nervous stumble. She expected applause, but the monitors indicated no noise levels in any of the worlds. Reassuring her, the mayor patted her twice on the back as she passed, stepping to the forefront.

"I am Mayor Chatoy. I regret his incident occurred in my city. Tonight, I want to thank Miss Menali for her courage to be here, to congratulate her for the personal fortitude it took to endure such an ordeal, and to appreciate her generosity in sharing this story with all of us. I also come with a deeper concern: How can we continue to live in the illusion that our cities are safe? The atrocity Miss Menali suffered should never have happened, and I will not tolerate a *status quo* that leaves it possible to repeat!" Now the cheering came again. "We have entrusted so much of our personal safety in the naïve belief that an enormous, profit-seeking corporation had enough goodwill to keep our safety foremost. Citizens of my country and of others, I say that Servi-Mod has failed us!" Inwardly, the politician grinned at the tumult of triumphant voices that answered her; she was indeed on as solid standing as she had hoped.

"I am reminded today of another great leader, one from a different era. One unafraid to go to battle with corporate giants that, in outgrowing their britches, became a threat to the public. I'm speaking of Theodore Roosevelt, a president of the United States. And I'm thinking about his unshakable determination to break down monopolies that put the public's best interests in jeopardy. And I have an announcement:" The expert lighting glowed around the mayor, catching glints of rich color from her jewelry. She paused and smiled to give a photogenic moment for history to pin down. It was no accident that she was likening her imminent actions to a president's. "It's time we go back to trust-busting! And if you are with me—" waves of voices cheered in duplicity across the worlds "—then let's start by taking down Servi-Mod!"

—

"It's mob injustice," gaped Servi-Mod's CEO in the ornate study of her country mansion. "One crazy person's actions don't mean that the whole company should be—" she cut off her words and sent a connect to her top attorney. Stiff and pale, the attorney responded with a brief apology and a briefer resignation. The CEO removed her mini-tab and threw it across the room, yelling at the ocean of activity on her display panels. "But we're efficient! We're innovative! Servi-Mod gave you everything you wanted! We've given it to you better than anyone else could, better than you yourself could! *You made us this! You chose with your money!* We are the creation of your spending, of *your choices*! How can you tear us up now? How can you rip apart the very company *you made so great*?"

Her voice bludgeoned the display panels, but the panels could not listen.

—

They'd gotten all the children inside. Raz sat in his home suite in the wobble wall building scratching Ufi behind the ear. Sodi stood in the room looking at him, hoping for his attention, but Raz never looked up. Sodi read nothing in him, just stillness, just an inert dearth of emotion, plus fondness for the dog.

The enforcement officers would be on the hill crests by now. They might break into the clearings around the buildings at any moment. Sodi pulled the blinds, turned the lock in the doorknob, stepped through the doorway, and closed the door with a small click. He sent up a quiet wish for the safety of his child before leaving his home to stand in the way of whatever was coming.

—

Kat thought she heard a rhythm in the undercurrent of mad cheering. A repetitive change in volume thudded forward on three beats, then yawned a pause. Although the phenomenon began in TruWrld2, enough of the attendees were present via multiple worlds that, after several moments, the rhythm caught in all the sims. The mayor stood on the platform, listening to the tri-beat pulse. Ceasing her speech, she strained to make sense of what she was hearing until the words became audible. "We want Kat! We want Kat!" cheered the all-world beings. "We want Kat!"

Breaking into a smile, the mayor turned back to Kat and

gestured her back to the physical and digital podiums. As she returned, the pulses of sound intensified, morphing into, "We love Kat!"

"Thank you," Kat said, her voice imbued with fresh innocence. The rhythm broke into chaotic glee. "You are all so very kind! Actually, I'm glad for the chance to come back up here. I have something for you: You won't have to miss me, because I am announcing the availability of my image, properly and legally licensed to the worlds you love most. But there will be a change: Instead of running from a murderer in a corporate uniform, I'll be running around *with* avatars dressed like the people who healed me. This means if you found joy in the sim-holograms—and hey, joy is a good thing!—you can go on having fun with them. Except now you can do so as a selectable option. And you can use it with confidence, because I consent to this, and never again will my avatar be a *hostage*." Ninety percent of the audience clapped respectfully; ten percent screamed with the berserk glee of hardcore fans.

"One more thing," Kat took a deep breath, but tried not to show it. This was the part that Mayor Chatoy told her not to script. She told her to speak from her heart, because her heart was good, because a good heart is the origin of every positive change. "The people I'll appear with are unlegitimized." Now the audiences went silent again. "This is the first time they've entered a real sim as themselves. We've been calling people like this *subversives* for a long time. But they did for me what legitimized people did not, and I'm alive and healthy because of it."

Next to Kat, a rectangle opened to show short video clips of the Moma hugging their children, playing games, and eating together. The people in the shots smiled at the camera, and the audience could look them in the eye, but many found it difficult to do so. "I've learned that the people around us, even if we don't interact with them much, have more goodness and commonality than we think." Across World One, neighbors who just met glanced at each other. Some patted each other on the shoulder when one was staring at the floor in guilt.

A murmur went up. Kat could not hear any of the words in the susseration, but she hoped she understood the meaning of it. It was the sound of millions of people exchanging compassionate words like, "I never did think the legitimization law was right," or "Yeah, those kids they just showed are not road bombers. Every kid deserves rights."

Kat continued, "So in honor of them—because they were generous with no expectation of return, because they were kind when others were hunting me—all of you will be allowed to use my image for free in all sims." Again the voices of approval rose. Kat thought to herself that the hard part was over. "And all I ask is that, when you see me and these wonderful people together, you ask yourself: Shouldn't these native-born people have the same rights of citizenship that I do?"

The pitch of approval peaked. Kat surveyed the audience's happiness as attendees slipstreamed their dancing or jumping or fist pumping. She felt herself standing before all worlds, soaking in their acceptance. *I have a place here,* she thought. *If this is everywhere, then my place is anywhere.* Something in Kat let go of worry. With all worlds listening, she laughed. She waved. She called out "I love you too!" and as their cheering continued, she laughed and laughed—the best sound in life. Across the worlds, people clapped and laughed with her, and for that moment they were all together.

—

The quiet jailor who had tortured Vol recognized him in the Moma clearing—and at last had something to say, albeit brief and rude. He had intended to put far more of his diamond-shaped pattern across the ex-inmate's chest before they'd been interrupted. Someone had pulled a string for this subversive and let him go free. But now it was Silent's turn to pull something for this subversive, and it wasn't a string.

He stabilized the barrel of his rifle against the trunk of a tree and curled his finger around the trigger. He did not have a clear shot: right behind the ex-inmate stood another subversive who was somewhat taller and maybe a few years older. If Silent took the shot, the round would go through both. They stood together like brothers. They could die like brothers, like twins. Silent peered through his scope and lined up his crosshairs on the same spot he'd worked with his pliers. The bullet wouldn't even have to go through skin to go through the subversive's heart.

"Abort mission," said a voice through his mini-tab. Silent did not change his stance. "Repeat: Abort mission." He pressed his lips together and tensed his trigger finger. He fired.

A few leaves fell out of the tree some twenty yards ahead, and Silent was stumbling back, not expecting to lose his balance. He realized that someone had knocked the barrel of his rifle upward, throwing his aim way off. "Abort the damn mission!" the person yelled. It was his co-worker at the jail, the button operator with the cushy job lining up inmates for identification.

"You know they deserve it," he said. "I had a shot. They said take any good shot."

"They said *abort*, ya dull-head fool! Ain't to us to say who deserves what!"

Having shoved Vol to the ground to get in front of him, Sodi now ran toward the treeline, having pinpointed where the shot came from. He could not see who was there, nor how many. He could not read the situation. He could not remember to zig-zag his running path. He could do nothing but hate. But when he arrived at the treeline, his senses kicked back in, and he heard at least eight people's footsteps—all retreating with speed and without caution. He tensed, choosing which set of footsteps to pursue, which person to obliterate. But he remembered Vol behind him, still injured and alone in the clearing. The fury left his muscles and returned to his mind, and Sodi returned to his dearest friend.

"What was that?" a squad leader yelled at the communications officer once the teams were all reassembled at their helicopters. "We were in position! Did you literally defecate on a fan? What was that!"

Communications shook her head. "That was us avoiding the biggest PR problem we'll ever see in our lifetimes. Did I actually hear a shot after I called the abort? Was anyone injured?"

"What PR problem? These are subversives!"

"I know you've been in the woods this morning, but you need to stop and watch the news. I'm not even sure if there still *are* subversives. Nobody is sure of anything right now except that *your team is not going to fire on anyone today*. We're leaving."

—

After the news conference drew to a close, Mayor Chatoy concluded privately to Kat, "Few people track when elections occur anymore, but I do. The next one is this November. I suspect that this time, many will *want* to vote!"

In the news arenas, idle avatars remained strewn about while their operators all tried to be first to the digital stock trading markets. There, they dumped their Servi-Mod holdings in favor of shares of the sim companies that would carry Kat Menali's sim-hologram.

Within the hour, there was considerably less of the Servi-Mod monopoly left to shatter.

Chapter 38

Pale paper crackled in Eva's fingers. It came folded in neat thirds inside a pale yellow paper envelope with a glue-strip closure. This envelope had only Eva's name written on it—by hand in blue ink. It had arrived by drone inside a cardboard box with some contraption that included an odd vented unit on a mounting brace.

Eva sat in a green-painted Adirondack chair facing a short clearing followed by deep woods. The back of the chair touched the clapboard siding of a drab, three-room cabin whose chubby, stone chimney puffed out a stream of smoke against the night chill of higher elevations. Earlier that day, like the day before, Eva had seen no other person. She had spent four hours lying prone on the hillside beside the small berm where the cabin perched. She had looked at the sky and done nothing. She had heard nothing. A few clover leaves had touched her when the breeze picked up. When she'd risen, she'd examined the crown vetch covering the short, steep side of the berm. The non-native plant clung to the rocky soil of the unnatural slope, sinking roots into unfavorable ground to fix nitrogen in the soil it held from erosion, and offer pale pink petals to the world. The plant did not belong here any more than Eva did. Somehow made a life out of hard scrabble. Eva had picked three flowers of crown vetch. She placed one flower behind her ear, and the other two between various toes on her left foot. She allowed herself to open the letter.

With the letter were printed pictures of Raz and Zati. The Moma children were smiling, something her own daughter never had a chance to do. Eva stared without thinking much.

She opened the letter and recognized Choti's handwriting.

Everyone understands you do not wish to be approached now. Any choice you make will be respected, even if Vol asked me to enclose this device. He says it is to reach out if you want. Nobody faults you. You helped Sodi for years, even if no woman could have been right for him. You didn't fail, Eva.

Raz is still fever-free and healthy. He spends a great deal of time with Zati. I believe the two are best friends. Most days about mid-afternoon he comes to keep this old lady company, too. We talk.

Five of us witnessed your adoption by our old healer as the mother of Raz. He wanted you to hear it from him directly, even if the rest of us already know you raised his grandson. Eva, the reason we marked you wasn't to limit your options, but to guarantee your welcome among us always. That stands.

However far you go, whatever time passes, our love will always be ready for you. You are welcome to send me a connect any time, particularly any mid-afternoon.

Eva rubbed the curling scar on her thigh. She felt nothing. She understood the letter, folded it up, and returned it to the envelope. She stared at the trees. Eventually, she looked at the photos in her lap again.

The healing never made sense to her. Raz caught fever by being unable to define himself, and was somehow healed of this deficiency. A breeze tickled past her bare feet, rustling the pointy petals of the flowers there. Eva also had been unable to define herself. She wondered if, because she never had the leeway to get sick from it, she also could never get healed from it. Eva wished for sickness.

Turning up her wrist, she placed a video connect to Choti, but hung up before the connect went through. She stared at the home screen, searching for nothing. Time passed for a while. Eventually she swiped on her banking app and noticed a deposit had been made for a sum roughly twice her weekly living expenses. The icon next to the deposit indicated it would repeat weekly, indefinitely. The deposit was made by Sodi. The sun touched the tops of the trees on the horizon, sinking slowly. She realized she could stay in this place, or in another, for as long as she needed without having to explain anything to anyone. She had not asked Sodi for this. She had not asked for anything.

Maybe she would try a connect again the next afternoon.

—

They called it a *nationquake* because the term *landslide* understated the intensity of voter response. Although the mayor-come-president's platform ostensibly hinged on attacking the Servi-Mod monopoly and eliminating certain legitimization restrictions, in truth her popularity soared on the angry righteousness of a people kept too docile for too long. They wanted change, so change was.

Just as none questioned whose choices had kept people pent up, none questioned the progress of her campaign promises. Nevertheless, President Chatoy honored her word to Kat. Legitimization restrictions on education disappeared, opening medical care, personal rights, and suffrage to all willing to pay their taxes. The result was that subversive societies like the Moma were restored to full citizenship, although they were still generally feared as being different. Not all made use of their full sets of rights; however, most voted. Most taught their children to vote as well. This pleased the president, who hoped for re-election.

President Chatoy found the public's lack of expectations convenient. It freed her to put the country together more as she saw fit—at least for the short stretch of time she could foresee.

—

"Kat! Where have you been, woman?"

"Remember that boyfriend, Mez?"

Mez's avatar slammed the tractor into neutral and turned his burly face full around to stare at the flat rectangle opened across the near distance. "Ohmigod, no way. He was the one who hostaged your avatar? I knew it! I told you!"

"Better, Mez."

The unshaven beard poked at the video connect frame as the brawny body snapped his head back and forth. "I was at three of the news conferences; I couldn't get in to the others. Servers were overloaded. I had one of you on every character before they all vanished. I can't believe he stole your World One body! That was just wrong, girl! But you're famous!" the farmhand jabbed.

"No; it's even better, Mez. I have a wonderful story to tell you, but you're going to have to turn off your panels for it."

Sitting in her cockpit, Mez blinked. "Well, you know what? I'm sick of the Servi-Mod ads anyway. They are so goody-two-shoes it hurts. Do you have any idea how evil the company is? I almost don't mind that my building is being sold to someone else. I mean, *ye-ah*, I will miss having the food always here, but can you guess how much weight I've put on in the past five years?" In jeans and flannel, the taut avatar gesticulated at his pert rear. "Besides, I feel like I've done just about everything there is on the sims. I'd love to see you. Like World One see you."

"Whoa, are you giving them up, Mez?"

"No way! But I miss you. And one thing gets old after a while. I guess everybody needs a change-up sometimes. Get over here and we'll have some quality time."

"I will. In fact, I can be right over. Oh, and do you mind if I bring a couple friends along?"

"They are, like, safe to have in my house, right?" asked Mez.

Kat avoided rolling her eyes. She worried it would take a long time for society to recover from the ugly concept of *subversives*. "One of them is an officer. I'm pretty sure you'll like them. Maybe we can hang out more regularly, see if a few more people want to join in."

"My place is never gonna be big enough for that."

"Oh, don't worry. I can get us all sorts of places now."

—

It was not the first note he minded. He'd been arrested. He'd lost his clearance. Pureforc accepted it; his firing was a logical decision based on the information Servi-Mod had at hand. If his services were no longer needed, it bore no reflection on how much they *had been* needed, nor on how much he had contributed to the company. Servi-Mod was comprised of its information. Therefore, it must be comprised of *him*. No withdrawn access codes could revoke that indivisibility.

But the second letter—the one delivered on an unsanitary lunch napkin, the impossible message written in scrawl—was outright blasphemy. *Servi-Mod will fail* was written beside casual ketchup smears with no boundaries to sort the two. He crumpled the obscenity. He refused to watch the comical newscasts. Yet the message dug into his mind, tormenting him with his utter impotence to rectify or reassess. In the end, he settled for public research. He found that the haggard note held sickening probability.

Pureforc flagged down the next guard and asked to give a discreet, accurate confession. If the elegant and efficient Servi-Mod was to be drawn and quartered like a common sinner of the old west—so too was Pureforc determined to find his quickest exit. He would not see his work become irrelevant. He requested the maximum penalty.

—

There was a dance that night.

Sodi had spent three days prior teaching Raz the steps, and

although the boy could reproduce every action consistently, it was not in the same style as his father. In every forward lunge-step, his growing frame arched outward and up, puffing his chest and chin slightly toward the sky. At that moment, Raz's eyes closed in a moment of delicate serenity. He looked as though he'd found a private sunbeam from somewhere beyond the ceiling. Despite his uneasy yearning for Raz to follow the steps in the older way or in Sodi's own raunchy interpretation, he wondered how elegant the uplifted respect-giving would appear when Raz emerged as a full-grown man.

Sodi and Vol made another change as well. The machine man teetered atop a ladder installing new lighting and hologram ports on a large arch over the dance floor. Boughs of twinkling color suffused the air. The holograms would provide one of the dancers: At the moment when the men stepped high and the women arched back, Kat's body-authentic avatar, piloted from her city apartment and clad in red with long ribbons, would be the one running through the tunnel of bodies. In turn, the new lighting on the archway would constantly monitor the shapes beneath it, mapping them and sending them as a live model to Kat's VR experience.

As part of the tech development, Vol and Sodi now wore beta-version light-tabs on their wrists instead of mini-tabs. By connecting over a light network rather than the much slower radio-based networks, they'd be able to move a lot more data around: They could model TruWrld2 in World One as holograms or VR—and not just one tree at a time. They could sim World One into TruWrld2. And they could model blended worlds—created out of parts of each, or even parts of many—wherever they wanted. They called it the Light Bridge.

—

"Well, what do you think of it?" Sodi asked Choti toward the end of the dance break. His eyes shone with the same boyish eagerness she had always adored in them. He smelled lightly of sweat and was breathing a little heavy, smiling.

She answered, "It's different. What do you think it will do, to have this sort of mixing, even in our dances?"

Sodi laughed. "I don't know. Maybe everything."

"Does that concern you, Sodi?"

He laughed more, and it was a good sound, the best sound. "Does it concern you?" he asked her back.

Her genial silence ended with a grin. "Oh, don't worry yourself about what bothers me. Go and make of your world what you will."

There was another figure there on the emptied dance floor. As though anticipating her, Raz walked toward the holographic figure being constructed out of the generators spewing color from their ports. Here, he stood under the lights as they mapped out his form and sent it in three dimensions to a much smaller device far away, nailed haphazardly to the ceiling of a cabin tucked in mountains.

Sodi could not hear their conversation, but he saw his son reach out to her. The child had peace in his face, that slight smile of contentment. She reached back as though to cup his cheek and tell him about his growing. Eva used Vol's device. Raz spoke to his mother, made out of light.

Later, the dancing recommenced. Seated beside the rhythmic stomping, Choti smiled at the adjustment in Raz's posture: a short bundle of great promise, defiant amid the grown men. She noted, too, that when twirling Zati noticed his pose, she answered it by raising her wrists, fingers uncurling like she were releasing a sparrow. The other youths began to emulate them. *By now I ought to know,* she mused to herself, *that the biggest tradition we ever had was to keep changing.* While treasuring the way the dance had been, she watched new beauty finding itself, as it would in any world that minds could create.

The Author

Vail Henry debuted as a writer in the first grade, where she scripted the same letter daily to inform her parents that she had not done her homework again. In the years following, she wrote a great deal of apology notes to a wide range of unhappy audiences. Having learned nothing, she now writes down things she made up. She lives in Fairfax County, Virginia and is a member of the Choctaw Nation of Oklahoma.

The Moma Language

The Moma people presented in this book, as well as their portrayed culture, are fictitious. However, the Moma language is based on fragments of Chahta Anumpa (the Choctaw language)—and characters' misunderstandings thereof. For those interested in learning Chahta Anumpa, there are publicly available classes, some of which are taught online, at the time of this writing.

Photo this page by Izolda T. *(digital manipulation subsequent)*

CPSIA information can be obtained
at www.ICGtesting.com
Printed in the USA
BVHW042110011221
623057BV00013B/826

9 781948 279000